Three More Months

Three More Months

Sarah Echavarre

LAKE UNION
PUBLISHING

Text copyright © 2021 by Sarah Smith
All rights reserved.

Published by Lake Union Publishing, Seattle

www.apub.com

Amazon, the Amazon logo, and Lake Union Publishing are trademarks of Amazon.com, Inc., or its affiliates.

ISBN-13: 978-1542031882
ISBN-10: 1542031885

Cover design by David Drummond

Printed in the United States of America

For you, Mom. See you next time.

Chapter One

Call your mom, Chloe. Seriously.

The bold black letters jump from the yellow Post-it note stuck to my refrigerator. It's like the words are screaming at me.

That's a new one.

It's not unusual for my best friend, Julianne, to leave notes for me tacked onto my refrigerator whenever she comes over for a girls' night. But they're usually reminders about picking up my dry cleaning or putting the bins out the night before garbage day. It's an old habit I'm thankful she kept up from our college roommate days. I don't even have to put reminders in my phone for errands like other people do. Julianne's always got me covered.

She's never reminded me to call my mom, though.

I check the calendar, which is pinned onto the wall next to the stainless-steel refrigerator. It takes several seconds of scanning the endless white squares before I even remember today's date.

When I finally remember that it's May 4, I sigh, then rub a fist against my forehead. The pressure eases only slightly. That tension in my head set up camp there a year ago when I was promoted to pharmacy residency program director at Nebraska Medical Center.

I loathe how one-track minded this job has made me. When I used to be just a staff pharmacist, I would drive to the hospital, clock in, report to whatever floor I was scheduled for that day, and verify medication orders. Sometimes I'd do rounds with the physicians and nurses. Yeah, days would be busy. I'd be occupied from the moment I walked through the doors of the hospital, but when my shift ended, I was done. I could go home and unwind with thirty minutes on the treadmill in my basement or a glass of wine before bed, then do it all over again the next day.

But now that I'm residency director, my life is even more work. I'm taking home a backpack full of papers and a work laptop almost every day. I'm reviewing residency and internship applications submitted by pharmacy school students. Or I'm reviewing projects that the interns and residents are working on. Or I'm proofreading journal papers or sitting in on job interviews. Things like eating, sleeping, charging my phone, and remembering to call loved ones have fallen by the wayside.

"Thank God I don't have kids," I mutter to myself, wondering how on earth anyone with a family manages a job like this.

That's probably the reason for Julianne's Post-it note. Mom likely texted her to see if I was still alive when I forgot to return her calls and texts. I left my phone on silent this past week so I could focus on reviewing a slew of residency projects and job applications. She's probably freaking out.

I need to fix this. Now. I swipe my phone from the kitchen counter, ignoring the missed call and text alerts, and dial her. She picks up on the second ring.

"*Anak!*" By the way she bellows her preferred Filipino term of endearment for me, I can tell she's grinning.

Her tone is a relief and a joy to hear. Then that familiar crushing disappointment hits me. This is the kind of love and forgiveness parents have for their kids, even when the kids are well into adulthood. If anyone else cut off communication with you for weeks on end, you'd likely not be in a hurry to talk to them.

But Mom is always excited to hear from me.

"Mom. Hi." I do my best to inject a dose of cheer into my voice.

"How are you doing? Good? You're not working yourself too hard, are you?"

Bombarding me with multiple questions at once is her trademark move whenever there's been a long gap in our conversations. I pause and swallow to keep from groaning out of fatigue.

"Only a little." I chuckle to make things sound light. It comes off like I'm being strangled.

The way she tsks on the other end of the line tells me she doesn't buy it one bit. "You sound tired."

"I'm fine. It's just . . . I'm on the interview committee for this job opening we have in the pharmacy. I got bogged down reviewing applications."

"Mm-hmm."

Her annoyed hum in lieu of actual words says it all. I can picture her disappointed stance perfectly because I do it when I'm annoyed too. That narrow gaze, crossed arms, the disapproving look on her face broadcasting just how much she hates that her only daughter, who used to visit home once a month, has become a textbook workaholic and hasn't seen her in months.

"I'm sorry it's been a while since I've called." I hope my apology is enough to get things back on track. I want this conversation to at least be pleasant.

"How is work going for you?" I ask when she doesn't say anything right away.

Mom's job is a safe direction to veer in. She's the overnight customer service manager for a grocery store in my hometown of Kearney, which is smack-dab in the middle of Nebraska. It's nearly three hours away from where I live in Omaha. Her store is part of a nationwide chain that's open twenty-four hours every day of the year. She always has plenty of stories to tell about bizarre customers or quirky employees.

"Busy as ever," she says, her voice a tad lighter. "You wouldn't believe what happened last night. Some customer came into the store so drunk he couldn't even walk straight."

"Really?" I spin around to the kitchen island and flip open my laptop, half listening as she recalls how the drunk customer crashed into a candy bar display in the middle of one of the aisles. I skim through an email from one of the pharmacy residents. She's asking me to proofread a PowerPoint slide that she's presenting at a regional conference next week about beta-blockers.

"There were chocolate bars everywhere," she says. "It was a mess."

I make a "hmm" noise as I skim through the info on my laptop screen.

"And then, he fell asleep!" Mom's high-pitched voice cuts into my mental review. "Can you believe that? On top of a pile of candy bars, he just started snoozing. How is that even comfortable?"

"Ha. Yeah, I don't know." I frown as one half of my brain attempts to read through the resident's notes while the other half listens to her story. Silently, I move my lips as I follow along with the text on the screen.

Beta-blockers are used to control heart rhythm, treat angina, and reduce high blood pressure.

Beta-blockers work by blocking the effect of the hormone epinephrine, also known as adrenaline.

Beta-blockers cause the heart to beat more slowly and with less force, which lowers blood pressure.

Side effects of beta-blockers include dizziness, weakness, fatigue, cold hands and feet, headache, upset stomach, dry mouth, or—

"Did you say something about blood pressure?" she asks.

My lips stop moving when I realize I must have been reading out loud.

"Are you even listening to me, Chloe?"

"Of course I am." My face heats out of pure shame. "How is your blood pressure these days, Mom? I've been meaning to ask." It's a shaky recovery, but I manage.

Her sigh rings heavy in response. My ears perk up, and all of my attention focuses on her. I don't like the sound of that. When she says nothing, I press her again.

"I'm fine."

"Are you? Like, the doctor says you're fine?"

"Yes." She practically spits out the word.

If there's one thing Mom is known for, it's this: she loves my younger brother, Andy, and me to the moon and back. She'd lie down in traffic for either one of us without a second thought. But when we try to tell her what to do, even if we know better, it drives her up the wall. She hates it even more than that annoying adolescent phase I went through where I used to call her by her name, Mabel, instead of Mom.

"Chloe. I said I'm fine."

I force myself to swallow through the sting of her annoyance. If I don't, I'll scoff. And if there's one thing Mom hates more than being fussed over by her adult kids, it's being scoffed at by her adult kids. It's disrespectful, she says. Every single time this has happened before, even when I apologize—and try to explain that I'm only concerned for her health and well-being—she doesn't care. She pulls her typical mom-guilt move. The one I'm one thousand percent sure she's pulling now, even though I can't see her.

It's the pursed lips and the brow furrowed so deeply that I wonder if the lines will stay in her richly tanned skin forever. But when she eases her expression, her skin is always smooth again. It's like the lines were never there at all. The disappointment lingers, though. Like an invisible damp fog in the air.

I try again, this time with a gentler tone. "Mom. I ask because I care."

"No, you're fussing. I don't need you to fuss over me, Chloe."

Whenever she says my actual name and not *anak* or *anakko*, I know I'm testing her last nerve. The punch she puts at the second syllable of my name signals I can't sweet-talk or apologize my way out of my comment, no matter how well intentioned. It lands hard and sharp, like a rubber band snapping against the inside of my wrist. It's enough to make the muscles in my neck tense just the slightest bit.

"The doctor says I'm fine," she says. Her harshness fades a notch. "At my checkup last month, my blood pressure was lower than at my appointment in the winter."

Despite the tension that still hangs between us, the muscles in my neck ease at the good news. "That's awesome. I'm so happy to hear that."

At sixty-one, Mom has no interest in slowing down, no matter how much Andy or I or her doctor want her to. She's worked overnight shifts ever since we were preteens. She always said it was because the inconvenient hours paid more, and she could use the money. It's true. She's been a single mom most of our lives. With two kids to support on her own, every penny counted.

But now that my brother and I are adults and are capable of supporting ourselves, we've tried to tell her countless times to ease back on her hours. She's always volunteering for overtime and working the holidays. Or, at the very least, we ask her to switch from overnights to the day shift. The graveyard shift is hell on sleep schedules and health— I know because I worked overnight hours most of my twenties when I was employed as a pharmacy technician and during my first couple of years as a staff pharmacist. And I still cover overnight shifts at the hospital whenever we're short-staffed.

But I'm relatively young. I can withstand temporary stress on my sleep schedule. Mom, on the other hand, is aging. She doesn't bounce back like she used to. I can see it every time I go home for a visit and catch her the morning after a busy overnight shift. I can see it in the crow's-feet around her eyes, how they deepen every time I see her. I see it in the way she moves gingerly around the kitchen while making her postwork herbal tea, the way she jokes about the never-ending aches and pains in her body.

But every time Andy and I ask her to switch to an easier day shift, she rebuffs us. She tells us she doesn't need her kids to tell her how to live. And then I bite my tongue and rack my brain for a different way to convince her to slow down, to take a break, because the older she gets, the more important it is for her to take care of herself.

It's a vicious cycle. I hate getting into arguments with her about it. But that's what happens every time. And I haven't figured out a better way to go about this yet.

That's why I always fall back into my old pattern of voicing my concern, enduring her disdain, and then crawling my way back into her good graces.

"I swear, you and your brother get on my case for the littlest things." Her tone turns curt. "You should know by now I can take care of myself."

I force myself to hum a yes.

"When do you think you'll be able to come home for a visit?" she asks.

"Oh." I clear my throat, embarrassed that I didn't see this question coming. Every single time we talk on the phone, she always wants to know when I'll come home. That shows just how much work mode has screwed me up.

"I'm not sure. I'll let you know, though."

There's a pause, then a sad sigh. The sound sends a painful squeeze to my chest.

"You always say that," she says.

The defeat in her tone cuts a million times deeper than when she snaps at me. Because it means I'm falling short of my daughter duties.

The duty list has always been brief, and up until last year, it was a list I could complete with relative ease.

It entails regular visits to see her once a month, at least two phone calls a week, and spending every major holiday with her and Andy at home. And if I'm scheduled to work a holiday, it's expected that I spend whatever days off I get in exchange at home.

With work getting more intense, I was bound to let the ball drop on one of her nonnegotiables. Unfortunately, it was the most important one.

"I'm sorry. I know I haven't been home since . . . since, um . . ."

"Easter," she says. "You haven't been home since Easter."

"That's only a month." I wince at my lie.

"A month and a half. More than a month and a half actually because it's already the beginning of May now. Easter was early this year, remember?"

There is zero sharpness in her voice now. Just something soft and longing. It makes my throat ache. I have to swallow twice to keep my voice from trembling when I respond to her. That long Easter weekend flows to the front of my mind. Mom, Andy, and I played card games into the wee hours of the morning, lounged on the couch watching Mom's favorite game shows, and ate honey ham and pineapple upside-down cake until our stomachs ached.

"I just miss you, *anak*."

I swallow, letting the quiet despair in her words pass through me. "You're always welcome to come visit me, Mom."

"And do what? Sit in your empty house while you go to the hospital and work those long, ridiculous hours? No, thank you."

"You can come when I have a day off."

"You hardly ever have a day off, Chloe. Not since you took that promotion."

Her retort hits like a sucker punch. She and Andy have only visited me a couple of times since my work schedule has gotten more demanding. And sadly, she's right . . . both times, I had to leave in the middle of catching up with them because I was on call.

"I'd rather have you visit here more often," she says. "That way you're away from the hospital and actually have to spend time at home with Andy and me. You can't run away to work."

"I'm sorry about that, Mom. Really." I sigh, wishing she knew just how much I really mean it. "This month is a little hectic, but I promise I'll come see you in June."

"You talk like you have to get on a plane to come see me," she says. "You live less than three hours away. You could actually take a day off and come visit. It would be good for you to get away. You'd be more relaxed and less stressed after a day or two at home, and do better when you go back to work."

"Mom, that's not—"

"Why do you always try to make an excuse not to come see me? You didn't use to."

Her voice sounds so small, so broken, so disappointed. It makes my eyes burn. I know this tone well. Because I've heard it more times than I care to admit over this past year.

More than anything, Mom values time with my brother and me. And for the last several months, I've failed again and again to give it to her. Because I'm scared of losing the financial stability I worked my entire twenties—my entire life—to have.

This promotion came with a bump in my salary that allowed me to pay off the bungalow I bought in the Dundee neighborhood of Omaha instead of stringing along the payments for another seven years. It means that I finally have a hefty emergency fund. It means making my monthly retirement fund contributions respectable instead of pitiful.

It means that, at thirty-three, I'm finally financially secure with a thriving career.

At the cost of my relationship with my mom.

"Mom." I take a breath for a second to regain my composure. "I'm working hard because it's how you taught me and Andy to be when we were younger. Remember? It's in our blood to work extra hard. You're the one we get it from. You spent your whole life being an example to us, always taking extra shifts and long hours to support us."

I don't elaborate because I don't need to. We both know why I am the way I am. Money was never plentiful for us, ever. With our dad out of the picture since my parents got divorced when I was in elementary school, Mom worked overtime constantly while raising us on her own. We were never destitute, but finances were always tight. I remember more times than I can count receiving past due bill notices in the mail and Mom quickly strategizing where in her budget she could pull from so that the electricity wouldn't be shut off or so that we could still afford to have internet. I remember seeing the paperwork she left on the kitchen table showing that she reduced her monthly retirement contribution to zero for the better part of two years to cover Andy's medical bills when he got appendicitis in grade school. I remember Mom venting in Ilocano to her sister, Auntie Linda, on the phone one day in her bedroom when our dad failed to send yet another child support payment, and she admitted she was going to have to work Thanksgiving, Christmas, and New Year's for the holiday pay to cover our expenses.

And this is why I bust my ass, why I'll willingly take on a stressful workload even though I know it will cost me my free time—time I could spend with her and my brother. Because I don't want to have to struggle like we did growing up. I want to financially weather whatever crap life chooses to throw at me.

"You're just making excuses," Mom says dismissively. "And I don't just mean with me. When was the last time you hung out with Julianne outside of work? When was the last time you went out on a date?"

I try and fail to stifle a groan. Mom has been bugging me about settling down and starting a family since I turned twenty-five.

"*Anak*, I know what happened with me and your dad makes you scared to date and have a relationship, but don't be so jaded! You're still so young and beautiful! You know, there's this very sweet and handsome young man I work with named Liam. He's one of the overnight shift managers. I was telling him about you—"

"Mom, can you please not set me up with your coworkers? That's humiliating."

"Oh, Chloe. I only do it because you clearly can't do it yourself. Work is your first love. But work won't hug and kiss you at the end of the day."

"Mom. Stop. I'm sorry I'm not married with kids, and I'm sorry I don't visit you enough. I'm doing my best to balance everything on my plate as it is. I'm sorry that's not good enough for you."

It's not until I'm done speaking that I realize just how hard my tone has become. My face heats yet again. I sound like I'm scolding her.

Just then, I see a reminder pop up in my email calendar. It's a note reminding me to get all the necessary paperwork ready for tomorrow afternoon's department budget meeting. Gritting my teeth, I take a breath. I completely forgot. I glance at the clock. It's nine at night. I need to get started on it now if I want to make it to bed before eleven.

"I have to go, Mom. I'll call you later, okay? Love you."

"Okay. I love you too."

Those last four words, spoken in that soft tone, land like an arrow in my heart. This conversation qualifies as one of the tamer arguments we've had. There was no shouting or door slamming. But even if we'd had the worst fight ever, she'd still say I love you. She always does. Every single interaction between us ends the same way, no matter if it was full of laughs or if we were so agitated that we could barely keep from hanging up on each other.

Because that's her above all. Whether she's mad or frustrated or happy or annoyed or any other emotion on the human spectrum, she's one thing when it comes to my brother and me: loving.

We hang up, and I spend the next hour sifting through documents. When I finish, I get ready for bed. The entire time, the sound of Mom's voice echoes in my mind. I fall asleep to the memory of her gentle "I love you too."

Chapter Two

I pick at my premade beet and goat cheese salad while sitting in the hospital cafeteria on my evening dinner break. I offered to pick up the first part of an overnight shift when my day shift ended today, so I won't be going home until probably close to three in the morning. I haven't eaten since breakfast, but I've only taken two bites since I sat down ten minutes ago. I'm still unsettled from my conversation with Mom last night, and when I'm feeling unsettled, it's hard for me to stomach food.

Julianne plops down across from me. She drops a paper plate of french fries and a side salad on the table. Her long legs hit my much shorter ones under the table. "Tell me why I decided to become a pharmacist again?" she mutters.

"Because you grew up watching your surgeon parents fail at striking a work-life balance and wanted to do something in medicine but less intense."

No one would ever guess that former party girl Julianne is the offspring of workaholic physicians. Both of her parents are trauma surgeons who, despite pushing retirement age, work an average of one hundred hours a week and left Julianne to be raised by nannies. Her parents love her and provided a cushy life for her but never spent as much time with her as she wished they would have. It's the reason Julianne chose to go the pharmacy route. It's a steady career with solid earning potential, but you can also see your family if you choose to have one.

She looks up at me, crinkling her perfectly arched eyebrows into a frown. "I swear to God, that's the last time I round with Dr. Hoechlin. Dude's a patronizing prick. He thinks all pharmacy does is count pills. Does he even know the difference between retail pharmacy and hospital pharmacy? Jesus." She gathers her shoulder-length light-blonde hair up into a ponytail, her movements jerky with annoyance.

I mock-frown at her. "There's a difference? No way!"

She cracks a smile and laughs before digging into her salad. "I bet he thinks IV drugs just magically appear, because clearly he doesn't realize that we're the ones prepping them."

"You should tell him that since he thinks all we do is count pills, you won't be showing up to rounds with him anymore. Or answering any questions he has about dosing and adverse reactions to drugs."

Julianne's eyes widen as she chews and points to me. "Brilliant."

"Maybe then he'll finally figure out just how much he relies on us lowly hospital pharmacists."

The tension inside of me melts the slightest bit at the boom of her cackle. A few people sitting at nearby tables turn to look, which makes me laugh. I'm silently so thankful my best friend and I have the same job and work at the same place with overlapping shifts. Workdays would suck without her.

"So, did you call your mom?" she asks.

"Yeah. Thanks for putting up that reminder on my refrigerator when you came over the other night."

"What are best friends for?" She flashes a winning smile at me, her glossed lips shiny under the lights. Even though we hospital staff pharmacists wear scrubs almost every day for our shifts—the least glamorous clothing in the world—Julianne refuses to de-glam the rest of her appearance. She's always wearing a full face of makeup. She says feeling cute helps her power through our long and grueling shifts. Even if she didn't, she'd still look more like a runway model than a hospital staff pharmacist. The stark white color of the cafeteria walls and the harsh fluorescent lighting can't diminish her effortless beauty.

"So how is she doing?" Julianne asks before digging into her fries. "You know she's getting next-level impatient with you when she texts me to remind you to call her."

When I became friends with Julianne in college, I took her home with me almost every holiday to celebrate with Mom and Andy because her parents were always working, and she's an only child. She hit it off instantly with Mom. Mom was ecstatic to have another person to feed and to fill up the house. Even now with a busy work schedule and traveling back home to see her own parents, Julianne makes it to Mom's house a couple of times a year. She's been unofficially adopted by my family.

But that also means it feels like I have another sibling to nag me whenever I'm falling short in my daughter duties.

"She's annoyed with me," I mutter before biting another forkful of salad.

Julianne directs her blue-eyed stare to me. "She just misses you, Chloe." She frowns slightly, her expression conveying a gentle concern. "Ever since you became residency program director last year, you've been in nonstop work mode. Actually, ever since you graduated and took this job at the hospital, you've been in nonstop work mode. You've just been even more work focused since becoming RPD. Even I have a hard time getting you to take a break for a glass of wine one night every few weeks. As your best friend, that drives me nuts. I can't imagine how it must make your mom feel to miss out on seeing you."

I sigh, then tell her exactly what I told Mom on the phone—how I'm focused on work because I'm trying to solidify my career and remain financially independent.

"My mom, of all people, should understand," I say, wincing at the slight bitterness in my tone. "We struggled so much financially when I was a kid. I thought she would understand me wanting that security."

Julianne pins me with her stare. "I get that. But your mom is the greatest. Like, literally the greatest. She just wants to see you. That's all."

She pauses to help herself to another few french fries and a couple of mouthfuls of salad. "I'm your best friend, and you know I've got your back forever. But your mom has made me feel like her third kid for the past fifteen years. She's always treated me like family when you've brought me home. I feel more at home at your house than I do at my parents' house." Her eyes shine bright with emotion. "You're lucky to have her, Chloe. You need to make the time to see her. I know you want to."

Julianne always has an insightful way of telling it like it is when I need her to. And she's always spot-on.

"You sound like my therapist," I say. "That's exactly what she said I should do when I told her during this morning's session about last night's argument with my mom."

She raises an eyebrow at me. "See? I know what I'm talking about. Look, I know how important job security and financial security is to you. But what's more fun? Reviewing applications and proofreading PowerPoint slides? Or hanging out at home with your mom?"

"Point taken," I say.

Julianne smiles and finishes the last of her fries and salad in a few quick bites before checking the time on her phone. "You've got ten more minutes of dinner, right? Call your mom now and tell her you're coming to visit her this weekend. I'll cover your shift."

I start to decline, but she shakes her head.

"No discussions. You covered for me last month when I decided to go on that weekend yoga retreat with my cousin. It was a total waste of time. God, can you believe she roped me into going there for one of her ridiculous private investigator excursions?"

I chuckle as Julianne rants once more about how her private investigator cousin took her on a trip to tail a client's cheating spouse.

"I'm never going anywhere with her again," she grumbles. "Anyway, none of that matters. The point is I owe you. I'll work your shift for you so you can go visit your mom."

"You're sure?"

"Positive. She's working now, isn't she? Call her up and surprise her with the news. She'll be so happy."

She smiles, and I wish her a good rest of her shift before she takes off. Then I pick up my salad container and walk out of the cafeteria to a nearby empty waiting room so I can FaceTime Mom. She's on her break right now, which means I can squeeze in a quick conversation.

When she answers, a wide grin stretches across her face. I recognize the bright-blue walls of the grocery store break room.

"*Anakko*! How are you?"

That happy, excited tone again, just like yesterday.

"Hi, Mom. I'm good. Just a few more hours at the hospital and I'll head home."

She nods before telling me for the millionth time to be extra careful when I walk out to my car and to text her that I arrived home safely. Then she starts to tell me how she was going through some old family photos and found my and Andy's baby pictures.

"Oh, *anak*, you were so cute."

She goes on about my chunky cheeks and thick black hair that was so fun to braid.

Just then, her stare drifts to the side. Her eyes go wide and she beams. "Look who's here!"

The image goes wobbly just before my younger brother, Andy, squeezes into frame. Mom turns to kiss his cheek as he smiles. At six feet tall, he towers over me and Mom since we're both barely five three with the same slight build. He's got our dad's giant midwestern genes that contribute to his long and lean build, but his face is all Mom's. So is mine. Our dark hair, tan skin, deep-brown eyes, dimpled cheeks, button noses, and thick eyebrows belong to her.

"Chloe! How's it going?"

"Good. You?"

"Doing a late-night snack run after my shift."

"Did you get good tips tonight?"

"One fifty. Pretty good for a Tuesday in this tiny town."

"Kearney is hardly tiny. The population is what, thirty thousand?" His eyebrows knit together in an exaggerated mock frown. "Compared to New York City, that's teeny tiny."

I roll my eyes and laugh. Typical smart-aleck comment from my baby brother.

Mom pats his shoulder, and he squeezes her into a side hug as he smiles at her. Whenever he grins, his face goes boyish. It always brings me back to us as kids, when he was my cute and chubby little brother who loved root beer and Ninja Turtles. He looks nothing like his baby pictures now that he's tall with wavy, shaggy dark-brown hair and an athletic build from years of youth sports.

"You know, if you ever want to quit the thankless industry of hospital pharmacy, you should join the service industry like me. They pay us the big bucks."

I let out a laugh while Mom lightly smacks his shoulder. "Don't say that to your sister. She's working hard and doing very well."

Andy rolls his eyes. "I know, I know. Chloe is the overachiever with an impressive job and paycheck to boot. I'm the disappointing mama's boy who still lives at home."

I'm chuckling again while Mom smacks his shoulder, this time a tad harder. "Ay! You're not a disappointment. You're working hard. I'm so proud of you. Both of you," she says with a frown on her face.

"Thanks, Mom," we say in unison.

If I'm the obnoxiously studious child in the family, Andy is the token free spirit. He's a smart kid and performed fine in school, but he's never been one for structure. He tried college at a state school a couple of hours from Kearney for a year but dropped out after he realized he didn't know what he wanted to study. Now he's bartending at a local bar and grill and living at home with Mom, saving money for whatever he decides to do next.

Andy pulls his phone out of his pocket and squints at the screen. "I'd better get going. I promised a friend I'd help move him into his new place tomorrow before my shift."

Mom gives him another kiss on the cheek while I tell him bye. He steps out of the frame, and she waves him off.

"You couldn't pay me to help someone move on a day I'm scheduled to work," I say.

"Andy is a good boy. So kind and helpful."

I can't help but laugh at how she talks about him like he's still a toddler. Even though he's twenty-five, she still thinks of him as her baby. It must be a mom thing.

"How's your shift going, Mom? Busy?"

She waves a hand dismissively before pushing up her dark-rimmed glasses. "Like always."

When she rubs the back of her neck, she pauses to yawn. It's such a slight, benign movement, but that's when I see it. Fatigue rests in the wrinkles of her forehead. Her rich-brown eyes take an extra second to focus with each slow blink she manages. She's so, so tired.

"How much sleep did you get today?" I ask.

She shrugs, glances at something to the side. "I don't know. Five, maybe six hours?"

I bite my tongue. That's nowhere near enough. But she'll freak if I lecture her. And I don't want to ruin two conversations with her in just as many days due to my overbearing concern.

Instead, I opt for something I know will make her smile. Something that will put her in a good mood. A way for me to make things right.

"What if I come home this weekend?" I ask.

Her thick eyebrows arch in surprise just as her entire face brightens. Everything from her skin to her eyes shines. Even the red lipstick she's wearing beams ten times brighter.

"Really? You're coming home?"

The disbelieving hope in her tone causes my heart to squeeze against my chest. Something this simple—something this silly—shouldn't bring so much joy. But it does. Because it's her.

"You were right yesterday when you said I need a break," I say. "It would do me some good to go home and spend some time with you. And I promise I won't bring any work with me."

"Oh, I would love that! I'll cook your favorite food too. It'll be ready the minute you get home. How does fried rice with wontons sound?"

My mouth waters at just the mention. "That sounds perfect. I'll be home Friday around five. Is that okay?"

"Of course that's okay. You never have to choose a time to come home, *anak*. You're always welcome, whenever you want. You know that."

I nod and smile at the serious tone of her reminder. "Right. Of course."

"I'm so happy you're coming!" she practically squeals. In the background, I see one of her coworkers jump at her screech.

"Me too, Mom. I'd better get going, though. My break's almost over."

She nods before waving a hand at me. "Yes, yes. Hurry up and go home so you can get some sleep."

"You need sleep, too, Mom. Promise you'll get at least seven hours after your shift tonight?"

I steel myself for the scolding she's about to give me for daring to lecture her on sleep yet again. But to my surprise, she nods in agreement. "Yes, I promise."

"Love you, Mom."

"Love you too!"

She waves goodbye, and we end the call. I power through the final hours of my shift, then drive home. As I wash my face and brush my teeth, a wave of sadness crashes at my feet, then slowly engulfs my legs, my chest, my arms, my head. It's so strong that my hand holding the toothbrush stills. I bite down on the head until my teeth ache. No more using work as an excuse. I need to go home more often. I only live three hours—less than three hours—away.

I burrow into my bedsheets, willing the remaining guilt away as I press my eyes shut. I'm going home this weekend. That's a start.

~

The shrill ring of my phone jolts me awake. Slowly, I reach for my cell phone, which is sitting on the nightstand next to my bed. I squint at the alarm clock right next to it. 5:07 a.m.

It's Andy. Why in the world is he calling me so early?

I take a second to clear my throat and then answer. "Hey. What's up?"

"Chloe."

He sounds out of breath when he says my name. I wait for him to say more, but there's no response. Just a shaky breath.

"Andy? Is everything okay?"

"Are you . . . can you please sit down?"

Another shaky breath bursts out of him. The sound causes every nerve inside of me to stand on edge. It's hard to place how or even why, since he's said so little, but something isn't right. When Andy calls me, it's to shoot the shit or to ask what gifts we should go in on for Mom's birthday and the holidays. That's exactly what we did two days ago when he jumped in on my FaceTime call with her. He's never once acted like this on the phone—breathless, nervous, and scared.

There's a strangled noise. Then silence.

"Christ, Andy. Are you choking?" I say as I sit up in bed. There's a tremor in my voice. If this is a joke, I'm going to strangle him when I see him in person this weekend.

He breathes, and I let out a huff of air in relief. I wait one second, then another.

Finally, he speaks. "No, I'm not . . ." His voice breaks.

"Crap, Andy. I'm sorry, I didn't mean to go off on you."

My heart is thudding at a million miles an hour as he sobs. What the hell is going on?

"Are you sitting down?" he asks again. His tone is that distorted whine it takes on whenever he's speaking and trying not to cry. I haven't heard it in years, not since our grandma died.

Andy's panic and sudden burst of tears can only mean one thing. Something is very, very wrong, either with him, or . . .

Terror lands in the form of an invisible punch, square in the center of my chest. It's agony to breathe. I can't speculate any longer. I need to know what's going on.

"Yes, I'm sitting. What's going on?"

I grip the edge of the bed with my free hand. It's like my body knows something is about to fall apart in the worst way right in front of me, and I'm going to need to hold on.

Andy still says nothing. My heart thunders.

"What is going on, Andy?" I nearly shout.

"It's Mom." His voice breaks, then he sobs once more.

Chapter Three

I don't say anything at first. I can't speak. I can't move. I can't even blink. My brain and my body are trapped in the terror of Andy's words.

It's Mom.

Those words are still making their way through me, still filtering through the deepest recesses of my brain. It's taking forever for my mind to soak it all in. The message moves like wet sand through an hourglass. It's a struggle for it to reach the rest of my body, to my arms and legs, to my heart and lungs, to my nervous system, to tell them all to keep functioning, to keep going, even though this is the worst possible news I could ever imagine.

I muster the energy to shake my head in an attempt to make sense of everything he's saying in between sobs.

Heart attack. Collapsed. Ambulance ride. Hospital. Some room on some floor I can't even begin to commit to memory.

My brain and my body lock up once more. Like a computer that crashes when too many programs are operating.

My heart is thudding, my ears are ringing, and there are spots in the corners of my vision. I open and close my mouth, but nothing forms. Not words, not even the sound of my breathing. Because I honestly don't think I know how to breathe anymore.

"Chloe."

Andy's voice is a faraway shout that I can barely hear.

"Chloe, did you hear me?"

This time, the booming volume pulls me back to real time.

"I heard you." It's my turn for my voice to break. I struggle to catch my breath.

"I'm on my way to the hospital right now. Just . . . just get here, okay?" He sniffles. "As soon as you can."

I nod instead of answering him, then hang up the phone. I jump up from the bed and run to the bathroom so I can pee, my head spinning, trying to figure out what I need to do first. I stumble to the closet while brushing my teeth and grab the closest overnight bag I can find, then start shoving clothing and toiletries into it. Minutes later, I'm dressed and somewhat clean.

I race down the stairs and slide on the first pair of sneakers I see by the doorway. Then, somehow, I walk out the door to the garage, throw my bag into the car, hop in the driver's seat, and open the garage door. Thank God I remembered to get gas yesterday. I don't know if I could figure out how to work a pump right now.

Just drive.

Drive to Mom. Drive to the hospital where she is.

And once I get there, I'll sprint to her room and sit by her side so that when she wakes up, I can hold her hand and give her a hug and a kiss.

At first, I can barely make out the darkened road at this predawn hour through the tears and snot covering my face. I'm making the drive from pure muscle memory.

But then Mom's voice chimes in through the crying and choking and sniffling noises I'm making, like an angel on my shoulder reminding me to make good decisions.

Be careful, anak! Not too fast.

It's so loud, so clear, I could swear she's right next to me. It's enough to halt my sobs and compel me to look at the passenger seat next to me, then twist for a quick second to check the back seat.

But there's no one. It's just me in the car.

Even still, her voice—her warning—echoes.

Be careful, anak! Not too fast.

So I do exactly what she says. I take a handful of slow, deep breaths and get my sobbing under control. It takes another minute, but I manage to steady the flow of air in and out of my lungs. I dig a tissue from the center console, wipe my eyes dry, then focus on the road. I have to squint to see, they're so swollen.

But I do it. Because her voice rings like a drumbeat near my ear.

Be careful.

"I will, Mom." I say it firmly, as if she's sitting next to me, and I want it to be clear enough that she can hear.

"Mom." It's a whisper, but it's all I can do. Because to speak louder, to say more, would send me into another fit.

"Mom." I say it again, swallowing until the squeeze in my throat starts to fade.

Tears pool in my eyes, but I blink them away.

"Mom. I'm coming."

∼

I jog down the hospital hallway, my head pivoting in every direction as I try to scan the room numbers.

When I find the right room, I push open the door to find Andy sitting in a chair at Mom's bedside, holding her hand.

I gaze at her face, her closed eyes, and the way her mouth—which is normally shellacked in bright-red lipstick—is a pale, thin line. Her shoulder-length raven-hued hair is a tangled mess against the pillow.

He glances at me with swollen red eyes, his lips trembling as he shoves a fist in his thick dark-brown hair.

"Chloe, she's . . . ," he says, his voice ragged and hoarse. "She's gone."

"What?"

"She . . . she had complications . . . another heart attack. Sh—she's gone."

I can barely understand his words through his sobs. A second passes, but I don't cry. This can't be.

My blood turns to ice, and then the ice turns to dread. It pumps hot and cold at once, causing the strangest tingling in my fingers and toes.

I dart over to her other side and grab her hand. It's still warm. "She can't be dead. She's still warm. Her skin—it's still so warm." The way I speak, I'm weirdly calm. "She's still hooked up to everything, all these machines. They're keeping her alive."

Andy sniffles, then looks up at me. "Chloe, I'm so, so sorry. She passed a half hour ago."

"She's gone?" I bark the words through gritted teeth, my voice breaking at the end.

His lips tremble again. "I didn't know what to do . . . I . . . I know I should have called you to tell you, but you were driving, and I didn't want to upset you or get you into an accident . . ."

My mouth starts to quiver as I soak in his words.

"I'm sorry. I'm so, so sorry." His voice breaks, which breaks me. My baby brother watched our mom die alone in this room because I couldn't get here fast enough.

I run over and hug him, letting him sob into my shoulder. I try my best to stand as still as possible and absorb the shakes of his body, but it's so hard. Because I want to break too.

He pulls away, and I gaze at Mom once more, taking in the state of her body. Nothing moves. There's not even a twitch of her finger or the slightest rise of her chest. I grip both of my hands around hers, running my gaze along her arms. They remind me of branches that have fallen off a tree: still and brittle.

It starts to register in my brain. She looks so lifeless, because she is. Because she's dead.

I huff out a shaky breath. "How did this happen?"

He swallows, then takes a deep breath. "I was asleep when I got a call from one of Mom's coworkers saying that she collapsed at work after complaining about chest pain. They called an ambulance and rushed her to the hospital emergency room. Apparently the paramedics were able to resuscitate her on the ride to the hospital. She was awake when they admitted her. They stabilized her. She was—" He stops to clear his throat. "She was stable but unconscious when I got here. But then . . . but then a few minutes after I sat down with her, she went into cardiac arrest."

He tries to clear his throat, but this time, he can't hide the sob that rips from his throat.

I set Mom's hand back down on the bed, then walk over and hug him.

"It's okay," I whisper to him. "Just take a breath."

My pharmacist brain goes into overdrive wondering how this happened. I think back to our FaceTime session the other night, our conversation on the phone the other day, how we argued about her not doing enough to reduce her stress and address her high blood pressure.

My throat goes dry. That was probably what caused the heart attack.

I release Andy from my hug but keep hold of his shoulders as I gaze at him once more, at his swollen eyes, his puffy red cheeks. He's wearing jeans and a T-shirt, and they're rumpled to hell.

"She seemed fine yesterday when I saw her at home getting ready for work," Andy mutters, his tone defeated. Heartbroken. "She was smiling and laughing. She didn't complain about chest pain or tightness or—"

"Andy. It's okay. No one could have predicted this." I say the words knowing that I need to hear them too.

I bite the inside of my cheek, angry at myself that I didn't push harder for her to go to the doctor more often. And Mom was notorious for denying that she needed medicine even when she was sick. Maybe if she had made an appointment this week for just a checkup, the doctor would have noticed something or advised her to change something in her diet or caught something in Mom's labs so he could have prescribed a medication that would have helped prevent this . . .

If that's the case—if all she needed to do was go to the doctor's office to get checked out—this all could have been avoided. She could have been okay. She could have been awake and—

"Do you want a minute alone with Mom?" Andy asks me. "I got to spend some time with her before you got here, so you should have some time alone with her if you want."

Wiping my nose with the sleeve of my hoodie, I nod. "Thank you."

After he leaves, I take the chair he was sitting in, then grab her hand in mine for the final time.

~

My hand twitches at just how cold her skin feels now, like she's been holding a bag of frozen vegetables. I have no idea how long I've been sitting next to her. Probably awhile based on the chill of her skin.

She lies motionless, every last bit of life drained from her. She won't talk or breathe or smile or say my name or laugh or hug me ever again. She's gone. Forever.

When I mull that thought over and over in my brain, something inside me shatters. It's not just a clean break; it's a dam bursting at every crack. It's a glass window smashed into a billion pieces.

Shattered.

It's a loss of everything I've ever known, everything that mattered. A loss of my center, my true north, my anchor. My mom was what grounded me—grounded us. No matter where Andy and I were in life, no matter what we did, how far we traveled, whatever foolish mistakes we made, she was always there for us. We could always call her; we could always come home.

Not anymore.

Shattered.

Not broken. Because when something's broken, there's the expectation that it can be repaired. But shattered means too far gone, not salvageable. Like me. Nothing in me can be saved without her.

I lean up and fall against her chest, hugging her one last time, crying into the thin hospital bedsheets that shroud her body.

Body.

I shake my head. Not a body, not anymore. Now that she's dead, she's a corpse.

My breathing turns ragged. I cry until my voice goes hoarse and my throat turns raw. I sob until my eyes are so swollen, I can barely see.

I reach up and smooth a hand over her thick, perfectly black hair that doesn't have a single gray strand showing because she always colored it. The scent of gardenia, her favorite perfume, the scent I remember smelling on her ever since I was a kid, hits my nostrils. It's comfort and torment all at once. Comfort because that floral musk always reminds me of her. Torment because it's now a reminder that she's gone. Forever.

I'm so sorry.

It's all I can think. It's all I can say.

If only I could have had more time with her. Just a few more minutes, and I could tell her how sorry I am. I could tell her how I plan to drive back home every day off I have from now until the end of time, work be damned. I'll tell her I love her more than anything and anyone, and if she wants me to visit her every day, I will.

I grip her hand with both of mine. "I'm so sorry, Mom."

For every excuse I made, for every time I chose work over her, for letting too much time pass between visits home.

"I'm so sorry." My voice is raw and barely audible, but I get it out.

I stare at her face, waiting for a response. I don't know why. It's not like she can answer me.

But in this moment, I actually catch myself wondering if she can hear me. And then I scold myself because I know better than to think that. She can't. Of course she can't.

She's gone.

Chapter Four

I open my eyes. All I see are pillows. They line the floor, the walls, even the chairs. When I sit up, I look around. But there's nothing. Just pillows.

And then Mom appears next to me, smiling. Her lips are bright red, her eyes sparkle.

That's when I know. This is a dream.

I move to hug her anyway. She squeezes back. All I can do is smile at her and shake my head. I can't believe she's here, that she's awake and smiling. Even though she's not—because it's all a dream.

But I don't care. Nothing matters. I get to see her again.

When she leans away, breaking our hug, I grab hold of both of her hands.

"How are you here?" I ask.

She frowns the slightest bit. But then she smiles, and the warmth of it shines over me. It's like I'm standing in the sun.

"*Anak*. I'm always here."

The sound of my phone ringing jolts me awake. I sit up from the couch in Mom's living room and rub my eyes, remembering through the grogginess of my late-afternoon nap that I'm at her house two days after she passed away.

The dread seeps back in slowly, like a trickle of water. It's like my brain is still so distraught that it doesn't want to remember losing her.

So every time I go to sleep, there's that fuzzy moment between sleep and awake where I'm blissfully unaware that things have changed for the worse. And then when it does come back to me, when I remember that she's gone, the grief hits like a kick to the chest. I lose her all over again.

The array of dishes and Tupperware on the kitchen counter and table at Mom's house clues me in as well. Ever since she passed, her coworkers and friends have dropped off food for Andy and me. Neither one of us has had an appetite, though. We're eating a few bites here and there, enough to keep us alive between crying, staring into space, and talking to each other about funeral planning. What we couldn't cram in the freezer and refrigerator crowds every available space in the kitchen.

It's the slightest bit comforting to see so much food. It's like a visible, tangible sign of just how many people loved Mom, how many lives she was part of, how her family extended beyond Andy and me. It's a reminder of how many people are going to miss her.

I swallow back a lump in my throat and answer the phone when I see it's Julianne calling.

"Hello?" I say, my voice scratchy from crying.

"Hey. How are you doing? Actually, don't answer that. What a horrible question to ask you right now. Sorry."

"Don't be sorry. You've done so much for me."

When I finally stopped sobbing in Mom's hospital room, I phoned Julianne to fill her in on what happened. She covered my shift today and yesterday at the hospital, on what were supposed to be her days off, and then emailed all the other staff pharmacists to cover the rest of my shifts for the next couple of weeks while I stay in Kearney and arrange things for Mom's funeral.

"You were so on top of things at the hospital," I say. "By the time I called our manager to let him know what was happening, you had it all covered. I didn't have to explain anything. I can't tell you how much I appreciate that."

"Chloe, you're my best friend. Your mom was like a second mom to me. It's the least I could do."

"You're still coming this weekend, right?"

"Of course."

"You sure you feel up to it? You've been working nonstop. I'm sure you could use a couple days to rest."

"Chloe." Her tone turns firm. "You don't have to worry about me, okay? I'm doing all this because I want to."

After crying to Julianne on the phone when I told her about Mom passing, she offered to come and stay with Andy and me before the funeral for moral support. I tried to talk her out of it, but she shut me down immediately. I was glad honestly. Having her here for just a few days would be such a support.

"Just focus on yourself and your brother," she says. "How's he doing by the way?"

"Not good." I think back to how Andy looks more and more run-down every time I see him.

"Poor guy."

"I sent him out to buy toilet paper a little bit ago, hoping that would be a distraction. I don't know if it'll work. We still have to figure everything out. Like, what to do with the things in her house, insurance, funeral stuff. I already called Mom's work, her family here in the States, and her relatives in the Philippines to let them know she passed, but after a while I started crying so hard I had to stop talking, then apologize, then hang up and call them back, then I fell asleep, but I still have so much to do . . ."

My head spins like a merry-go-round when I think about our endless to-do list. I glance up and spot Mom's purse sitting on the coffee table. I set it there when we got home from the hospital and haven't bothered to look through it because just the thought of going through her belongings seems so wrong.

"I just—I feel like I need to be the strong big sister, but I'm such a mess right now." I pause to wipe my nose.

"Chloe, it's okay." The calm in Julianne's voice instantly soothes me. "You *are* the strong big sister. I promise you that's what Andy thinks of you, okay? He's just not saying it because he's sad. And you don't have to do everything right now. Forget about calling people. Just take today for yourself and Andy. Then eat something. Cry. Watch TV. Take a shower. Eat again, then cry again. That's all you're responsible for doing today, okay?"

I sigh, sniffling as I blink back tears. "Okay. Thank you."

"When I get there, I'll help you with your to-do list. You guys won't have to do this alone. I promise."

I whisper a thank-you before we hang up. I set my phone down, but it immediately buzzes with a text from Julianne.

You're being an amazing big sister to Andy. Your mom would be so proud.

My eyes water as I text her to say thank you. Then I glance over at the mountain of food in the kitchen and contemplate eating something when my phone rings yet again. When I see it's Auntie Linda, mom's older sister, calling, I answer right away.

"*Anakko.* How are you?" The fatigue is clear in her scratchy voice. I remember how she wailed when I called to tell her that Mom passed away.

I say that I'm okay and ask her the same.

"I'm okay too. I just . . ." She clears her throat. "I'm so sorry to ask you this because I know you're hurting, but . . . I was wondering what you and Andy were planning to do for your mom's funeral service."

I close my eyes, bracing myself for what she's going to say when I tell her. "Yes. I think we do know. Mom had always said she wanted to be cremated, and Andy and I would like to honor her wishes."

There's a heavy sigh on her end of the line. "I see." Her voice trembles. "She never said anything about a traditional Catholic service when she talked to you kids?"

"No, she didn't. I'm sorry, Auntie."

She sniffles, then dives into an explanation of how, in her and Mom's Filipino family culture, it's important to have a Catholic funeral with all the sacraments. I nod along, even though I know what I'm going to say at the end of all this. It makes sense why Auntie Linda wants this. She and Mom were born in the Philippines to a strict Catholic family who went to Mass multiple times a week. The habit held up even after they moved to the United States and settled in a suburb in Denver when Mom and Auntie Linda were teens. Their belief systems were never in sync, though. I'm too exhausted to remind Auntie that Mom hasn't been a practicing Catholic since she turned eighteen and could control how she spent her Sundays. That's one of the clearest memories I have of her, how she preferred to spend Sunday mornings playing with Andy and me instead of dragging us to church.

"It's not that I don't believe in God. I do," Mom said when I asked her as a kid why we never went to church but Auntie Linda and her family always did. "I just never liked church. So serious and boring and all about praying in a way that I never liked. And I don't think I need to go to church or Mass or whatever in order to feel connected to God. I pray plenty on my own, and I feel closer than when I recited any of those prayers growing up. I don't need a priest or rosary beads to tell me how to do it."

The few times we did go to church were whenever Auntie Linda, Uncle Lyle, and our cousins visited us or we visited them in Denver. Looking back now, I recall all the stern glances Auntie Linda threw Mom's way when she didn't go up to accept communion or repeat the prayers during service like everyone else. Now I understand that for someone as religious as Auntie Linda, it must have been so difficult to see her younger sister's disinterest in something she held so dear.

"So no viewing of your mom then? No communion?" Auntie Linda says, her voice breaking.

"I'm sorry, Auntie. It's what Mom wanted. We're just trying to honor that."

There's a few seconds of sniffling and a muffled sound, probably Auntie wiping her nose. "It's okay. I understand, *anakko*. I just . . ." She pauses again to blow her nose, the sound thundering in the receiver of my phone. "I just . . . I just want to make sure her soul is taken care of."

"I'm sure it is."

"Will there be a prayer at least?"

"Of course there will be."

"That will be so nice." The sigh she lets out sounds a tad lighter than before. "I'm sorry. I know this must be so hard for you. I didn't mean to give you more things to worry about. I shouldn't have asked."

"Auntie Linda, it's okay. She's your sister. I understand why you'd want to know."

"Thank you, *anak*." She lets out a soft cry.

My eyes well up just hearing how much she's in pain. What would it be like to outlive your younger sibling? For a split second I contemplate the grief that would consume me if someday, somehow Andy passes before me. My gut seizes, it's such a distressing, heartbreaking thought. I have to press my eyes shut for a few seconds before refocusing.

"I just . . . I just wish things had been different," Auntie Linda says. "There were so many things I should have said."

"I know." My throat tightens. "I feel the same way."

Listening to Auntie break on the phone makes me wish I could drop everything and go to her so I could give her a hug. It's a whole new kind of unnerving to hear my normally upbeat and cheerful aunt sound so completely ripped apart. Every memory I have of her, she's smiling or laughing. Every visit with her, Uncle Lyle, and their sons was full of laughter, playing, and good-natured bickering between her and Mom. Tears only happened when it was time to leave each other, and even then they were short lived because we always knew we'd see each other again.

Maybe because now we both know we'll never see Mom again, that's why her cries sound all the more wrenching.

She sniffles, then there's a soft, muffled noise. "I never got the chance . . . I shouldn't have waited so long to make things right. And now it's too late . . ."

I wait for her to finish, but all that follows is silence.

"Make what right, Auntie? What do you mean it's too late?" I shouldn't pry, but Auntie Linda sounds so distraught. What was too late for her to do concerning Mom?

But she doesn't answer. Instead she clears her throat. "Nothing, *anak*. I just . . . Once you figure out the date and time of the funeral, you call me, okay? Me and Uncle Lyle and your cousins will be there for you and Andy."

She promises to relay the funeral details to Mom's family as soon as we finalize them so that Andy and I don't have to. I thank her once more, we exchange I love yous, and I hang up.

Then I warm up a small plate of food but only manage a few bites as I try to untangle the mess in my brain. That cryptic thing Auntie Linda said, that dream I had about Mom. I'm too exhausted to make sense of any of it, though. So I fall back down on the couch, close my eyes, and hope I dream of Mom again.

～

"That was . . . weird," Andy says as he drops his car keys on the kitchen table.

"This whole situation is weird," I say.

Andy slumps into a chair while muttering a "yup."

We spent the morning touring the funeral home where we decided to hold Mom's service next week on May 20. All the plans have been finalized. We decided on a simple yet respectful ceremony to honor her memory. There will be a display table at the front where we can showcase photos of Mom and mementos if we want.

I silently hope that Auntie Linda will approve, since she wanted something more formal and Catholic. But then I remember how after *Apong* Selene's funeral and memorial service, which was hours long, Mom remarked how she'd never want something so elaborate. That stress knot in my stomach eases. Even if everyone disapproves, it's okay. Because this is what Mom wanted.

The funeral director we met with said she'd be happy to give the opening and closing remarks. I let out a sigh of relief when she offered that because it meant that I wouldn't have to make another round of awkward phone calls where I'm fighting not to cry as I talk to potential officiants.

I fall into the chair next to Andy. He twists his head, and I catch that dead-behind-the-eyes stare I've grown used to seeing him display these past few days. It's like he's looking around him but not really seeing anything.

When I focus my gaze on him, I notice he looks even more exhausted than he did this morning. There are bags under his eyes, and his hair flops every which way. The five-o'clock shadow he typically sports is slowly turning into a patchy beard. I wonder if he got any sleep last night, or if he just cried off and on until the sun rose like I did.

I bite my tongue to keep from saying anything. I'm in no position to lecture him about taking better care of himself. The glimpse I caught of myself in the bathroom mirror this morning made me blink in shock at just how hard I'm failing at taking care of myself too. My reflection tells me I'm a strange combination of haggard and childlike. Haggard because I'm sporting some hefty undereye bags due to days on end of crying and lack of sleep. I haven't bothered with styling my hair at any point. All I do is throw it up into a bun or ponytail.

And childlike because I haven't had the energy to do my makeup. When I'm disheveled and without makeup, I look like a lost kid who's also been working overtime in a factory, even though I'm well into my thirties.

"Do you want to talk about anything?" I ask him.

He shakes his head.

"It's not good to bottle everything up."

"Yeah, but . . . I don't know what to say. I just feel so sad. And empty. And hopeless."

I reach over and place my hand over his, then wait until he looks at me. "Do you want to talk to someone about how you're feeling? You don't have to talk to me, but I think it would help if you had someone you could confide in. Maybe a counselor?"

He pulls his hand away from mine and rests it in his lap, his eyes darting to the floor. "I don't need to do that. I'm fine."

The urge to tell him that it's okay not to be okay and to ask for help—to talk to a professional so that he can process his grief—takes hold. But I ignore it. Now's not the time to push him.

A quiet beat passes between us before I say anything else.

"Okay, well . . . if you ever want to talk, I'm here. And if you ever want to talk to someone who isn't me, I can recommend a therapist. I see one sometimes—"

"Got it. Thanks."

That's the most conviction I've heard him express in days.

A heavy sigh bursts from his mouth as he leans back and runs a hand through his hair. "Do you think we need to tell Dad?"

Just the word *Dad* coming from Andy's mouth sounds odd. Wrong, even.

It's been years since I've given any thought to him. Bill Howard was never an involved father, even when he was around. I remember distinctly how detached he seemed around us—when he wasn't drunk. Mom was always loving and joyful in every interaction with us our entire lives. Even when I was a little kid and Andy was a baby and Mom was frustrated with all our misbehaving and crying, I could still tell she cared. It was clear in the way that she looked at us, in how she rearranged her work, her social life, her everything to accommodate us kids. How she never left us, no matter how tough things got.

But Dad was a different story. Mom often had to tell him to play with me or change Andy's diaper.

Most of my memories of Mom and Dad involve them arguing about Dad's drinking. I can only recall a handful of times when they smiled and laughed with each other.

And then, one night, Dad left Andy and me in his car in the middle of winter while he got drunk at a bar for hours before driving home with us, getting pulled over, and then getting arrested. Mom filed for divorce at that point—when I was eight and Andy was still a baby. She got full custody; Dad hardly ever showed up for his scheduled weekend visits. He moved a million times and only gave us his updated address half the time. We'd see him once or twice a year when he randomly felt like coming to a graduation or soccer game or recital. The last time I saw him was at my undergraduate graduation, when he sheepishly congratulated me after the ceremony, then disappeared when Mom's family came to greet me. He reeked of booze even then.

"I . . . honestly don't know. I don't even know how to get a hold of him. I don't have his phone number. I don't even know where he lives now."

"It's probably for the best," Andy says. "He doesn't deserve to come to her funeral after how he left, how he treated her."

The tip of my tongue itches with the urge to tell Andy to talk more. He hardly ever talks about him, since he was still a baby when Dad left. And even when Dad would visit us after the divorce, it was always so sporadic that it was almost impossible for Andy to form any kind of meaningful bond with him.

Then the impulsive part of my brain acts—the same part that yells "ow!" when I stub my toe or when I automatically right myself after I stumble.

For a fleeting second, I think this should have been Dad instead of Mom.

But I catch it midthought and kick it away before it can fully process and take hold in my brain. Because to wish anyone dead, no matter who they are or what they've done, is just plain evil.

"I guess we need to think about what kind of music we want to play during the service," he says, pulling me back.

"Oh. Right," I say, recalling that the funeral home asked us to email back a few songs to play before and during the service. "I can't think of anything appropriate for a funeral. Mom liked listening to disco songs by Donna Summer and Gloria Estefan."

The corner of Andy's mouth twitches up into a ghost of a half smile. In his eyes is a dazed look, like he's remembering something. I wonder if he's thinking of all those times when Mom would dance to her favorite songs while cleaning the house.

He looks up at me, his eyes brighter all of a sudden. "Could you imagine blaring 'Turn the Beat Around' as people arrived at the service?"

He chuckles, which makes me laugh too. "I actually love that idea. Let's not rule it out."

Andy's expression turns pained once more. "Who's going to do her eulogy?"

I rack my brain, wondering if any of Mom's relatives would be comfortable speaking about her publicly. But after talking to most of them on the phone and hearing them so distraught at suddenly losing her, I don't think any of them would be in the right emotional state to do it. I consider saying that we should ask one of Mom's coworkers but think better of it. I don't want to put anyone on the spot like that.

The only people that make sense for the eulogy are Andy and me. But I don't want to put that kind of pressure on my younger sibling while he's grieving.

That leaves me.

I hold my breath at the thought, at somehow getting myself to the point where I will be steady enough to speak in front of loved ones, friends, and coworkers. Even when I just imagine it, my stomach curdles. I've never been comfortable with public speaking. To do it on the day of my mother's funeral seems like the most daunting task on the planet. I'd rather attempt to fly to the moon. It sounds more doable.

But before I outright reject the idea, I pause and let myself imagine just for one moment what it would feel like if I could get myself together and speak words that would do her justice—if I could stand and sing her praises in front of everyone who ever loved her, one last time.

The knot in my stomach loosens. I take it as a sign. At least part of me thinks I can do it. And I have a few days to prepare.

Maybe I can do this.

My eyes connect with Andy's. "I'll do it. I'll give her eulogy."

A concerned frown fills his face. "Are you sure?"

"Positive."

He opens his mouth and hesitates, but I stop him.

"I'm the oldest, Andy. It's my job to do stuff like this."

"Yeah, but . . . we're both adults, Chloe." There's the slightest petulance in his voice. "You shouldn't feel like you have to do things just because you were born first."

"I don't feel that way at all," I say with a newfound conviction rising within me. "I want to."

As he nods, his eyes grow watery once more. He swallows, then reaches across the table for my hand and squeezes it. He doesn't say thank you, but he doesn't have to. I know exactly how much my offer means to him.

I give him a quiet nod in return.

~

The pile of crumpled papers overflowing from the trash can in my bedroom stares back at me, taunting me.

One whole day of trying to write a eulogy for Mom, and I've got nothing to show for it.

I tried everything. All those standard phrases people employ when they lose a loved one.

She was the most wonderful person.

She loved her kids more than anything.

We miss her every single day.

They're all true, of course. It's just that every single one of those phrases falls short of how I feel about her. Mom was everything to Andy and me, to her sister, to her cousins, to her friends, to the people she worked with. She was more than words could ever express. How am I supposed to use just words to describe her?

I shove aside my notes and scoop up my phone, then head out to the kitchen. Maybe getting out of my old bedroom, which I've confined myself to the entire day, will be the change I need to break the logjam in my head.

I grab a glass of water, sit at the table, then do a slow scan of the small open-concept space of Mom's house, as if gazing at the framed paintings of flowers, the light-colored kitchen cabinets, or the endless knickknacks displayed on the bookshelf and end tables will magically help me think of something to write. It doesn't.

I've drained my glass when the scent of gardenia hits me once more. It's so strong that every limb, every muscle in my body freezes. My heart races, and my breathing picks up.

Before, that scent indicated one thing: Mom was nearby.

My eyes burn with tears when I remind myself that it's impossible. This is just another instance of my emotions playing tricks on me. That scent is my brain acting out in desperation. It's going to happen again. I just need to gently remind myself of the truth every time it does.

I wipe my face, then walk back to my room.

Chapter Five

"Thanks again for making all those calls," Andy says from across the kitchen table while nursing a mug of tea.

It's been a handful of days since Mom died, and we've been slowly wading our way through a to-do list. Contacting people to let them know the funeral date and time, which is in three days. Contacting health insurance companies and life insurance companies and the social security office. Remembering to eat and shower and sleep.

It's barely seven in the evening and already my entire body feels like it's been wrung out. But my main concern is Andy. Every day he looks more and more run-down. It doesn't matter how many times I make him sit down to eat a meal or drink water or sleep, it doesn't seem to do any good. Grief is ravaging every part of him. It's like looking at a plant that continues wilting no matter how many times I water it or put it out in the sun.

He sighs, his shoulders rising and falling with the slow movement. When he looks up at me, there's a glint in his eye, like he's embarrassed. "I know I should have . . . done more. I promise I'll try to help out more from now on." He fixes his eyes on the tea as he speaks.

My throat squeezes at how red his face is from day after day of crying, at how the only time he's been able to hold it together ever since losing Mom was that hour we spent touring the funeral home. Every other time, he's been either crying or sitting in a stupor of grief, staring blankly at nothing in particular. It's such a far cry from the grin he almost always sports, that sparkle in his eyes that never used to go away. I barely recognize him.

I reach across the table to gently grab his arm. "Andy. You're doing enough as it is. I promise."

I rub the back of my neck, wondering if I'll sleep any better than I did last night. It was another night of tossing and turning until I finally drifted off. I've lost count of the number of times I've jolted awake the past several nights, eyes wide and searching in the pitch-black darkness.

My phone buzzes with an email alert. I check and see that it's a message from my boss, Malcolm, asking how things are going and when I'll be able to come back to work. I quickly answer that I'm not certain, but I'll do my best to keep them posted. Just then, my phone rings with a number from the hospital. I stand up and go into my old bedroom to answer it.

"Chloe? It's Malcolm. How are you doing?"

I bite back the annoyed sigh I ache to let loose. Malcolm is the newly christened pharmacy manager as of three months ago. Ever since he took the position, he's been a textbook micromanager, sending out emails over the littlest things, from cleaning out the break room refrigerator to thinking of team-building activities the department can do every quarter. Today is not the day I want to deal with an unnecessary phone call from him.

"I've been better," I answer him.

"Of course. I just want to say on behalf of everyone in pharmacy, we're so sorry for your loss."

"Thank you."

"It's just . . . well, here's the thing, Chloe." He sighs. "We understand this is a challenging time for you and your family. You're allowed to have a weeklong bereavement leave, per hospital policy. But we're going to need you to come back next week."

"Sorry?"

"It's just that . . . well, as healthcare professionals, we're essential personnel. You know that. We can't just take time off like in other jobs. Even if there's an extenuating circumstance, like a loss in the family, we'll do our best to accommodate, but there needs to be a return date on the schedule. You understand, don't you?"

I grit my teeth as he speaks, only easing up when I feel the beginnings of a tension headache.

"Fine, yes, that may be true, but come on, Malcolm. Not even seven days ago I got the news that my mother died suddenly of a heart attack. And now you're on my ass about going back to work? We haven't even buried her yet. What the hell is wrong with you?"

Instead of responding, Malcolm just stammers.

"Can't you just take time out of my PTO accrual? I've got at least two months banked."

"I'm sorry, but you need to make requests for time off ahead of time."

The no-nonsense way he recites those words makes me want to scream.

"Malcolm, I've worked damn hard for this hospital. I've busted my ass for the past seven years to be a reliable and hardworking staff member. I've covered more open shifts than anyone else in the department on top of being the residency program director. Whenever someone calls in sick or wants to take time off at the last minute, I'm the first to volunteer to cover those shifts. I've never asked for anything in return. Until now. Now I'm asking for you to give me some extra time to grieve my mother."

It hits me that this is exactly how Mom was, always picking up shifts and working holidays.

Again Malcolm stammers, but I don't have the patience to listen to what he has to say. Anger steamrolls my insides. Inside my head a loud voice screams, *Fuck it!*

"You know what? I'm not dealing with this. I quit."

"Chloe," Malcolm says, his voice softer. "You're not thinking clearly. You're just upset and sad and—"

"I've made my decision. I'm done. Please don't call me again. I will expect a call from HR in the next few days. Not you."

I hang up, then quickly type an email of resignation on my phone and hit send. An unfamiliar numbness washes over me. I just burned a bridge. I just lost the job I had worked my entire adult life to earn. The job that I used to pride myself so much on—the job that used to define me. I just walked away from it.

The job that I used to put first, before everything—before my social life, before my sleep schedule, before time at home, before my family . . .

My insides catch fire with an infuriated mix of anger, frustration, and regret.

All those extra shifts I took. All those calls I missed from Mom because I was working. All those times I opted to stay in Omaha on my days off because I was too tired from work to drive home for a quick visit.

None of that was worth it.

Because of my job, I wasn't able to see her before she died. I wasn't able to say goodbye.

But I have no one to blame other than myself. I'm the one who prioritized work before everything else—before her.

My chest aches, and I start to pant. Tears flood my eyes until everything is blurry. I try to walk forward, but I hit my leg on something—my desk, I think—and fall to the floor with a thud and a yelp.

Seconds later, heavy footsteps sound from behind my closed bedroom door. Andy bursts in.

"Are you okay?" he asks. "What was that noise?"

My head spins as I rub the sore spot on my leg, biting back another yelp. The reel of memories swirling through my brain halts on that FaceTime conversation I had with Mom last week when I told her I'd be home to visit at the weekend, and she promised to make fried rice and wontons for me.

I was so close to seeing her again. I should have dropped everything that night and gone to her. Then I would have seen her one last time, I could have hugged her and kissed her and smelled her hair and told her I loved her while looking into her eyes . . .

Sobs shake me to the core. Soon Andy is crouched down, bracing me with his hands on my arms. I try to breathe, but it comes out like a broken sob. I tremble like I'm standing outside in the dead of winter with no clothes.

"Mom's wontons," I say, my voice a ragged whisper from my cries. "I—I don't even know how to cook them. She's gone and . . ."

A million times I've stood in the kitchen while she cooked, and not once did I think to ask how to make them. I scour the contents of my brain, struggling to come up with one single recipe of hers that I remember. Not one comes to mind.

All I ever did when she cooked for us was eat and say thank you. I should have asked her to show me how to cook them. I had so many chances.

Andy turns my head to look at him. I blink until his blurry image starts to come into focus. "Chloe, I know. I know she's gone."

"Do you know the recipe?" I babble.

The pained expression on his face deepens. "I never thought to ask."

I force air out of my mouth, which buys me a second to speak more clearly. "She's gone, Andy. Mom's gone."

My voice ricochets off the walls. His eyes grow even wider as they fill with tears. "I know! Chloe, I know! Fuck, I can't . . ."

He pauses before gulping and taking a breath. One tear, then another tumbles down his full cheeks.

"Christ, Chloe. I know she's gone. It's tearing me up, too, okay? I'm a goddamn disaster. But we can't just fall apart."

For a moment I'm heartened at my brother's show of strength. But the pain from Mom's loss runs so deep, it surpasses any burst of hope.

I drown in a fresh wave of grief. "How can we not fall apart? Look at us. We're so broken, and it's only been days since she's been gone." I have to stop and gulp air, my throat aches so badly. "How can we do this without her?"

His lip trembles as he opens his mouth, but a long moment passes and he says nothing.

I'm grabbing at his arms like I'm about to fall and holding on to him is the only thing that'll keep me steady. "She's gone and we don't know any of her recipes and I didn't get to say goodbye or tell her that I loved her one last time and it's not fucking okay. None of this is fucking okay."

Every word comes out stilted because I'm gasping for air between sobs.

"It was almost two months since I came home. Two fucking months." The words pour out of me like runny, snotty soup. "I could have come home more often, but there was always an excuse, a reason to put it off."

"Chloe." Andy gives my arms a gentle squeeze as he holds me. He shakes his head, glancing down at the ground as the tears drip from his face. "Chloe . . ." All he can do is say my name in a broken voice.

My heart cracks even more. My baby brother is sitting next to me, watching as I completely fall apart.

"I gave you so much shit for living at home with her. But you made the right choice. You got to see her every day."

With the last of my words goes the last of my energy. My head is so heavy I can barely hold it up.

"Chloe, stop." He gives me the slightest shake, probably to jerk me out of my grief hysteria, but it doesn't do anything. I'm sinking deeper and deeper into the abyss. I don't care if I ever get out.

"You can't beat yourself up like this. Mom would hate it if she were here and saw you acting like this."

"But she's not here. And that's the whole point." I speak with an eerie, defeated calm. I've never heard myself sound like this before.

Andy's pained expression turns dejected. He lets go and we both sit on the floor, hunched over and cross-legged and staring at the ground, clearly exhausted from screaming and crying. For what feels like minutes, we alternate between sniffling and wiping our noses. We're both beyond shattered, both sinking into the depths of something I'm not sure we'll be able to climb out of.

"I quit my job," I blurt.

In my peripheral vision, I see Andy's head jerk up. "You can't quit your job. You've worked so hard—"

"And look where it got me," I say, cutting him off. "I missed saying goodbye to our mom on her deathbed."

"That's not . . ." He shakes his head. "Mom would be so disappointed in you."

A line that normally would have cut me to the core elicits zero reaction from me. I can't compel myself to feel anything at his words.

"I don't care," I say in that same eerily defeated tone. "I don't even want to go back. I don't give a shit about that or anything right now."

Andy shakes his head before standing up and hauling me to my feet. Then he lowers me onto the bed and says something about me getting some rest as I turn to lie on my side. He shuts off the light and starts to walk out of the room but stops in the doorway to look back at me. The light from the hallway frames his silhouette, highlighting just how tall and lanky he is.

"You'll feel better tomorrow. Promise," he says before shutting the door behind him.

I sit up and decide to change into the shorts and oversize T-shirt that I always sleep in. Then I crawl under the covers. As exhausted as I am, it's hell falling asleep. Everything in my room is a reminder of Mom. That flimsy baby-pink bookshelf she helped me assemble in high school that holds books I haven't read in years. The walk-in closet that contains all of the overflow from Mom's own closet because she loved shopping sales. The small brown desk in the corner that displays a trio of framed photos—one of me as a toddler playing in a sandbox with Mom, one of Andy and me riding a carousel together, and one of the three of us huddled together on a family road trip when Andy was in kindergarten and I was in middle school.

I zero in on the photo of Mom and me, fixating on how the bridges of our noses both crinkle when we grin wide. How did I never notice that before?

My eyes burn, and I choke through a cry. I toss and turn in the full-size bed. Even it reminds me of her. I remember the squabble we had at the furniture store while choosing a new bed. I was sixteen and wanted a queen, but Mom insisted on just a full-size one because even though my bedroom was technically big enough to hold a queen, it would feel cluttered with all the other furniture I had in it. The moment we brought the full-size bed home, assembled the frame, and put it together, it was the perfect fit. She was right. Like always.

When I finally fall asleep, I dream. Mom and me and Andy are sitting in the kitchen, playing cards. A plate of her famous wontons sits in the center for us to snack on. Everything smells like gardenia.

She discards two cards, then looks at me, pushing her glasses up the bridge of her nose. The smile she flashes is so happy and pure. "Your turn, *anak*."

But I don't take a card. All I can do is stare at her. I want to hug her, but dream-me can't move. A second later she reaches over and touches my hand. And then it's all okay.

~

A splitting headache is my wake-up call. I roll over in bed and check the time. Five past eleven. I'd groan at sleeping in so late, but I don't have the energy. When I swallow, my throat burns. It's raw from how hard I cried.

I'm in desperate need of water. Then coffee. Then maybe I'll have the energy to collapse onto the kitchen floor and cry there.

I pad to the bathroom, then to the kitchen. I press a hand against my head. I'm so light-headed, gripping the counter is the only way I stay standing as I fill a glass with water. One gulp, then two. Then a third. I set the empty glass down on the counter. It lands with a soft clanking noise. And now both my hands are free to grip the counter, to keep me upright, to help me stay standing.

"What does it even matter?" I mutter to myself, knowing full well that at some point today, I'll end up curled into a ball on the ground, whimpering until I'm gasping for air.

Behind me I hear the soft shuffle of footsteps. Taking a breath, I wipe my runny nose with the back of my wrist. I owe Andy an apology for how I flipped out yesterday. I need to get my shit together. Julianne is coming later today; then Auntie Linda, Uncle Lyle, their sons, and the rest of Mom's family are arriving tomorrow for Mom's funeral, which is happening the day after.

I turn around, ready to face Andy, to tell him sorry and then ask him how the hell we get through this day, yet another day without our mom, when we've barely made it through the ones we've had so far.

But when my eyes focus on the person who just walked into the kitchen, I nearly double over.

What's in front of me can't be.

What I'm seeing isn't real.

This . . . it's not possible.

She's not here anymore.

But she is.

I open my mouth, but there are no words. Just the sharp intake of air. And then I choke. A second after that, my eyes are blurry again. They burn worse than before.

One second after that, I sob.

Mom is here, standing two feet away from me, in the flesh. Somehow, some way.

Chapter Six

As I stand and watch her place a fresh filter into the coffee maker, I try to make sense of it. What . . . why . . . how the hell is she here?

I stumble toward her, my legs wobbly and disbelieving until I pull her into a hug. The feel of her body against mine almost makes me believe. There's warm skin on mine. Her thick shoulder-length hair is soft along my cheek. Her gardenia perfume hits my nostrils, and I cry even harder.

She's here, in the flesh, all her flesh, in my arms. It's real—she's real. I can feel her and smell her and hear her surprised "good morning, *anak*" as I squeeze her as tight as I possibly can.

This is comfort. Pure comfort.

"*Anak*! What are you—" Her last few words fall muffled against my shoulder.

"You're here." My words are barely audible through the blubbering cries I let out. "I'm so, so happy," I babble.

But happy is so not the right word. More like the most overwhelming mixture of bliss and relief a human being could ever feel.

She pats my back, like a wrestler tapping out during a match. It's only then that I realize how I'm squeezing the air out of her.

When I release her, I see a look of wild shock in her eyes. "Chloe!" she yells before smacking me on the shoulder.

That familiar frown burrows deep in her face. I let out another happy sob. I don't even let myself blink. I can't endure one more nanosecond without her.

"I could barely breathe," she says, chest rising with a breath. "What are you thinking?"

With both hands, I wipe the tears from my face. And then her frown shifts from annoyed and bewildered to concerned.

"What's the matter?" She grabs me by the arms. "What's wrong? *Anakko*, tell me."

I shake my head, clasping my arms behind my back to keep from mauling her yet again with a constricting hug.

"You can tell me anything, remember?" she says.

Endless questions swarm my brain, making my head feel heavy and dizzy.

How is it possible that I can see you?

Are you real?

Are you a ghost?

How come when I touch you, you feel real?

How are you standing here, in front of me?

Aren't you supposed to be dead?

How are you alive?

And if you really are alive . . . why do I think you died?

"Mom, what . . . what are you doing here?" is the best I can sputter out.

Her frown of confusion is back. "What are you talking about? It's morning time. I'm always home in the mornings."

I do a frantic scan of her face, then of her slight five-foot-three frame for any clue as to why she's standing in front of me and not lying in the morgue of a funeral home, like she should be.

"But . . . but how?" I stammer, then sniffle.

The expression on her face indicates that she's utterly mystified by me, like I have a tree growing out of my head.

I contemplate another question to clarify. But then I think *screw it* and hug her against me once more.

"I don't even care." I kiss her forehead. "You're here and I'm so, so happy. I love you so much."

I see Andy come stumbling down the hall from his room to the coffee maker. "Morning," he mumbles, rubbing a fist against one eye.

"Mom's here!" I practically scream the words. They're only slightly muffled by my tears of joy.

Around me, Mom's arms tighten, then loosen. Then she pats my back and says a muffled, "Okay, *anak*. That's enough. I need to breathe, remember?"

But it is physically impossible for me to let go. Nothing on this planet or in this universe could compel me to release her from this hug.

I bury my face in her thick jet-black hair and breathe in. Gardenia again, this time mixed with her favorite honeysuckle shampoo. When I look up, I spot Andy frowning from behind his coffee mug. His eyes are only a little puffy—from sleep, not crying. But they've been swollen nonstop for days . . . What in the world is going on?

When I finally let her go, she backs up and smooths out the wrinkles in her blouse. "Chloe, what in the world was all that about?"

"Seriously," Andy says. He glances between Mom and me before his stare settles on me. "What is up with you?"

A bout of dizziness hits before I can say anything. It's so sudden and strong, I have to grip the edge of the counter to stay standing.

A second later, I let go, thinking I can answer this question just fine while standing, but then I start to teeter over. I grab at the counter again, wondering what is causing my head to feel so heavy.

And then my vision goes cloudy. I blink until I can just start to see in front of me again. There's Andy and Mom, both staring at me, confusion rife in their expressions.

Mom takes a step toward me, her hand outstretched. "Chloe, are you okay?"

My legs give out completely. Her question is the last thing I hear before I crumble to the ground. I blink again, but then everything around me goes dark and soundless.

~

When I open my eyes, I'm lying on the cold ceramic tile floor of Mom's kitchen. She's crouched on my right side, and Andy's crouched on my left.

The first sensation I register is their warm hands on my arms. I blink again and again until I can make out the image above me clearly.

Their mouths are moving, but I can't hear anything. Just a soft ringing.

And then, a long second later, I hear it. Their voices raised in panic.

"*Anak*, are you okay?"

"Chloe! Chloe, look at me."

It's a struggle to heed all the directions they shout at me. I try to answer that I'm fine, but then my brain processes that Andy just asked me to do something too. When I realize I can't do both at once, I close my eyes and take a breath.

"Don't close your eyes." My brother's voice booms around me, causing me to peel open my eyes even though I don't want to.

"Yes, I can hear you," I groan. "And yes, I'm okay, Mom."

The worried lines that fill Mom's face ease a tad. Andy tells her to step back so he can haul me up, which he does easily with both of his hands under my arms for support.

He leads me to the couch in the living room, Mom scurrying behind us.

"Maybe she hit her head. She needs to go to the doctor," Mom says behind me.

"She didn't. I was able to put my hand behind her head and cradle it as she fell. My hand took most of the impact."

The loud sigh she lets out indicates she's relieved. "Okay, good," she says to Andy. "If you hadn't woken up, I don't even want to know how your sister would have hurt herself."

Mom sits next to me while Andy straightens up to stand in front of us. He frowns down at me, like a watchful guardian. "Well, thankfully she didn't," he says before putting his hands on his hips.

"Maybe she had a bad dream about me, and it felt so real when she woke," Mom says before handing me a glass of water and telling me to drink it all.

They discuss a few more possible options for why I fainted all of a sudden, not once asking for my input. But even if they did, I wouldn't have a reasonable explanation. I haven't the slightest clue what happened to me a minute ago. Just like I have no idea what happened to Mom.

And I have no idea what the hell is going on right now.

Mom hugs my arm and smooths my hair with her hand. Normally, being fussed over makes me want to shed my skin just to get away. And even though I'm not a fan of how they're talking about me like I'm not even in the room, it's more than okay. I'll happily sit here and take it. Because I'm sitting next to Mom. She's physically here—with me. With us. This is what I've been wishing for.

Questions from earlier seep back into my brain.

What the hell is happening? How is she alive and here again? *Is* this a dream? Am I having some sort of breakdown because I was so stricken with grief the past few days that my brain just couldn't take it anymore, and this is the result? Did I dream up an alternate reality where my mom is somehow still alive?

I scan through my mental Rolodex of medical conditions I've learned in my career that can alter a person's state of mind. But running through endless symptoms in my brain just confuses me. Nothing seems to line up. Absolutely nothing makes sense.

Except maybe an emotional breakdown. In my intense grief, I could be hallucinating the image of Mom. But even that doesn't fully explain what's happening to me. The world around me is too real. I can touch the objects surrounding me. The fact that I can hug Mom and touch her proves she's not a hallucination.

Mom and Andy continue their assessment of me, chattering about whether or not I need to go to the doctor.

I stand up and shake my head. "I don't need to go to the doctor."

"You sure?" Mom asks. "You're acting very strange."

"I just need a minute, okay?"

I lean down and give her another long hug, but this time I'm careful not to hug her too tight.

"I'm so, so glad you're here," I whisper.

When I release her, she's flashing that bewildered expression at me once more. She tells Andy to walk me to my room, but I wave him off, saying it's not necessary. I shut the door behind me, plop down on my bed, and grab my laptop. But before I can turn it on, my text alert goes off. It's a message from Julianne.

Quick, I need you to talk me out of keying Dr. Hoechlin's car. That condescending ass made a pill counting joke during rounds this morning and I'm going to lose it on him, I swear.

I wish you were here to talk me down during my lunch break! What will I do without you for the next month?? LOL

I frown at the message. What is Julianne talking about? When did I take a month off work?

I exit out of my text messages and glance at the date. March 30. What the . . . ?

I shake my head and squint at the date again. That's not possible. Yesterday it was May.

I turn my phone off, then turn it back on again. Maybe something glitched in the software and the dates are wrong. But when I turn the phone back on, it says the same thing. March 30.

I bolt out of the room, run to the kitchen where Mom tacks a brand-new monthly calendar on the wall every year, and check the date. March 30.

When I look up, I notice Mom and Andy have paused their conversation to gawk at me in confusion.

"You sure you're okay?" Mom asks from where she's sitting on the couch.

I ruffle the messy bun on the top of my head. "I am completely fine."

Then I run to the bathroom to look at myself in the mirror. I look the exact same as I did when I fell asleep last night—in May. I'm still wearing an oversize T-shirt and a pair of plaid sleeping shorts, the outfit I crawled into bed last night wearing.

Every single thing is the same. But everything is different. And nothing makes sense.

I dart back in my room and check the date and the day of the week ten more times. Then I fire up my laptop and visit more than a dozen random websites to make sure they're listing today's date as the same too.

I look up a dozen random businesses online, call them, and ask them what day it is. They all say March 30. When I ask if anything crazy happened yesterday or the day before, half of the people on the phone ask me to repeat the question. When I explain that I think something weird has happened to the days of the week, half of them hang up on me. One asks if I'm high. One asks if I need medical attention.

And then it pops into my head that I should call the hospital where Mom was. And the funeral home.

But when I ask the hospital if they have a record of the patient Mabel Howard checking in, they say there's no record of her.

"But . . . how can that be?" I stammer. "She had a heart attack. One of your ambulances picked her up from her place of work when she collapsed. You resuscitated her on the drive to the hospital, but she lost consciousness when she was admitted . . ."

There's a long pause on the other end along with the sound of fingers hammering away on a keyboard.

"Ma'am, I'm so sorry, but I can't find any information for a patient by that name."

I stammer a few more sounds of disbelief before mumbling a thank-you, then call the funeral home. My ears perk up at hearing the gentle voice of the director. Andy and I just met her in person a couple of days ago.

"Hi, yes, um, I want to double-check on a service that my brother and I arranged for our mother. Mabel Howard."

There's a shuffling paper noise.

"We toured your funeral home a few days ago," I say, trying to keep my tone from hitting a panicked register. I almost say that we scheduled Mom's funeral for May 20, but then I remind myself that it's not May anymore. It's March again.

"I'm so sorry, dear, but I don't have any services in the books for an individual by that name."

In the seconds that follow, I hold my breath, my head spinning.

"What date is it today?"

"March 30," she says.

"And you . . . you don't remember speaking to me or my brother? Chloe and Andy Howard?"

"I'm sorry, dear." Her tone is just as sincere as I remember it. "I don't mean to imply anything by this, but I make it a point to meet every person and every family that schedules a service with our establishment," she says. "I promise I'd remember you and your brother, and your mother, if you came here."

She's so sweet and comforting in her tone. Just like she was the first time she met Andy and me—even though apparently she doesn't think we've met at all.

I open my mouth but say nothing. My brain is a mass of confusion. Nothing is making sense.

I quietly thank her, then hang up. And then I jolt out of my bedroom and to the living room where Andy and Mom are sitting together.

"Andy," I bark.

They both turn to look at me.

"I, um, need you to help me with something. In my room."

Both of them frown at me.

"There's a spider on the ceiling. I can't reach it."

Andy sighs and stands up, then walks over to me. I grab him by the arm and drag him to my bedroom, shutting the door behind me.

He's frowning as he scans the ceiling. "I don't see a spider."

I tug his arm to get him to look back at me. "There's no spider. I need to ask you something serious. You can't tell anyone, though."

He scrunches his face.

I grab him by the arms, then take a breath. "Do you remember what happened to Mom?"

His head falls forward as his brows wrinkle together. "What are you talking about?"

"I'm serious, Andy. Do you remember what happened to her? Do you remember her dying?"

He jerks out of my hold. "What the hell . . . Mom isn't dead. She's sitting in the living room. Why would you even think that?"

I hold up a hand to cut him off. "I know, but . . . something happened to her a few days ago and . . ."

His eyes stay fixed on me, like they're searching for something.

"It was like she died," I say, knowing full well I'm not making any sense.

His thick eyebrows furrow as he scoffs and backs away from me. He rests his hands on his hips. "This isn't funny, Chloe. Why would you joke about something as fucking awful as that?"

My hands fly up to my hair. I make dual fists near my scalp and try to hold back a scream. "I'm not joking. This is real. And I'm telling the truth. Yesterday, Mom was gone. We lost her. But she's back now, like nothing happened. I'm just . . . trying to make sense of it."

He says nothing, his expression morphing from disbelief to disgust. "Obviously Mom's not gone. She's sitting in the living room. She's perfectly fine."

He reaches for the knob but then twists back to look at me. "I don't know what is going on with you, Chloe. But whatever it is, figure it out. I don't want you saying any of this crap to her."

When he leaves, he shuts the door behind him. I fall into a sitting position on the edge of my bed, struggling with the mess inside my brain. Just then I remember that Julianne texted me. I should ask her what the hell is going on.

It's half a dozen rings until she answers.

"Julianne! Julianne, what day is it?"

She lets out a chuckle. "Wow. Hello to you too. What's with the terrified tone?"

When I don't say anything, she answers. "Okay, um. It's March 30."

"March 30," I repeat to myself.

It tumbles over and over in my head.

"Are you okay, Chloe?"

My chest heaves as I try to get my racing heartbeat under control. "No. I mean, yes, I'm okay. I'm not hurt or anything like that or . . . I just . . . It's just that something weird has happened and it's March 30, even though it's not supposed to be . . . I just don't even know what to say or what to think or what to do."

There's silence on the other end of the line. "Shit, is this a joke?" She booms out a laugh. "Gotta hand it to you. You got the element of surprise on me. You're always so serious. Nicely done."

I shake my head, even though she can't see me. "No, Julianne. Just listen to me." I kick my legs forward and settle into a cross-legged position. I don't want Mom or Andy to hear me right now. "Listen, I'm not joking. I woke up today, and things were weird. Like, completely, off-the-wall weird."

"How do you mean?" All lightness has left Julianne's voice. I can picture her furrowed brow perfectly, her inquisitive blue eyes, a wrinkle at the top of her ski-slope nose broadcasting her confusion at what I'm saying.

I open my mouth, ready to divulge everything that's happened since I woke up minutes ago. But then I stop myself. I can't be totally honest. She'll think I've completely lost my mind.

So instead, I decide to work backward from the point where it all started.

"Do you remember when I took off to drive home to Kearney? It was May 7. I had to drive home because of . . . family stuff. Do you remember that?"

There's a pause on her end.

"What do you mean May 7? It's March, Chloe."

"Right, I know that, but . . ." I press my eyes shut and breathe. "Okay, so you—you don't remember me calling you about something weird that happened at home?" I keep my tone even. I need to be calm.

There's nothing but silence.

"Chloe, I'm really sorry, but I have no idea what you're talking about."

Julianne has been my best friend since we met freshman year of college. I know when she's lying, even if I can't see her face. And right now, she's not lying. That confusion and uncertainty in her tone is real. She's telling me the truth.

I tug a hand through my hair. "Okay." I take a breath, my mind racing as I try to think of where to take our conversation next. "Can you tell me what I did last week, then?"

"You worked, then you went home to visit your mom and brother for Easter." She pauses to chuckle. "And when you came back to the hospital, you put in a request to take three more weeks off so you could spend more time at home."

"I did?" My voice hitches up.

"I was as surprised as everyone. Workaholic pharmacist Chloe Howard never, ever takes time off. But you told me that weekend with your mom made you realize how you work too much, and you wanted to spend more time with her. A whole month."

"Oh." I can't believe I did that.

Julianne chuckles about how upset our manager, Malcolm, was at my last-minute request to take time off immediately, but then a group of our coworkers who I've covered shifts for multiple times this past year offered to cover me while I was gone as a thank-you.

"Malcolm was speechless, don't you remember? It was awesome."

A few seconds of silence follow before I answer her.

"Yeah, um, it definitely was. You sure you don't remember sending me any texts about my mom?"

She says no.

"You don't remember—wait, hang on."

I switch my phone to speaker, then swipe through my text messages. When I get to my text chain with Julianne, I scan for the exchange where I told her about Mom passing away. But those texts are nowhere to be found. I stare at the screen in disbelief. How the hell did they disappear?

Instead all I see is a text where I tell Julianne that I'm planning to take a month off work to stay home with my mom. She replies with a mind-blown emoji, then a text that says, We're talking about this on our lunch break!

I gaze at the exchange until my vision goes hazy. "What the . . ."

"What is it?"

I don't answer. I quickly swipe to my recent call list. There should be a call from Andy on the morning of May 7 when he told me about Mom's heart attack, but since it's still March, there's nothing. No call from Andy. No texts from Julianne. No texts or phone calls from Auntie Linda or anyone else in the family or Mom's coworkers. It's like all of those events disappeared from the current timeline.

"Chloe." Julianne's tone grows hard and panicked. "You're scaring me. Did something happen to you? If something happened to you, please tell me. Whatever it is, I'll do everything I can do to help you."

I take a deep breath, hoping it steadies me. Instead my voice shakes when I try to talk. Taking a moment, I swallow. This can't be right. How in the world did I go to bed last night and travel back in time to March? How did I lose almost two months of time, but no one else did?

I'm stammering to myself again. There's no way I can say any of this out loud, not even to Julianne. Clearly something in the world—something in the universe—hit some unexplainable glitch.

"Chloe." Julianne's voice jolts me out of my panicked thought process. "Chloe, what's wrong? Tell me."

I swallow, then try to rein in the uncertainty in my voice. "Nothing. I think . . . I think I might have had a bad dream or something. And then I must have woken up and thought it was real. Or something. I'm sorry."

"Jesus," she says through a sigh. "As much as I miss you, I'm glad you're taking a month off work. You need it."

"Yeah, I, uh, I'm glad I decided to come home. Maybe some time here will do me some good."

"You had me freaking out for a second there." She lets out an exasperated breath. "You didn't sound like yourself. Get some rest, okay? Do something completely mindless. Like, go shopping or binge something on Netflix."

"Okay, yeah, will do. Thanks." We say goodbye, but then one more question pops in my head. "Wait, Julianne?"

"Yeah?"

"Who's watching my house while I'm away?"

She laughs. "I am. I'm staying there while my condo gets renovated. Remember?"

"Oh. Right."

"You're going to have a hell of a time getting me to move out when it's finished. I love that you live only a ten-minute drive from the hospital. I don't miss my forty-five-minute commute from my place at all. And most of my favorite restaurants in the city are just a few blocks from your house. It's so much more convenient ordering dinner now. You'll have to force me out of here."

I try to laugh, but it sounds strangled. I clear my throat.

I thank her again and hang up. Tossing my phone on the bed, I hug my knees to my chest and stare blankly ahead.

There is not one single logical explanation for what has happened. The rest of the world is operating like normal—except for me. That thought, that single realization, slingshots me back to reality. To right now. To the miracle happening in the room right next to me.

Mom is alive. She's here with us again. Somehow, some way.

Yes, this entire scenario is unexplainable. But that doesn't matter. Nothing except her comes close to mattering.

I jolt up from the bed and walk down the hall. Behind the closed bathroom door, I can hear the water running. Andy's in the shower.

I walk to the living room, where Mom is playing solitaire on the coffee table. She gazes up at me, her brows at her hairline.

Instead of attacking her with another hug that robs her of oxygen, I give her a small smile and sit next to her on the couch.

I gently pat her knee. She's still real, still here. With me. With us. Right now.

I clear my throat so my voice won't break when I speak. "Sorry about earlier. I just had a bad dream, I think."

She chuckles, her gaze trained on the cards in front of her. "I'm glad you're feeling better."

I can't help but stare at her skin, the deep-tan hue shining brightly. Days ago it looked waxy and dull as all life left her body.

"Are you busy today?" she asks, snapping me out of my flashback.

I shake my head no. She swipes the cards into a pile, signaling the end of her game. She takes off her glasses, which she almost always wears when she plays cards or watches TV.

"I thought we could get lunch at that new Mongolian grill place," she says.

Twisting my head to look at her, my eyes water. I grin in an attempt to keep the tears of disbelief from falling once more. "That sounds perfect. I'd love that."

Chapter Seven

For the third time this morning, I pinch the flesh on my forearm. Nothing.

I try pinching the skin on my thigh. Still nothing.

It's been three days since I woke up in this new reality where Mom is still alive. Each day I wonder how any of this is possible—I wonder if there's a glitch in the universe or a glitch in me. If everything and everyone around me is acting normal, like nothing out of the ordinary happened, then I must be the issue. And I need to figure out what exactly is going on.

That's why I'm holed up in my childhood bedroom on a Skype call with my therapist, Dr. McAuliffe, after I called her and asked for an emergency session. The only time she could fit me in was this morning for fifteen minutes before her first client session of the day. I take a breath before asking her the question I need the answer to above all.

"This is going to sound nuts, but I swear it's true," I say.

Dr. McAuliffe frowns before adjusting her glasses, her expression unmoved. Clearly she's used to people asking her weird questions during therapy sessions.

"Have you ever had a client who had a dream that felt so real that when they woke up, they thought they were living in two different realities?"

"Not that exact scenario, no. But I've spoken to individuals who think they can time travel. Or who question the reality around them."

"Really?"

"Yes. Some people with bipolar disorder or schizophrenia or other disorders can experience similar things. Or clients who are having a mental breakdown of sorts."

I swallow back a wave of panic. What if that's happening to me?

"You've been my client off and on for years, Chloe. You don't have bipolar disorder. Or schizophrenia. And it doesn't seem like you're having a mental breakdown either," Dr. McAuliffe says, as if she's reading my mind.

She runs her fingers along the edge of her sandy-blonde bob. I lean back against the squeaky office chair, relieved yet also deflated that I'm no closer to figuring out what's going on.

"Have you by chance been under a lot of stress lately?" she asks after a moment.

"Yeah, actually."

"What kind of stress?"

"Work mostly. But that's nothing new. Work has always been pretty stressful for me. Especially ever since I got promoted."

She hums her understanding while nodding, fist under her chin.

I open my mouth, then hesitate. I need to be careful how I word this next part. "But honestly most of my stress is coming from the fact that . . . I thought that my mom died." I cringe inwardly, aware of how awful that sounds.

"I see. Well, that's probably the issue right there. Combined, those are two incredibly stressful things that very likely could have taken a serious toll on you emotionally and mentally. That could have thrown your sense of reality completely off for a bit."

"Really?"

"Yes. But I think as long as you take care of yourself—sleep regularly, exercise, maybe even meditate—you should be just fine."

I let out a quiet sigh, disappointed that she doesn't elaborate. "Okay. Thank you."

I check the time on my computer. Our session is nearly through.

I open my mouth to tell her thank you for meeting with me at the last minute, but then I stop myself just as my inner voice nags at me. Maybe I just need to be blunt. Yes, I'll sound out of my mind, but it's the truth. And she can't help me if I don't divulge absolutely everything to her.

"Actually, can I just say one more thing?"

She replies with a tight smile and a quick look at the clock. "Sure."

"Just . . . I'm going to tell you something, and I need you to be totally honest with me, okay?"

"All right. Go ahead." There's a tinge of hesitation in her voice.

"Almost two weeks ago, I thought my mom died. It was devastating. And it was very, very real. I can tell you the hospital where it happened, what room number was hers, the names of the doctors and the nurses who took care of her. I can tell you the date and time. All of this happened in the month of May. But then a few days later, I woke up and it was the end of March again, just after Easter. And she was here. She was alive again. It was like her death never happened. I can hold her and talk to her and it's amazing. I just . . . I just can't make sense of any of it. It all felt real—her dying felt real, and seeing her come back to life felt real too. And now I have this panic inside of me at all times. It feels like she somehow got a second chance at life, but I don't know if it will last—or if it's even really happening. I'm so, so happy to be with her, but at the same time there's this sense of dread I can't shake—because I'm afraid that I'll wake up one day and she'll be gone again. It's like . . . ever since I woke up and saw that my mom was here again, there's been an invisible timer ticking in the back of my head. I have no idea what it's counting down to, though—I have no idea if it will ever stop ticking—but I feel this sense of urgency to spend as much time with her as possible and at the same time do everything I can to help keep her safe."

Dr. McAuliffe says nothing in response.

"I feel like I'm losing my mind," I admit.

This time, when she frowns at me, there is something curious behind her eyes. Like I've said something that's given her pause, and it's making her think extra hard.

"I know all of that probably sounds outrageous," I say.

"It doesn't actually. You know, Chloe, our brains are incredibly powerful. They can make us see things that aren't there. They can make us think something is real when it's not." She pauses and shuffles. Her chair squeaks in the background.

"As a pharmacist, you're familiar with the placebo effect, correct? And how powerful it can be?"

"Yes, absolutely."

"What you described isn't what I'd call a placebo effect necessarily. But it sounds like an instance of a thought or a fear you've harbored manifesting in your real life somehow. I know that quite a few of the sessions we've had together this past year, you've mentioned feeling guilty and stressed about not spending enough time with your mom because your career was taking off. Maybe that's related to what's happening to you right now. Maybe some part of you was so stressed and guilty about that, it manifested in your worst fear—you thought you lost your mom. And maybe you were so devastated that you wished she could come back to you, which ended up happening. But really, nothing in real life changed at all. It was all in your head."

I say nothing as I let her words soak in. I don't know if I believe her, but this is the most insightful explanation I've gotten about what it is that I'm experiencing.

Dr. McAuliffe glances at the clock on the wall once more. "I'm sorry, but we should end the session here. My next appointment is due in a couple of minutes, and I want to make sure I give them ample time."

"Of course. Thank you for making time to see me on such short notice."

I say goodbye and am about to end the Skype session, but she stops me.

"Try not to think too hard about all this, Chloe," Dr. McAuliffe says, the expression on her face softening. "Every time you hear that invisible timer ticking away in your head, stop. Take a breath. Focus on something else, whether that's talking to your mom or going for a run. And then just try to enjoy the time you have with your mom now. And feel free to make another appointment with me if you want to talk anything out again. I'm happy to do this again with you via Skype."

"I will. Thank you."

When I end the session, I close my laptop and slump into my chair, mulling over her last bit of advice.

Just enjoy the time you have with your mom.

I wish I could stop overthinking, stop freaking out, but I can't. It's impossible for me to sit back and be relaxed about this whole thing because I don't know what's going on, why it's happening, or how long this time with her will last. And that above all is the most unsettling thing about it . . . that I could lose Mom all over again.

I pull out my phone and mark May 7 on my calendar. And then I grab a notebook from my desk and scribble down a list of goals to accomplish now that Mom is here with us again.

1. Prevent Mom from having a heart attack by improving her health
2. Repair the rift between her and Auntie Linda
3. Spend more time with her
4. Learn how to make her recipes
5. Tell her I love her every day
6. Do everything I can to keep her here with me and Andy as long as possible

Then I open my laptop, do a quick internet search, and make a phone call. She's going to hate me for this, no doubt. But it'll save her life.

~

Mom gazes around the doctor's office waiting room, her expression a mix of confusion and annoyance. "What in the world are we doing here? I thought you said we're going to breakfast."

"It's a surprise," I say while filling out the form for her. When she's this annoyed, it would be pointless to ask her to fill it out. She'd just refuse.

She frowns. "What kind of surprise? Why did you bring me to the doctor? I feel fine."

"I know." I pause to quickly scribble down Mom's general information. "It's just a precaution."

Inside I wince. Any reasonable person would probably say I'm in the wrong for tricking her into coming here. But this was the only appointment I could get for her at the last minute, and I don't have time to waste. It's already a few days into April; May 7 is only weeks away.

Yes, it's bad that I lied to Mom and told her this morning that I was taking her to breakfast and instead I drove her to the clinic for a surprise doctor's visit to get her checked out.

But if I have any hope of changing the course of history, her health needs to be a priority. This checkup needs to happen as soon as possible so we can find out where she is health-wise in order to prevent the heart attack that took her away.

When I finish filling out the form, I walk to the receptionist's desk to hand it back to her. Mom stays sitting in her chair, arms crossed. She directs her glare across the waiting room, scanning the sterile white chairs lining the wall, the haphazard stack of magazines littering the table in front of us, and the messy pile of children's toys in the corner.

When I sit back down, she turns to me. "I know what you're doing, Chloe."

"Oh?" I stare at my phone. I'd rather not get into an argument with her in the middle of a doctor's office waiting room.

"You think I'm clueless? You think I don't remember all those times you asked me questions about my health?"

I turn to her and keep my expression cheery. "I do it because I care about you. Because I love you."

She shakes her head and looks away, her mouth twisted in distaste. "You are something else, Chloe Howard."

I say nothing because it's true. "Something else" is what Mom used to call Andy and me as kids when we were being little shits and she didn't want to use profanity.

A nurse in blue scrubs opens the door to the waiting room and calls Mom's name. We stand up and follow her to an exam room down a long hallway. She instructs Mom to stand on a nearby scale.

She takes Mom's height and weight, then her blood pressure and temperature, then instructs her to take a seat on the exam table, which is covered in a sheet of paper. She listens to her breathing and draws her blood for a cholesterol test.

"Have you eaten anything today?" the nurse asks as she carefully inserts the needle into a vein at the inside crook of Mom's elbow.

"No. I haven't actually." Mom directs a pointed look at me. "I had plans to, but my daughter had a different idea."

I let out a long sigh. I deserved that.

"That's good," the nurse says as she secures the vial of blood shut. "It's always best to do a cholesterol panel after fasting."

"We'll get brunch after this, Mom," I say.

She doesn't say anything in response. Instead she gazes at a nearby chart explaining the importance of mammograms for women in their late forties and older.

The nurse glances up. "Dr. Massey will be in to see you soon."

When she leaves the room, Mom and I sit in silence. She looks everywhere but at me—at the ceiling, at the floor, at the glass container of tongue depressors, at the BMI chart. I bite my tongue and try to pretend that her blatantly ignoring me isn't annoying.

The door opens, and in walks a sixtysomething doctor with thinning salt-and-pepper hair. He introduces himself, then flips through the pages of her medical chart.

"Well, Mabel." He adjusts his thick-rimmed glasses. "Let's have a look at things."

He tests her reflexes, then asks her to lie back on the exam table. He presses against her abdomen, asking her to gauge the way the pressure feels.

"Any pain?" he asks.

"Nope," she answers.

The entire time, I'm holding my breath, balling my hands into fists, hoping that if there's anything medically wrong with her, he'll catch it right now, when it's hopefully early enough to do something about it.

He squints at the paperwork on his clipboard. "You're at a healthy weight for your height. And it says here that you walk ten thousand steps every night for your job. That's good. That means you're active."

Mom nods proudly.

Before I can hesitate, I blurt out the question I've been aching to ask. "What's the risk for a heart attack for someone her age?"

Mom directs an are-you-kidding-me expression at me. I haven't seen this one in years. That's the same hard look she used to flash me and Andy as kids when we'd misbehave in public.

Dr. Massey turns slowly to face me, his brow lifted in what I can only assume is shock.

"Um, I don't think there's reason to be overly concerned about that. It says on the chart there's no family history of heart disease."

"Overly concerned?" I repeat.

I've always hated when patients' families question the authority of medical professionals who have spent years of their lives training to administer the best care possible. But now, given this situation, I'm starting to understand why people do it.

Dr. Massey lets out a sigh instead of answering me, rubbing his wrinkly brow with a hand. Then he gazes back down at her chart. "Mabel, it looks like your blood pressure is a tad bit high, and your cholesterol was high last time you had blood work."

She crosses her arms, an unconcerned look on her face. "That's strange. I feel fine."

Dr. Massey glances up at her and patiently nods. "The fact that you feel good is a positive sign. That counts for a lot. But sometimes high cholesterol and blood pressure aren't things that you can necessarily feel."

When he starts to mention the names of drugs that lower cholesterol and blood pressure, I hold my breath. This might be it. This might be the ground zero of health issues for Mom. And if we can tackle them right now, this could change her course for the better and help her avoid a heart attack.

Dr. Massey scribbles something on the paperwork. "As easy as it may be to write a prescription, I don't think that's what we need to do in your case," he says. "I'm one of those old-fashioned physicians who thinks you should modify your diet and exercise before taking a slew of pharmaceutical drugs."

My breath catches in my throat, but I keep from questioning him. I want to hear more of what he has to say.

He hums for a few seconds while writing. "The good news is that you're not at dangerously high numbers for your cholesterol or your blood pressure. What I'd recommend is that you make some changes in your eating and activity level, and then come see me again next month."

My thoughts skid to a halt. All I can focus on is his decision not to give her medicine of any kind.

"Wouldn't an ACE inhibitor be a good idea, though?" I say.

Dr. Massey twists his head to me, wrinkling his bushy eyebrows. The movement reminds me of a caterpillar inching its way along a sidewalk. I'm guessing he isn't pleased to have his recommendation questioned by someone young enough to be his child.

I glance up at the clock on the wall. It's so quiet for a second that I can hear the second hand tick away.

Tick. Tick. Tick.

It matches the timer in my head that's been ticking in the background of my racing thoughts ever since I woke up and Mom was somehow here again.

It's a reminder that time is passing, and each second that ticks by brings May 7 closer and closer. And if I have any hope of saving Mom—of keeping her here with us—I need to do everything I can think of.

"Do you work in the medical field?" he asks.

"I'm a pharmacist at Nebraska Medical Center in Omaha."

"I see," he says, with a slight sigh at the end, like he's tired of me already. "Well, I appreciate your concern and insight, but pharmacists and physicians have different scopes of practice, as I'm sure you're well aware."

"It's still a valid question, though. Many physicians wouldn't hesitate to prescribe," I say.

He takes a long breath, like he's refilling his stockpile of patience before dealing with me again.

"I understand why you might think an ACE inhibitor is the appropriate solution," he says with a tight yet polite smile. "But I honestly see more success with patients who implement lifestyle changes than those who just take pills, never change a thing about their lifestyle, and then wonder why their health doesn't improve."

The pointed way he speaks and looks at me quells that surge of worry. He's right. Lifestyle changes are what will make the biggest difference. If I can get Mom to eat better, get more restful sleep, and be more active, that will make a world of difference rather than her taking a bunch of pills and engaging in the same behavior.

He taps his pen against the clipboard and turns back to Mom. "Mabel, if nothing has changed by the next time you see me, then we'll get you on some meds. But you're already at a decent starting point health-wise. Add more whole foods to your diet, cut out the processed stuff, get more restful sleep, and do a bit more exercise, and you should be golden."

He grabs two pamphlets out of a nearby drawer. I lean forward slightly and see that one is about healthy eating and one is about blood pressure lowering activities.

Judging by the petulant scowl on her face and the way she tightly crosses her arms over her chest, Mom's not one bit pleased about any of this. She death-stares the pamphlets in Dr. Massey's outstretched hand, so I quickly scoop them up.

"Thank you," I say. "I'll make sure today is day one of new healthy habits."

"That's great. Getting fit and healthy is even easier when you can do it with someone." He turns to Mom. "You're very lucky to have your daughter here helping you."

I let out a sigh of relief, appreciative that Dr. Massey is recommending what I've been telling Mom all along. Maybe now she'll actually listen.

Mom responds with a tight smile. We finish up, and then Dr. Massey leaves the room. Mom doesn't say a word when we gather our things to leave, then walk to the reception desk. The receptionist makes a follow-up appointment for four weeks from today.

When we get in the car, she turns to me from the passenger seat and wags her finger. "No making me eat flavorless food."

"Got it."

"And no crazy workout classes. I'll break a hip."

I pull out of the parking lot and into the street, heading toward downtown Kearney where her favorite breakfast café is. I owe her a yummy brunch for this. "Fine. But you're not exactly elderly. You're capable of being active."

"I'm not as young as you think I am, *anak*," she says while staring out the window.

Her words land like a punch to my gut. I blink and recall her lying still in a hospital bed, her body unmoving and lifeless.

She absolutely isn't as young or resilient as I always thought. But there's still so much she can do—so much I can help her with.

"You can still do a lot, Mom."

"I hope so," she mumbles.

I hope so too.

"I promise this will be okay, Mom." I swallow back the lump in my throat. "I'll be with you the whole way."

She takes a second before looking at me again. When she does, that tightness in her expression fades the slightest bit. I can tell she's a tad less frustrated with me right now—and I hope it's because she can tell from my words and my actions that I'm doing all of this because I love her more than anything.

For a moment, I contemplate telling her what happened. Maybe if I lay everything out on the table, she'll understand.

"Mom. I—"

She waves a hand at me, cutting me off. "You don't have to keep lecturing me," she says. I clamp my mouth shut, my nerve fleeing after a few seconds.

Then she turns to me. "Thank you for caring so much about me," she says. This time when she smiles, it reads soft and sincere.

At least I know she'll be happy about the next surprise I have planned for her.

Chapter Eight

"I'm so excited to surprise your mom, *anak*." Auntie Linda checks her makeup in her compact mirror while sitting in the passenger seat of my car as I pull into the driveway of Mom's house.

"I'm so happy you had time to come visit. Mom's gonna be thrilled to see you."

I flash back to how pained and broken Auntie Linda sounded when we spoke on the phone after Mom died.

I never got the chance . . . I shouldn't have waited so long to make things right. And now it's too late.

I shove aside the memory, my head still spinning when I think about how in this world that conversation with Auntie Linda never happened.

It's going to be okay. They'll repair whatever this rift is between them and make up.

The last time Mom and Auntie Linda saw each other was over a year ago when Auntie Linda came to stay with her for a week. Whatever squabble they had, they'll be able to hash it out now. I've arranged for her to stay with Mom for the rest of April so they can have plenty of time together.

She waves a hand. "Oh, *anak*. I'm retired now, so my schedule is free. I'm always happy to come out here to see you and Andy and your mom." She pats her hand over mine. "But even if I were still working,

I'd always make time to see you all. I'd come visit all the time, but we know how that would drive your mom nuts."

We share a chuckle as she digs for her lipstick, then reapplies it. She offers it to me, but I tell her no thanks.

She pats my hand. "You know, I remember when you were little and you loved playing with my makeup. It would make your mom so mad. She'd say it was a waste to let you try on all that expensive makeup since you were just going to wash it off right after. But I loved it. You looked like a little doll every single time."

I smile at the memory.

"It was a nice break from all the toy trucks and dirt and mess from your cousins. Speaking of my boys, they're too busy traveling to come see their mom," she says in an exasperated tone as she smooths lotion on her hands. "So don't you worry about me clearing time to come visit. I've got plenty of it and not a whole lot else to do."

"They're in the military, Auntie. It's hard for them to take time off."

"Oh, I know that, but still. I'm a mom. I always want to see my kids."

The conversation I had with Mom on the phone just a few days before her heart attack resurfaces. I swallow back the ache in my throat and focus on the moment and how I'm going to do everything differently now.

I pull the keys out of the ignition just as Auntie Linda reaches over to give me a hug. Then she claps her hands in excitement and laughs. "Your mom's going to be so shocked to see me."

I smile at how much I've missed her impromptu hugs. She's always made it a habit to hug Andy and me at the most random times whenever we see each other: when we're sitting in the car, cooking in the kitchen, walking past her in the house. I breathe in the scent of her light citrus perfume, her curled shoulder-length hair tickling my nose.

She kisses me on the cheek, her mauve lipstick leaving a print that I can't see but can definitely feel. I quickly wipe it away before jumping out of the car to grab her luggage and leading her into the house.

When I walk in, the first thing I see is Mom sitting at the kitchen table, squinting at a few rows of cards while sipping a cup of coffee, her usual routine before she gets ready for work.

"Hi, *anak*," she says without looking up.

"I have a surprise for you. Just flown in from Denver."

She glances up just as I step out of the way to reveal Auntie Linda walking in behind me. Mom's mouth falls open, and her eyes go wide. She pops out of her chair and walks over while shrieking "oh my gosh!"

I step out of the way so they can hug. They chatter and laugh and squeal while wiping away happy tears, and then a few more hugs follow. And just like that, the timer in my head silences. The tension melts, giving way to a warmth that pulses inside my chest. Mom and Auntie Linda are together again. This is worth every trouble, every stress, every moment of worry.

From the side I take in the scene of Mom and Auntie Linda's embrace, noticing like I do every time I see them together how much they look alike. They're the same height with a similar slight stature and loads of thick black hair, though mom prefers to straighten hers while Auntie Linda uses hot rollers every morning. They share full, expressive faces and eyes so deep brown they could pass for black. Even though Auntie Linda is three years older than Mom, they look the same age. The only major physical difference they share is how they dress and style themselves. While Mom prefers to wear leggings and blousy tops when she's not dressed in her work uniform of a polo and khakis, Auntie likes walking shorts and jeans and button-up tops in bright colors.

Mom grabs my hand, grinning. "You planned this?"

"It's been a while since you've seen each other. I thought you two could use a visit."

So you can hug and laugh and make up and bicker over only silly, inconsequential things like you normally do, and make even more happy memories together.

She pulls me down to hug me so tight before turning back to Auntie and pulling her into the kitchen. Their excited chatting echoes through the hallway as I drop off Auntie's bags in the guest room and stop by Andy's room to say hi since I've barely seen him this past handful of days. The longest conversation we had was the day that I woke up and saw that Mom was back. Every other time I've seen him at the house, he's barely spent longer than fifteen minutes to shower and eat before heading out to work or seeing friends.

Inside I deflate. I hate that the last time we had a proper conversation, it was so unpleasant. I need to get us back on track.

But there's no sign of him when I walk in. Just his comforter shoved messily on top of his unmade bed and an array of rumpled clothes on the floor.

I pull out my phone from my jeans pocket to text him.

Hey. It's been a while. We should catch up. Free tomorrow at all?
Auntie Linda wants to see you too.

I'm walking down the hallway back to the kitchen when I hear Mom's tone turn low and charged.

"I'm sick of talking about it, okay? Enough is enough, *manang*. Leave it alone."

I halt in my tracks at the sound of Mom and Auntie Linda arguing in Ilocano.

Just then there's a long, sharp sigh. "*Adingko*, how can you just forget about it?" Auntie Linda's tone is sharp with impatience.

"Because it was years ago. And he was my husband. That's how."

Every molecule in my body stills.

"He hurt you all so badly," Auntie Linda says. "But he hurt our mom, too, when he took that from you. Don't you understand? How could you let him get away with it?"

My mind races as I try to figure out what she's talking about. Mom starts to speak, but then drifts off. "I said I don't want to talk about it."

A long silence follows. I can't stay standing in the hallway forever, so I wait a moment, then walk into the kitchen and pretend I didn't hear anything.

"So! What should we do for dinner?" When I look up, Mom and Auntie Linda are sitting on opposite sides of the kitchen table. Even though they're staring at me with smiles on their faces, I can feel the strain between them like an invisible cloud floating around us.

Auntie Linda pops up. "I'll cook pansit, *anak*."

I ask if I can help so I can learn the recipe, to which she says yes. Out of the corner of my eye, I see Mom stand up from her chair. She announces that she's going to take a shower before dinner.

As Auntie Linda and I chat about how things are going in Denver and how Uncle Lyle is doing, I try to wrap my head around the charged conversation I overheard. If there's any hope of them resolving their rift, I need to figure out what they were talking about—and how exactly my dad factors into it.

~

"I can't believe you want me to take a healthy cooking class." Mom crosses her arms while staring out the windshield of the car as I drive.

It's two days into Auntie Linda's visit, and I haven't overheard them fight again. They've fallen back into their normal vibe whenever they visit each other: chatting and laughing, playing cards, cooking, watching game shows and soap operas, and going for walks.

Since Auntie Linda is attending Mass right now, I figured this would be a good opportunity to spend some time together while also doing an activity that's good for Mom's health.

And hopefully by the end of this class, I'll feel brave enough to ask her what she and Auntie Linda were fighting about the other day. But that will involve mentioning my dad, about whom my mom hasn't spoken in years. I grip the steering wheel extra tightly at the idea. The last time Mom talked about him was when I was in my twenties, and she was complaining about how he failed to send his child support payment for Andy for the seventh month in a row. I can't imagine her being delighted to chat about the guy who caused so much financial uncertainty for her and her kids—and the rift between her and her only sibling.

"I think taking a cooking class together will be fun," I say, focusing back on our conversation. I twist my head and give her a quick smile.

She says nothing at first and just crosses her arms. But then she turns to me, her expression softer. "I spent my whole life cooking. You think I can't cook for myself?"

"That's not it at all," I say, trying to keep my tone cheery.

I turn right at the stoplight down from Mom's house in the direction of the local rec center a few miles away, which is where today's cooking class will be held. A few minutes of silence follow, underscoring the tension between us.

"You are the best cook I know, Mom. All I wanted was to add a few more recipes to your lineup." I pull into the parking lot at the rec center. "Just try to give this class a chance, okay?"

"I'll try," she says before climbing out of the car and shutting the door. "But I can't make any promises."

She ties her hair up while walking ahead of me to the front entrance. I check my phone and see that Andy still hasn't texted me back. I haven't seen him at the house either. The only way I know he's been home is by the state of his room. There are new piles of clothes strewn across his floor and bed, indicating that he's stopping by to shower and change, probably late at night or early in the morning when we're all asleep.

Mom and I make our way to a large room at the far end of the building. It boasts the look of a sleek and modern home economics classroom. A half dozen islands adorn the middle of the room, each one decked out with two sinks and two stove tops. Already there are several folks Mom's age standing at the stations. At the front of the classroom stands a sixtysomething woman with the cheeriest neutral expression I've ever seen. Everything from the slight upturn of her mouth to the sparkle in her eyes conveys that she's brimming with excitement at teaching the fifty-plus crowd how to cook healthy meals.

I smile at her and say hello while I sign Mom and me in on the registration sheet.

"So happy to have you two join us today!" she says, her short and curled golden-gray hairstyle shining in the overhead light. "Feel free to set up at any open station you'd like."

I thank her and go back to Mom, who's standing at the island in the back corner. We store our purses on the lower shelf built into the cooking station as other attendees filter into the classroom. The clock hits nine, and the cheery instructor begins.

"Welcome to Healthy Cooking for Seniors 101! My name is Sharon, and I'm a healthy senior!"

"Hi, Sharon," everyone says.

She dives right into the objective of today's class, which is to learn how to prepare quick and easy dishes with superfoods.

She points to an impressive spread of fresh fruits and vegetables that sits on her counter. "All of these yummy items are superfoods. Does anyone know what a superfood is?"

Someone answers that it's a nutrient-dense food, which earns an excited handclap from Sharon.

"That's right. And I'd like to kick off today's class with my very favorite superfood." She scoops up a bundle of kale and holds it up in front of her. "Does anyone know what this is?"

"Kale," someone in the front says.

"Very good! Yes, it's kale, which is a super-duper food. Did you know that just one cup of kale exceeds your daily recommended requirement for vitamin A?"

"You know I don't like kale," Mom whispers to me, the slight frown on her face giving away how mildly annoyed she is. She crinkles her nose in disapproval, then adjusts her glasses.

I don't blame her. Every time I attempt to eat kale, I have to choke it down. But I can't deny how insanely healthy it is. I'll pretend to like it if it helps convince Mom to eat it.

"Just give it a try, okay?" I ask.

Sharon instructs everyone to sample a bite of the raw kale in each of our serving bowls. She closes her eyes, chewing slowly while making "mmm" noises.

"Oh my goodness, isn't that delicious, you guys?" Her voice rings through the room.

I chomp down on a leaf and resist the urge to gag. Instead, I force every muscle in my face to keep a neutral expression while I chew and nod yes. I swallow, then I turn to Mom to make sure she's eating it too. She's chewing slowly, her distaste for it written all over her face. It reminds me of what little kids look like when you tell them they can't leave the table until they finish all the veggies on their plate.

"How does it taste?" Sharon asks.

"Like dirt," Mom blurts out.

A handful of chuckles echo across the room.

"Mom," I scold with a quiet, shrill whisper.

She shrugs, a disinterested expression on her face. "I'm just speaking the truth."

I turn back to Sharon, who's still cheerily smiling, seemingly unfazed by Mom's brutal assessment of her favorite superfood. Sharon rolls up the sleeves of her peach blouse. "Kale is definitely an acquired taste. But no worries, because today I'm going to teach you how to make it delicious by incorporating it into three different recipes."

She claps her hands, then begins to explain how to make a tropical smoothie using kale. She instructs us to dump the ingredients on the trays at each station, which include pineapple, banana, frozen berries, and kale. The sound of a dozen blenders buzzing at once reminds me of a horde of bees. When we all finish, Sharon instructs us to pour the smoothie into small cups, then sip them.

"Mmm," I say through a long swallow.

Bits of kale coat my tongue. It's like I'm chewing the remnants of an artificial plant. It's a struggle not to groan in dissatisfaction, but I manage. I wipe my mouth, and then I peer over at Mom and grin, like I'm in a commercial and I'm trying to convey just how scrumptious this healthy smoothie is.

"Good, right?"

She takes a sip, then looks down at the glass. "It's not bad."

Sharon dives into the next recipe, which is kale sautéed with lemon and garlic. For the next ten minutes, we chop and stir. The smell of lemon and garlic wafts throughout the room.

"Doesn't that smell yummy?" I say to Mom, who's busy wiping down the counter.

"I guess," she mutters.

I plate up a serving for her to try. In the row ahead of us, Sharon walks by and observes how everyone is managing at their cooking stations. When she stops in front of our station, she aims her hopeful smile at Mom, who's about to take a bite.

"So? What do you think?" Sharon asks, clasping her hands in front of her as she watches Mom.

I hold my breath as Mom sighs and looks at both Sharon and me before trying a bite. She chews, her unimpressed expression never leaving her face.

"It tastes fine," she finally says with a shrug.

I direct an apologetic smile at Sharon.

She chuckles. "Like I said, kale is an acquired taste. But I promise, you'll learn to love it."

She turns around and heads for the front of the class again.

"I doubt that," Mom says under her breath.

"Mom. Don't be rude."

She sighs. "Are we almost done?"

I shake my head, thankful that Sharon's too deep into her explanation of the next recipe, kale with whole-grain pasta and tomato sauce, to hear my and Mom's whisper-fight.

"No, we're not almost done. And it's very rude how dismissive you're being just because you don't like kale."

Mom scoffs. "I'm just being honest."

"You can be honest and also polite." I have to remind myself to keep my voice low. Mom's indifference-turned-annoyance at this healthy cooking class is starting to wear on my nerves.

"I just think it's ridiculous how we're all trying to pretend kale is yummy. It's not."

My jaw falls at her biting comment. "That's such a terrible thing to say." The last word slips out of my mouth at a slightly higher volume. I look around to make sure no one heard me.

"The only terrible thing is that you're making me take this class when I've told you that I'm fully capable of cooking," Mom says. "I don't need to be taught how to cook. I'm not an infant."

The way she shakes her head and waves her hand at me, like she's dismissing me, makes my blood start to boil.

"You think helping you be healthy is ridiculous?" It's a strain on my throat to keep my voice at a whisper, but I manage.

"It is! I don't need help. I'm perfectly fine."

"You are not perfectly fine, Mom. Not according to your doctor." This time my voice surges forward before I can remind myself to control my volume.

Her frown turns into a full-on glare. "You know, Chloe. I didn't even want to come to this class, but I did because you made it seem like you wanted to spend time with me. But now that I know it was for some sneaky reason, I don't want to pretend anymore. This healthy stuff you're making me do is annoying. I can't stand it."

The invisible floodgate holding back all of my frustration has burst. There's no use holding back now. Normally I wouldn't bring up Mom's health in such a heated context, but if she's going to take this attitude, then I need to make it clear why I'm doing this.

"Well, that's too bad. Because of your bad habits, you have high blood pressure and cholesterol. You know what those things can lead to? A heart attack."

I have to remind myself not to think of her lying in that hospital bed, her eyes closed, her body still. The invisible clock that's set up shop in my brain ticks louder than ever, even as I tell myself to take a moment and calm down.

"You need to do something about your health, and that's why we're here. I care about you, Mom. I love you, and I want you to be with us for as long as possible. Don't you get that? All I'm doing is trying to help you, but you're acting like a spoiled child."

Mom's eyes bulge wide. Her shock at my words is written all over her face. And then that's when I realize Sharon has stopped speaking entirely. Instead she's standing at the front of the room, eyes wide. Everyone else is at their cooking stations and has stopped chopping and stirring to observe our spat.

My mouth falls open, but I don't say a word. I'm too embarrassed that I lost control of myself in front of all these people.

A beat later Mom sighs, then reins in her expression before grabbing her purse and marching out the door. "I'm done, Chloe."

I don't have the energy to follow her, so I stay standing at our cooking station. I'm about to offer a public apology, but Sharon claps her hands and gets everyone back on track with a cheery fact about the low glycemic index of kale. Everyone finishes cooking while I clean up my station. Sharon ends class by giving an enthusiastic preview of the next class's featured ingredient: sweet potatoes.

At the end of class, everyone nibbles on their pasta while chatting. I slink up to Sharon, who's looking through a cookbook at the front of the room.

"I'm so sorry about what happened earlier with my mom and me." My face feels like it's on fire, I'm so mortified. "Our behavior was disruptive and immature."

Sharon responds with an understanding smile. "It's all right. It's not the first time a loud conversation has happened in this class."

"Really?"

"Oh, honey, this is a class for senior citizens. Half the time they're hard of hearing. Do you know how many times I've overheard awkward comments spoken way too loud? I'm used to it."

I let a small smile slip at her reassurance. "Still, though. It's no excuse for how we behaved. I shouldn't have let myself get so upset."

Sharon reaches a hand to my shoulder and gives me an encouraging squeeze. "It's all right, honey. To be honest with you, it's nice to see a young person like you get involved in your mom's life like this."

She pauses, and the look in her hazel eyes turns sad. She gazes around the room, the crow's-feet in the corners of her eyes deepening when she flashes a small smile. "Every person in this room would love to have what your mom has—their loved one by their side. When I stop and chat with them, they're always talking about their kids or grandkids and how much they wish their families would visit them more. And here you are attending a cooking class with your mom because you want to help her be healthy. That's nothing to be sorry about."

The tiniest bit of tension that I've been holding inside of me every time Mom and I argue about food or exercise or sleep or doctor's visits melts away.

"Thanks, Sharon. Really."

She pats my hand. When people start filing out of the class, I follow. I head for the car but notice Mom's not sitting in it or standing nearby like I thought she would be.

I peer around, then spot her sitting on a bench near the other end of the building. As I walk toward her, that's when I see it. A brown bag—a fast-food bag.

I jog over and plant myself in front of her just as she shoves another fry in her mouth.

She looks up at me. "Hello."

"What. Are. You. Doing." The stilted way I speak does little to hide the anger coursing through me.

"Eating french fries. Want some?"

She holds out a handful to me. I grab the fries, then throw them on the ground.

"Ay!" she yells. "That's wasteful."

"That"—I point to the bag—"is disgusting. You shouldn't be eating that."

She shrugs. "I thought a few fries would be okay since I ate so healthy in the cooking class."

I open and close my mouth a half dozen times, but no words come out. Just invisible steam from the anger and frustration colliding inside of me.

Mom brushes the chunk of jet-black hair that's fallen loose from her ponytail out of her face, then crosses her arms. "You know, wontons are fried, too, just like these fries." She juts her chin at the bag. "You love wontons, *anak*. Remember? You should be more understanding."

"Homemade wontons don't have the disgusting preservatives and additives that fast food has. Are you kidding me right now?"

I snatch up the bag of fries, then march to a nearby trash can.

"Chloe! What are you doing?"

Mom's annoyed voice follows behind me as I shove the bag to the very bottom.

"I wasn't done eating!" Mom booms from behind me.

Wiping my hands on my shorts, I march toward the car. "I don't care." I spin around. "How did you even have time to run and get french fries? You were out here for ten minutes tops." My voice squeaks with disbelief.

She squares her shoulders. "Uber Eats."

"How do you know how to use Uber Eats? You don't even know how to check your voice mail."

She narrows her gaze at me, her expression turning indignant. "My coworker Liam taught me how. It's very easy. Remember me mentioning him? He's the one I wanted to set you up with."

Through gritted teeth, I force out a breath. "That's just great."

We walk in silence to the car. After a few minutes of driving without talking to each other, she speaks.

"You can't hide from me, *anak*," she says softly.

"What do you mean?" I ask, trying to maintain a patient tone as I keep my eyes on the road.

"You hated that kale as much as I did. I could see it in your face."

I take a breath and then admit that she's right. "Of course I hate kale. It's disgusting. It tastes like plant garbage. But it's very nutritious."

She lets out a chuckle. "You made the same face you used to make when you were little and I'd try to get you to eat a vegetable you didn't like."

The corner of my mouth twitches up into a small smile. It's another long silence, but this time, there's less tension in the air.

"I eventually came around to eating more vegetables," I say. "Just not kale."

She lets out a laugh. I turn to look at her. She's staring out the window.

"You have to admit that fries taste better than kale."

"Fine. I'll admit that. But you have to admit that they're unhealthy."

"Of course they're unhealthy."

She shakes her head. "Just look at us," she says through a breath. "So stubborn, both of us."

Her words hit something deep inside of me.

"We're stubborn because we care. Because we love each other," I say.

I pull into the driveway of Mom's house and park. Then she unbuckles her seat belt and looks at me, patting my arm with her hand.

"That's true. It'll be the death of us both," she says with a chuckle before stepping out of the car.

Her comment unleashes a wave of dread inside of me. The ticking inside my head echoes louder and louder with each second that passes. I have to sit in the car for a minute until the feeling fades, until it doesn't feel like my chest is going to collapse into itself, until I feel like I can stand on my legs again. When I shut the car door, my hands are shaking.

Chapter Nine

It has been two hours since the failed cooking class, and I still can't shake the dread from Mom's morbid joke. So I changed and threw on my running shoes and am attempting to expend all my anxious energy with a jog and a vent session with Julianne.

"Your mom hates being told what to do. Especially when it's by one of her kids. You know that."

"I know, it's just . . . I wish she would take her health more seriously."

"We all wish that about our parents, Chloe. But you can't force anyone to do anything, least of all your mom."

I'm on the route I normally run when I'm visiting Mom, about a mile away from her house near the local college campus in town.

"Any word on why your mom and your aunt were arguing about your dad?" Julianne asks in my earpiece.

"Not yet. I was going to ask her about it after cooking class, but it didn't seem like the best thing to bring him up after we argued."

"Yeah, I get it." She sighs, then there's a gulping sound as she takes a drink. "Can I just point out how annoying it is that you're in such good shape that you can jog *and* talk on the phone? I'd be dying if I tried to do that."

I let out a chuckle and wipe the sweat from my brow with my free hand. I jog past a brick duplex and spot Andy walking down the driveway.

"Let me call you back," I say to Julianne as I slow down to a walk.

I wave and reach the end of the driveway. "Hey, stranger. Haven't seen you in a while."

Instead of the goofy smile and wave I expect from him, his eyes go wide before he frowns. I almost laugh at his startled reaction. But then I spot a tallish twentysomething woman with light-brown hair walking after him. She halts when she sees me standing a few feet from Andy. Judging by the strained look on the woman's face, they were in the middle of something before I came along.

A shy smile tugs at her lips as she waves at me. "Hey."

"Hi. I'm Andy's older sister, Chloe."

I walk over to shake her hand as her smile widens.

"It's so nice to finally meet you. I'm Hannah," she says as she lets go of my hand. "Andy's told me so much about his impressive big sister."

I turn to Andy, whose cheeks are flushed red.

"So is this who you've been ditching Mom, Auntie Linda, and me for the past few days?" I turn to Hannah. "Kidding."

Andy frowns and glances at the ground while Hannah chuckles.

"Yeah, um, sorry. It's been kinda busy. We've been kind of busy, I mean. Hannah and me." Andy clears his throat after stammering through his explanation.

I wait for him to elaborate or to introduce Hannah as the person he's dating. But he just stands there shuffling his feet, then shoves his hands in his pockets. Clearly I've interrupted them during a tense moment.

I back away on the driveway, trying to keep my tone light. "Sorry to bug you guys."

"You didn't at all." Hannah beams at me. There's a joy to her expressive face that instantly perks me up. "It was so nice to finally meet you." She looks between Andy and me. "You two have the same smile. It's so cute."

"Told you we're related." When I nudge Andy with my arm, he cracks a grin. "You should come by the house sometime and have dinner with us, Hannah. Our mom would love to have another person to feed and fuss over."

I don't miss the unblinking stare Andy levels at me as I pivot toward the sidewalk.

"I'd really like that," Hannah says.

"Anytime you want, come over!" I holler as I jog away.

The entire rest of the jog, I try to make sense of whatever the hell my little brother is up to.

Hours later I'm scouring Mom's fridge for something to make for dinner when I hear keys jingling in the front. I pop up and spot Andy, who doesn't bother to look at me.

"Hey."

"Hey," he mutters as he walks into the living room and tosses his keys and wallet on the coffee table. "Mom and Auntie Linda around?"

"They're out shopping."

He grunts an "okay," then plops on the couch. I wait for him to say something—anything—about my text that he never answered or that awkward introduction to Hannah. But he just stares at his phone in silence.

I sigh and peer at him from a few feet away as I lean on the kitchen island. "Are you seriously going to do this?"

"Do what?" His stare doesn't budge from his phone screen.

"Sit there and pretend you haven't been acting completely out of character these past few days."

"Don't talk to me about acting out of character. Weren't you the one who thought Mom was dead?"

The sting of our conversation from a week and a half ago hits once more.

"Other than that, I've been acting perfectly normal, which is more than I can say for you."

He finally sets his phone down and falls back into the couch with a sigh, then looks at me. "I've just been busy at work."

I twist the cap off a bottled water with extra force. "You've been busy at work plenty of times before without turning into a complete jerk. Why are you ignoring my texts? And what is up with the way you acted around Hannah? Clearly you two are dating. Why have you never mentioned her to me or Mom?"

Andy leans forward to rest his elbows on his knees, his head in his hands. He groans softly before looking over at me. This is the first time I've gotten a proper look at him in more than a week. There are bags under his eyes, and his cheeks are starting to look sunken in.

"You know, I'm not legally obligated to tell you about my dating life," he says.

I pause midsip at the biting undercurrent in his reply. I swallow. "Wow. Okay."

A sigh rockets from him. "Sorry, I just mean . . . it's complicated," he finally says. "Way too complicated to bring to a family dinner."

"I'm sure Hannah would love to be thought of as a complication," I mutter as I take a long pull of the icy cold water.

"No, that's not . . ." His shoulders rise and fall with yet another deep breath. "I didn't mean it like that. Hannah's amazing."

The way his mouth turns up as he says those words restores a bit of my fuzziness for my baby brother.

"It's just been tough lately balancing work and some . . . relationship stuff."

I nod, not wanting to pry further. "I get it. Sorry to hear that."

He shrugs.

"I'm not someone who has any right to lecture you on relationships or dating, Andy."

I try not to scoff or laugh at myself. Because I haven't been on a proper date in more than a year, and it's been a handful of years since my last long-term relationship. I can count on one hand the number of long-term relationships I've had in my life—one was in high school and one was in college. I'm no one's guide to dating or relationships. But I can't just stand by and watch my brother brush off the woman he's dating.

"I just wanna say that Hannah seems really sweet. And I can tell by the way she looks at you that she likes you. Whatever's complicating things for you two right now, uncomplicate it. Then bring her over for dinner."

He shakes his head as he stands up and mutters, "Easy for you to say." He starts to walk in the direction of his bedroom right as Mom and Auntie Linda walk inside.

Andy plasters on a smiley face and greets them both with a hug. He laughs and lets Auntie Linda pinch his cheeks and go on about how tall he is before excusing himself to take a shower.

Mom walks over and pulls me into a hug, letting the tension from our argument this morning melt away. I close my eyes and savor the moment, how comforting it feels to have her hair tickle my nose, how soft she feels in my arms, how she smells like gardenia. It's been over a week, and I still can't shake the disbelief that washes over me like a tidal wave when I realize over and over again that she's still here.

"I'm going to go take a nap before work," she says.

When she walks off and closes the door to her bedroom, Auntie Linda sits on the sofa while going through her purse for her ChapStick. When she finishes, she walks into the kitchen and starts pulling out the ingredients to make *lumpia*.

I pause. Maybe I can ask her about their argument. I don't want to get into two arguments with Mom in one day, and I'm scared that might happen if I bring up Dad to her.

I take a breath and walk over to Auntie Linda, who's standing at the kitchen counter seasoning the ground pork.

"Can I help you?" I ask.

"Oh sure, *anak*. Here." She hands me a spoon and directs me on the right amount of seasoned pork to put on the *lumpia* wrapper.

"No more than a couple of spoonfuls. I like to make mine a bit smaller than your Mom's."

"Right." I make a note of how Auntie Linda adds minced carrots and shredded cabbage in her meat mixture, just like Mom does with her own *lumpia* recipe.

"Do you make the same recipe that Mom does?" I ask, suddenly sidetracked from my bigger mission of asking her about my dad.

She nods as she starts spooning the meat onto wrappers. "The exact same one. It's the one we used to make with your *Apong* Selene when we were little."

For just a moment, my nerves ease. "I've been meaning to ask Mom to write down the recipe so I can have it always."

"Oh, you don't need a recipe. You learn by making. It's just some pork, salt and pepper, garlic powder, maybe some extra seasoned salt if you have it, carrots, and cabbage. That's it. So delicious."

I finish rolling one *lumpia* and start on another, confident that I'll be able to remember Mom and Auntie's unofficial recipe forever.

She beams up at me. "How was your run earlier, *anak*?"

"It was good. Um, can I ask you something?"

"Yes, of course."

"I, um, I overheard you and Mom arguing the other day—the day that you arrived actually. Something to do with my dad."

The smile drops from her mauve lips as her brow wrinkles. Her hands still as she reaches for another *lumpia* wrapper.

She looks at me. "You heard us? Talking about that?"

"Yes. I'm sorry. I didn't mean to, but I was in the hall and the sound from the kitchen carries sometimes. And I just . . . I hate that you and Mom are fighting. You've always been so close, and I don't want anything to come between you two. Especially not my dad."

Auntie Linda nods and sighs like she knows exactly what I mean. Then she wipes her hands on her apron and takes my hand in hers. "Your mom would kill me if she knew I told you this."

"I won't tell her you said anything. I promise."

She pats my arm in thanks, then looks in the direction of the hallway to Mom's room. "Our mom, your *Apong* Selene, gave me and your mom her most precious jewelry before she died. A beautiful gold diamond ring and bracelet. Your mom was keeping it for us. And one day years ago, when your dad was drunk and needed money, he stole it from her jewelry box."

My heart and lungs plummet to my feet. Of course he would steal from his own wife. He left his kids in a car in the middle of winter to drink himself to death at a bar, then tried to drive. Stealing is small beans compared to that.

"Your mom didn't tell me that he had taken it until after they got divorced. I was so mad. That jewelry meant so much to me and your mom. I wanted to wear it to your cousin Marco's wedding, so I asked your mom if I could borrow it, and that's when she finally told me what he did. I was so upset. I must have yelled until my voice was hoarse. I wanted to try and track him down to get it back. Or at least make him pay for it. They were so valuable. *Apong* Selene wore that jewelry on her wedding day to marry our dad, your *Apong* Gerald. But your mom didn't want to. She said she didn't even know where to find him at that point. She tried to track him down a couple of times for missed child support, but he had moved so much. By the time she tracked down one address, he was already gone. She finally said it was best to leave it alone. It's always been a sore point for us. We still fight about it from time to time . . . and sometimes, we say some terrible things to each other because of it." Her voice shakes as she speaks.

Then she wipes her eyes, and I'm instantly transported back to that moment when we were speaking on the phone after Mom died.

I shouldn't have waited so long to make things right. And now it's too late . . .

Something inside of me ignites. It's like that fire that sparked within me when I woke up and Mom was alive again, and I decided I'd do everything in my power to help her stay with us forever. Except this fire is hard. It's angry.

I want to make this right for Auntie Linda and Mom now. I don't care what I have to do.

I rip a paper towel from the roll and hand it to Auntie Linda. When she finishes dabbing her eyes and nose, I hug her and thank her for telling me. Once we're done rolling all the *lumpia*, I excuse myself to my bedroom and call Julianne.

"Hey. I need a favor."

~

I stare at the calendar on my laptop while sitting in my bedroom. I'm due back at the hospital in just over a week, but there's no way I can leave and go back to work now. Not when I just hired Julianne's private investigator cousin to track down my dad so I can try to get Mom and Auntie Linda's jewelry back. Not when Andy is being weirdly cryptic about his relationship with Hannah. And definitely not when Mom is refusing to take care of herself properly. She's been begrudgingly eating the healthy meals that I've cooked her and taking walks with Auntie Linda. But as soon as she's left on her own, she'll go back to eating whatever's convenient, like the snack cakes and coffee with sugary creamer that she normally prefers to eat when she's slammed during a work shift and sleep deprived—and that's most definitely not going to help ward off a heart attack.

I need to stay with her and help her every single day—like I have been—to make sure she makes it past May 7.

Sitting on the edge of my bed in my room, I call my manager, Malcolm. We exchange pleasantries, then I take a silent breath, feeling my muscles tense in anticipation of what he'll say when I ask for even more time off.

"I have a favor to ask you. I know I asked for three weeks off already, but I'm going to need more time."

"Sorry, what?"

"I have enough time saved to take the rest of April, all of May, and most of June off. So I'd like to do that."

"Um, Chloe." He pauses to take a sip of something. "Do you realize what you're asking?" He chuckles, like he thinks I'm joking.

"I know exactly what I'm asking. I'm asking you to let me take some extra time off after I've spent the last seven years busting my ass for the hospital—for your department."

"There's no need to use language like that."

I pause. "Sorry. But Malcolm, I've spent my entire time at the hospital working hard for this department. I'm the first one who offers to cover an open shift. I don't flood your inbox with frivolous complaints. When I took over the residency program last year, I helped make it into one of the most desirable programs for pharmacy graduates to apply for. Top students from around the country want to study at our hospital because of how I overhauled that program."

A déjà vu feeling hits. I had a very similar conversation with Malcolm before—right after Mom died. It's going exactly the same. Why did I think it would be different this time?

Malcolm lets out a sigh, like he's tired and only hearing me out as professional formality. "That's all true, Chloe. I'm not trying to refute any of that. It's just that I have a schedule to fill, and I can't just allow a pharmacist to take all of spring and the first part of summer off with zero notice and leave a hole in our schedule. It's not realistic. And it's not fair to the other pharmacists. They deserve to take time off too."

Even though I'm annoyed, I silently admit that he's right. What I'm asking is too much. I can't just take months off work with zero notice.

That means there's only one option left. I should have known.

"You're right, Malcolm. Sorry to put you in that position."

"It's all right. We all have those moments—"

"And I'm sorry to have to do this to you right now," I say, interrupting him. "But I quit."

There's a choking sound on the other end of the line.

"You—you what?"

"I quit, Malcolm. I need this time off. It's nonnegotiable."

He spends a few more seconds stammering.

"Chloe, what the hell!" he shouts.

"Language, Malcolm."

"Oh, that's nice. Real professional of you to up and quit last-minute like this." His tone turns pouty. "And what about the residency program? The schedule? How am I going to cover all these open shifts without you?"

"I'm sure you won't have any trouble finding a replacement."

"Easy for you to say."

There's a crashing noise in the background. Possibly Malcolm shoving something off his desk. If this were normal me, I'd be freaking out. Actually, normal me wouldn't have quit my job on zero notice. But that was before all this happened with Mom. It feels like a totally different lifetime.

Right now my heartbeat doesn't even spike at the sound of Malcolm losing it. It's like I've been sedated with something that gives me an automatic sense of calm. In this moment nothing else matters. Not my job, not my boss, not my résumé or my job prospects. If I can't guarantee that Mom is alive and okay, nothing in the world means anything.

"Sorry, Malcolm. I have to go."

I hang up and toss my phone on the bed. Then I stand up and walk out of my room to start breakfast so it's ready for Mom by the time she arrives home from work.

～

"I'm tired of all this healthy food." Mom sits at the kitchen table staring at the bowl of steel-cut oats with organic berries I served up for her.

Auntie Linda taps Mom's hand and gives her a look that I recognize right away. It's the same look I gave Andy when we were younger and he was being fussy—I still employ it once in a while.

On the inside I soften at seeing how the four of us share that. Auntie Linda and me as the watchful older siblings; Mom and Andy as the fussy younger ones.

I lean against the kitchen counter. "Mom. It's not that bad. It's one meal out of the day."

She frowns at the porridge before stabbing her spoon into it. "One meal *can* be that bad when it's bland oatmeal."

I roll my eyes at her comment. This must be what it feels like to be a parent with a kid who refuses to eat their dinner, so you end up forcing them to sit at the table until they take enough bites that you're confident they ingested something healthy into their body.

"Mom, just try to eat some of it, okay?"

She swallows a spoonful, then makes a face.

Auntie Linda shakes her head as she happily eats her own oatmeal. "Don't be like that, *adingko*. I'm eating the same thing right now, and I think it tastes great. Very nutritious."

"There's something wrong with your taste buds," Mom says before forcing herself to eat another spoonful.

Her phone rings and she squints at the screen, then she grins and answers. "Julianne! Hello! How are you, hon?"

For a minute, she chats and I clean up the kitchen, wondering if Julianne's private investigator cousin has found anything on my dad yet.

I glance over at Mom, who's happily gabbing with Julianne. As much as I want to be open with her, I don't want to stress her out by telling her that I've hired a private investigator to find her ex-husband so I can try to take back what he stole. This whole situation is upsetting enough, and I don't want to further upset her, which could cause heart issues.

"Oh, it's going fine," Mom says. "Chloe's just trying to get me onto oatmeal. I'm kicking and screaming with every bite."

Julianne's boisterous voice echoes softly from Mom's phone. Mom holds up the phone and puts it on speaker.

"*Anak*, Julianne wants to say hi."

"Hey, Julianne," I say, trying not to groan.

"What's this I hear about you trying to force-feed your mom flavorless foods?"

"It's not like that. At all."

"Oh, come on. Let her have at least one fun thing to eat."

"I'll think about it," I say.

"Shoot, I've got another call incoming," Julianne announces.

She makes a *muah* noise on the other end of the line, Mom tells her to be safe and have a good day, and I holler bye. When Mom hangs up, I glance at her.

"You should really finish that oatmeal, Mom."

She purses her lips, groaning before she takes a bite of the oatmeal. It plays out like that for a few minutes with Mom wincing after every reluctant bite.

I shake my head and think about what Julianne said. "If you finish that bowl of oatmeal, I promise I'll cook something yummy for dinner."

Mom perks up in her chair. I almost laugh at her sudden straight posture. That's exactly the way I'd react as a kid when she promised me a cookie if I finished all my dinner.

"What will you cook?" she asks.

"What do you feel like?"

Her face wrinkles as she thinks, then she smiles. "I want corn dogs."

"Ay, corn dogs?" Auntie Linda says, wrinkling her nose. "They're no good. Too salty. And chewy. Like gum almost."

I add that I agree with Auntie's assessment, but Mom wrinkles her nose before insisting that it's one of her favorite comfort foods because it's yummy and quick to prepare.

I bite my tongue, already regretting the trade-off I've made. "Fine. I'll make corn dogs for dinner."

I start to say that I can run to the store and pick up these vegetarian corn dogs I've seen in the freezer section, but Mom wags her finger at me.

"No vegetarian corn dogs. What even is that? I want a proper one made of pork."

I sigh, wondering if she would have even been able to tell the difference if I had just kept my mouth shut and bought those vegetarian corn dogs without telling her. They're both processed to hell.

"And you have to fry them, not bake them," Mom says. "They don't taste the same baked."

"Okay. I'll fry them. But you have to eat a vegetable with it too. Or a salad. And a piece of fruit."

She beams at me before happily taking another spoonful of oatmeal. "I can do that."

I cross my arms, then shake my head in disbelief at how the parent-child dynamic has changed between us. Now I'm the one constantly bargaining to make sure Mom eats all her healthy food.

I leave the kitchen and head back to my room to tackle the next item on today's to-do list. An hour later I'm sitting at my desk staring at my laptop, my vision blurry as I try to focus on the local YMCA fitness class schedule.

A fitness class could go a long way in improving Mom's overall heart health. And prioritizing her health is more important than ever, since May 7 is less than three weeks away.

I quickly text Andy.

Me: Hey. I need your help with Mom.

Andy: Okay. What's up?

Me: Will you come to a fitness class with us?

Andy: Um, why?

Me: Duh. To help get her on the right track health-wise. Doctor's orders, remember? She's fought me every step of the way so far. But if her baby boy is on board, too, she might be more receptive.

Andy: Ugh fine. But only if I'm not working. I'm not taking off work for this.

Me: Deal.

My phone rings with a call from Julianne. She's probably calling me to tell me to ease up on Mom.

"Hey," I say through a breath. "What's up?"

"You quit the hospital?"

I'm jolted by Julianne's nearly shouted greeting. "Um, yes. I did."

I didn't expect to have to talk about this with Julianne so soon. I guess Malcolm must have delivered the news to the staff this morning. That was quick.

"I can explain."

"Did something happen with you, Chloe? This is so unlike you. Never in a million years would you have ever just quit your job with zero notice."

"I know." I take a breath. "But things are . . . different now."

"Is everything okay with you? Look, I tried not to say anything because I didn't want to upset you, but ever since you called me freaking out about what day it was, things have felt off."

I let a silent moment pass between us, wondering just how I'm going to word this. The last thing I want is to lie. Julianne is my best friend, and I've never been dishonest with her in my life. I don't want to start now. But I can't tell her the truth. She'll think I've lost my mind.

"And look, I'm one hundred percent behind you on your whole mission to track down your estranged dad. He was a jerkoff for stealing from your mom and aunt, and they deserve to have closure about that. But I gotta admit, something's been different with you these past few weeks."

I say nothing, still struggling to find the right words.

"Chloe, answer me." Julianne's tone turns worried. "If it's not something with you, is there something going on with your mom? Is she okay? Is it Andy?"

"No, they're fine and I'm fine."

"Oh, thank God."

I opt for telling her the truth, but modified.

"It's just that . . ." I rub my fist against my forehead, careful of how I word things. I can't tell her that Mom came back to life after dying, and now I'm trying to make everything right so we don't lose her again. "Mom's getting older, Julianne. I need to spend more time with her now before it's too late."

Julianne pauses. I can tell she's unmoved.

"I had a nightmare about my mom, Julianne. But it felt so real. She died . . . of a heart attack. And it completely wrecked me. I was devastated. And even though it wasn't real, it made me rethink some things. I need to spend more time with her and do a better job of taking care of her."

Another pause follows, but this time it's longer. I know Julianne is processing what I've said. "That's awful, Chloe. I'm sorry. And now that you've explained it, I get it. I know how much your mom means to you." She hesitates for a moment. "But do you really think you can put your life on hold like this? Are you really ready to sacrifice your goals and dreams?"

Her words set off a million memories in my mind. I recall how Mom would often work long hours when Andy and I were kids because it paid overtime and we always needed the money, how she would miss some of Andy's sports games growing up to pick up an extra shift, how she refused to spend money on herself because she always wanted to save it to buy sports gear for him or to pay college application fees for me.

"She sacrificed for me and Andy growing up. A lot," I say with renewed conviction in my voice. "This is the least I can do for her."

Julianne's heavy breath echoes on the other end, like an unspoken and reluctant acceptance of my reasoning. "Aren't you worried about money at all? How are you going to pay your bills if you're not working?"

"I have enough saved. All those years of overtime are finally paying off. I can afford to be impulsive for a bit and say screw it to working, at least for the summer."

"What about your house? Aren't you worried that you won't be there to make sure everything is okay?"

"You're there for the month. After you're back in your condo, can you just stop by once a week to check the mail and make sure it doesn't catch fire or the pipes don't burst?"

She lets out a chuckle that sounds tinged with disbelief. "Sure."

"You can stay there as long as you want. I won't be using it, obviously."

"I guess there's no point in trying to talk you out of this." She groans. "You say your mom is stubborn, but you could give her a run for her money. You know that?"

"She's the one I get it from. Blame her."

Julianne goes quiet for a bit before speaking again. "Have you . . . have you thought about what you're going to do? Like, when you eventually go back to work? Malcolm is pretty pissed. I don't think he'd hire you back, honestly."

"I don't expect him to. The way I quit definitely burned that bridge with the hospital. But I'll figure out something. I'll get a retail job at a drug store. Or maybe I'll do telepharmacy."

"Do you honestly think you'd be okay with working from home approving orders online all day? Or counseling patients via Skype? You are so good at your job, Chloe. You were one of the most accomplished and knowledgeable pharmacists on staff. Anytime someone had a question about a new drug or dosages, or a patient had an adverse reaction to some random med, you were the person they went to. You were up to date on every recent medical journal article about new drugs."

I take a moment to think about all those evenings I spent at home, glued to my laptop reading studies just so I was as informed as possible for anything that would pop up at the hospital. Yeah, it helped widen my knowledge base as a pharmacist . . . but I could have done a better job balancing it all. I could have spent some of that time chatting with or visiting Mom.

"Look, I used to think all that stuff was what mattered most. And it did for a while. But now I know time with my mom is the most important thing for me," I say. "I need to do this. It's the right thing to do."

"Okay." Doubt colors her tone as she says it.

"Please don't tell my mom I quit, though, okay? Or Andy. I'm going to tell them, but I need to figure out how. I know they're going to be upset."

"I won't. Promise. But try not to blame them if they're angry when you tell them. You've always been the sensible firstborn child and oldest sibling who worked so hard. You always made all the right choices. You've never done an impulsive thing in your life. They're probably going to have a hard time accepting what you've decided."

"You're right," I say with a sigh.

I think back to how as a kid I followed the rules to a T and planned almost everything I ever did. I never skipped class or faked an illness to stay home on a day when I just didn't feel like going to school. In all my years of school, I never got a single detention. No teacher even had to shush me for talking out of turn in class. Any vacation I've ever gone on I planned for months. I never even took a spontaneous road trip as a teenager or stayed out past curfew.

When I eventually break the news to Mom and Andy that I've chosen to quit my job and live with them for the foreseeable future, it's going to jolt them for sure.

I thank Julianne and promise to call her next week, then hang up.

I refocus on the YMCA fitness class schedule still on my laptop, silently hoping that what I'm doing will actually make a difference.

Chapter Ten

"I don't see why we have to go to this." Mom stares out the window of the passenger seat as I drive us to the water aerobics class I signed us up for.

Because it's two weeks until May 7, and I'm going to do everything in my power to keep you alive.

My real answer—the answer I don't dare speak out loud—tumbles in my head for a second before I clear my throat.

"I thought it would be fun."

She makes a scoffing noise. My hands tighten around the steering wheel as I try to keep my cheery tone.

"I asked you before what sorts of classes you'd like to go to, Mom. You never told me. You always said you weren't interested in anything. So I had to make a choice."

"My blood pressure and cholesterol are only a little high," she mutters. "I don't see why I need to start working out like a maniac. I would have gone to Mass with Auntie had I known you were going to make me do aerobics in the water."

"Mom, come on."

Mom has never been interested in exercise, ever. She's never had to. She's always been able to maintain her figure with zero effort. The one time I got her to do an aerobics workout video years ago, she quit after five minutes, saying she was bored. And every other physical activity I've pitched to her over the last few days—weight lifting, ribbon dancing, regular dancing, martial arts—she's shot down.

"Besides, it's been so hot lately," I say. "Water aerobics will be a great way to cool off."

She crosses her arms, still refusing to make direct eye contact with me. "Mm-hmm."

I had to drag her away from her solitaire game this morning to make it to the class on time. She's giving me snarky comments and the cold shoulder in return.

"Andy's really excited about today's class," I lie. She says nothing in response.

It's silent the rest of the drive to the YMCA. I park the car, unbuckle my seat belt, then turn to her. I rest my hand gently on her forearm. Still, she stays turned away from me, staring out the window.

"I feel just fine the way I am. Without water aerobics," she mutters.

I bite down to keep from saying anything. That's exactly why her heart attack was such a shock—for so long she looked good, felt full of energy, and never had to worry about her health. But now I know how misleading that can be.

"I know this isn't what you're used to," I say. "But can you please try? For me and Andy. We love you, and we want you to be healthy."

She twists to me, brow lifted, clearly surprised at my tone and words.

Then she blinks, and her dark-brown eyes turn tender. "Okay."

Then I check my phone to see if Andy has texted me. He was already gone from the house when I woke up this morning. I've texted him multiple times reminding him to come to water aerobics today, but he hasn't responded.

"Where's Andy?" Mom asks while glancing out the window.

"He said he'd meet us here."

When there's no reply, I try calling him, but I get his voice mail. I swallow back a curse, then plaster on a smile for Mom.

"We should head inside," I say to her.

The tender expression Mom gave me in the car evaporates as soon as we walk into the massive indoor swimming area and hit the water. Her face turns sour the minute she lowers herself into the pool.

"It's so cold," she whines.

I tie my hair up into a bun and shake my head. "It's a pool of water. It's supposed to be cold. And you were just complaining about how humid and hot it was this morning."

A voluptuous woman with graying hair in a red one-piece swimsuit smiles and walks to the edge of the pool. In the water are a dozen women plus Mom and me. I do a quick scan for Andy, but he's nowhere to be found. I grit my teeth, annoyed that he decided to blow this off—and annoyed at how detached he's been from us lately. Yeah, he's busy with work—and whatever is going on with him and Hannah. But he has never completely ignored my messages or stood Mom or me up when we've made plans to meet, not even when he was a moody and temperamental teenager. Something is up with him.

"Good morning, ladies!" the instructor shouts, interrupting my thoughts. She pulls on a swim cap while beaming at us. "Who's ready to get physical?"

She instructs us to run in place as a warm-up, then demonstrates the movement herself. It's a surprisingly rigorous activity trying to move your legs when you're weighed down by water. My heart rate is up after a minute. I turn to check on Mom, who is frowning and constantly wiping her face with her hands.

She sputters out water from her mouth. "All these people in the water. This is so unsanitary."

I bite my tongue to keep from replying, instead focusing on the instructor's directions. She runs us through intervals of a side-to-side skiing movement with breaks in between sets. We repeat the same format with wide-legged jumps, then do the same with a move she calls the washing machine, where we twist our torsos while jumping up and down.

"And now, jump up with your legs together! Keep your arms high!" she bellows.

I follow along with everyone else in class as they jump up and down while keeping their arms straight up in the air. My lungs pump harder and harder through the intervals. This is one hell of a workout.

I spot Mom barely moving in the water, her arms at her sides. I whip my head around to check on her, my heart racing. But when I see her deadpan expression and that she's not even breathing that hard, I grit my teeth. Then I grab her arm in an attempt to lead her along with my movement.

"*Anak*, stop grabbing my arm!"

"Higher, ladies! Higher! Higher!" The instructor sings the commands like she's a choir director.

"You have to at least try," I say to her, but she jerks her hand away.

The instructor directs her stare to Mom. "You can do better than that. Higher!"

Mom rolls her eyes but concedes by actually jumping.

Around us the other ladies in the class splash and splash with each animated movement.

"You're doing great, ladies!" the instructor sings.

When the last interval ends, she gives us a minute-long break to catch our breath before we start the series of intervals over again. I glance over and see Mom performing the moves with excellent form this time. I smile, heartened. She's moving quicker than me even. The instructor singles her out to applaud her effort.

Several minutes later, we hit the final interval series. But I catch Mom heading for the edge of the pool.

"Mom, where are you going?" I ask.

"I'm done with this," she says through a gasp. It's barely loud enough for me to hear her above all the splashing.

I grab her hand to get her to turn around to talk to me. "You're leaving? But you're doing so well."

"Yes, well, I'm done now." Her hard tone echoes through the swimming area.

"Mom—"

"I said I'm done!" she yells, jerking her hand out of mine.

I'm paralyzed at her tone, at how angry she sounds. Everyone else is, too, it seems, given the way every other class participant has frozen midmovement to gawk at us.

If we were on land, she'd be jogging away right about now. But since we're in the water, her getaway is slower. She wipes a hand over her dripping wet face and pushes back the wet hair stuck to her skin. Then she pulls herself out with the metal ladder at the edge of the pool and marches to the women's locker room, not once looking back at me.

My face heats as I stare down, fixated on how distorted my legs look through the water. Thankfully the instructor simply clears her throat and carries on with singing out the exercise intervals for us.

I follow along, thankful that I'm in the back so I don't have to endure the feeling of a dozen eyes on me, wondering what in the world is wrong with Mom and me since we clearly can't get through one forty-five-minute water aerobics class without losing our cool.

When it ends, I jump out of the water as fast as I can, head to the women's locker room, dry off, and get dressed. I pull my phone out of my bag and shoot Andy a quick text.

What the hell happened to you? You were supposed to come to the YMCA with Mom and me, remember?

When I walk toward the entrance, there sits Mom on a bench, hands folded in her lap, frown on her face, looking at nothing in particular.

In that moment, my chest folds in on itself, and it all sinks in. This whole time everything I've been doing was to try to help her and bring us closer together. But she's so upset that we're more distant than we've ever been.

"You ready to go?" I ask her once I walk up to her.

"I guess so." She makes it a point to look at her sandals and not at me when she answers.

We walk out to the car and head home in silence. When I park in the driveway, she moves to step out of the car, but stops and turns to face me.

"What happened with you, Chloe?" she asks, her face twisted in concern. "The way you're acting is ridiculous. I wish you'd just be normal like before."

Her words land at the center of my chest, where my heart is. I could try to explain it all, to tell her how I watched her die and how I'm scared it'll happen all over again if I don't at least try to make her change her habits . . .

I could tell her that every day I'm terrified I'll wake up and she'll be gone again. I could tell her that every day I live with a silent timer ticking in the back of my mind, counting down to May 7, when her time with me and Andy could be up again. I could tell her that even though I have no idea what's going on and I have no idea if anything I'm doing will make a difference, I can't just sit back and do nothing.

"I just care about your health, Mom."

She frowns, her brown eyes curious. "It's more than that. I can tell."

She's relentless—just like I am.

So I take a breath and tell her what I hope she'll understand.

"I know this is going to sound strange, but just hear me out, okay? I had a dream that you died. Of a heart attack."

"What?" She scoffs. It almost sounds like a laugh.

"I had a dream that you died of a heart attack. And I—I thought it was real."

She shakes her head. "*Anak*, obviously that didn't happen. I'm right here."

"I know that. It just—I thought we lost you forever, Mom. And it destroyed me."

When my eyes start to water, I glance away. In the extra second, I press my eyes shut until I'm certain I won't cry.

I turn back to face her. "That's why I stayed home. To help you and make sure that nothing like that happens to you."

She blinks, then glances off to the side. She shakes her head before turning back to me. "*Anak*, whatever you thought happened, it didn't. I'm still here."

She reaches over and squeezes my hand. I'm warm from the inside out.

"I appreciate how much you care about me. And I know that you're doing this because you love me," she says before letting go. Then her eyebrows furrow into a stern frown. "But you don't get to order me around and tell me what to eat or what to do. I'm your mom. That won't ever change, no matter how old you get or what you think you know."

"Mom. I've never asked you to do things like this before. I've always listened to you and supported you. Can't you do this one thing for me? Can't you try to start taking better care of yourself?"

She purses her lips together, fixing her stare ahead.

I grab her hand, and she looks at me. "I love you, Mom. I just want you to be okay."

Her expression softens. Maybe what I'm doing—what I'm saying— is finally resonating with her.

She taps my hand. "I love you too. And thank you for caring about me so much. But I'm doing just fine."

Clenching my jaw, I ease out a silent breath. Then she grabs her purse and moves to open the door. Something yellow sticking out of her purse catches my eye. When I focus and see the golden arch logo, I bite the inside of my cheek to keep from saying anything. Mom must have ordered Uber Eats again after storming out of water aerobics.

Closing my eyes, I huff out a breath and pinch the bridge of my nose. Lecturing her now would be hopeless. She just told me she's not interested in listening to anything I have to say when it comes to her well-being.

But I need to do something about this.

She slams the car door and walks into the house, leaving me sitting alone in the car. I'm two minutes into staring at the white exterior of her ranch-style house before I come up with a plan. An underhanded plan that will make her loathe me even more, but it's the only thing that will work. I just need to figure out the right timing.

~

With my laptop on my lap, I type my dad's name into the search box of my browser. There are hundreds of Bill Howards.

I groan as I rub my face with my hands. Why did I think a Google search was the way to go? And then I silently scold myself for being impatient at the fact that Julianne's private investigator cousin hasn't managed to track down any leads. It's only been a handful of days since I hired her to locate him. I need to be patient.

I text Julianne anyway.

Me: Anything yet from your cousin?

Julianne: No, sorry. I promise she's working hard, though. Bill Howard is a common name. That's probably why it's taking so long.

Me: You're right. Sorry for being impatient.

Even as I type, doubts linger at the back of my mind. Because the cynical part of me thinks that trying to track down my dad is akin to finding a needle in a haystack. He's got one of the most common first and last names a guy in North America could possibly have. When he and Mom split, he used to move constantly, never updating his information. And he's never been able to hold down a steady job.

The only information I could give Julianne's cousin were his date of birth, the dates of his and Mom's marriage and divorce, and a copy of an old driver's license I found in a box of family photos in the hallway closet. The single most helpful thing I offered was his middle name, which is Taplin. I'm hoping that its uniqueness will help narrow down the search. But barring that, he's probably one of the hardest humans to trace.

I resist the urge to pull out my own hair in frustration. I may as well call it off. What's the likelihood that I'll be able to find one missing deadbeat dad in all of the United States—in all of the world? But then I think of my mom and Auntie Linda, who are both napping in their rooms after spending the morning playing cards. They deserve their mother's jewelry back. And if I can't get it back, I need to know that I tried everything I possibly could.

I let out a breath and walk to the kitchen. I have exactly four hours until Mom wakes up and starts getting ready for her overnight shift.

All I have to do is act normal. Make dinner for her and pack her lunch to take to work with her, like I do every other night. And then I can carry out that plan I thought of yesterday after the water aerobics fiasco.

From the refrigerator, I tuck carrots, cabbage, a head of celery, mushrooms, a container of brown rice, a bottle of low-sodium soy sauce, and a carton of eggs into my arms, then carefully place them on top of the counter.

A beat later, Andy walks in the front door and says hello.

I spin around to look at him. "Hey. What happened yesterday?"

He frowns at me, like he doesn't know what I'm talking about.

"You were supposed to come work out with Mom and me at the YMCA, remember?"

For a long second, he stares, like he's confused at what I've said.

"Do you not remember all those texts I sent you reminding you about that water aerobics class?"

Eyes closed, he lets out a heavy sigh. "Sorry. I . . . forgot. A friend asked me to help them with something, and I just lost track of time."

"By 'friend' do you mean Hannah?"

"Chloe, don't start." A sigh rockets from him as he plops down onto the couch. When he blinks, I notice how heavy his eyelids are. I wonder if he's been sleeping enough lately. He doesn't look like it.

"If you're busy with Hannah, just say so. But quit standing me up. It's rude."

He says nothing and just rubs a hand against his forehead while staring off into the distance.

"Is something up with you? You've never been this MIA or evasive before and I gotta say, I'm not a fan."

He rubs his eyes with the heels of his hands. "It's nothing. Just . . . work. It's been busier than usual."

For a moment, I consider pressing him, but I don't. He's clearly going through something and doesn't want to talk to me about it. Badgering him never works—and it's a shitty, invasive thing to do. I need to just let him sort it out on his own and stop pestering him.

I turn back around to the stove and start prepping a healthy version of fried rice I looked up on my phone earlier. I sauté veggies in a tablespoon of extra-virgin olive oil and ask Andy to double-check the amount of soy sauce I'm supposed to use in the recipe. I give him my passcode, and he unlocks my phone just as it dings with a text message.

"Is it two tablespoons or two teaspoons?" I ask.

When he doesn't answer right away, I turn around to face him.

"Hey, why aren't you . . ."

When I look at him, he's standing behind me frowning down at my phone. He looks up at me, a bewildered look on his face.

"What?" I ask.

"You quit your job?"

He doesn't even blink when he looks at me, he's so shocked. "What? How did you . . ."

That's when I see the text message from Julianne still unopened on the screen.

Still can't believe you quit. The pharmacy dept. is in shambles without you. Sorry, not trying to be a mopey jerk, I know you made your decision and there's no use in trying to talk you out of it . . . but we miss you, damn it!

Julianne texted me right when Andy unlocked my phone. I almost mutter a curse word, but instead I turn back around to the stove, turn off the burner, and walk over to him.

"I can explain, but not here." My eyes dart down the hall where Mom is sleeping. I eye the front door. "Come on."

I tug Andy by the arm out the front door. With the door shut behind us, I settle on the porch swing. He sits next to me. I swipe my phone out of his hand.

"Chloe." The stare he pins on me is part indignant, part surprised. "Why did you quit your job? I thought everything was going well."

"Yeah, well . . ." is all I say.

"Did something happen?"

"No."

"Did you get a new job?"

"Not yet."

"So . . . you just quit?"

"Yes, Andy."

He frowns, his brown eyes bewildered. "But . . . why?"

I take a moment, careful how I word things. "So I could spend more time at home with Mom. And you too," I quickly add.

Andy rolls his eyes. "Do you know how insane that sounds?"

I look away, shaking my head.

"You can't just stay here and be Mom's handler," he says. "You really just want to spend your life cooking for Mom and annoying her about going to exercise classes?"

"Why not?" Crossing my arms, I direct my gaze to the street. I wave at an elderly couple out for an early evening stroll.

"Chloe," Andy says, jerking my attention back to him. "I swear to God, something has gotten into you. I get that you want Mom to be healthy. I do too. But you've been acting really weird lately. You plan her meals for her like she's a five-year-old. You drive her to all these random things like cooking classes and fitness classes, and she always comes home in the worst mood. You guys are fighting more than I've ever seen you fight before. Now this?"

"So?" I snap at him. "It's bad that I'm taking an interest in our mom's health? That's a pretty messed up mentality, Andy."

"You know that's not what I mean."

He ruffles his hair, then leans his head back and groans. "Okay, fine, Mom's stuff aside, what are you going to do with your life if you're not going to work? Just hang around here forever? What will you do?"

"I'll get a job again eventually. I can do telepharmacy and work from the house."

He tilts his head to the side, unimpressed by my plan. "Then what? You're just going to sit around and continue micromanaging her life? That's your plan?"

At least until I get her past May 7.

"I don't agree with how you've worded it, but yes. Essentially, that's what I'm planning to do for now."

He shakes his head and looks away from me. I'm clearly frustrating the hell out of him.

"Andy, I'm not a child. I'm almost eight years older than you, actually."

Judging by how he gives me zero reaction, he's still unconvinced.

"I just needed a break from all the stress, okay? I spent eight years in school studying to be a pharmacist. And then I jumped straight into working at the hospital after I graduated. I haven't taken more than a week off at a time. The last vacation I had was in my twenties. I got burned out after all that and needed a breather. You of all people should understand," I say.

Andy rolls his eyes at me. "First of all, I of all people know just what a load of crap that is. You loved school, and you love your job."

"I loved the security of my job," I say, cutting him off. "And I liked the challenge of it. I went into pharmacy because I was good at science, and the job prospects were solid. But I was never passionate about it, Andy. There's a difference. And yeah, I was one of those kids who was good at school, but that doesn't mean I loved it. I liked a lot about my job. But liking something is different from feeling fulfilled."

This is the first time I've spoken the words that have been rolling around in my head ever since I decided to quit.

"You sure as hell sounded fulfilled," Andy says. "Chloe, every time you came home you would always talk about whatever project or paper you were working on for the hospital. When you got that promotion to residency program director, you were so excited. I remember how pumped you were when you called Mom to tell her. You've always kicked ass in academics and in every job you've ever had. You've always taken pride in your work. Always."

"Of course I took pride in my work. But do you realize that the reason I was so dedicated to my job was because I wanted stability, Andy? The kind of stability we didn't have when we were growing up. And now that I have it, I can take a break and spend more time with Mom."

"You didn't have to quit your job to see Mom more often," he mutters.

"Yes, I did. The way I want to do this—the way I want to be there for Mom, I absolutely had to quit."

Andy shakes his head like he doesn't believe a word I'm saying.

"I'm not good at school stuff. I've known that about myself ever since I was a kid," he says. "But you are. You're a high achiever, and your dreams align with that. You can't just stay home and screw around like me. Whatever life crisis you're going through? Tell it to fuck off. Otherwise, it's going to ruin everything for you."

"Believe it or not, Andy, I'm more than school and work. I always have been. I'm just realizing that now. Maybe that's on you that you haven't been able to see me as anything more than your one-dimensional older sister who's good at taking tests and working myself to the bone."

The sharpness in my voice catches the attention of a neighbor on a walk with her baby in a stroller. Andy and I both hesitate for a second before waving at her in an awkward attempt to show that this exchange isn't as charged as it seems.

"Look." I turn so that I'm fully facing him. "I know it's unexpected of me to do this, but . . ."

The expression on Andy's face softens. Emotion hits me like a choke hold. I clear my throat. "I had to ask myself what was really important: work or spending more time with family. The answer was pretty clear for me."

For several seconds, Andy says nothing. He just stares ahead, like he's thinking deeply about what I've said.

He lets out a tired sigh, then finally turns to me. "You're making a huge mistake, Chloe."

"I know what I'm doing, and I have a plan."

Standing up, he walks back into the house, leaving me alone to sit on the front porch and ponder his words.

Chapter Eleven

Under the fluorescent lights in the produce aisle, I check the time on my phone. Almost three in the morning. I stand behind the display of bananas situated in the center of the produce section, pick up a bunch, then pretend to examine them carefully in the light.

It's hours after Andy and I had it out about my decision to quit my job, and I still can't shake the way we left things. He's never looked at me like I've completely disappointed him, like he looked at me earlier today. Yes, we've had a million arguments before—we're brother and sister, after all. But we've always fought a bit less than your average siblings. Probably because of the gap in our ages. I was almost eight when he was born. I remember being so excited the day Mom and Dad brought him home from the hospital that I made a card that said, "I love you, baby brother." I read it to him as I sat next to Mom on the couch, not realizing that he was too little to understand me.

Whenever my parents would let me hold him, I'd whine when they asked me to give him back. And when our dad left, I felt a new protectiveness for him. I promised him that I'd never let anyone, or anything, hurt him. I've carried that feeling ever since. I never let him cross the street without holding my hand when he was little. When I turned sixteen and got my driver's license, I scheduled my classes to have the last period free so I could pick him up at the elementary school on time and he wouldn't have to take the bus. Yeah, we had little spats here and there, but not like other kids.

I was always so proud of our closeness and how different we were from other siblings. That's why it cuts so deep that we're on the outs with each other.

I shove the thought aside and try to focus on my current mission. The tricky thing about coming to Mom's store in the middle of the night is that there aren't a ton of customers like there are during the day. Though I'm a bit shocked to see the dozen customers shopping at the store currently. Who knew so many people liked to go to the grocery store in the middle of the night?

Tonight, I could actually use the cover of a busy crowd as I navigate this gigantic store.

I'll have to be extra sleuthy to keep off Mom's radar, especially since she's about to take her lunch break.

I look up and fix my gaze on the empty sitting area at the front of the store next to the main entrance, just before the produce section. That's where Mom likes to spend her lunches. I know this because of the countless times I've called and FaceTimed her to chat during all-night study sessions I've pulled. She spends her first fifteen-minute break in the break room, then her lunch in one of the booths in the sitting area. She does it because she says she likes the change in scenery.

I check the time again and start to make my way to the other end of the store. I zero in on the canned-goods aisle. That should give me the perfect cover and vantage point. All I have to do is position myself at the end of the aisle and peek over at the sitting area in front of the produce section. And then I'll know for sure if she's eating the healthy lunches I've been packing for her or if she's ordering fast food via Uber Eats. Staying in produce would give me the clearest view, but there's no question she would spot me. And she can't see me spying on her. She'll flip out even worse than she did at water aerobics.

I speed-walk to canned goods, fully aware of how ridiculous this is. I'm spying on my mother in the middle of her overnight work shift to make sure she's eating the healthy lunch I've packed for her. That's borderline nutjob behavior, no question. That's why I'm relieved when I see there are no other customers nearby—that means no one can witness what an overbearing weirdo I am.

I dart to the end. With the wall of canned corn at my back, I inch my head forward to get a better look while keeping my body inside the aisle. Leaning out, I crane my neck to get a better view. Mom sits in the corner booth, examining the edamame salad I packed for her earlier today. She raises a forkful to her nose, sniffs it, then makes a face. I hold my breath, tensing my legs to keep myself in place. If she rejects those ultra healthy veggies lightly doused in organic red wine vinegar, it's going to take everything in me not to march up to that booth and spoon-feed it to her.

But then she sighs and takes a bite. After a few seconds of chewing, she makes a "not bad" face, then finishes two-thirds of it before moving on to the seared piece of salmon in the other Tupperware container.

The corner of my mouth lifts in a smile. She actually looks like she's enjoying it.

"Can I help you?"

I jump, then whip around to the voice behind me.

A guy who looks to be in his early thirties backs up a step, both hands held up so that his palms are facing me.

"Sorry," he says, his brow lifting up all the way to his golden-hued hairline. "I didn't mean to scare you."

My hand falls on my chest. For a second, I can feel my thundering heartbeat hit lightly against my hand. A second later it eases, and I take a breath before focusing on the stranger standing in front of me. He's wearing the same blue polo my mom wears, which means he must work here too. He's easily half a foot taller than me, so just under Andy's height. But this guy's got more lean mass. I can tell by the tone of his forearms and the spread of his shoulders. He's got thick lips, a slender nose, and a jawline that looks like it's been carved from marble.

In my old life, a guy this cute would have elicited an immediate swoon from me. I would have admired him from afar, silently hoping he'd approach me at whatever bar or restaurant or shop I was at. But in this life, I simply take a one-second mental inventory of his physical features before I remind myself why I'm here in the first place.

Then I register his eyes. They're an arresting shade of light blue. I've only seen this particular color in a handful of people and have had one of two reactions: either the light blue is such a stark contrast to the inky-black pupil that the person looks like a maniac, or it's so eye-catching that I'm hypnotized, unable to tear my eyes away from the person.

This guy is in the second camp.

His frown deepens with concern. "Are you all right?"

I swallow, then realize I've just been staring at him for the past several seconds while saying nothing.

"I'm fine. I just . . . was looking . . . for the, um, radishes."

He frowns and swallows before taking a second to process my random request.

"Canned radishes?" he asks.

I nod, even though I'm certain those don't exist.

"Do you mean pickled radishes? We have those in glass jars in aisle six."

"No. I mean, um, regular unpickled radishes. In cans."

"I'm sorry, we don't carry those."

He ruffles his thick golden-blond hair with a hand, then pivots his gaze to the side, as if he's trying to look right through the section of canned peas on the other side of the aisle. "We have fresh radishes, though, in the produce section toward the front of the store."

"Okay, great. Thank you," I say quickly.

"Do you want me to show you where they are?"

"No!" The loud bark I let out makes his eyes bulge for a half second. If I head back to produce, that'll blow my cover.

"I just—I don't want to bother you. You're clearly working. I'm sure I'll be able to find the radishes on my own, thanks a lot"—I squint at the name tag clipped to the left side of his shirt—"Liam."

His name rings clear in my memory. This is the guy Mom mentioned to me on the phone all those weeks ago—the guy she wanted to set me up with. He's also the person who taught Mom how to order fast food via the Uber Eats app on her phone.

His mouth turns up in a half smile. It almost makes me choke, it's so pretty. "No problem . . ."

"Chloe."

I start to walk down the aisle and away from Liam, but then he stops me.

"Wait."

I turn around to face him.

"You're Mabel's daughter, aren't you?"

"Yeah. How'd you know?"

"You look a lot alike. You have the exact same eyes and smile."

His easy grin instantly relaxes me from the surprisingly stressful activity of grocery store sleuthing.

"I've heard a lot about you," he says with a smile that radiates gentleness.

I offer a flustered smile in return. "Oh, I bet." I let out a soft chuckle. "My mom talks about my brother and me nonstop. Sorry you have to hear it."

"I'm not. She tells me all about her brilliant pharmacist daughter. She's really proud of you. It's very sweet."

Inside my chest squeezes so tight, like a hug from the inside out.

"Thanks for saying that," I say quietly. "I should go."

I move to turn around, but he stops me once more. "Don't you want to say hi to your mom? I think she's on her lunch break."

I shake my head. "I don't want to bother her. And she'd be annoyed if she knew I was here."

"Oh. Okay." Judging by his expression, he looks like he wants to say more.

I step toward him. "Actually, would you mind not mentioning that you saw me tonight? I know that's a weird request, but it's just . . ." I try and fail to think of a way to explain this situation and not make myself sound like a weirdo. "Just trust me, okay? It's better if you don't say anything to her about me."

He nods, but there's something so sincere about his confusion that makes me want to be genuine and honest with him, even though I've only just met him. So I say screw it and decide to be honest.

"I know this is going to sound bonkers, but I'm trying to get her to eat healthier these days. Aging and health issues and all that."

Liam's expression eases. He nods.

"I started packing these healthy lunches recently, and I just wanted to stop by and make sure she was eating them and not chucking them into the garbage and then buying potato chips instead. Or ordering fast food from Uber Eats. She's developed a habit of doing that."

He lets a sheepish grin loose, then tugs at the collar of his work polo as if nervous. "I guess I'm partly to blame. I showed her how to use the app."

"So I heard."

We share a chuckle.

"Say no more," he says. "I'm kind of a health nut, too, so I understand."

I walk forward and take one final peek at Mom as she finishes the last of her salmon. When she starts to peel the orange I packed, I know I can leave, satisfied that she's eaten the majority of the lunch.

I turn back to Liam. "Well, she ate it. I can sleuth my way back home then. Thanks for being cool about this."

"No problem. Maybe I'll see you sleuthing around here again?"

His raised eyebrow does the strangest thing to the middle of my stomach. I have to swallow to keep the jumping at bay. "You definitely will."

"Your secret's safe with me."

He lingers for an extra second, and I almost ask him if he knows that Mom tried to set him up with me.

I even start to speak, but then I clamp my mouth shut and let out a flustered chuckle when I lose my nerve.

"I appreciate it," I say instead.

He offers a two-finger salute and a grin before pivoting and disappearing around the corner. I wait until Mom leaves the booth, then I walk quickly out of the store and to my car, my cheeks flushing the entire drive home.

~

I stumble from the garage to the kitchen after running to the store again to grab groceries and dump the bags on the counter.

Out of the corner of my eye, I see Mom lying on the couch. That's where she was when I left her to run to the store, flipping through a magazine to unwind after work.

"Mom, I was thinking of lentil soup for lunch after Auntie Linda gets back from Mass. What do you think?"

Tonight's super healthy recipe is sure to be met with a groan from her and then probably also a comment about how it's too hot for soup since recent daily highs are near the nineties.

"Or we can do lentil salad with fish if you want something different," I offer.

While unloading the groceries into the cupboards and the refrigerator, I wait for her to answer. But nothing.

When I glance up, I catch an image of her arm dangling from the sofa. Immediately I cup my hand over my mouth. She fell asleep.

I almost say "sorry" but catch myself. I need to be quiet.

I finish unloading all the groceries, then grab a glass of water. I'm down to my last gulp when I zero in on my mom's limp arm once more. And that's when something inside of me flips.

A visual surfaces of her in the hospital bed, her arms hanging off the sides. They hung like broken branches, lifeless and still. Just like they are now.

An alarm sounds in my brain. It blares like a million invisible sirens around me.

I ran out of time. She's gone again.

All this time, all these days spent trying to spend more time with her and get her healthy were for nothing because she's lifeless right in front of my eyes—

I freeze, my eyes glued to her left forearm. No. She can't be gone. She's alive. I saw her lying on the couch reading a magazine when I left this morning. I saw her wave goodbye to me. It's not even May 7 yet . . .

She's alive. She has to be.

But every time I blink, the image of her dead in the hospital bed seeps into every rational recess of my brain, making me doubt everything.

Her arm then looked just like it does now. Still and empty and completely void of life.

For a minute all I can do is stand, sweat beading at the back of my neck while the hairs on my own arm stand on end.

I direct my focus to her chest. It doesn't move. That means she's not breathing.

I drop the glass in the sink, then bolt to the couch. Falling at her side, I grab her arm with one hand and her face with the other.

"Mom! Mom, wake up!"

I try to be gentle when I shake her, but adrenaline has taken over. My touch is urgent and desperate because I need it to be. I need to know that she's okay, that's she's still here. That she's alive.

Her skin is still hot to the touch. The tension in my chest eases the tiniest bit. Because if she were dead, she'd be cold. I know that—I know what she feels like when she's dead. I felt it weeks ago, and it broke me.

One second passes, then two.

She still doesn't move. Why isn't she moving? If she's warm and alive, then she needs to be moving. She *has* to be.

This can't be happening. Not again. Please not again.

"Mom!" I cry out, my eyes filling with tears.

Please no. Not like this. Not when I just got her back and—

Just then her eyes pop wide open. Even through their dark-brown hue, I can tell her pupils are dilated. That's how shocked she must be. A second later, she's frowning. For a moment, I'm confused, wondering why she looks so displeased, but then I register it's because I'm still holding on to her arm, shaking her.

I let go and fall back on the edge of the coffee table, hitting my back. Leaning forward, I hug myself with both arms wrapped around me. Then I let go and fall forward so I can hug her instead.

"Chloe! What in the world are you doing?"

I sit down and take a breath. "Nothing. Sorry. You just, um. Well, I came home from the store and was talking to you, but you weren't answering. And then when I looked up, I saw you with your eyes closed . . . So I—I tried to wake you up to make sure you were okay, but you weren't waking up and it freaked me out."

Mom's expression grows more bewildered the longer I babble.

Then she shakes her head and waves her hand at me dismissively. "I was taking a nap, Chloe. Oh, for crying out loud." She sits up, her face scrunched up at me in disbelief and annoyance. "I had to stay late at the store this morning to sit in on a job interview. I was so tired when I got home that I fell asleep on the couch. I was out cold."

"Oh."

"Until you started shaking me and shouting like a maniac."

"Mom, I'm sorry, I just—"

She darts up from the couch and heads down the hallway to her room. She stops just before her door, then turns around to face me. "I don't know what's gotten into you, Chloe. You're freaking out about the strangest things now, and it's got me very worried."

She pauses, scanning me with her rich-brown eyes. "You had another dream about me, didn't you? You dreamed that I died again."

I flinch at how flippant her tone is. "No, I didn't." I bite my tongue. Because I can't say that I'm still operating off the fear and terror that the first "dream" unleashed in me. That's not any better.

"I'm just . . . having an off day. I'm fine." I try to smile when I say it, but she just shakes her head.

"You're not acting fine."

For a few seconds we say nothing. Mom just stares at me, the look in her eyes a mix of concern and confusion. My chest aches that I'm the cause of her worry now. I'm supposed to be making her life easier and better, not more stressful.

"Here, why don't you lie down on the couch and I'll make you some of that herbal tea that helps you sleep. Some rest would do you good."

I hold up a hand. "No, that's not—I don't need to sleep right now, Mom."

"Maybe you do, *anak.*"

I repeat that I'm fine, and she responds with a doubtful expression.

I stand up when I can't think of anything else to say. "I'm going to make myself a snack. You want something?"

She sighs, shaking her head. "No. I'll just go to my room and rest."

I wish her sweet dreams before heading to the kitchen to lean against the counter and hope a few deep breaths will calm my racing heart.

That night I spend hours tossing and turning in bed until I fall asleep. When I finally do, I have the most disturbing dream. I'm standing in a room across from Mom, and we're staring at each other. I wave, but she doesn't see me. She just stares straight ahead, her face expressionless. I run forward to get to her, my arms and legs pumping as fast as they can go. But I don't move. I look down and see I'm in the exact same spot, and she's still so far away.

And then there's a crashing noise above me. I look up and see nothing.

And then I look forward and she's gone.

I open my mouth to call after her, to scream, but no sound comes out.

I move to run after her, but suddenly I have no arms or hands. I look down, and my legs have disappeared.

I try to breathe, but I choke.

Then I see my chest is hollow, like a cannon shot straight through me and annihilated absolutely everything.

Including my heart. It's gone too.

~

"I think I might be losing it."

"Losing it?" Dr. McAuliffe says.

She doesn't even frown at what I've said. Her expression on the screen of my laptop during our Skype therapy session is one of total composure and professionalism. Her eye contact is steady, and her mouth doesn't even twitch up.

"Sorry, I don't know if that's the proper way to put it," I say. "It's just . . . how I feel at the moment."

"When you say 'losing it,' what exactly do you mean? Are you questioning your state of mind? Do you mean that you're having a difficult time processing the events around you?"

I pause and think about how to answer her honestly without sounding even more convoluted.

"Can I just describe something that happened, and you can help me try to process it?"

"Of course."

I take a breath. "I thought my mom died. Again."

Again, there's no discernable reaction from her, just her thoughtful expression that indicates she's listening to me.

"Go on," she says.

"I had just come home yesterday morning and saw that she had fallen asleep on the couch. I didn't think anything of it at first. But then I didn't see her chest move—it looked like she wasn't breathing. She wasn't moving at all. And then it's like my brain jumped to the worst possible scenario."

"I see," she says, nodding. "Can you describe your emotions of that moment?"

"Panic. Dread. My heart started racing. It was difficult to catch my breath. I kept . . . I kept thinking of that moment from before when I thought she died and I . . ." My chest tightens as I recall the hurricane of emotions in that moment. "And I wanted more than anything for her to wake up."

"Did she wake up? Or did you wake her up?"

"I woke her up," I say quietly, remembering how rough I was when I shook her awake.

"And how did you feel when she woke up?"

"Relief. This huge, overwhelming wave of relief. I started to cry. It completely freaked her out."

"What was her reaction?"

"She was upset. Obviously. There she was taking a nap one minute, and the next I'm in tears shaking her awake."

"Did you tell her why you woke her up like that?"

"Yeah. It didn't help. She was still really mad."

Dr. McAuliffe nods. "Chloe, do you think there's still a part of you that's extremely afraid of your mom dying, even though you see her alive and well every day?"

"Yes." I contemplate whether I should tell her about the unspoken deadline of May 7 that lingers at the back of my mind all day, every day. Maybe if I explain that, she'll get a better idea of what I'm going through.

So I do. She nods along like she understands exactly what I mean.

"That fear you're experiencing is perfectly normal," she says. "Most people are terrified at the thought of losing a loved one. Just imagining it can send people into a panic. You're definitely not alone in that."

"I have this fear that I'm going to lose her again on May 7," I blurt.

"Why do you think that, Chloe?"

I clear my throat. "That was the date that she passed away. I mean, when I *thought* she passed away," I quickly correct. "And I think . . . in some weird way it makes sense to me that if she can make it past May 7, my brother and I won't lose her again."

I exhale, the tense muscles in my shoulders loosening. I probably sound out of my mind—like I think I'm living in a movie or the Matrix or some ridiculous nonsense like that.

It feels good to say it out loud, though, to tell that to someone instead of keeping it inside of me.

"The timer in my head is still there too. Not always. Like, it's not like I hear it constantly. Only sometimes, usually when Mom and I are arguing or she's upset with me. And then last night I had this awful nightmare where she and I were in the same room, but I couldn't get to her. She couldn't see me either. And then all of a sudden, she was gone. I couldn't see her anymore. And then when I tried to look for her, I couldn't move. My arms and legs were gone. There was a giant hole in my chest too."

My heart's pounding as I explain this to Dr. McAuliffe.

"I know dreams can be so weird and random . . . but I feel so shaken up by it."

"I see." She nods, seemingly unfazed by what I've said. "I don't have a lot of experience with dream analysis, but it doesn't surprise me that you dreamed that after experiencing such a stressful moment with your mom. And I can also understand why May 7 would hold significance for you."

When she pauses, I blurt the other thing that's been on my mind. May as well get it all out in the open.

"I'm also trying to find my dad."

Her eyes widen the slightest bit. "Really?"

In the past I've talked about my dad to Dr. McAuliffe, specifically how he was an alcoholic and absent father. She knows I haven't spoken to him in years and am not interested in having a relationship with him.

"Yeah. I, um, learned something about him pertaining to my mom."

I explain how dad stole Mom and Auntie Linda's heirlooms, how it caused a strain in their relationship, and how I'm tracking him down without my mom knowing.

"It all kind of plays into that goal I have of doing as much for my mom as possible before May 7." I shrug.

She pauses for a moment, thoughtfully processing what I've said. "Tell me how that makes you feel, the prospect of seeing your dad."

"Uneasy. Anxious. Upset. Sad."

There's a long pause before I say more. "I'm still really mad at him. I know it was a long time ago that he stole it. And I know my mom wants to let it all go. But I just can't."

"Why can't you? If it's your mom's wishes to leave this issue alone, why pursue it?"

Her gentle tone causes me to reflect instead of becoming defensive like I probably would if someone else were to ask me this same question.

"My mom's been through so much. She was married to an alcoholic who took her for granted and left her alone to raise two kids. Life has never been easy for her. She was an immigrant who moved to the United States from the Philippines when she was a teenager, then helped her parents build a store from the ground up. She worked there every day when she was a kid, until she moved out on her own. She helped take care of both her parents when they got sick, till they passed away. She works hard every day of her life. She doesn't deserve one more bad thing to happen to her. That's why."

There's a conviction in my tone that I don't notice until I finish speaking and can feel just how hard my heart is beating. I exhale and order my hunched shoulders to relax.

"You think this is a bad idea, don't you?" I ask Dr. McAuliffe.

"That's not for me to say. I'm here to help you work through whatever feelings you want to address. And if this feels like the right thing for you to pursue, then that's what you should do."

I almost laugh at her diplomatic therapist answer.

Dr. McAuliffe straightens in her chair. "What I will say is this. You're implementing a lot of stressful things in your life right now, what with quitting your job to live with your mom full time and now trying to locate your dad. It's important that you have an outlet. An escape."

"I do. I go running."

"That's great. Exercise is a wonderful release, but I mean something more than that. Like a friend."

"I have my best friend Julianne."

Dr. McAuliffe nods her approval. "I like to tell my clients that they should have three people they can call at any time, no matter the day, and they know that person will be there for them emotionally. A 'no matter what' person. Who are your three?"

"Julianne. My mom." I almost say Andy but stop myself. I love him, but he's my younger sibling. No matter how old he gets, I'll always think of him as my little brother—someone I should always look out for. And because of that I won't be able to fully lean on him as an emotional support.

"It sounds like you need a third 'no matter what,'" she says with a soft smile.

"I'll work on that."

"I think it would go a long way in helping you cope with the stress and anxiety you're feeling right now. The more people you have in your life you can count on for support, the more at ease and fulfilled you'll feel. I promise."

"That makes sense."

"As upsetting as it is, we can't control how long our loved ones are with us. Everyone wishes they could, but it's just a harsh reality of life. What you can control is how you spend the time you have with them now. The longer you allow your emotions to be controlled by your fear—specifically your fear of losing your mom—the less you're able to truly enjoy that time you have with her. If you're always operating with this fear in the back of your mind, it's going to make it hard for you to be fully present with her whenever you're spending time together. It makes it harder to enjoy that time you're spending with her because you're always worrying about a million what-ifs. You're always wondering how much time you have left with her instead of appreciating the time you have together now."

"It's just hard because there's this constant terror in the back of my mind that I'm going to wake up one day and she'll be gone again."

"I understand. That's a very common fear that a lot of people have. But there's not a magical solution to that issue unfortunately. All you can do is focus on the time you have with her now."

I nod my understanding even though I'm frustrated she doesn't have a better answer.

But what can I expect really? I can't reasonably expect anyone to guarantee that my mom will stay alive no matter what.

I can't even presume that anything I'm doing to help Mom currently will make a difference.

I think of the handful of times when Mom and I argued—at cooking class, water aerobics, when I mistakenly thought she died and shouted her awake.

My stomach churns at how our time together has been marred with moments of conflict and arguing. That needs to change.

"We're reaching the end of our time," Dr. McAuliffe says. "Do you want to make an appointment for next week?"

"I'd like that."

She offers a soft smile. "It'll be okay, Chloe."

I thank her and close out of our session, hoping that she's right.

Chapter Twelve

I rush to wipe the counter as the garage door sounds, signaling Mom is home after her overnight shift.

It's been a couple of days since I saw her sleeping, mistakenly thought she was dead, and freaked out. I've caught her looking at me a bunch of times since then, almost like she's studying me to make sure I'm okay. I shove away the thought and the unease it sows through my gut, and instead I focus on the moment, on the fact that it's the beginning of May and she's still here. When she walks through the door, I'll get to see her and hug her.

It will all be okay.

I hear the sound of her car door closing, then hurry to place the plate of chicken parmesan that I whipped up for her as an after-work treat at the kitchen table. When she walks in, I look up at her with a wide smile and point my hand at the plate, like I'm a game show host revealing a grand prize.

But instead of the smile I expect, she just stands there, looks at me, then sighs. After a moment, she walks over and chucks her purse on top of the kitchen table, then stomps her feet on the tile floor, as if she doesn't plan on leaving this spot ever.

When she props a hand on her hip, that's when I notice the scowl on her face.

"Is everything okay?" I ask.

"Were you ever going to tell me about your plans?"

"What plans?"

"Your plans to quit your job."

My heart skids to a halt. Quickly, I turn, head to the sink, and start to scrub the pan clean to give myself a moment to plan my response.

I hear the bathroom door open and see Auntie Linda walk out from her morning shower dressed in a muumuu, her jet-black hair damp.

"Who quit what?" she asks, halting at the entryway of the kitchen next to Mom.

Mom mutters in Ilocano that I quit my job while I turn my back to them.

"Chloe, I'm still talking to you. Don't ignore me."

Her voice takes on that hard, unrelenting tone that tells me she means business.

Taking a breath, I turn back around. "Who told you that I quit?"

Despite my question, I think I already know. Only two people know I quit the hospital: Andy and Julianne. But only one of them is bitter enough to tattle on me, and that's Andy. I glance down the hallway to his bedroom door. Lucky for him, he's not here. He's spending the morning helping a friend rebuild the fence in their yard before he heads to work. Otherwise I'd march down the hall, kick his door down, then punch him in the arm for taking it upon himself to tell on me. That is such an immature move. He could have just come to me to talk things out instead of going behind my back and ratting me out to Mom.

She waves her free hand in the air. "Who told me isn't important. What's important is the fact that my daughter quit the job she's brilliant at to move back home and do nothing more than pester me about eating and exercising. Would you like to tell me why?"

I'm met with the angry knit of her eyebrows. Auntie Linda's expression goes sheepish as she mutters something about getting all packed up before her flight home tomorrow. She slinks back to the guest room to let us have it out in the kitchen.

"Mom, I know what you're thinking."

"Do you?" she says, tilting her head to the side. She tugs at the hem of her top. I can tell even in her sharp, jerky movements how angry she is. "Do you honestly know what is running through my head right now? Because I bet you don't."

Taking a breath, I try to gauge where her anger, frustration, and impatience are coming from. I'm the oldest—I'm her first baby. As a kid, I always studied hard and earned high grades in school. I was always the student in elementary school who cried because I got an A-minus and not an A. I was the kid in high school who chose to stay home studying on weekend nights when other kids were partying because I wanted to ace all my tests and papers.

I was the kid who took community college classes in high school to prepare me for college and won enough scholarship money to cover most of my tuition.

I was the kid who was on the honor roll every year of university, who graduated summa cum laude and got admitted to my first-choice pharmacy school. I was the kid who was happily dedicated to my job for years.

And now, after all that, I quit. I can't be surprised that she's pissed and shocked. And if I'm being honest, if I were in Mom's shoes and my gold-star kid suddenly announced that her new life plans were to quit her steady job and move back home, I'd probably be pissed too.

"Mom." My voice is measured, steady, calm. "I understand why you're upset. But I'm thirty-three years old. I can make my own decisions when it comes to my life. And I've decided to quit working for now because it's the right thing for me to do."

She's still shaking her head, still monumentally disappointed in me and seemingly unmoved.

"You're lying to yourself, *anak*. I know you, better than anyone knows you." She tugs a hand through her ebony hair while sighing and shaking her head. "I'm your mom. I know that you're happiest when you're working hard, when you're busy and challenging yourself. You're not someone who can be content just sitting around and doing random things here and there. You're not like Andy. You'll go out of your mind."

I frown at her, annoyed that she would think to insult him. But before I can say anything to defend him, she speaks.

"I don't mean it in the way you think I do. Andy is my baby. I love him to death just like I love you. But I know my kids. I know how different you are. Andy is smart, but he never liked school. It never suited him the way it suited you. So he found a job that he's good at that fulfills him. I'm so happy and proud of him." She points a finger at me. "But you."

I swallow, my throat suddenly dry. It's been so long since I've been on the receiving end of a hard scolding from her that I've forgotten how it makes me want to crawl out of my skin.

She wags her index finger, the red polish on her fingernails glistening in the sunlight that's filtering through the windows in the living room and kitchen. "*You* are different. And you know you are. You thrive in your job. It's where you shine. You get bored when things get too easy. Yes, you get stressed out when there are challenging things in your way, but that's your motivation. That's your fuel. You'd be bored to tears if you tried to live otherwise for very long."

Standing in front of her, I have nothing to say in response. Because she's right. That's exactly the kind of person I've been. But I want to be different now.

"We're the same in that way," she says after a moment. "We may work different jobs, but our attitude is the same. We don't like to just sit around and do nothing. We're driven, and we like to stay busy."

"Mom—"

"I always liked that we had that in common," she quips. "But now . . ."

Her disappointment is evident in the dismissive way she shakes her head at me. My gaze falls to the floor. We may have that in common, but even with a busy schedule, she always made as much time as she could for her family—unlike me.

It takes a second before I can look at her again. When I do, she's still frowning, but there's a bewildered look in her eyes now.

"Wait . . . does this have anything to do with what you told me before?" she asks.

My chest tightens. I sigh, then start to explain, but she cuts me off.

"You quit your job because of that dream you had, didn't you? You dreamed that I died, and you thought it was real at first, but even though it's not . . . that's why you quit your job, isn't it?"

She crosses her arms, clearly disappointed in me.

"It's fine if you think my reasons for doing this are silly, but I do want to spend more time with you, Mom." My voice shakes as I try not to cry. "I feel bad about living so far away and missing so much time with you."

The hardness melts from Mom's face. She steps toward me and holds me by the shoulders. "*Anak*, you don't need to quit your job to see me."

"But you even told me you wish I visited more. I know . . . I know I wasn't very good about coming home this past year with how busy I was after I got promoted. Or even before that really."

My nose tingles, a telltale sign that I'm close to tears. I take a slow, silent breath.

A sad smile tugs at her lips. "I'm your mom. I want to see you as often as possible. There will never be a time when I think I'm seeing you often enough. I admit that I get a little over the top when I call you and tell you how much I wish you could come home. But to quit your job? That's ridiculous."

"Not to me."

Her hands fall to her sides. She shakes her head. "You're making a mistake."

"I'm really not."

She turns around to grab her purse from the table, then starts to walk out of the kitchen in the direction of her bedroom. But she stops and turns back to me. "You had an amazing career. And you threw it all away."

I shake my head at her, knowing that even though she means well, she couldn't be more wrong. Here, at home with her, is where I need to be for the foreseeable future. I can feel it in my bones, in every breath I take, every morning when I wake up and see her and hug her and talk to her.

The right thing for me to do is to stay, even if she thinks I'm wrong. Even if she doesn't want me here.

"I can see why you think that," I say. "But this is what I want. More than anything. Life is short, and I want to focus more on the things that actually matter."

On the inside I wince at my poor phrasing with "life is short," but it's still the truth.

A defeated sigh is her response.

"Sometimes people need a break, Mom. I needed one. I was burned out. You should think about taking one before you burn out too."

She ignores my appeal by turning away and walking into her bedroom. Down the hall I hear a door open, then the low conversation between Mom and Auntie Linda in Ilocano.

"Why are you so mad? Your daughter wants to spend more time with you. That's wonderful."

"No. She wants to live here and babysit me."

"Ay, *adingko*. Don't say it like that. She loves you."

There's a muttered exchange that I can't make out, then Auntie Linda's voice grows louder.

"I'm lucky if my boys call me once a month. Their schedules in the military are so crazy. And here your daughter quit her job to be closer to you. You're a fool for being upset."

Mom makes a disapproving noise. "You always have something to criticize, don't you? First, you're mad that I didn't call the police on my own husband for stealing our jewelry, and now you're mad about how I don't just sit back and watch my own daughter ruin her life while belittling me?"

I wince at how bitter Mom sounds, at how this fight between us has caused an argument between her and Auntie Linda.

Auntie Linda sighs. "That's not how I mean it. *Ading*, I'm not criticizing you. I only say this because I care about you."

A dismissive "uh-huh" from Mom follows, then a door slams.

I let out a breath and notice just how tense the muscles in my neck and shoulders are.

Auntie Linda walks out of the hallway and into the kitchen. She flashes a sad smile to me before pulling me into a hug.

"Your mom will come around. I promise."

"Thanks, Auntie."

"You're a wonderful daughter. Don't let anyone tell you otherwise."

She kisses my cheek before heading to the living room to sit down and read the newspaper. Her sweet embrace and words have left me the slightest bit heartened, but most of me is still fuming from what Andy did. I tell Auntie I'm off to run an errand, then swipe my car keys from the coffee table, walk out the door, and hop in my car.

~

I walk into Crowler's Bar and Grill in downtown Kearney and scan the space for Andy. It's a simple setup with wooden tables and booths in dark, rich colors. A couple of flat-screen TVs adorn the area right above the bar.

The tables are empty since it's only a minute past opening. I spot Andy just as he pops up from behind the counter at the bar. When he sees me, he squints.

"What are you doing here?" he asks as I walk up to him.

"We need to talk. Now."

He frowns, then turns to a random glass and starts drying it with the tea towel in his hand. "I'm busy."

"You can spare a few minutes."

He continues to polish the glass while staring at it for a solid minute. But I stay standing there and cross my arms, making it silently clear that I'm not going anywhere.

Andy sighs, places the glass on the counter, then finally looks up at me. "Fine. Let's go out back."

I watch as he ducks his tall frame to avoid hitting the low doorway and follow him out to the alleyway. The sounds of passing cars from the nearby street fill the air.

Again he frowns as he plants himself in front of me, arms crossed. "What is it?"

I take a breath, then punch him in the shoulder.

"Ow!" he yelps, his low voice echoing against the brick walls that line the alleyway. He rubs the spot on his arm. "Chloe, what the hell?"

"What the hell me? What the hell you!" I boom. "You told Mom I quit my job after I told you not to. What did you do that for?"

His face falls. For a long moment, he says nothing.

Glancing at the ground, he shakes his head. "Would you believe me if I told you it was an accident?"

I scoff. "Nope. Explain. Now."

He sighs, rubbing his temple with his hand. Then he reaches in his back pocket and pulls out a pack of cigarettes and a lighter. He lights one up and takes a long puff.

I glare at him, wrinkling my nose at the smell. "Since when did you pick up that disgusting habit?"

"Since I became the token underachiever in the family."

He takes another long drag, making sure to face away from me when he exhales a cloud of smoke. He hides this habit well. I've never once smelled smoke on him the times that I've been home to visit. Either he must change every time he does it, or he really doesn't do it that often.

"I only do it sometimes. When I'm super stressed out," he says, as if reading my mind.

"And what exactly is stressing you out right now?"

"The fact that my big sister quit her successful job to live at home, just like me."

He doesn't look at me when he speaks, but I can tell by his defeated tone and his downcast eyes that he's sad.

"Andy—"

"You're not supposed to be like me, Chloe." He bends down to put out his cigarette in a puddle of muddy water, then tosses the butt into a nearby empty coffee tin filled with sand and cigarettes.

"And what exactly am I supposed to be?"

"Something better."

"Do you honestly think being a pharmacist makes someone a better person? Because I've worked with plenty of jackasses who prove that theory dead wrong."

He shakes his head. "I don't mean it like that. It's just . . . You say you'll be fine living at home, that you'll get some other job someday. Do you know how many people say that? So many people quit their jobs or drop out of school, then they never go back. Half of my friends who dropped out of college said that. *I* said that. Look at me."

He shoves his hands in his pockets, his face twisted in a pained expression. My chest squeezes just watching him, and suddenly my arms ache to hold him, to comfort him. He's clearly hurting. But then he pivots away from me for a second.

He turns back around. "You're the smart one. You've never messed up or made a rash decision that cost you everything. But this decision you made to just up and leave your job could be a huge mistake. Who knows what it could cost you?" He looks off to the side. "Who knows what it could lead to?"

Sirens wail in the distance as we stand and say nothing. That faraway look in his eyes remains. The longer I stand there, the longer his words soak in, and the more I realize that he's not talking about me anymore.

I touch his arm. "Andy, what are you talking about?"

He finally looks up at me. "I don't want you to end up making a snap decision that costs you everything."

"What do you mean? Did something happen?" My tone is no longer impatient and annoyed. It's gentler, in the hopes that he'll open up about whatever is bothering him.

He takes a breath and looks me in the eye. "Remember Hannah? We've been seeing each other on and off for a while now and . . . we had a pregnancy scare not too long ago."

"What? When?"

"A couple of months ago." He swallows, the expression on his face falling.

I hesitate to ask him to elaborate. As curious as I am about this whole situation, I'm not sure I want to hear about the details of my brother's love life.

"How did you meet her?" I ask instead.

"Here. During a bar crawl for her friend's bachelorette party. We hit it off and started seeing each other casually. But there was one time where we weren't careful." He swallows. "Hannah texted me one day in March asking if we could meet up. It was weird because she's always so bubbly and upbeat, but she sounded so serious in her message. When we met, she told me she missed her period. And I just kind of went . . . numb."

He pauses, and I touch his arm. It seems to help because after a second he starts speaking again.

"She told me she was going to take a pregnancy test and wanted me to be there with her when she did. I didn't say a word. I just nodded, like a jerk. Can you believe that?"

He lets out a soft, bitter laugh.

"Andy . . ."

He shakes his head. "And then I left. I don't even remember what I said to her, but I jumped out of my chair in that coffeehouse where we met up and just took off in my car. I didn't even know where I was driving. She tried to call me, but I didn't answer. It was like my head was trapped in this weird fog."

"You were in shock."

"I was. My brain was a mess. It was like all these thoughts were crashing into each other over and over, and I couldn't make sense of anything. What if she's pregnant? Should we get married? I can't afford a wedding. But then I thought, what the hell am I worried about a wedding for? How will I support a baby on my crappy bartender salary? How will I take care of a baby when I live with my mom still? I couldn't think straight."

"Andy, it's okay."

"It's not okay." His tone turns firm. "I should have comforted her. I should have told her that no matter what, I'd be there for her. I should have held her hand in that coffee shop and told her it was all going to be okay. I should have been her rock. But I was so freaked out that I ended up saying nothing, and that caused this strain between us. Because she thought I was abandoning her. I swear, I wasn't. I just . . . I needed a minute to process it all. But now I realize how awful I made her feel with how I acted."

I nod my understanding. I've never had a pregnancy scare before, but I know exactly how I'd feel if I had thought I was pregnant in my early twenties and the guy I was seeing had acted so detached. I'd feel abandoned and alone. And I'd question if we should even be together in the first place.

"I didn't call her or text her for days, I was so frozen with fear. I was such a piece of shit." Andy's eyes glisten as he looks up at me. "Sound like anyone you know?"

The sad smirk that tugs at his mouth sends a jolt of pain to my chest. I know exactly who he means.

"Andy. Don't say that. You're not like our dad."

"I kind of am, though. He ditched Mom with two kids. But I didn't even wait until actual kids showed up. I ditched Hannah when just the possibility of kids came up."

I squeeze his arm. "Stop. You didn't ditch her. Yeah, you could have handled things better for sure, but you showed up to be with her when she took the pregnancy test, right?"

He nods and wipes his nose. "Yes."

"And you're together now still. You're working it out."

"Trying to," he mutters. He blinks away the tears pooling in his eyes. "You know what the fucked-up thing about all this is? When I saw that the test was negative, I was sad. Like, I actually felt disappointed. In that moment, as panicked as I was, I realized that deep down, I think I wanted Hannah to be pregnant. I always thought I'd like to be a dad someday. I just didn't think it would happen so soon. Even though it actually didn't."

I tug Andy's arm so he looks at me. "Andy. Listen to me. It's okay that you felt panicked and mixed up. Something like this, an unplanned pregnancy, can conjure up so many emotions. Sometimes they conflict or they don't make sense. That's totally normal."

Even as he stares at me, the look in his eyes reads empty. It's like he's hearing me but not quite taking in what I'm saying.

"You're not like Dad. Don't even think that." A lump lodges in my throat, but I swallow it away. "Yeah, you messed up by how you responded when Hannah first told you that she might be pregnant. I'll be the first person to tell you that was a shitty thing to do. But did you apologize to her?"

"Yes."

"Good. And you were there for her the day that she took the test. And you've been there for her ever since, right?"

He nods. "I promised her that I'd never leave her like that again. I don't know if she believes me, though."

"Have you talked about why you bolted on her?"

"Yeah. A few times. But I always feel like the biggest piece of garbage when I do. Because yeah, I was scared and that's understandable. But she was scared too—and she had it worse than I did because she was the one who would have been pregnant. So it doesn't really matter how freaked out or unprepared I was. It pales in comparison to what she was going through."

I nod in agreement with him. Because he's absolutely right.

"She says she understands why I reacted the way I did," he says softly. "But she said it still hurts her. She wanted some time to herself to think things through after we found out she wasn't pregnant. So we stopped seeing each other."

The skin on his neck flushes as he swallows. His eyes water again. "We didn't see each other for a couple of weeks after that. I was a wreck without her. So I reached out to her and apologized again, told her that I wanted to give things between us a proper shot. We got back together right after Easter."

I rack my brain for any memory of Andy seeming down recently, but nothing comes to mind. He still joked and laughed while spending time with us over Easter weekend.

I pull him into a hug. Despite his large frame that dwarfs mine, he feels so small and frail in my arms—like he's my tiny, scared baby brother all over again.

"I'm so, so sorry I didn't realize what you were going through."

"It's okay," he mumbles, patting my back. "I honestly wouldn't have been able to handle it had you and Mom fussed over me."

We pull apart. His eyes still glisten, but no tears fall.

"It was nice actually that you were preoccupied with work stuff, and Mom was busy cooking Easter dinner and Skyping with Auntie Linda and all the family. You both were too distracted to interrogate me about anything."

His words land like an anvil ripping through my heart. I know there's relief in his words—he's always hated being doted on. But I'm destroyed at the thought that I wasn't there for him, that I didn't even notice the smallest sign of what he was going through.

"Is that why you've been away so much? To be with Hannah?"

He nods. "I think she's still having a hard time trusting me. I know she wants to be with me—she wouldn't have taken me back if she didn't—but I think part of her is still skittish. I think she wonders if I'll ever ditch her again."

"Did you guys have a fight about that when I saw you that one day?"

"Yeah," he says through a heavy sigh.

"All you can do is show her that you're different now, that you're committed to her one hundred percent no matter what. She'll forgive you eventually. I promise she will."

We both take a second to breathe. A truck revs past us, the deafening sound of its engine echoing against the alley walls.

Andy shoves his hands in his pockets and looks at me, the expression on his face sheepish. I reach for his arm. "Don't worry, I won't tell Mom."

"Thanks. I know—I know I probably deserve to be ratted on, especially after I told her about you quitting your job. I realize what a piece of crap I am for doing that to you—in addition to what I did to Hannah." He rubs the back of his neck.

"No, you don't deserve that. That's not how this works."

He shakes his head as if to dismiss my reassurance, but I grab his arm. "Listen to me. You're an incredible person. One of the best I know. And I'm not just saying that because you're my brother. I'm saying it because it's true. Yeah, you fucked up. You did something hurtful. But we all do. The things you did aren't unforgivable. You've made it right with me, and you'll make it right with Hannah too."

He flashes a sad smile. "Thanks. It's just . . . when you told me you quit your job, I guess I panicked. I thought that was going to kick off a landslide of irresponsible decisions for you, too, like quitting school did for me—as irrational as that sounds. And I thought that telling Mom would be one way to stop you. But I know now that wasn't the right thing to do. I think I was projecting my own hang-ups onto you. It wasn't right. I'm sorry for that."

"I understand now. And it's okay."

He lets out a tired sigh. "I still wish you'd reconsider, but you know what's best for you. I respect your decision."

"Thank you."

"Call me crazy, but I always pictured you doing something incredible. Like, helping develop some breakthrough drug or taking over the hospital. You were amazing at your job, Chloe. I bragged to everyone about what a big shot my sister is."

He shrugs. There's a sincerity in his voice that makes something inside my chest pull tight.

"Maybe someday," I say.

He tugs at the neckline of his black polo with the word *Crowler's* stitched in gold over the right chest pocket. "I'd better get back to work."

He turns and heads for the door. Just before he reaches for the knob, he turns back to me.

"Thanks, Chloe. For everything."

"Of course."

The door shuts behind Andy, and I make my way down the alley and around the block to where my car is parked. My head is still swirling at Andy's revelation—at how my little brother was almost a father, even though he really wasn't that close.

On the drive home, all I can think about is how thrilled Mom would have been to be a grandma. Tears flood my eyes. Even though I blink quickly, I can't stop them from falling. By the time I park at Mom's house, I can't get out of the car right away because my face is soaked.

And then I pull my phone out of my purse and dial Julianne, the no-matter-what person I can count on to talk me through this.

Chapter Thirteen

"I thought we could try something different," I say while pulling into a parking space in front of Riva Meditation.

Mom squints at the purple sign above that boasts the huge lettering in Papyrus font. This guided meditation studio sits in a run-down strip mall between a payday loan place and a gyro joint.

"What in the world . . ." She trails off, her squint turning into a frown.

Meditation is one of the recommended activities for improving heart health, and I've been meaning to get Mom to go ever since her checkup with Dr. Massey. But honestly, I need it too. Ever since our argument several days ago about me quitting my job, we haven't spoken much. I can feel the tension between us like an invisible fog. I want things to be normal between us again. One meditation class won't fix everything, but maybe it'll put us in a calmer state.

Especially since today is May 6—one day before the unofficial deadline I've been holding in the back of my mind. It's the finish line that Mom absolutely has to cross—if she makes it past May 7, I can breathe easy. We all can.

One piece of heartening news concerning this is Mom's follow-up appointment with Dr. Massey yesterday morning. He congratulated her on lowering her cholesterol and blood pressure through diet and exercise, then told her that she wouldn't need meds if she kept up her new healthy lifestyle. When he asked me if I was helping her, Mom made a comment that yes, I was because I had all this free time to boss her around now that I was jobless.

But I ignored her quip and instead focused on the fact that health-wise she's where she needs to be. It can all work out. She just has to make it past tomorrow.

Slowly and quietly, I let out the breath I've been holding in and follow her gaze up to the Riva Meditation sign. I'm still surprised that she agreed to go anywhere with me this morning when I asked if she'd be up for something easy and relaxing. But as I unbuckle my seat belt, I'm grateful.

"This looks ridiculous," Mom mutters.

"You didn't seem to be into the idea of that online guided medita-tion class I suggested at first," I say.

"Because that's such a ridiculous idea. I'm not going to pay money to lie on my living room floor while someone on a computer screen whispers to me."

"Then an in-person meditation class was the next best choice." I try not to groan. "You didn't really seem to enjoy anything else I've sug-gested, like the cooking class," I say. "Or water aerobics. Or anything else I've come up with so far. This is me thinking outside of the box."

When I step out of the car, I catch the beginnings of her annoyed scoff.

"You're lucky I love you," she mutters, slamming the car door before following me into the studio.

The door opens to a small reception space with a desk in the front. Nearby is a padded bench with curtains draped over the wall behind it as a sort of makeshift waiting area. On the other end of the front entrance is a dark shelving unit that boasts a bevy of meditation-related items. On one shelf sits a mini Zen garden. The tiny tray of sand and wooden rake looks like it's sized to sit on a desk or side table. On the other shelves rest books about meditation, Buddhism, massage, and related topics. Vials of essential oils line one shelf.

Mom spends a few seconds gazing around, taking it all in. She tugs at the loose white T-shirt she changed into after she arrived home from work. She mutters a comment about how weird it feels to wear my yoga pants.

"We're the same size, Mom," I say after closing my eyes for a minute to gather my patience. "I'm wearing that exact style, and they're perfectly comfortable."

In the corner on the floor is a rock sculpture the size of a fire hydrant with a stream running through it. The soft sound of water trickling down the rocks echoes in the small space, creating a relaxing type of white noise.

Mom turns her nose up at the water rock sculpture. "If I had to listen to that thing all day, I'd have to pee every five minutes."

I let out a quiet chuckle. This is the first time I've laughed since Andy told me about Hannah's pregnancy scare. I still can't believe he kept that to himself.

Just then a tall guy in his early twenties with a man bun walks down the hall that must lead to the actual meditation room. He greets us with a soft smile and intense, unblinking eye contact.

"Namaste. Are you ladies here for this morning's hour-long guided meditation?"

I'm about to tell him yes, but then the door opens behind us.

"Hey," Andy says from behind me.

I spin around, stunned to see him. I texted him earlier today that Mom and I were headed here this morning, but I didn't think he'd be up for coming. When I see Hannah step out from behind him, I'm in shock.

"Sorry I'm late."

"It's okay," Mom says with a wide smile on her face. "Who's this with you?"

Mom beams at Hannah, who's fidgeting with her hands in front of her.

"This is my girlfriend, Hannah."

"Ay, I didn't know you have a girlfriend!"

Not even a second later, Mom pulls Hannah into a hug.

I stand back and laugh quietly as Hannah introduces herself while pinned in Mom's embrace.

Mom finally released her but still holds her by the shoulders. "Look at you! So pretty."

Hannah's cherub cheeks turn pink at the compliment. Andy grins at the floor as he shoves his hands in his pockets before looking at me.

"I hope it's okay that we both came."

My heart swells. This is the first time I've seen Andy's smile reach his eyes in weeks. This means so much. It means that he and Hannah are official. It means that he's comfortable enough to introduce her to Mom and me. It means that he's happy, Hannah's happy, and Mom's happy. It means that I'm so, so happy too. It means that everything is starting to feel a bit less chaotic and uncertain, and a bit more complete.

"Of course it's okay," I say. "More than okay."

Mom finally turns to Andy and pulls him into a hug.

"Hannah and I were just talking about how we've been so busy lately and wanted to unwind. This should be perfect." He tugs at the hem of his T-shirt.

I spin back around to the man-bun guy and hand over my credit card to pay for the session and say that there will be four of us instead of two. Hannah starts to object, but I wave a hand at her and tell her it's my treat.

She says a soft thank-you and fumbles with the hem of her tank top, then pulls at her yoga pants. When I finish paying, I turn around and give her a soft pat on the arm. It must be odd as hell to meet your significant other's mom at a guided meditation class.

"You're a good sport for coming to this," I say.

Hannah laughs while tying her long, straight hair into a ponytail. Mom takes her by the arm and starts to ask her a million questions about herself as the man-bun guy, who's also the instructor of the class, leads us to the back.

"Mom is in love with Hannah," I quietly say to Andy as we follow behind Mom, Hannah, and the instructor, who introduces himself as Logan.

"I warned Hannah that Mom would be fawning all over her. She didn't seem to be worried at all. She actually seemed like she was excited about it."

I glance up and see the two of them chuckling about something. My chest squeezes even tighter than before. I look up at Andy. "I'm really glad you guys came."

He smiles at me, then looks between Mom and Hannah. "Me too."

"It saves me from having to continue listening to Mom grumble about the fact that we're spending money to sit in a room and close our eyes for an hour."

Andy laughs. "Oh, she definitely would have done that."

We walk down the hallway, which leads to an open space. It's dimly lit with no windows. It's just off-white walls and a smooth hardwood floor that shines like glass.

Two dozen people, mostly women, sit cross-legged on the floor on top of yoga mats.

Logan asks us to each grab a yoga mat from the basket in the corner, then choose a spot to sit on the floor.

A few more people trickle in, then Logan walks to the front of the room, where he sits on his own mat.

He stretches both arms at his sides, like he's about to hold hands with two imaginary friends flanking him.

"Everyone. Thank you for coming to today's morning class. It is a joy and an honor and a privilege to practice mindfulness with you all here today."

Mom lets out a loud yawn that echoes in the room. A handful of people shoot her looks. I narrow my gaze at her while Andy tries and fails to hold back a laugh before yawning himself. All she does is wave her hand in dismissal of me. After a second, I chuckle too.

With his hands pressed together like he's about to pray, Logan stares ahead, saying nothing, the expression on his face a content sort of neutral. He blinks slowly, like he's drowsy with sleep. The corners of his mouth are curved up in a not-quite smile. Even though this dude is unquestionably over the top, I admire him. He seems so completely at peace, so calm in his movements and his expression that stress must not even register on his radar.

After a full minute of staring at nothing, Logan grabs a tiny stick and hits a golden gong the size of a saucer sitting to his left side. Everyone in the room closes their eyes and takes a deep breath in. I do the same.

When I hear zero breathing noises from Mom, I open one eye and pivot my head to her. She sits, frown on her face, arms crossed, like an annoyed child who's been banished to time-out.

Before I can say anything to her, Andy turns to her.

"Mom," he whispers. "Close your eyes and breathe."

I'm heartened at just how seriously Andy's taking this. Mom sighs but complies a second later. I turn my head to face the front once more, then close my eyes and force myself to breathe in and out in a slow, steady rhythm.

It takes a few minutes for my mind to stop racing. I don't know if I'll ever get to the state of complete mental relaxation that Logan wants us to aim for. The entire time I'm sitting on the floor, eyes closed, I'm thinking of Mom. Is she breathing like she should be? Are her eyes closed the way they're supposed to be? Is she putting in the effort to clear her mind like everyone else is? Or is she just sitting there and stewing like usual? What about Andy? Is this helping him at all? How does

Hannah feel? Is she completely weirded out that as a family we're going to a guided meditation class?

But then I consciously halt every errant thought I have. Every time a worry or concern about Mom or Andy pops into my brain, I shove it away. I focus on the darkness in front of me, on the slow rise and fall of my chest with each breath.

Logan rings the mini gong once more. "Okay everyone," he says in a low, soft tone. "I want you to slowly, very slowly, lie down on your mats."

When I open my eyes to lower myself down, I'm happy to see Mom following the instructions too.

"Close your eyes," he chants in a whisper. "Think of the beat of your heart, how it slows down. Think of your breath—the air—entering and leaving your body. Try to make it as slow and deliberate and relaxed as possible."

The steady, whispered rhythm that Logan employs when he speaks starts to take effect on me. Every muscle in my body relaxes. Soon my limbs and my back feel heavy, like they're sinking into the floor.

Every so often I start to drift off but wake when I hear someone clear their throat or when Logan rings his gong.

But then all the noise around me turns cloudy and muffled. And then I'm asleep.

The sound of chuckling wakes me. When I open my eyes, upside-down Logan greets me, smiling wide.

"Looks like someone was completely zenned out."

I blink, then rub my eyes before sitting up. "Oh. Sorry," I quickly say before a yawn takes hold of me.

"Don't be sorry," he says.

When I steady myself enough to stand, he presses his palms together and gives me a slight bow.

"It's impressive that you were able to let your mental stresses completely go like that in your first class. I'm in awe."

I tell him thank you. Logan turns away and nods at Mom, who's snoring on the floor beside us. I cup my mouth to muffle a chuckle. Andy smiles as he quietly stands up.

"Your mother has mastered the art of clearing the mind." The continued look of awe on Logan's face tells me that he's completely serious and impressed at our ability to fall asleep so easily.

"She sure has."

I'm about to explain that she just got off a night shift, but then someone waves Logan over across the room to ask him a question.

I crouch down and tap her gently on the shoulder. She wakes with a jolt, eyes wide, then a beat later it's back to her frown.

"Did you have a nice nap?" I ask, unable to hide the smile on my face.

She shakes her head at my amused tone. "Yes. I'm ready to go home and sleep now."

We walk out of the classroom after telling Logan thanks once more. When we're in the parking lot, Andy and Hannah walk to the car with us.

"All I learned from that young man is how to fall asleep to annoying dinging noises while lying on a hardwood floor."

"That's actually a good sign," I say. "You were relaxed enough in your mind and body to fall asleep in an unfamiliar environment. That shows you were able to tune out stress well."

She shrugs.

"I think this would be good to continue. Regular meditation could help continue to lower your blood pressure," Andy says.

I turn to him, impressed. He's clearly been researching things related to Mom's health.

I catch a thoughtful look in Mom's eyes, but when she blinks, she's back to her neutral expression. "I don't know if I want to pay money to take a nap on that guy's floor," she says.

"I'll pay it then."

"No. It's a waste."

"We don't have to go all the time," Andy says gently while leaning against my car. "Just every once in a while."

She says nothing for a second, only crossing her arms and glancing around, like she's thinking about it.

"And it's a lot more fun than water aerobics," I say.

She lets out a laugh. "That's for sure."

"And you don't have to force yourself to eat anything you don't like during it. Like kale," Andy adds.

Mom looks at me. "You told him about the kale incident?"

"Of course I did."

The three of us laugh.

She takes a deep breath in through her nose, like she's savoring the morning air. "Maybe we'll go next week then. But only if someone comes with me. I don't want to go alone," she says before turning to Hannah. "And only if you come over for dinner tomorrow night, Hannah."

Hannah, who's been standing off to the side and quietly observing while the three of us politely argue about the merits of guided meditation, looks slightly caught off guard judging by the gentle raise of her eyebrows.

But then she smiles at Mom. "I'd love to."

Mom pats her hand. "Great! I'll make fried rice, Andy's favorite!"

She hugs Andy and Hannah goodbye, then hops into the passenger seat of the car and glances down at her legs. "I think I like these yoga pants actually." She pats the top of her thigh.

"You can keep that pair," I say. "Wear them the next time we go to a meditation class. Or when we go for a walk."

She looks up at me, grinning. "Thanks, *anak*."

Hannah's phone rings, and she excuses herself before walking off to take the call. I tell Mom that I left something in Andy's car that I need to grab.

We walk across the parking lot to his car. "Thanks for coming today," I say.

"Sure thing. It was actually kind of relaxing," he says, rubbing his hand along the back of his neck. "My head feels a bit clearer now."

"That's really good. Things between you and Hannah seem to be going well too."

"Today's a good day."

He glances over at her talking on the phone several feet away on the sidewalk in front of Riva Meditation.

"Are you sure she feels okay coming to dinner tomorrow? Mom kind of put her on the spot, but I can talk to her later if Hannah's not comfortable."

Andy shakes his head. "No, she wants to. She's been asking about it ever since you invited her, actually. Sorry it took so long to do this—to introduce her to you and Mom."

"It's okay, Andy. I'm glad she's here now."

Hannah walks over and we say our goodbyes, then I head back to the car and drive Mom home.

"I'm so happy that Andy has a girlfriend," Mom says, grinning as she looks out the window.

"Me too. She seems really sweet."

"She does. Now we just need to get you someone."

I roll my eyes and groan. "Mom. Don't start."

She holds her hands up. "I'm just saying. You're such a catch, *anak*. Beautiful, smart, hardworking, independent, you own your own house. Any man would be lucky to have you."

I mutter a thanks.

"You know, that young man Liam I mentioned before, the one who I work with at the store who taught me how to use Uber Eats, is single. Remember when I mentioned him to you—"

"Yes, Mom. I remember." I exhale so hard, I feel my breath hit the tops of my thighs.

"I'm just saying. He's very handsome. And single." She speaks while looking out the window.

I think back on the one run-in I had with Liam. He's handsome for sure, but I'm not here to date or get into a relationship. I'm here to spend more time with my mom.

I pull into the driveway of her house and turn off the car before turning to address her.

"I appreciate the thought, but I don't need to be set up. I'm perfectly happy single."

She flashes a knowing smile before getting out of the car. "We'll see."

~

"Do you think this is enough food?" Mom asks as she stands next to the stove, stirring a giant wok of fried rice.

"Mom, that's enough food to feed ten people. It's more than plenty."

I look over at her as I set the kitchen table. Her arm shakes as she struggles to stir the mountain of rice, peas, carrots, scrambled egg, chicken chunks, and bacon.

I walk to the stove and take over stirring duties.

"I hope Hannah likes it," Mom says.

"She'll love it. Promise."

She fusses over the *bibingka* she whipped up for dessert, and my mouth waters. The chewy glutinous rice cake is my favorite dessert that she makes, and I haven't had it in months.

She jokes about the jiggly consistency of the cake, how it reminds her of her thighs. As I laugh, I feel a lightness I haven't experienced since I woke up that morning and saw her alive again. Because it's May 7, and Mom is still here. This morning I woke with a knot in my chest that didn't dissipate until I saw her walk out of her room and fetch a cup of coffee from the kitchen. And as I chatted with her, laughed with her, and spent the day with her, little by little the knot loosened.

I walk over and give her another hug.

"So many hugs today, *anak*." She chuckles, squeezing me back. "What's the occasion?"

"Nothing." I try my hardest to keep my voice steady. "I just wanted to say thanks for cooking for us."

Leaning back, she holds me by the arms as she gazes at me. Her smile reaches all the way to her rich-brown eyes, like it always does when she's truly happy. "I'll always cook for you kids. Anytime you want."

The front door opens, and in walks Andy with Hannah. Immediately Mom runs over to hug them and makes them sit at the table while she scoops a mound of fried rice onto a serving platter.

"Hope you're hungry!" she singsongs as she walks over to the table.

As we dig in, I take in the scene. Mom listens intently as Andy and Hannah explain how they met. Andy reaches for Hannah's hand as he recalls how he saw her immediately in a busy Saturday night crowd at Crowler's.

"It must have been the hot-pink bridesmaid's sash I was wearing," Hannah jokes as she sips her water, winking at him.

Andy grabs her hand, his heart in his eyes when he looks at her. "I think it was more like you were the most beautiful woman in the whole place."

Mom cackles, her shoulders shaking as she laughs. "Listen to you. Such a charmer."

They joke about how long it took Andy to call Hannah after asking for her number when he ran the check for the bachelorette party.

"By the time you called, weeks had passed. I had completely forgotten about you." She nudges Andy with an elbow good-naturedly.

He shakes his head, laughing. "I was trying not to come off as too eager."

"There's a fine line between not too eager and completely disinterested."

Andy turns to Mom. "You sure about that whole charmer thing? Clearly I messed up the when-to-call-her part of all this."

We all burst out laughing. I ask Hannah what she does for work, and when she answers that she works at a day care center, Mom rests a hand on her chest and *awws*.

"What a sweetheart you are for doing a job like that. Working with kids all day isn't for everyone. I could never handle that. The only kids I could ever put up with were my own."

Hannah asks me about my work and thankfully doesn't prod when I explain that I'm a pharmacist who's taking some time off. I shoot Andy a grateful smile. He probably filled her in on what a sore subject my work is among the family at the moment, so she likely knows not to dwell too long on it.

Conversation flows naturally the rest of the meal. And for a moment, I sit back and relish just how well everyone is getting along, how natural it feels for the four of us to share a meal. I look over at Hannah, who finished all of her fried rice save for a few bites.

"More?" I reach for the serving platter, but she shakes her head. Under the sunlight streaming in through the nearby kitchen window, I notice small beads of sweat glistening along the delicate ridge of her brow.

"No, thanks. I'm just gonna run to the restroom."

Andy directs her down the hall.

I fetch the pan of *bibingka* from the counter and bring it to the table.

"So are you gonna leave any for us, or is this sheet pan just for you?" Andy asks while squinting at me.

I smack his arm. "You're so annoying. I've never eaten an entire sheet pan of *bibingka* before. Ever."

"But you've come pretty damn close. Maybe the three of us can split a single square while you take the rest."

He laughs when I smack him again.

"Ay, no fighting, you two!" Mom scolds before chuckling.

I'm laughing as I fall back into my chair but stop when I hear a thud down the hall. All three of us whip our heads in the direction of the hallway.

Andy shoots up from his chair. "You okay, Hannah?" he calls as he walks to the bathroom.

Mom's face furrows when there's no answer. The silence stretches for seconds. And that's when my heart starts to race.

"Hannah?" Her name is a soft inquiry in Andy's voice. But a beat later it becomes a shout. "Hannah!"

At his scream, Mom and I jump up from our chairs and run down the hall. When we get to the bathroom, the door is wide open. Andy's on the floor.

"Andy, what's—"

But before I can say anything else, my throat dries. I lose all the air in my lungs. My hands won't stop shaking.

All I can do is stand and stare at the scene before me, frozen in place, my heartbeat crashing in my ears.

There's blood—so much blood—on the tile floor of the hallway bathroom.

There's Hannah lying face down, her head near the edge of the bathtub.

There's blood running down her legs, her feet, on the palms of her hands.

There's Andy shouting something, but I can't understand what he's saying. My ears are ringing too hard.

There's Mom falling to the ground, grabbing Hannah's arms, then her shoulders, then her cheeks.

Andy turns to me. When we lock eyes, something inside of me breaks loose, and I can finally hear him.

"Call 911."

I pull out my phone and do exactly that. I tell the operator everything that's happened—that Hannah collapsed while using the bathroom, that she's bleeding vaginally, that she's barely breathing.

Andy yells for me to tell the operator that Hannah missed her period a month and a half ago. I relay the information while Mom's head snaps up at Andy. But then she turns her focus back to Hannah, whose breaths are rapid and shallow now.

"You're going to be okay," Mom says.

Chapter Fourteen

Sitting in the waiting room at the hospital, I can't get warm. I rub my hands over my bare arms. It's almost summer in Nebraska, which means it's hot and muggy most days. It also means that places crank the AC to stay cool.

But right now I'd give anything to be outside, sweating my face off in the heat and humidity that remains even in the dead of night, instead of sitting in this icebox ER waiting room.

I'm shaking. Not just because it's cold, but because just hours ago we saw Hannah almost bleed to death.

I'm shaking because the last time I was at this hospital, Mom was here, on this exact date—as a deceased patient. And now she's sitting next to me, healthy as can be, like that visit—like that day—never happened.

I'm shaking because I think Hannah's miscarriage and Mom's presence here on Earth could be connected.

Mom's alive—but her grandchild is dead.

One in, one out.

My face, neck, and chest grow hotter and hotter with the thought, at how maybe this senseless world all of a sudden makes sense. Hannah's miscarriage happened on May 7, the day that Mom died . . .

One in, one out.

It's a phrase that I've heard a million times before for a litany of insignificant things like bar capacity and department store dressing rooms. It's never meant anything to me.

But right now it means everything. Other than the waves of sorrow crashing inside of me, that phrase is the only other piece of information my brain can process right now.

It means that Mom being here isn't the purely joyful miracle I think it is.

One in, one out.

It means that there was a price that needed to be paid for her existence. A price that I didn't know existed. Until now.

I glance down at my hands resting on the tops of my thighs. I try to lift them slowly from my legs, but I'm still shaking too hard. I quickly shove them under my thighs. I can barely process what the hell is going on.

Closing my eyes, I take a long, quiet breath and exhale slowly. I can't think about this right now. I need to focus on being present in the moment so I can support Mom and Andy. And Hannah.

I look over at Mom, who's sitting with her legs and arms crossed, her eyes red and swollen from crying. She stares at the ground. There's no focus in her deep-brown gaze. It's like she's sleeping with her eyes open.

I take her hand in mine. "Are you okay?"

She nods. "I'm just worried about Hannah."

"She'll be okay. The doctor said so."

"What a horrible thing for her to go through. And Andy."

After paramedics arrived and took Hannah to the emergency room, I drove us all to the hospital. Thankfully paramedics were able to stabilize Hannah before she arrived. When we got there, Andy went straight to Hannah while Mom and I waited in the emergency room. The ER physician on call who treated Hannah discovered that she was miscarrying a very early pregnancy—just a handful of weeks.

My heart shot to my throat when Andy first came out and told us what happened, though I'd had a good sense earlier.

"She didn't even know she was pregnant," he said through trembling lips.

Mom did her best to hold back tears but broke after a few minutes. Andy and I hugged her as she cried, then he left to go back and be with Hannah. Even though Hannah's stable and conscious, the doctor is keeping her overnight to monitor her, and Andy wants to be by her side.

I grab Mom's hand as we wait for Andy to come back out and update us on Hannah's condition. "I'm sorry, Mom."

"You don't need to tell me sorry, *anak*. I'm okay," she says with a sniffle before slowly pulling her hand out of my grip.

Her words ring like a well-timed flashback. I've heard her utter that phrase countless times my whole life. When I'd see her furiously punching at a calculator at the kitchen table as she figured out how to stretch her paycheck to pay our bills. When she was so tired from pulling double shifts all the time because Dad couldn't keep a steady job to save his life. When I caught her crying in the bathroom after Dad got arrested for drunk driving with Andy and me in the car. It was always, "I'm okay."

I sigh and nod instead of telling her that she doesn't have to pretend, that she doesn't have to plaster on a brave face. But saying that would just make her defensive. It's not worth an argument right now.

Just then Andy walks out from the sliding glass doors on the far side of the floor over to us.

"Hannah's resting. I just wanted to come down and tell you guys thanks again for coming. You should go home and get some rest yourselves," Andy says. "Hannah wanted me to tell you thank you so much for dinner. And that she's sorry for how things ended."

Mom shakes her head. "She doesn't need to apologize. None of this is her fault."

"Yeah, but . . . that's just the kind of person she is. She feels bad for stuff that's never her fault."

Mom and I nod our understanding.

"You take care of her, okay?" Mom says.

"Call us if you need anything," I say as we hug.

"Promise I will."

On the drive home, Mom doesn't say a word.

"Are you okay, Mom?"

"Yes. Fine."

"You sure you don't want to talk about anything?"

The subject I'm hinting at lies in the silence between us. Mom just learned a handful of hours ago that she could have been a grandma. This is the kind of devastation that would weigh heavy on even the strongest person. She should at least try to talk about it.

"Yes, I'm sure. I'm fine."

"You sure you don't want to take a couple of days off work? What happened is serious, and it's fine to take some time to process it. I know you're scheduled to go back tomorrow night, but you could call in and—"

"I don't need to call in, Chloe."

Her biting tone and the way that she tugs on her seat belt tell me she's done talking. And that's all we say to each other the rest of the night when we arrive home and go to bed.

~

"Can I ask you a weird question?"

"Of course." Dr. McAuliffe's neutral, professional expression remains unmoved on my laptop screen.

I clasp my clammy hands together in my lap. I don't know why I'm so nervous to ask this. I've brought up so many strange and off-the-wall subjects to her, and she's always taken them in stride. This won't be any different.

"Do you think the universe . . . has a need to . . . balance things out?"

She squints at me and I bite back a wince, annoyed at how convoluted I sound.

"I'm not sure I know what you mean by that," she says.

"Okay, well . . . when a baby is born . . . it's almost like they're replacing the life of someone who has died on that same day or around that same time. I mean, you could look at it that way, right?"

Dr. McAuliffe takes a moment to blink, like she's trying to make sense of what I've said. "I don't know how popular that belief is, but I'm sure some people ascribe to it."

"Right, well . . . do you think the opposite could be true? Like, if someone was supposed to die, but then somehow lived, then wouldn't there be some sort of life debt to be paid to the universe?"

"*Life* debt?"

I open my mouth, but it's hard to even say it. It's only been a day since Hannah lost her baby. But I have to know if this could be the reason why Mom lived and the baby didn't make it. I can't sleep, I can't eat, I can't think about anything else right now. That's why I messaged Dr. McAuliffe for this last-minute session.

"As in a miscarriage," I finally say, my throat tight. "Like, what if a baby was supposed to be born, but then someone who was supposed to die all of a sudden survived? So then the baby couldn't be born anymore . . . because it would throw off the balance in the universe."

I swallow, painfully aware of how absolutely out of my mind I sound to someone who doesn't know what I know. But to me it makes complete sense—the same day, the same place, so many of the same people. How can I overlook all this?

Dr. McAuliffe frowns at me, like she's trying to sort out the word salad spilling from my mouth.

"Did someone you know have a miscarriage, Chloe?"

I sigh and nod, then explain what happened with Hannah and how I think it could explain why Mom's still here.

Dr. McAuliffe's face twists in a pained expression. "I'm so sorry to hear that. Truly." She pauses and looks away for a quick moment, like she's choosing her words carefully before speaking them. "I don't mean to sound insensitive when I say this, but people die every minute of every day. Just like how they're born every minute of every day. It doesn't mean anything more than what it is: birth, life, and death."

She says it so simply, without an ounce of hesitation in her voice.

"I know you want to find the meaning in this, Chloe. And many times there is a lot of meaning to derive from many kinds of events, both joyful and tragic. But this? I honestly think you're looking for something that's not there. Yes, the timing is coincidental. But that's all it is: a coincidence. Because some things in life don't have a special meaning. Sometimes they just happen, both good and bad. And you should accept them for what they are instead of trying to search for a meaning that may not be there."

I take a few seconds to process what she's said. To her and everyone else, it's a coincidence because they haven't experienced what I've experienced—waking up one day and seeing Mom, who was dead, come back to life. But maybe since I'm the only one who sees the connection in what has happened, I need to let it go. I need to try and move on like everyone else is.

"The more time you spend struggling over this, the more time you miss with your brother, his girlfriend, and your mom. I think it's better if you spend your energy supporting them, Chloe."

Dr. McAuliffe's advice hits like a pillow smack to the face. Even if there is a significance in what happened, what difference does it make right now? Because this timeline, this existence, and the people in it— Mom, Andy, and Hannah—are what count.

That means letting Hannah and Andy know that I'm here for them in any way they need me.

That means taking care of Mom and trying to convince her that she needs to take a break so she can process her emotions about Hannah's miscarriage.

And getting back what's rightfully hers from my dad.

A renewed sense of urgency ignites inside of me. "You're right. I—I don't know why I fixate on these things."

"It's okay, Chloe." A reassuring smile appears on her face. "You shouldn't feel bad about your feelings and emotions. It's important to talk about them. That's exactly what you're doing. And it's a good thing."

I thank Dr. McAuliffe, then end the session. And then I pick up my phone and call Andy. I get his voice mail.

"Hey. It's me. I know I haven't called since we left you guys at the hospital yesterday, but I didn't want to bother you two when you're going through so much. I just . . . if you guys need anything, tell me, okay? I'm here for you both. And I know—I know that's a completely unhelpful and mildly infuriating thing to have to hear after what you guys have been through, but I honestly don't know what else to do. Or say. And I'm sorry for that. I just . . . want to be there for you guys. So let me know whatever I can do, okay? Love you."

I hang up, then stand up and run to the kitchen for a glass of water. When I walk back in my bedroom, I see my phone flashing with a new text from Andy.

Andy: Hey. Just got your message. Thank you.

Me: Are you guys hungry? Want some home-cooked food instead of whatever bland hospital stuff you're eating?

Andy: That sounds amazing. Thanks.

I put my phone away and get to work whipping up pansit for Andy and Hannah. It's not much at all, but it's something. A small way to support him and Hannah. But right now, that's what counts.

~

I pull into an empty spot in the parking lot at Mom's grocery store and turn off the car.

"I know she's not okay," I say to Julianne as I talk to her on the phone. "She's in denial and needs to take some time to process her grief instead of just going about her day as usual."

"Maybe this is her way of grieving the loss of her unborn grandchild, Chloe," Julianne says. "I'm not saying it's healthy. But it would make sense. Your mom's not one to slow down."

That's the understatement of the week. For a solid week since Hannah's miscarriage, Mom has refused to talk about it or take a day off work. Every time I try to broach the subject, she shuts me down with a stern "I'm okay," then walks out of the room. Even Andy trying to get her to take some time for herself didn't work.

But despite her claims, I know she's struggling. She hasn't been able to sleep well at all. I've caught her awake hours before her alarm goes off. And she's been forgetting things she normally never does. Like tonight when she forgot her lunch, which is why I'm at the grocery store in the middle of the night, right before she takes her lunch break. Hopefully when I bring her lunch, I can sit with her and convince her to take a day or two off or at least slow down. Maybe even talk.

"How is Hannah doing?" Julianne asks.

"Andy said her recovery is going well. She's pretty distraught and sad, though."

"I can imagine. God, poor girl."

"I haven't talked to her since dinner last week. I don't want to pry or overwhelm her."

I tell her how Andy reassured me that Hannah's seeing a specialist to help manage her recovery and also a therapist to help her through the depression she's experiencing.

"And Andy?"

"He says he's okay, but it's clear he's hurting. Every time I see him, his eyes are swollen. I know he cries when he's alone. And probably when he's with Hannah too. Which is completely understandable given what they're going through. I just . . . don't want him to feel like he has to hide his pain. I'm his big sister. I want to be here for him."

I've been trying to get Andy to talk to me about how he's feeling for the past few days, but he's barely been at home. He only stops by to grab clean clothes since he's been staying with Hannah at her apartment ever since she was discharged from the hospital several days ago. It's never long enough for me to have a frank conversation about his emotional state.

Julianne's sigh echoes through the interior of my car. "I wish I knew what to say. Or what to do. I'm sorry, Chloe."

"You're doing more than enough by letting me call you in the middle of the night and unload all of this to you. You're an amazing no-matter-what person."

"Damn straight I am."

She chuckles, and I crack my first smile in days. I'm tempted to ask her how things are going in the search for my dad, but I hold back. I asked her a couple of days ago and still nothing from her cousin, and I don't want to keep pestering.

I promise to call Julianne again soon. We hang up, and I walk into the store, Tupperware in hand. I scan the front of the store and spot Mom at a register assisting one of the cashiers with an alcohol purchase.

I wait until she's done helping, then walk up behind her and tap her shoulder.

"Chloe." She tucks a few strands that have fallen around her face behind her ears. "What are you doing here?"

I hold up the Tupperware. "You forgot your lunch."

The smile she flashes is tight. "Oh. Right. Thank you. Here. Come walk with me to put it in the break room."

We walk in strained silence through the quiet aisles.

"You didn't have to come all the way here. It's the middle of the night," she says, staring straight ahead. "I could have figured out how to scrounge up a meal for myself."

"I know that, but I was still wide awake anyway and figured this would be easier."

"Always looking after me. Thank you."

I clear my throat before I bring up the topic she dreads most. "Have you given any more thought to taking some time off?" I try to keep my tone light. "I think it would do you some good to rest for a couple of days."

A heavy sigh rockets from her. "Nope. I don't need to."

I stop her with a hand on her arm. "Come on, Mom. Stop pretending. I know you're reeling from what happened with Hannah. We all are. But you need to stop pushing yourself. It's not good for you."

"Says who?"

"Says me."

"Oh, so you think you know better than me?"

"In this situation, yes."

She rolls her eyes and starts walking away from me.

I catch up with her. "Mom, you know I'm right. You're forgetting things. You're having trouble sleeping. It isn't healthy to keep going on like this."

"Here we go with the health nonsense again. What do you want me to do, Chloe? Take another meditation class? Maybe force-feed me kale? That'll cure me right up."

My skin pricks at the sarcasm in her tone.

"Mom, don't say that. That's rude."

She stops walking and turns to me, frowning. "No, you know what's rude? Acting like you know better than me. I'm your mom. I know what's good for me, and I don't need your or anyone else's opinion on it."

"Mom, just because I'm your kid doesn't mean you always know what's best in every situation. Sometimes you don't, and that's okay. That's why I'm here—to help you."

She purses her lips, her chest rising with her breath. "You think I'm not handling my sadness well? I know what we lost, Chloe. Hannah lost her baby . . . I lost a grandbaby. That makes me so sad, I can barely breathe sometimes when I think about it."

My eyes water as her voice quivers.

She swallows. "But what good would it do for me to sit around and feel sad about it? I'd rather move on."

I tug a fist through my hair, wishing that Auntie Linda were still here. I bet she could get Mom to slow down for at least a day. Or at the very least, she would sit Mom down and they could talk and have a long cry about what happened. Because it's one thing for me to lecture my mom and an entirely different thing for her older sister to do it. Mom might actually listen to her.

Just then a midforties man in coveralls juts his head out from the end of the nearby aisle. "Christ. Finally," he mutters as he looks at Mom.

I cock my head toward him. "Excuse me?"

He huffs out a breath and stomps to the end of the aisle, like he's annoyed. "I had a question I wanted to ask an employee of this store, but there is absolutely no one around. I've been looking for someone for almost five minutes. This is ridiculous." He crosses his arms, an indignant look on his face.

I'm about to tell him off for his entitled tone and ridiculous expectation that retail workers should be at his beck and call, but Mom speaks before I can.

"I'm sorry about that, sir," she says, reeling in the frustration and pain that plagued her expression just seconds ago. "What can I help you with?"

I bite down, annoyed that Mom essentially has to put on a happy face to deal with this rude jerk.

The guy points to an empty shelf nearby. "Why are there no paper plates left? I came all the way out here to buy them, and they're not even in stock."

"I'm sorry, sir, but the stockers are running a bit behind tonight. Someone called in sick and we're a worker down, so the food aisles get restocked first. Paper goods should be stocked by morning, though."

He shakes his head. "That is not acceptable. I need them now."

When he points his finger down at the ground, like he's commanding a dog to sit, my blood turns to lava.

My head spins when I realize how often Mom and the other employees at this store must deal with awful customers like this guy. Yes, the majority of customers are friendly and polite, but that doesn't take away from how upsetting one demanding and rude customer can be.

I take a breath as Mom holds her hands up to ease him. "I understand you're frustrated. But there's nothing I can do about it at the moment. Please just be patient with us, we're all doing our best."

He scowls at her. "How about instead of wandering around the store and chatting away, *you* go to the back, get some paper plates, and restock the shelves. That's your job, isn't it?"

This fucking guy, likening grocery store employees to servants.

"Or do I have to complain to the store manager that you're not doing your job?" he says, crossing his arms again.

I watch as Mom's expression hardens, as she takes a deep, steady breath. This is probably what she does every time she has to deal with a shitty customer.

But tonight, she won't have to. Because I'm here. No one gets to be a rude prick to my mother in my presence.

"Hey, Dick," I bark.

He jerks his head to me.

I point to the name on his coveralls, which reads *Richard*. "Dick is short for Richard, isn't it? And actually, you're acting more like a dick than a Richard."

He turns his scowl at me. "You have no right to speak to me like—"

"Wrong!" I bark the word so loudly, he jerks back. "I do. I absolutely get to speak to you like that, since you speak just like that to other people. So listen here, *Dick*. You will apologize to my mother for being a rude asshole, and then you will leave this store quietly."

I scan the large white stitching across the chest of his gray coveralls. Bellamy Mechanics.

"Or I will call your boss and tell them that their employee *Dick* was escorted out of the store by security because he was harassing and berating their employee."

He huffs out a breath. "Good luck with that. I own Bellamy."

"Even better." I pull out my phone and take a quick photo of him. "I'll post this lovely picture of you on my Facebook, Twitter, and Instagram accounts and let the world know what a prick the owner of Bellamy Mechanics is."

His jaw drops. I take a step toward him. Yeah, he's a handful of inches taller than me, but I don't care. No one disrespects my mother. Fire coats my lungs. I'm confident that in this moment I could maim him.

He stumbles back, probably because of that crazed look in my eye that says if he so much as looks at her wrong, there is no way on this earth that he will leave this store in one piece.

"I'm a millennial, Dick. Do you know what that means? I'm on social media. A lot. And I grew up in this town. I have tens of thousands of social media followers who live in this area. I'm going to post this photo of you with a caption explaining how you think it's okay to harass retail workers at the most popular grocery store in town. Do you have any idea how hard their jobs are? They come to work every single day to make sure this store is operating so you and other customers can shop here at all times of the day, every day. They come to work when the rest of the world shuts down due to bad weather or a freaking pandemic. They come to work every day even when jerkoff customers like you berate them over the most nonsensical crap in the middle of the night."

Dick stands unmoving, his mouth hanging wide open.

"Get ready, Dick," I growl. "The minute this picture goes viral, every person in this city is going to see it—they're going to see *you*. This town will learn that you are a disrespectful jerk to the employees of the grocery store that they love to shop at. You're going to lose business. You're going to lose money. All because you didn't want to say sorry."

I turn back to my phone and upload the photo on Instagram, then begin to type a caption.

"It's your call, *Dick*." Bellamy Mechanics' Instagram account pops up when I type it into the caption. I turn the phone screen to him. "It was nice knowing you."

This time his eyes bulge so wide, I'm surprised they don't pop out of his head. "Okay!" he says through a breath. "Please don't post that!"

I wiggle the phone at him. "Say you're sorry."

He turns to Mom, who's standing next to me, her brows all the way at her hairline, stunned at the scene unfolding before her.

"I—I'm sorry. For being so rude. I'm very, very sorry," he stammers while holding both of his hands up at her.

She nods once. "Apology accepted."

Dick's chest rises and falls rapidly as he stares at the ground.

"Take this as a life lesson, Dick," I say. "Don't be a jerk to kind people, because some very horrible things could end up happening to you."

He darts an embarrassed stare at me before slowly nodding and scurrying away.

"Everything good?" a low voice says from behind me.

I turn around and see Liam standing a few feet behind Mom and me, his eyes darting between us before looking at Dick as he scurries away.

I start to answer him, but Mom holds up a hand.

"Everything's great," she says. "My daughter took care of it."

She pulls me into a side hug, then gives me a squeeze before speaking quietly into my ear. "I understand you're worried about me, but I'm fine. Okay, *anak*? Thank you for what you did."

She turns to Liam. "This is my daughter, Chloe." She wags her eyebrow. "He's the one I wanted you to meet. Over Easter."

"Oh. Right." My face grows hot as I remember how she insisted that he and I would hit it off.

"Actually Mabel, we've met before," Liam says.

"Oh yeah? When?" Mom smiles cheerily as she looks back and forth between us.

Panic hits me. I can't tell her that we met while I was spying on her. She'll kill me.

But Liam saves me before I have to scrounge up a lie.

"She was shopping here one night a few weeks ago, and we bumped into each other. I knew right away she was your daughter. You two look a lot alike."

Mom grins. "Oh! How nice." She grabs the Tupperware from my hand. "Well, I'm off to take my break. Thanks again for my lunch. I can't wait to eat it."

She walks in the direction of the sitting area where she usually takes her lunches, leaving me and Liam standing together.

I can feel my cheeks start to heat. My chest feels like Jell-O. It's a scramble of emotions and sensations inside of me right now. Frustration at my mom being so stubborn and refusing to slow down. An adrenaline rush at going off on Dick. Surprise and excitement at seeing Liam again.

"The way you took that guy down was epic," he says.

"It wasn't really that epic."

"It was. I heard the dude's voice from five aisles away and was about to jump in and help, but I didn't have to. Ruining him via social media, huh?"

I shrug. "It probably wouldn't have done anything to his business honestly. But sometimes all you have to do is sound scary to get your point across."

Liam holds up a hand. "I'm definitely terrified of you. No question."

My second laugh of the day happens right then and there. "Thanks for that."

"For what?" His mouth quirks up into a half smile that I like better than any half smile I've ever seen before.

"For making me laugh. It's been a hell of a day."

"One of those, huh?"

"You don't even know the half of it."

We share a quiet moment of standing and smiling until my phone rings.

"Sorry, one sec," I say to Liam as I answer Julianne's call.

"Hey. When I said call me soon, I didn't mean it literally," I joke.

"My cousin found your dad, Chloe."

The next words she utters I barely take in. Something about an address in Kansas City. Something about managing a furniture store. Something about getting married two more times. Something about two divorces.

The words float around me like slow-moving clouds. I can't catch them. All I can do is stand there and observe as they float by and try to take it all in.

"Chloe, can you hear me? Are you okay?"

It's a long second before I can answer. I must look as unbalanced as I feel because soon Liam is frowning at me. He takes a step toward me. "Hey. Are you okay?"

I nod, even though I feel like I'm about to pass out. Why the hell do I feel this way? I asked for this. I asked Julianne's cousin to track him down. I asked her to find an address and a way for me to get in contact with him. This is exactly what I wanted—so why do I feel like I'm about to be sick?

I try to shake my head, then I remember I'm on the phone and Julianne can't see me. "Um . . . let me call you back, okay?"

Then I hang up and notice my trembling hands.

"Do you want some air?"

I nod at his question. I blink and Liam's got me gently by the arm, leading me through a side door. Once we're outside, an invisible wall of humidity hits me. I take a breath and cough, then Liam guides me to sit on a nearby bench and kneels down in front of me.

"You want some water?"

"No, I . . ."

"Did you get some bad news on the phone? Would you like me to go get your mom?"

My hand lands on his shoulder. I make a fist in the thick fabric of his polo. "No. Don't. Please."

I focus on Liam's icy-blue eyes. They're like an anchor for my brain, which is currently bouncing around in my skull, scrambling every single thought I attempt to form.

The longer I look at him, the surer I feel. It's the strangest thing, the sense of calm he gives me.

"Do you want to talk?"

"Yeah." I say it before I realize what I'm doing. I *do* want to talk to Liam. Something about him makes me want to share the madness inside of my head. Maybe it's the kindness in his eyes or how caring he's being to me, a near stranger in this moment.

"This is going to sound crazy."

He doesn't even blink, he's so unfazed. "Hit me."

And then I spill everything. How I hired my best friend's private investigator cousin to track down my MIA alcoholic deadbeat dad because he stole my grandma's jewelry when I was a kid before ditching the family, how it caused a rift between my mom and aunt that I've been trying to figure out how to repair. How this is all related to the decision I made to quit my job and spend more time with Mom and get her healthier, which is why he saw me spying on her in the store the first time we met.

I leave out the part about how all this is part of some nonsensical and impossible second timeline that kicked off when I woke up one day and my mom was still alive. He doesn't need to try to make sense of that craziness.

Liam doesn't say a word, he just stays kneeling in front of me, nodding along, blinking only every so often, like he's captivated by the nonsense spilling from my mouth. But not in a morbidly curious way. In a caring way. I can tell by his unwavering eye contact and the kindness glistening in his stare. He's listening to me because he wants to. Because he cares.

When I finish, he sits on the bench next to me.

"So, um . . . yeah. Sorry for unloading on you. I'm just trying to process all of this."

"Don't be sorry. You're going through a lot right now. It's not good to bottle it all up."

"Yeah, but—I don't know how healthy it is to unload on a complete stranger." I let out a joyless chuckle. "You're a really good listener. It felt so . . . natural to word-vomit on you."

I twist my head and catch him smiling.

"Maybe in another life, we knew each other. Or we were best friends. Maybe that's why it's so easy to talk to me."

I can tell by the way he tilts his head and that almost-smirk on his face, he's joking. But what he says resonates. Because even though that sounds impossible, it could be true. Anything could be at this point. And just the thought that we could have known each other before somehow, in some impossible way, settles the nerves whirring inside of me.

"And actually, we're not technically strangers," he says. "We've met. Twice now."

"I guess that's true." I feel myself smiling, and the stress knot in my stomach eases. It feels good to smile. It feels good to smile with Liam.

"And I know you in a way. Your mom talks about you a lot, about her brilliant pharmacist daughter who's so smart and successful. She says the hospital you work at would fall apart without you and that you graduated at the top of your class. So I know you better than a stranger."

I shake my head. "That's not even close to true. I was in the top ten percent, not the top of the class."

"Still pretty impressive."

"Yeah, well, I'm not so impressive currently since I'm not working."

"You're doing well enough to take some time off. That's pretty successful."

I look at him, appreciating the kind way he words things.

"Would it make you feel better to know some things about me?"

"Actually yeah." I lean back against the bench and pivot so I can face him a bit better.

"Okay well, I'm a thirty-one-year-old college dropout. I played baseball in college. Didn't really have much of a career plan outside of hoping to make it pro one day. Typical naive college athlete mentality. But then I injured my shoulder, and it never healed properly. Kind of wiped out any chance for me to go pro."

"Oh. Sorry to hear that."

"It's fine."

"So how did you end up here?"

"I tried a million different jobs and quit every single one of them until I stumbled upon this one. I liked it so much that I stayed on for a few years and applied for an overnight manager position when one opened. The work culture here is really supportive—way more than any other job I've had. A lot of that's due to your mom. She's not just about pointing out mistakes and hitting numbers like other managers. She makes it a point to pull you aside and tell you what a great job you're doing regularly. I've never had any boss do that before."

"She's pretty great."

"I think someday I'd like to go back to school and get a business degree. Maybe even my MBA." He lets out an amused laugh. "Your mom is always getting on my case to enroll in school. She says it annoys her when young people like your brother and me don't take advantage of education when we're young. She always says it's easier to do it now than to wait when you're older."

"She's definitely a stickler about that sort of thing."

"Anyway, that's the gist of it. Now you know me. That's how I ended up sitting next to you on this bench."

He kicks his legs forward and plants his sneakers on the ground.

"Thanks for that."

A long silence passes between us before I look over at him.

"It's okay that you're not sure what you want to do about your dad," he says.

"You think so?"

"Yeah. Sometimes things are weird like that. You spend so much time thinking you know what you'd do in a certain scenario, but then that scenario actually happens and it ends up throwing you off."

"That's exactly how this feels. I know I want to see him and confront him. I'm just nervous. Because I don't know what he's going to say or do. I don't even know if he still has my grandma's jewelry. I have no idea how this is all going to turn out."

"That's completely understandable."

Just then the side door opens, and a guy with a scruffy beard looks at Liam. "Dude, where have you been? We're having a crisis in the dairy aisle."

The guy disappears back inside, and Liam stands up. "I should get going."

Just then I realize I've taken up a good twenty minutes out of Liam's shift to unload my personal problems onto him.

"Of course. I'm so sorry for bothering you." I stand up so we're facing each other.

"Don't be. It was nice talking to you."

"Thanks for listening."

"Anytime."

He leaves me with that half smile before darting back inside.

My stomach and chest flutter at once. I quickly dart my eyes away. That's never happened before. And then something inside me heats to a fiery ember. I know that feeling well, even though it's been a while. It's a spark. Attraction.

But then I remember where I am and what I'm here to do.

To confront my dad and reclaim what's rightfully Mom's—and to spend as much time with her as possible. Nothing can get in the way of that.

Slowly, the ember inside me dies out. I speed-walk around the side of the building to the parking lot, then hop in my car. When I get home I call Julianne and get all the information I can on my dad.

Chapter Fifteen

When Andy walks in through the front door, I take a breath. I have a lot to unload on him, but I can't do it right away.

"Hey." I sit up on the couch and shut my laptop. "How are things?"

Andy's been working long hours these last handful of days and spending his free time with Hannah. I've been dying to ask about her, but I don't want to intrude or bombard him with texts. They need to spend this time together to mourn their loss.

"Busy, but good." He grabs a sparkling water from the fridge before sitting down on the other end of the couch. "Mom doing okay?"

"Yeah, she's in the shower getting ready for her shift."

"Still refusing to take any time off, huh?"

"I tried to talk to her, but she won't listen to me."

We let out dual sighs, like a silent acknowledgement of just how stubborn our mom is.

"I think it pisses her off that her kids are trying to tell her how to live," Andy says before taking a long swig of water.

"I get that, but we're not kids. We're adults. And sometimes we know better than her."

"That's true, but we'll always be her kids, no matter how old we are."

I quietly accept the accuracy of my little brother's assessment.

"How's Hannah?"

He explains that she had an IUD implanted, and she's had a good first session with her counselor.

"Let us know if there's anything we can do."

Mom has been cooking large batches of meals for Andy to take to Hannah when he stays with her. She hasn't been over since dinner that night.

"I will. Thanks." His response is tight and brief. He probably doesn't want to talk anymore. But I need to know that he's okay.

"Andy. How are you feeling? Like, really feeling?"

I can tell by the way he pulls his lips into his mouth through a breath that he's trying to rein in his expression. He's gearing up to brush me off.

I rest my hand on his arm. "Seriously. Tell me."

His head drops and he nods, like he understands that I simply want to be there for him. "I don't know. Not good. But not as sad as I was."

"It's okay, Andy. You can be sad. What you lost . . ."

His eyes water, and I pull him into a hug. When we break apart seconds later, he sets his bottle of water on the coffee table, leans back on the couch, and rubs a hand over his face. "I'm worried about Hannah. She's having a hard time. Some days she cries a lot. I think it's because of her work at the day care—she sees all these babies, and it's hard for her because it reminds her of what we lost. Sometimes I think she tries to pretend that it never happened. She tries to stay busy and distract herself. But then it's like she's so one-track minded. She'll forget to eat or drink enough water. And when I try to get on top of her about taking care of herself, she gets upset. We've argued about it a couple of times."

I let out a sad chuckle. "Sounds familiar. Like me with Mom."

A small smile tugs at Andy's lips as he nods along before it falls from his face and his expression twists in sadness once more. "I just don't know if anything I'm doing helps. I'm physically there for her—I do things around the apartment for her, I hug her and tell her I love her. But I don't know if any of it makes a difference."

"Of course you're helping her," I say. "You're doing the right thing by being there and supporting her, I promise. It helps so much, even if she can't verbalize it right now."

A moment passes before he pats my knee.

"I think the fact that you two are supporting each other so much says a lot about how strong you are as a couple."

"I want to be there for her for everything. I just . . . don't want to smother her, you know?"

"I don't think you are. I think you're just being a good boyfriend."

He flashes a sad smile. "Thanks."

He grabs his water from the table, falls back against the couch, and looks at something on his phone. The timing of this couldn't be worse, but I have to tell Andy right now.

"I need to talk to you about Dad."

Andy pauses midsip and turns to me. "What about him?"

"This is going to sound outrageous."

I tell him about the conversation I overheard between Mom and Auntie Linda, how Dad stole grandma's jewelry, and how I hired Julianne's cousin to track him down. I tell him that Dad lives in Kansas City now and manages a furniture store. I tell him he's been married and divorced twice since Mom and has no more kids.

"Wow." Andy falls back against the couch, the look on his face the shocked side of bewildered.

"Sorry—I know you're already dealing with so much. The timing of this is the absolute worst. But I'm going to confront him. To try to get the jewelry back. For Mom and Auntie Linda. I'm not telling you this to make you feel like you need to be part of it or anything like that. I'm fully prepared to confront him on my own. I just thought you should know. He's your dad too."

"To be honest, Chloe, I barely remember him. I was little when he left for good. I can count on two hands the number of times he actually showed up to pick us up for his weekend visitations."

"I know."

"I really just don't want to see him. Or have anything to do with him."

"That's totally fine."

"You sure this is what you want to do?"

"Yeah. It's the right thing to do."

"But Mom already said she's fine leaving it alone." He runs a hand through his floppy hair like he's frustrated.

"I know, but . . . this is something I think she'll get on board with eventually. Maybe she doesn't see the point in it now, but I think she'll be glad about it in the end. I have to at least try to get back what's rightfully hers."

A tired smile tugs at his lips. "Okay. I support you one hundred percent. I just can't be part of it."

"That's fine. Can you just cover for me while I'm gone? I'm leaving early tomorrow morning. I'll be back in the late evening. The plan is to tell her I'm visiting a college friend who lives there now."

"Damn, you're like a spy with all the planning you're doing for this."

We share a laugh that adds a lightness in the air between us that I didn't know we needed. I look at my baby brother again. This time I see past the full cheeks and unkempt hair that make him look so young. I see fatigue in his eyes and the faintest wrinkles in his forehead. I see the beginnings of crow's-feet along the edges of his expressive eyes. I see someone trying to figure out the complicated shit going on in his life, making decisions for himself, taking care of his partner. And in that moment, it's like I'm seeing a whole new person.

He's not just my little brother anymore. He's a young man—a totally different human being than I've known my whole life. It's weird and surreal and wild and comforting.

"Sure, I'll cover for you no problem." He stands up and walks back into the kitchen. "If I've learned one thing in my life, it's never to stop you from doing anything. Because no matter what, you're going to do it."

"You're right about that."

Just then the doorbell rings. When I answer it, I'm shocked to see Hannah.

"Hannah. How are you?"

She offers a timid smile when she answers that she's doing okay. She fidgets for a moment before folding her hands in front of her. The silver bangles on her slight wrist jingle together.

I invite her in, and Andy comes up to the door.

"Hey." He pulls her into a hug. "Is everything okay?"

"Yeah, I just . . ." Hannah looks at me. "I came here to see your sister. And your mom."

"Oh. Sure." Judging by the slight surprise in Andy's tone, he wasn't expecting her to say that.

He says he's going to run out to the garage and straighten a few things up. Hannah and I sit on the couch. I offer her something to drink, but she declines.

"I just wanted to come by and talk to you. The last time I was here, things were a bit chaotic."

The small laugh she lets out sounds the tiniest bit strained. She tucks her long light-brown hair behind her ear and glances down at the tops of her jean-clad thighs. Then she tugs on the hem of her tank top. I wonder if that's a nervous habit of hers.

"Sorry, I didn't mean to drop by with zero notice."

"You don't have to apologize, Hannah. You can come by whenever you want."

"I just wanted to say thank you for how you guys helped me the night I . . ."

Her eyes water. I reach over and grab her hand in mine, hoping I don't choke up. I need to be strong for her. She's been through so much.

"You don't have to thank us."

"It's just been really hard to know what to do at this point."

"I don't think there's an instruction manual for this sort of thing. Unfortunately."

She chuckles through a sniffle. "That's true. I just wanted to say how much it meant that you and Mabel waited at the hospital for me. You had just met me, and you were so supportive."

I squeeze her hand in mine. "That's how it works. You walk in this house, and you're family. You couldn't get rid of us if you wanted to."

This time when she laughs, her shoulders shake. It makes me feel a million times lighter.

"I just want you to know that if you need anything, you can come to us. You're family now."

"Thank you." Her lips quiver as she smiles. "My family lives on the East Coast, and I really miss them. It means everything to have Andy, you, and your mom. And actually"—she shifts slightly against the plushy couch cushion—"Andy mentioned that your mom is having a hard time with what happened."

I nod and explain how she's refusing to talk about it or even take time off.

"It's not that we want to make her talk about something that upsets her," I say. "It's just that . . . I wish that she would just let herself have a day or two to process it all. Andy and I both think it would help."

"I totally agree. I can talk to her if you want. That's part of why I came here."

For a moment I hesitate. It's not Hannah's job to have heavy, emotional conversations with our mom. But then I remind myself that she came here, she reached out—she's one of us now. And if she wants to talk to Mom, she absolutely can.

I hear the shower turn off in the bathroom.

"I think that might help." I excuse myself to go check on Mom, who's now in her robe and standing at the dresser in her room, her hair wrapped in a towel.

"Mom. Hannah's here. She wanted to talk to you."

Her perfectly arched eyebrows fly up her forehead. "Oh. Is every-thing okay?"

"Yeah, everything's fine. She just wanted to see you."

Her face lights up the slightest bit. "Of course. Let me just get dressed."

I tell Mom Hannah's in the living room, then I walk out of the house to give them privacy.

My phone buzzes in my pocket as I step onto the front lawn.

Hey, it's Liam. Sorry for how awkward this is going to sound, but I asked your Mom for your phone number under the guise of asking you a pharmacy-related question . . . but what I really wanted was to check and see how you're doing.

I smile down at my phone. I'm surprised to hear from him. But also really, really happy.

Me: Hey. Thank you. I'm doing okay.

Me: I've decided to confront my dad. Tomorrow actually. Wish me luck.

He texts back right away.

Liam: I really admire you for what you're doing. You're very brave.

Me: Brave, out of my mind, same difference, right?

He sends back a laughing emoji. I scrunch my face to ward off the smile aching to let loose. This shouldn't feel so fun. This check-in text shouldn't feel so much like flirting.

Liam: Brave, hands down.

Me: I'm a little nervous. I'll be confronting him on my own. I haven't seen him in more than ten years.

Liam: Do you want me to come with you?

My eyes bulge at the boldness of his offer.

Me: Are you serious?

Liam: Yeah. Sorry, did that come off weird?

Liam: I'm off this weekend anyway. If you want moral support and no one else can come with you, I'd be happy to.

Me: But you barely know me.

Me: We'd be driving, like, five hours one way. Then another five hours back.

Liam: I've made the trip to Kansas City before, I'm well aware of the drive time.

Liam: It's part of my duties as your mom's underling, accompanying her daughter on impromptu road trips.

I snort a laugh.

Liam: In all seriousness, I'm down to go if you're up for the company.

Me: You sure you want to spend a full day in the car with someone you barely know?

Liam: I thought we already established that we know each other a lot better than that. We were friends in another life, remember?

Me: I'll think about it.

I have no intention of dragging Liam on this trip with me. But the more I think about it, the more at ease I feel. The less daunting the prospect of confronting my estranged dad seems when I think about having Liam by my side.

Just then Hannah walks out of the front door with Andy.

"How did it go?" I ask her.

"Well, I think. She said she's going to take some time off."

"Oh my gosh, really?"

I pull her into a hug.

"You're seriously amazing. Thank you. For everything."

I watch Andy walk her to her car, which is parked on the street in front of Mom's house. I take in how he faces her, his back to the road to shield her, how he opens her door, how he makes sure she locks her door and straps on her seat belt. Something inside me swells. In that moment, I know without a doubt that Andy is going to be an amazing husband and father someday.

I swallow back the emotion in my throat and walk inside the house. Mom sits on the couch, wiping her eyes. I sit down beside her and hug her. When she squeezes me hard, she sniffles.

"You don't have to say anything, Mom. Just know that I'm here for you. We all are."

"I know, *anak*. Thank you."

And even though we don't speak a word about what Andy and Hannah lost, what we've said is enough in this moment.

She pats my leg and stands up. "I'm taking some days off. I'm arranging it tonight at work."

"I'm so glad to hear that."

When I look up at her, at her misty eyes and her smile, I almost tell her what I have planned, that I'm going to confront Dad to try and get back what's rightfully hers. But I stop myself. I don't want to ruin this moment with the mention of someone who hurt her.

She walks off to her room to finish getting ready. And I look back down at my phone and skim my text conversation with Liam. It's nighttime when I finally work up the nerve to call him.

"If the offer still stands, I'd like for you to come with me."

"I'd be happy to."

~

"How are you feeling?" Liam asks as I pull into the parking lot of Big Russ's Furniture Store in Overland Park, a suburb of Kansas City.

I squeeze the steering wheel. "Weird. Nervous. But less so that you're here."

Liam has been the perfect companion to have on this weird and unconventional road trip. He brought a whole paper bag of snacks, plenty of water, and offered to drive the first half of the trip. He hasn't annoyed me with a terrible playlist or badgered me with a million annoying questions. We've chatted easily about my plan as well as enjoyed the silence of any lulls in conversation.

I'm starting to wonder if in some weird parallel universe—different than the one I may very well be in right now—we actually were friends, and that's where this natural ease comes from.

But the moment I pull into the parking lot of my dad's workplace, every muscle in my neck and shoulders tenses. I'm gripping the steering wheel so hard my palms start to cramp. I let go and wring out my hand.

"Hey." Liam grabs my hand. "It's okay if you don't want to do this. You made it this far. That's huge."

"No, I want to do this."

He releases my hand. I scoop up the papers that I placed on the dashboard, which are printouts of all the info Julianne's cousin gathered on my dad.

"He's working till two p.m. today, then he's due for a break."

"How did Julianne's cousin find that out?"

"She hacked into their work database and found the schedule."

"Damn," Liam mutters.

I watch the clock on the dashboard hit 1:57 and go over the plan in my head. Wait until he walks out. Politely reintroduce myself to him. Calmly explain that I'm here to collect the jewelry he stole from my mom. Collect the jewelry. Then leave and drive back to Kearney.

I fix my stare on the entrance of the furniture store. I don't say a word. I barely blink. And then at 2:02, I see him.

He walks out with his hands shoved in the pockets of his dress pants, his tie flapping in the wind. He's just as tall as Andy but thinner. Frailer. His once-wavy chestnut hair is now mostly gray and cropped close to his scalp. And he shaved his mustache. Now there's just a sheen of gray stubble covering his face.

Then a frown appears that jolts me back to childhood the longer I stare at him. I'm five again, and he's staring blankly at the wall while I'm playing with my toys. I ask him to play with me and he does—he tries. But he's so drunk that when he reaches for a doll, he loses his balance and lands face-first on the carpet. I yell, "Are you okay, Daddy?" But there's no answer. Just snoring.

My legs feel as stable as two jellyfish, but I force myself to walk out of the car.

"Chloe. You okay?"

I mutter a yes at Liam's question, shut the car door, then walk the twenty feet to where he is in the parking lot, which is at the first row of parked cars.

"Bill Howard?" I holler.

His head jerks up, but he's looking in the opposite direction. A second later when he finally twists his head in my direction, I freeze in place. Recognition flashes across his face. He remembers me.

"Chloe."

He says my name like it's too precious to speak loudly. He looks at me like I'm a ghost come back to life. It makes the lump in my throat lodge deeper. It's like I've swallowed a rock. Because in this single look, in these three seconds of seeing me, there's more emotion in his face than I remember after an entire childhood with him.

"Chloe." He says it clearer this time and with a smile. "Hi."

"Hi." I can barely get it out. It's like my head is trapped in a fog but my heart is bouncing along the concrete parking lot.

I take a second to blink and steady myself.

He walks closer to me but stops just a few feet away. "Wow. Look at you. All grown up."

"And look at you." It almost sounds bitter, the way I say it.

A sheepish expression takes over the awe on his face. "It's called getting older." And then he smiles, and his whole face lights up. "You look so beautiful, honey. Just like your mom."

I lift my chin in response to the niceness he's directing at me. I can't stand such a compliment, not from someone who abandoned his entire family.

"Speaking of Mom. You stole something from her. The heirlooms from her mom, *Apong* Selene. The bracelet and ring. That's why I'm here, to get them back."

It takes a minute for his smile to drop, but when it does, I'm shocked at the way my chest pings.

"Right." He glances down at the ground. "I'm sorry about that."

"Don't be sorry," I say, cutting him off. "Just make it right. Give them back."

His entire chest rises as he breathes. Standing this close to him, I notice just how splotchy his pale skin is. Maybe from all those years of drinking?

He shakes his head. "I don't have them with me, honey."

"Do you have them at all still? Or did you sell them? Because if you did, I want the money for it. You need to pay for what you did."

My eyes water as I finish speaking. I stop to swallow, determined for my voice not to break.

His salt-and-pepper eyebrows wrinkle. "No, I didn't sell them. I—I'll admit I was going to, but then my conscience caught up to me. I kept them. It was the one decent thing I did."

I grit my teeth at how it sounds like he's trying to reframe things to make it seem like he did something noble and upstanding.

"Well, I'd like them back, please. So I can give them to Mom."

"Okay, but . . . can we just talk for a bit first? It's been so long. I'd like to catch up."

He has the audacity to smile, to look happy, to act like this is a joyous reunion instead of the sad exchange it actually is. And it unleashes a silent wave of fury inside of me that I suspect has been brimming ever since I was a kid.

"You had years to talk to us. You chose not to. You could barely manage the every-other-weekend setup you had with us when we were kids. You could barely make it to a game or a recital or a graduation. You could barely remember to call us on our birthdays. Why should I want to catch up with you now?"

He rubs a hand over his face, grimacing. "I was sick back then. You were better off without me."

The wave inside of me crashes, spilling over every cell, every organ, every fiber that makes me who I am. It causes the tears to fall down my cheeks in uncontrollable streams. It causes my face to twist as I fight back cries.

"No, we weren't better off, Dad. Do you know how much of a struggle it was for us? Mom worked so hard to support us. Long hours and weekends and holidays just to make sure we had food in the house and a roof over our heads. Because you left. She had to do it all herself. And it broke her sometimes. Sometimes she didn't sleep, sometimes she didn't go to the doctor so Andy and me could afford to go instead, some nights she didn't get to tuck us into bed and kiss us good night because she had to work extra shifts. So don't tell me we were better off. You don't know the first goddamn thing about what life was like without you, how hard we struggled. The only way we would have been better off is if you had given a shit about being a father to us."

I don't realize I'm practically screaming until I pause to catch my breath.

Just then Liam walks up beside me, but I wave him off.

"I don't give a shit what you think about us. All I want is what you stole from her."

When I look into my dad's eyes, I can tell I've broken him by what I've said. I haven't looked at him face-to-face in more than ten years. But that heartbroken gleam in his eyes is impossible to miss. I'd be able to see it from across the highway, it's that glaring.

He gives a sad nod. "It's okay, honey. You have every right to be mad, and—look, I can't give you the jewelry until tomorrow morning. It's in a safe at the bank. They're closed, but I can get it first thing in the morning."

"Fine," I bark while wiping my nose with my wrist. "I want it in my hands tomorrow morning, here. Before your shift at work."

"I promise I'll be here."

Liam leads me with a gentle hand on the arm back to the car. He drives somewhere along the highway, not saying a word. I don't have the energy to speak either. All I can do is stare off into the distance and watch the buildings fly by.

Chapter Sixteen

"I'm so sorry." It's the millionth time I've said this to Liam since the disastrous reunion with my dad.

And for the millionth time, he tells me I have no reason to apologize.

I slump against the headboard of the bed I'm sitting on. We checked into a motel after driving around for an hour. After I started to come out of the shock of blowing up on my dad, I realized we needed a place to stay if the plan was to meet again in the morning.

Liam sits on the other bed and hands me a container of Chinese food. "You should eat something."

I thank him and take a few bites of the saucy chunk of breaded chicken. Then I set it on the nightstand between us.

"Beer?" Liam holds a can up.

I glance over at him as he sits, his legs hooked over the side of his own bed, take-out box in his other hand.

"God, yes."

I take a long swig, then sigh.

"I just . . . feel awful for making you spend your day off like this."

"Like what?"

"Observing the trashiest, saddest father-daughter reunion in the history of Earth."

His lips scrunch in a small smile as he chews. "I think you're overstating things a bit."

"And I think you're being too nice."

His eyes cut to me. "I'm not nice."

There's a thrill that flashes through me at the slight firmness in his tone.

"Nice is so passive, so meh."

"You're right. You're not nice. You're kind and sweet and a goddamn angel for accompanying your boss's daughter at the last minute on a daylong road trip that turned into an overnight shit show."

This time he doesn't laugh at what I've said. He clears his throat. "Chloe. I'm not an angel. I'm a guy who knows what it's like to have a strained and complicated relationship with my parents. And I just wanted to offer support to someone going through something similar because I honestly never got it when I went through my own shit with my parents, and I wish I had."

His candid admission jolts me. I sit up straighter on the bed and face him. "I'm sorry. What happened? If you want to talk about it."

He rubs the back of his neck. I wonder if that's a tell that talking about this makes him uncomfortable. "I feel like a jerk for bringing it up when you're going through this difficulty with your dad."

"Liam. This isn't a competition. Whatever your experience, whatever pain you feel is valid. And if you're comfortable, you should talk about it. I'm here to listen."

He takes a swig of beer before he speaks. "I don't have a very good relationship with my parents. And it's for a pretty ridiculous reason. They've been pissed at me since I dropped out of college. We haven't spoken much in the last few years because all we do is argue about it."

"Are you serious?"

"I'm serious. They've always been the kind of people who think that college is the be-all, end-all. And they don't have a lot of patience for people who don't know what they want to do with their lives after a career-ending sports injury, even if it's their own son."

"Shit, that's—I don't even know what to say."

"Neither do I, honestly."

"What is it that your parents do?"

"They're corporate lawyers. When baseball fizzled out, my decision to leave school was like a punch to the gut to them." He stares straight ahead, taking another long pull of his beer. "I think they thought I'd come to my senses and go to law school, follow in their footsteps. But I didn't have an interest in that. I tried a lot of different jobs. Working at the grocery store was the first I actually enjoyed. They weren't happy about that. And honestly after a while, I just got sick of them lecturing me and getting into arguments about it."

"Liam, I'm so sorry."

"It's all right. It's not that big a deal."

"It is, though. If they're not speaking to you because they don't like your job—a perfectly respectable job—then that's infuriating."

He shrugs. "They can be pretty goddamn infuriating at times."

I huff out a breath, frustrated. In the short time that I've known Liam, he's proven to be kind and selfless in a way that I haven't witnessed before. How can his parents dismiss him when he's such an incredible person?

"That's absolutely not okay. I mean, what if something were to happen to you? What if you got into an accident? Or what if one of them had a serious health issue? Suddenly you have no more time left. All that time spent refusing to speak to or see each other—it could have been time spent together."

My eyes start to water as the weight of what I've said sinks in.

"I'm sorry," I say, blinking the tears away. "It's just that . . . family is the most important thing to me. And it just always makes me sad when I hear about families not getting along. Life is too short for that. You never know how much time anyone has."

"You're right. I should reach out to them."

"It shouldn't just be on you," I say. "They're the ones who should reach out since they're the ones who have a problem with you and your job."

There's a long silence. I glance around the motel room, which looks like a beige fest. Everything from the laminate flooring to the nightstand to the door to the bedding is beige. It's weirdly calming after such a chaotic day.

We both gulp more beer, and I take a few more bites of food.

"Maybe they should be the ones to reach out, but what you're saying is true," Liam says, running a hand through his hair. "Anything could happen to us at any point. If they don't want to make the first move, I should. All three of us are guilty of shutting each other out over the past few years. Maybe I just need to be the bigger person and make that first call."

I move to sit next to him and squeeze his arm, hoping that it's somewhat of a comfort to him.

"My worst nightmare is getting into a fight with my mom or my brother or someone else close to me, not speaking to them, and then losing them out of the blue. I don't think I could live with myself knowing that I wasted all that time when all it would have taken was one phone call or one visit to fix everything."

I have to swallow back the emotion that lodges in my throat as I recall just how close I was to that happening. The memory of arguing with Mom right before her heart attack hits like an invisible meteor. If we hadn't had that middle-of-the-night phone conversation during my work shift the day after, which was prompted by Julianne . . .

Liam's focused stare brings me back to the present. "When you put it that way, it makes a lot of sense."

I move to hold his hand in mine. His skin feels warm and comforting. Normally, I'm not a hand-holding kind of person. But with Liam, it feels right.

"I don't mean to tell you what to do. I'm the last person who should lecture anyone on family dynamics. I mean, look at how I acted in front of my dad just now. Ten-plus years of not seeing each other, and I have a breakdown in front of him."

"You had every right to be upset at him. He was a terrible father to you and your brother. And a terrible husband to your mom. And on top of that, he stole from her. I say you went a little easy on him."

I start to smile. It's such an unnatural movement after my mouth spent the entire day in a tense line in anticipation of seeing my dad. The upward curve doesn't remain long. But for the few seconds that it lasted, it felt weirdly good.

"I hate how much his absence affected me."

Liam says nothing, he just nods.

"For the longest time I thought I didn't need him. And in a way, I didn't. I mean, growing up without him was hard. Money was always tight, and it always bothered me to know that my mom had to work twice as hard almost her entire life to take care of us because he would rather drink himself to death. But we made it. I went to school and got a good job. My mom worked her way up at the store. She was able to pay off our house. Andy is stable, too, now. I just . . ."

I stop and swallow when I feel the tears burning in my eyes.

"I hate that he made me cynical about relationships. I have the world's shittiest dating record because my entire life I didn't want to open myself up and fully trust someone in a relationship. I was afraid that at some point, they'd just leave, like my dad did. I know that's the most ridiculous thought. It makes no sense."

"It does, though. When what you have modeled to you is a disastrous relationship as a kid, what are you supposed to do when you grow up? You don't just innately know how to be in a functional relationship. You learn it from the adults who raise you. It's okay to be mad at him for that."

"Yeah, but it's up to me to fix it. I can't keep blaming him as the one responsible for my shortcomings."

I slip my hand from his and take a swig from my beer can. He does the same. Liam sets his can on the nightstand and eyes me. "I don't think it's possible that you have a shortcoming."

"Ha. That's because you don't know me very well."

His gaze says he doesn't believe me.

"I'm overbearing to a fault. Just ask my mom and brother."

"That's not a fault, Chloe. That's a sign of how much you love your family."

The buzz from the beer starts to kick in. I can feel my tongue loosen the slightest bit. I'm headed straight for the honesty portion of tipsy. But I don't care. Being with Liam, I don't feel the slightest bit self-conscious or nervous. I feel like I could say anything to him and he would sit patiently and listen, like he has every other time I've unloaded on him.

I shift so I can look him straight in the eye. "How's this for a fault? As angry as I was to see my dad today, part of me was happy. It was a tiny part. I was still so mad at him. But it was kind of nice to see him and know that he's still alive and doing okay. Because after all these years, that tiny part of me missed him. Even after all the awful things he did, after everything he put my mom through, a tiny part of me still loves him."

I stop talking when my lip quivers uncontrollably. I set the beer down on the floor and cover my face with my hands as I cry. A second later I feel a warm, soft touch around both of my wrists. Liam gently pulls my hands from my face, slips his arm around me, and turns me into him so I can sob into his chest.

And for the next several minutes, that's exactly what I do. I sob so hard my entire body shakes. I soak through his light-blue T-shirt. And he lets me. He doesn't say a word. The entire time he wraps his arms around me, cradling me.

When I finally catch my breath, I lean away. Liam reaches for the tissue box on the nightstand and hands it to me. It takes three tissues, but I'm slightly drier than I was.

"Do you want to lie down and go to sleep?" he asks in a soft whisper.

I nod yes. He scoots down the bed to make room for me to lie down. When he starts to stand up, I reach for his wrist.

"Stay. Please."

It's sad and desperate, but I don't care. I want Liam cuddled into me. It's the only comfort I need in this moment.

The corner of his mouth quirks up. "Of course."

A second later he's spooned behind me, his head tucked on top of mine. I close my eyes and instantly melt into him, my entire body relaxing at his embrace.

"You loving your dad isn't a shortcoming, Chloe," Liam whispers. "It's even more proof of what a wonderful person you are. Don't ever think otherwise."

I drift off to sleep, his whispered words echoing in my head.

~

The next morning, I wake up alone in bed with a monster headache and swollen eyes. I start to sit up and yawn, then notice there's no sign of Liam.

My bladder screams at me, so I scurry off to the bathroom. When I'm washing up, I hear the squeak of the door as it opens. I instinctively hold my breath. What the hell do you say to someone you've known for a total of a handful of days, who supported you through one of the most personal and emotional moments of your life, who held you as you cried yourself to sleep?

Hiding out in the bathroom indefinitely won't do me any good, so I open the door and face him with an awkward smile and even more awkward wave.

"Good morning," he says, his voice low and growly. He holds up a handful of floss, mini toothbrushes, a tube of toothpaste, and some face wipes. "Got it from the front desk. In case you wanted to freshen up."

I almost *aww*. Instead I thank him and take his offering. Standing this close to him, I notice a sheen of silvery stubble along his cheeks. His eyes are puffy, his shirt and jeans are rumpled, and he's got a serious case of bedhead, but he still looks devastatingly handsome.

I quietly scold myself for checking him out. He starts to turn around, but I grab his arm. "Thank you. For everything you did last night."

There's a warmth in his face I've never seen before as he smiles softly at me. "You don't have to thank me. I hope I offered some kind of support."

"You did. It meant . . . everything. I was such a mess."

"You weren't a mess, Chloe. You were human."

I lean in to hug him and breathe in his musky, spicy scent. He squeezes me against his broad chest.

"You're the best, I swear."

He chuckles. When we release, he looks down at me. "We've got an hour till we're due to meet your dad. Do you want to get cleaned up and grab some food on the way?"

"Sounds perfect."

Nerves swirl inside my chest and stomach. But not just because I have to see my dad again. It's because I think I like Liam.

~

Liam pulls my car into the parking lot of the furniture store. He turns off the ignition and looks over at me.

I glance over at him, fully aware that the dynamic between us has changed since last night. Nothing technically happened. We just cuddled and fell asleep—we didn't even kiss.

But now I'm realizing that you don't always have to kiss someone to feel an intimacy with them. I've kissed plenty of guys in my life who I didn't feel anything substantial for.

Yet what I feel for Liam is strange and foreign and makes my heart race and my skin tingle. There's something about this weird bond between us. Maybe in this world where I woke up and my mom was alive again, certain things are different—and maybe in this world things are different for *me* too. Maybe in this world, I can meet a guy, feel an instant comfort with him, and know beyond a shadow of a doubt that we're meant to be something more.

"Do you want me to come out there with you?" he asks.

"It's okay. I'd like to talk to him alone."

A gray sedan I recognize immediately pulls up into a spot in front of us. Dad climbs out, and I focus on his expression. Sadness is evident in the furrow of his brow and his glistening eyes. But there's also hope in them.

Liam gives my hand a soft squeeze before I climb out of the car. It's early morning, but the humidity is already killer. Sweat beads along my exposed skin. I glance up and see sweat along Dad's brow and upper lip.

I walk the few feet over to him and spot a small, flat, rectangular black-velvet jewelry box in his hand.

I stop short and cross my arms. "Is that it? Mom's bracelet and ring?"

He says yes and hands it over to me. I open it just to make sure. The gold and diamonds sparkle in the sunlight.

"Thanks."

"I know you're not gonna believe me, but I was going to try and give this back to your mom someday."

"Really?" I scoff.

He flinches at the sharpness in my tone. "Yes. And I don't blame you for not believing me, after all that I did."

"No, you can't blame us. Because you didn't really set things up well for us to trust you. Or count on your word."

He purses his lips, his expression pained. "I didn't mean to upset you yesterday with what I said, Chloe. I just wanted to explain. I was really messed up for a long time. And I'm so sorry that things were such a struggle for you all when I was gone. But I would have just made it worse."

I take a moment to breathe instead of lash out. When I pause and think about it, he's right. Even though things were hard with him gone, they were better than when he was with us.

"I know you probably don't care, but I just want you to know: I'm sober now. I have been for the past three years. Three years and forty-seven days, actually."

"That's good." I actually mean it.

The smallest smile tugs at his lips. "I love you and your brother so much. And your mom. I'm sorry I wasn't the father you deserved. Ever since I got my life together, I've been wondering about making amends. Telling you all how sorry I am. I . . . I'm sorry I waited so long. I'm sorry you had to be the one to find me first."

I study his face as he pauses. It's the strangest thing how I can't see one bit of him in Andy or me. Other than his height and frame, Andy has none of our dad's features. Not his light eyes or pointed nose or fair skin or attached earlobes. I don't either. We both look so much like Mom.

I think back on the brief conversation Andy and I had about possibly contacting Dad when Mom passed away, how neither one of us wanted him at her funeral. I think back on the anger that took hold of me from the inside out at the thought that he got to outlive her.

Now as I stand before him, I don't feel that same anger anymore. Yeah, I'm still mad at him. But the bitterness isn't there anymore. It's like a cloud of smoke that remains stagnant in the air until a gust of wind blasts it away. All these years I held on to that anger, I shoved it down deep so I wouldn't have to think about it every day. But it was always there. And when it surfaced yesterday, it nearly wrecked me. But I've had time to reflect, to process and think. Seeing him in person as he exists now—an old man doing his best—makes him seem all the more real and human and flawed.

I don't know if I'll ever be able to forgive him for what he did. But I'm done being upset about it.

A sad smile appears on his face. "You were always so determined and tenacious. I should have known you'd figure out a way to get a hold of me. What do you do now?"

"I was a pharmacist at a hospital in Omaha. I'm taking some time off now, though. Andy's still living with Mom at home. He's a bartender."

There's a long moment when he pauses. It takes me a few seconds to process what he's reacting to: the son of an alcoholic is a bartender.

"He doesn't drink all that much, if you're worried about that," I say.

His shoulders relax the slightest bit.

"That's really good. I'm so proud of you kids."

"Thanks."

For a second we just stand and look at each other.

"I know you're not interested, but if you ever want to get together and go to lunch or have a visit, I'd love to do that with you, Chloe. And Andy too. I'd love to see him—to see you both, together."

Yesterday those words would have sent me into a rage. I'd have thought he was an entitled, smug, out-of-touch jerk for assuming we could attempt to have a normal father-daughter interaction after shirking his parental duties. But now, even though I'm not interested in taking him up on his offer, I don't feel rage. I don't feel anything really. And that's something—because at least it's not anger.

"I don't know if Andy is ready for that. He knew I was coming here today . . . I asked him if he wanted to come, but he said no."

I have to fight back a wince when I say all that because I know just how much it hurts him to hear this. I can tell by the tremble in his lips and the slow, hard swallow that makes its way down his throat.

"And honestly, I don't think I'm ready for that either."

Even though he nods his understanding, it looks like it kills him to know that we aren't ready to have him back in our lives. His blue eyes read sad as he glances at the cement below his feet.

"Maybe someday, though."

My quiet words elicit a hopeful smile from him. He pulls out a piece of paper from his pocket and hands it to me. "My phone number. In case you ever want to get in touch."

I tuck the paper in the pocket of my jean shorts and do something I didn't think I'd have the strength to. I step forward to give him a hug. It's a half second before he embraces me back; he's probably shocked that I would hug him after all this. But some tiny part of me, the part that still loves him, wanted to.

He squeezes me tight. "I love you, Chloe."

When I release and step away, I don't say anything in return. I just nod. I don't know if I'll ever be able to say that to him. But I know on the inside that I love him too.

I tell him goodbye and hop back in the car with Liam, and then we drive away.

~

Five hours later Liam pulls my car into Mom's driveway.

I turn to him when he turns off the ignition. "Thank you so much for coming with me. I know that must have been so weird."

"I was happy to. Thanks for asking me to come with you."

Those icy-blue eyes of his radiate warmth and send goose bumps across my skin all at once. It's nearly June and muggy as hell out and still this man can make me shiver.

"What's weird is that I drove you to your house even though I should have driven straight to my place since you picked me up, and I have no way of getting back to my house now." He laughs, rubbing his face with his hands. "I don't know what I was thinking."

I laugh, the exhaustion of the past day and a half catching up with me. I slow-blink, my eyelids heavy. "Christ, I didn't even realize—sorry, I'm just so out of it after all that's happened."

"It's okay. You've been through a lot these past couple of days."

We sit there, staring at each other, soft smiles on our faces.

My heart thuds as I contemplate bringing up last night.

"How are you feeling?" Liam asks.

"Okay. A little weird. Emotionally drained. But also relieved. I just hope that last night wasn't weird for you—or that I made you uncomfortable."

His sandy-blond eyebrows crash together. "Not at all. I wanted to be there for you."

He opens his mouth, then shuts it, then opens it again. "It's weird how drawn I am to you, Chloe. Maybe it's all those times your mom talked about you at work. I feel like I knew you pretty well even before we met."

"I can always count on my mom to talk me up."

We both laugh.

"I like you." There's a glimmer in his eye that makes my heart tumble all the way to my stomach.

"Good. Because I like you too." I shift in my seat so that our faces are a bit closer. I can feel his deliciously wet breath on my skin when he exhales.

And then something inside of me takes hold. I hesitate to call it desire because I've felt that before with other guys—but with Liam, it's stronger and deeper, more meaningful.

I grab his cheeks with my hands and press my mouth to his. It's been ages since I kissed someone. But my mouth obviously has excellent muscle memory because everything comes back to me. The rhythm I like to set, the teasing way I slip my tongue in his mouth, the way I move slowly because I've always liked to take my time and savor the taste, the feel, the softness of another person's mouth on mine.

Liam's hand cups my cheek softly for a few seconds before moving to my hair. His fingers curl, and there's a heat against my scalp. I moan in response. And then I let one hand slide down his body. Even through the cotton of his shirt, I can feel just how firm his chest is. It makes my mouth water.

I run my tongue along his bottom lip. He tastes sweet, almost like candy.

"Ay my God!"

A shout from outside my car breaks us apart instantly. When I look up I see Mom, Auntie Linda, and four of their cousins who I haven't seen in years because they're scattered across the country—Auntie Mel, Auntie Rita, Auntie Lorna, and Auntie Kay. They're all standing at the head of the driveway, right in front of my car, staring at us with their jaws on the floor.

For the slightest second I wonder what in the world they're all doing here, but then I remember that my face is on fire because they just witnessed me and Liam going at it.

"Oh my God," I mutter at the same time that Liam mutters, "Shit."

"Drive."

He turns to me. "What?"

"Drive! Go! To your place!"

"Wh—now?"

"Yes, now!"

Liam backs out of the driveway, and we speed in silence to his house. After he puts the car in park and turns off the engine, he jumps out of the car and I slide into the driver's seat.

He leans down to look at me through the open driver's side window. "So, um . . ."

Inside I'm a battlefield of warring emotions. Mortified, shocked, confused, and the slightest bit turned on.

I make eye contact with him, and then we both burst out laughing.

He clears his throat. "That was . . ."

"So damn awkward."

"Yeah." He says it through a laugh, which eases the tension between us a bit.

We lock eyes once more, and for a second the tension is back. I feel it in my chest, like an invisible string is pulling me closer to him. I quickly turn on the car and look straight ahead.

"I'll call you later, okay?"

I back out of his driveway without waiting for his reply and drive back home, wondering how the hell I'm going to look my mother and aunties in the eye after they caught me making out with Mom's coworker.

Chapter Seventeen

I walk back in the house to something akin to a mini celebration. Mom's cousins crowd the kitchen table playing their favorite card game, forty-one, while Mom and Auntie Linda roll and fry *lumpia* at the stove.

"*Anak*! You're back!" Mom hollers. When she looks at me, there's a glint in her eye that makes me want to hide my face in my shirt and run straight to my room. I feel like I'm in high school again.

Auntie Linda beams at me, then runs over to give me a hug. "Hi again, *anakko*!"

I do my best to pretend like I haven't just experienced the most mortifying moment of my life in front of my extended family and ask her what's the occasion for her surprise visit.

"I took a page out of your book! I wanted to surprise your mom with a visit from our cousins. Since we're all retired now, we always have so much free time. You inspired me, *anak*. I asked myself, Why not have everyone come to Nebraska to see your mom? It's been ages since we all got together. And the timing was perfect because your mom even took some days off work. Can you believe it?"

I glance up at Mom as she dunks a half dozen *lumpia* into a pot of frying oil, reflecting for a moment how I conducted a surprise visit of my own, too, over the weekend. I make a mental note to tell Andy about how things went with our dad—after I give Mom her jewelry back.

"I can't believe it. How great." Warmth courses through me as I smile in Mom's direction.

It takes me a few seconds to remember when the last time was that Mom and her cousins got together like this, and even then I'm not totally sure. Maybe for one of my cousins' graduations? But that would have been a handful of years ago. This reunion is long overdue.

Mom's cousins all shoot up from their chairs to greet me with hugs. The warmth in my chest grows with each hug. They tell me how happy they are to see me, how it's been too long since we last visited each other. Auntie Mel and Auntie Rita even pinch my cheeks, a holdover from every time I'd see them as a kid. Unlike before when I rolled my eyes at the gesture, I soak it in this time and smile. I'm grateful they're so thrilled to see me after years of being too busy to visit them.

They're all chattering at once, asking me how I'm doing and who that handsome guy in my car was.

I bite the inside of my cheek and grimace-smile in an attempt to ride out this fresh wave of humiliation. "Oh he's . . . a friend."

"He's my coworker," Mom says with pride. "I knew you two would hit it off. See how things work out when you listen to me?"

Mom explains to them how she's been trying to set us up for months. There's another wave of excited chattering and laughter. After visiting with the aunties for several minutes, I walk over to Mom.

"Mom, can we talk? I have something to show you."

She wipes her hands on the cherry-red apron tied around her waist. "Sure, what is it?"

"Um, well . . ." I glance over to the kitchen table, where everyone is gathered. "Actually, can we go someplace quiet?"

"Okay, let's go to my room."

Mom shuts the door behind her, and I take in the space. Her perfectly made queen-size bed is the focal point with its dozen throw pillows and bright floral duvet. I take in the gardenia scent that hits every single time I walk into her room. This is where she gets ready every night before work, at her oak vanity that sits in the corner. Endless makeup palettes, lipsticks, and perfume bottles adorn the mahogany surface. There's a bottle of hair spray and a curling iron teetering at the very edge, looking like it's about to fall off.

She turns to me. "So. What did you want to show me?"

I pull the velvet jewelry box from my back pocket and hand it to her.

"Oh, you got me a present? *Anak*, you shouldn't have!"

"No, actually . . ."

I trail off when she opens the box and the recognition flashes across her face.

"Oh my God."

She squints down at the gold and diamond bracelet and ring for five seconds, not uttering a word.

She finally looks up at me. "How did you get this?"

"I found Dad. I got it from him."

"But how did you know he had it? I never told you kids that he had it."

I sigh, then lead her by the arm to sit with me on her bed. And then I tell her everything—overhearing her argument with Auntie Linda in April about *Apong*'s jewelry, how I hired Julianne's cousin to track him down, how I drove to Kansas City to find him and demand it back—with Liam.

She listens without interruption. When I finish, Mom stares off to the side, looking at nothing in particular.

"Well. That's quite something."

I wait for her to say more, but she doesn't.

"Are you mad?"

She frowns at me. "Why would I be mad?"

"I just . . . thought you might be upset that I planned all this without telling you. But I figured you'd try to talk me out of it. I wanted to at least try to see if I could get this back for you."

The smile she flashes at me is tender; her eyes are full of emotion. It's the same look she'd give me or Andy anytime we did something to make her proud.

"I'm not mad at you. Thank you for getting this back. I'm so happy. Auntie Linda will be, too, when I show it to her. I'm just thinking about all the trouble you went through for me. And it makes me a little sad."

"It was worth it to get this back to you." I gesture to the jewelry box, which is now sitting on the bed next to Mom. "Besides, Liam was with me. I had the support I needed."

I tell her that the night Julianne called with the info about Dad is the same night I brought her lunch to the store and ran into Liam. I was so distraught at first that Liam helped calm me, then he called days later to check on me—and offered to accompany me for emotional support.

"I know it's probably a little weird that he came with me."

"I don't think it's weird at all."

"We haven't known each other for that long, though."

Mom flashes her trademark knowing look. "Sometimes you don't have to know someone for very long to know what kind of person they are. Liam's a wonderfully kind and supportive person. I remember getting that feeling about him right away when I hired him."

I nod, agreeing that I got that vibe from him right away, too, when we first met.

"Sometimes you just click with a person," Mom says. "You know right away that you like them and will get along with them. That's a good thing."

I think of Liam and let Mom's words marinate in my mind.

"How was your dad?"

I'm thrown by her out-of-the-blue question but answer it anyway. "Fine, I guess. He says he stopped drinking."

"That's good." There's a detachment in her upbeat tone.

"I kind of went off on him, though."

"What do you mean?"

"I think I just . . . had so many feelings pent up over the years concerning him abandoning us. And I think when I saw him, it just kind of spilled over."

"Believe me, *anak*. You have every right to be angry at him. He was a terrible father to you. And you were too little to know what to do or say at the time, so it only makes sense that you'd tell him now as an adult."

"Yeah, but I think I'm done being angry. I'm not ready to have a relationship with him or anything like that. But I don't want to be bitter about what he did to us anymore. That takes too much energy, I've realized."

She pats my hand. "You're right."

Then she stands up and pulls me into a hug. "Thank you so, so much, *anak*."

She picks up the jewelry box, her eyes scanning the bracelet and ring once more. "I can't believe he didn't sell these."

"It's one of the few decent things he's done."

She lets out a chuckle. "I guess I shouldn't be too surprised. He couldn't keep his word to save his life. You know he promised me that we would move to Hawaii after we got married?"

"Seriously?"

"Yup. It was my dream to move there. I was planning to move there after I graduated high school, before I met him actually." She says it offhandedly.

"Wow, really? Why didn't you ever tell me?"

She shrugs, like it's no big deal. "It was before you were born. And then it never worked out so I never thought it was worth mentioning."

She starts to walk toward the door, but I stop her. "Wait, tell me more about Hawaii."

"Oh. Well, let's see." She plops back down on the bed. "A couple of my girlfriends and I had been obsessed with Hawaii ever since we saw that show *Magnum, P.I.*," she says with a smile.

I let out a laugh.

She frowns at me and smacks my arm lightly. "It was an excellent show. Tom Selleck was so handsome when he was young."

I nod along, trying to remember if I've ever seen what a young Tom Selleck looks like.

"That and *Hawaii Five-0* were our favorite shows," she says. "Hawaii just seemed like this beautiful tropical place that was so different from where I lived at the time."

A wistful smile takes over her expression as she talks.

"Here," she says, pointing to the door. "Let's go for a walk around the park while I tell you more. I could use some air."

She closes the jewelry box and sets it on top of her vanity. Then we walk out, and Mom tells everyone we're going for a quick stroll. We throw on our sneakers and head out. The trademark heat and humidity of early summer hits instantly the moment we step outside. Sweat beads pop up on my skin in just seconds with the sun beating down on us. She marches toward the nearby park across the street.

"So *Hawaii Five-0* and *Magnum, P.I.* made you want to move to Hawaii?" I ask.

She nods, her stare focused on the sidewalk ahead. "Oh, absolutely. We couldn't get enough of the beaches and the beautiful weather and how crystal blue the ocean looked. It reminded me a lot of the Philippines, actually."

"You didn't want to move back there?" I ask.

"I wanted to explore someplace different. I was young and wanted to see as many places as I could. But I had only ever lived in the Philippines and Denver. I thought Hawaii would be an exciting next step. So, my friends and I, we all agreed to save our money so that after high school, we could move there, rent a small apartment together— maybe close to the beach if we were lucky—and find jobs. We were so excited."

We turn at the top of the hill.

"Wow. That's so . . . spontaneous of you," I say.

She twists her head to me, a sly smile on her face. "I was pretty spontaneous before you came along."

"What other spontaneous stuff did you do?"

She shakes her head, laughing. "I used to sneak out with my friends on the weekends."

My jaw drops. "No way."

"Your *Apong* Gerald and *Apong* Selene were so strict with your Auntie Linda and me. And Auntie Linda was always so good and obedient, going to Mass all the time and hanging out with her church friends. They didn't like me to go out with my friends on school nights or stay out late on the weekends. If I wasn't studying or in school, I had to help around the house." She shrugs. "But I had to get away every once in a while. It was my way of blowing off steam."

I've only ever known my mom to be a hardworking parent who hardly takes time to do anything for herself. I figured she was a rule follower her whole life. Hearing that she had a wild streak as a kid is eye-opening—and relatable. It's like I'm getting to know her as a completely different person.

"What would you do when you'd sneak out?" I ask.

"Oh, all sorts of things. Sometimes we'd just drive through the city at night. Other times we'd go to friends' parties."

"Did you ever get caught?"

"Never. I was always very careful," she says matter-of-factly. "Auntie Linda always threatened to tell on me, but she never did. She loved me too much."

"So you were a rule breaker that was going to uproot your life to Hawaii." I take care with how I word the next part. "What happened? You said you met Dad and . . ."

"Well, my dad, your *Apong* Gerald, got sick, so I stayed for a few years to help your *Apong* Selene take care of him." There's a tinge of sadness in the expression in her face when she speaks. "But that was okay. I got to spend more time with him before he passed."

I swallow back the ache in my throat.

Like how I want to spend more time with you.

"I'm just sad you kids never got to meet him," she says. "Damn cancer. And damn him for chain-smoking all of his adult life."

I rub her arm, hoping it comforts her, then make a mental note to tell Andy he needs to stop smoking cigarettes ASAP.

She waves a hand, as if to dismiss the sadness. "It was fine, too, because it gave me more time with my mom. And then I could save money to move. Hawaii is very expensive, so my friends had to live at home for a few years and save more money too."

"Mom, can I ask you something?"

"Of course."

"You stayed to be with *Apong* Gerald. But you didn't want me to stay with you at first. Why not? Isn't that kind of a similar situation?"

I brace myself for a defensive response, but she just pats my hand. "I guess it is in a way, huh?"

She says nothing else, and I don't press further. Because her small admission is enough. She's acknowledging that she feels differently now—that she's completely fine with my choice to stay with her.

We walk along the sidewalk, our pace increasing as we get comfortable.

"So then what happened? You were still planning to move, but then you met Dad?"

"Exactly. We met and fell in love. When I told him I wanted to move to Hawaii, he was one hundred percent behind it. But it just never worked out."

I realize now that I don't even know how they met, so I ask her.

A wistful smile tugs at her lips as she picks up the pace. "I was working as a barista at a coffee shop, and your dad used to come in almost every morning. He was a construction worker at the time. He always made it a point to tell me how he was blown away that I could look so pretty so early in the morning. We flirted like that for a couple of weeks. Then he asked me out. And the rest is history."

"Oh. Wow." I take a second to process the rom-com-worthy way my parents met. It's almost bizarre considering how badly their relationship ended.

"How come Hawaii never worked out?"

She makes a face and shakes her head. "It was a lot of things. First we said we were going to save money, but then we thought that buying a house would be better so we could build some equity, but we bought a fixer-upper that ended up needing so much more work than we realized at first. And after a while Denver was getting to be so expensive, so your dad suggested moving to Nebraska because it was more affordable but close enough that I could still visit Auntie Linda's family and our cousins, aunties, and uncles who lived in the area. And then after a couple of years, we had you, and the idea of uprooting us all across the ocean seemed like too much trouble."

We make our way down a hill along the perimeter of the park.

"He promised we'd take a family vacation to Hawaii someday, though," she says. "But then he had trouble keeping a job, then his drinking got worse and worse. Obviously it never worked out. And by the time it was just me and you kids, money was so tight. It didn't make sense to spend all that money on a trip to Hawaii. But it's okay. We took so many road trips to Denver to visit family. That was just as nice."

She pats my arm.

"But aren't you mad?"

Mom whips her head toward me, still keeping her impressive speedy walking pace. Her eyebrows wrinkle. "Mad about what?"

I reach for her arm, pulling her to the grass. Then I take a second to catch my breath, wiping my sweat-soaked brow with my forearm.

"Hawaii was your dream, but you never got to go because of Dad."

I think of every vacation our Mom ever took us on when we were kids. They were usually within a few hours' driving distance because traveling by car was cheaper than flying. And the one time we flew, it was to Disneyland, a trip that was solely for me and Andy.

Something inside my chest pulls. All that vacation time and money she saved, it was always for Andy and me. Never for herself.

"I just think I'd be mad at my husband if he broke a really important promise to me," I say quietly, hoping I don't sound too bitter.

Her chest heaves as she catches her breath. The small frown on her face melts away, leaving behind a smile that is all joy, zero trace of anger or regret.

"Well, I wasn't. I was so happy because I got you and your brother instead." She pats my hand. "A million times better than Hawaii in my book."

We round the corner to the other edge of the park, which is right across the street from the house.

We walk up to the porch. Before I get to the door, I turn to her. "I'm sorry that Hawaii didn't work out."

She lets out an easy laugh. "It's okay, *anak*. Maybe we'll get to go someday, together as a family."

We walk in the house and breathe in the aroma of *lumpia*, wontons, and pansit. Auntie Linda gestures for us to sit and eat. All the while I think about what Mom told me. How unbitter she is about her dream to move to Hawaii being taken away from her by a guy who turned out to be a terrible husband and father. Mom's cousins chat about how Mom's birthday is coming up, and an idea hits.

We need to do something special to celebrate. After everything she's been through—after everything that's happened, even if she doesn't know it happened, she deserves it.

The couch cushion next to me sinks down. "So! When are you seeing Liam again?" Mom asks.

"Um, not sure," I say around a mouthful of pansit.

She tsks. "You young people. Always so noncommittal."

"Mom, can you not?"

"I'm just saying." She holds up a hand as if to absolve her of how nosey she's being. I almost laugh. "I saw the way you were looking at each other earlier. You like each other. A lot. You should see each other again."

I groan at how insistent she is. "I'd definitely like to see him again. I'm just not sure when."

There's no doubt I like Liam and feel an attraction to him I can't fully comprehend. In the back of my mind, I wonder how he's feeling. Did his skin catch fire like mine did when we kissed? Is he still thinking of me, like I'm thinking of him? Is he completely turned off by the way I left things? Is he regretting spending his weekend off with me, the weirdo who kissed him, freaked out, then kicked him to the curb?

But none of that is my focus; it can't be. My focus is my mom. She's my priority above everything, and I don't want to let a distraction get in the way like I did before when I allowed work to take over my life.

"Sooner rather than later, *anak*," Auntie Mel says as she fusses with the barrette in her wavy dark-brown hair. Auntie Kay nods in agreement, adjusting her glasses.

I nod politely at the advice everyone chatters at me, but my mind is focused on something else: it's Mom's birthday in three weeks. I need to text Andy and Julianne right away. As I'm reaching for my phone, I think of Hannah. If she's feeling up to it, I want her to be part of this too. Then I need to get in touch with Liam. If I'm going to pull this off, I'll need his help. I just need to work up the nerve to talk to him again after the way I left him today.

~

"It's been over a week, Chloe," Julianne says. "When are you going to finally call Liam?"

I sigh into the phone as I weave through the crowded living room and kitchen. She's been on me to reach out to him ever since I filled her in on what happened with my dad and Liam. I told her I've been busy catching up with Mom's cousins every day since coming home from Kansas City and haven't had the time. She's not buying it, though.

Even though I don't outright admit it, Liam has been on my mind every day since we arrived back in Kearney. Every night when I'm lying in bed trying to fall asleep, I think of him and wonder what he is up to. I could text him—but I'm too much of a coward. Because what would I say?

Hey, what's up? Remember when we made out and my mom and aunties saw us, then I practically threw you out of my car?

Just thinking of having to broach the subject with Liam has me aching to crawl under the nearest rock.

But I still can't get him off my mind. Not his kindness, his sweetness, how he cradled me in his arms in that motel room and made me feel so safe and cared for and understood. I can't forget that smile or the way his icy-blue eyes peered right into me and made me feel like he truly understood every single crazy feeling I was going through.

I just need to grow a spine and figure out a way to pick up my phone and call him.

I pin the phone between my cheek and shoulder while helping Mom make wontons. I glance around the open-concept space. The aunties are in the living room playing mah-jongg while Mom and I are in the kitchen preparing food with Auntie Linda.

"You know you want to see him again, Chloe," Julianne says.

"Of course I do. I just—honestly, I don't even know what to say to him at this point."

"Um, I think all you need to say is, 'Hey, thanks so much for being my rock during that emotional roller coaster of a weekend with my dad. Also, I really enjoyed kissing you and would like to kiss you some more. Wanna meet up?'"

I stifle a laugh as Mom's ears perk up. "Is that Julianne? Put her on speaker, I want to say hi."

When I do, Mom says hello and introduces Julianne to everyone. They all holler hello. Julianne says hi in return, then says to give her a second so she can go to a quieter spot to talk.

Mom directs me to dump the ground pork in a large bowl so we can mix it together with her special spice blend. I do what Mom does and pour half a palmful of pepper and garlic powder into the ground meat, then five shakes of the soy sauce bottle. The other day I asked her to write down her recipe for wontons, along with her *lumpia*, adobo, pansit, and fried rice recipes. Like Auntie Linda, she balked at the idea of writing down her dishes because she said she never followed a recipe. But when I explained to her how much it would mean to have her food, which is so special to me, documented in this way, she relented and jotted down general directions on note cards for me to keep. We've cooked each of those dishes at least once since Auntie Linda and their cousins have been visiting. I've helped prep each dish, which fills me with a kind of joy I've never experienced before. I now know how to cook Mom's recipes—recipes from her family, that her sister and her cousins cook too. It makes me feel that much closer to her, to all of them.

"Thanks for teaching me how to make this, Mom," I say amid the chatter and laughter.

She beams up at me. "You're welcome. I should have taught you this ages ago. Every time I tried when you were a kid, we'd always get so frustrated with each other."

"I could never get it to turn out like yours. It always tasted different."

"That's because you didn't listen when I would tell you the recipe. And you would always try to add something extra. Like red pepper flakes." She makes a face, then nudges me with her hip.

"I tried to teach you again when you got older, but you were always so busy with school, then work."

"Not anymore," I say, wrapping my arm around her and giving her a hug. I've nailed this recipe twice since she taught it to me, and today as we prepare it together, I have no doubt it will be as delicious as ever.

Just then Julianne jumps back on.

"What have you been up to, Julianne?" Mom asks.

"Oh, you know, same old stuff." Julianne's singsong voice echoes in the kitchen. "Staying busy with work, staying at Chloe's house and making sure I don't burn it down every time I try to cook something, and trying to convince Chloe to call Liam."

"You'd better not burn my house down," I holler.

Mom frowns up at me. "You haven't called him yet?"

Everyone else's head whips up to look at me. Six pairs of deep-brown eyes bore into me before they bombard me with questions.

"Why haven't you called him?"

"Did something happen?"

"Don't you want to see him again?"

"Don't you want to finish that kiss?"

"He's so handsome, why don't you want to see him again?"

I bite back a groan and instead focus on seasoning, then stirring the ground pork mixture. "Thanks for that, Julianne."

She chuckles. "I know, I know. That wasn't fair of me. But we've gotta get you back in the dating game, Chloe."

"I agree with you there, Julianne," Mom says as she hands me a stack of flour wrappers so I can start wrapping the wontons.

Despite the mild frustration at my love life being the topic of my entire family and best friend's current discussion, I smile. Because Mom and I have the same size hands, I don't have to use spoons and cups to measure; I can follow her recipe exactly as she does it, and the comfort of that lands like a warm hug to my chest.

I dollop the pork mixture onto a flour wrapper square, dab egg wash along the edges, then fold it in half diagonally so it forms a triangle.

"You all leave her alone. She's a smart and capable young lady. She can do what she wants," Auntie Linda says as she hugs me from behind.

I twist around and smile at her, appreciative of her defense of me in this good-natured family discussion of my love life. Earlier in the week, after Mom showed her the bracelet and ring, Auntie Linda hugged me while crying.

"I can't believe you did this, *anak*," she said. "You gave us a part of our mom back that I thought we lost forever. That means everything. Thank you."

Her eyes are full of emotion now as she beams at me and gives my hand a soft squeeze before darting off to the hallway bathroom. "Thanks for your thoughts on my dating life, everyone," I say as politely as I can. "But I've got this under control."

"Then call him," Mom and Julianne say in unison. They're definitely not going to give up anytime soon.

I exhale so hard, it almost sounds like a groan.

Auntie Lorna and Auntie Mel start chattering about the importance of going after what you want when it comes to dating just as Auntie Kay and Auntie Rita mention how playing hard to get is more fun.

"It's what I did when I was your age, *anakko*," Auntie Rita calls from the living room while staring at her mah-jongg tiles.

"Don't listen to her," Auntie Lorna says as she twists her wavy gray-black hair into a bun. "Playing hard to get is for children. You're a grown woman. Say what you want, and if he's a real man, he'll give it to you."

"Oh, I think he'll give it to her no matter what," Auntie Mel chimes in.

Mom scolds her while I laugh and shake my head. Julianne bursts into uncontrollable giggles.

My family's unsolicited advice is well meaning and has been a constant throughout my entire life. Growing up, whenever we would go to big family gatherings, it was inevitable that no matter what life issue Andy, our cousins, or I were going through, big or small, we could always count on Mom and the aunties to pipe in and offer their advice—whether we wanted it or not.

I almost laugh at how overbearing our entire family dynamic is. When I was younger it drove me nuts. And even now I realize that if I hadn't fallen asleep in May and woken up in March that one crazy, mysterious morning, I would probably still find my family's antics annoying. I'd be rolling my eyes at Auntie Mel's sensational comments and faking a smile while the rest of my aunties pried. But now all I feel is joy and gratitude. The two collide in a warm wave at the center of my chest as I gaze up and beam at my aunties and Mom. It took losing my mom and then getting her back in an impossible way to make me realize just how lucky I was to have what I have—how lucky I *am* to have what I have.

Their meddling and chattering and constant barrage of comments and questions are proof of how much they care about and love me. I understand now why Mom was never annoyed at any family gathering, why she always smiled and laughed along with everyone's comments and questions—because everything was rooted in love. All that time spent together was a gift because it didn't happen often. Even in this moment when everyone is teasing me and butting into my personal life, I relish it. Because it's more time we can all spend together—and more importantly it's one more joyful memory Mom can have with her family.

"Okay, okay," I finally say in a good-natured tone after a minute of letting everyone babble away. "I'll call him."

A chorus of yays and Julianne's "woo-hoo" over speaker phone follow. Mom and Julianne chat for a few more minutes while Mom and I make wontons. When they finish, I tell Julianne goodbye and wash up.

I swipe my phone from the counter and walk out of the kitchen. "I'm calling him. Wish me luck!"

"Good luck, *anak*!" everyone calls after me.

I shut the door to my bedroom, sit on my bed, and take a breath before dialing Liam.

When he answers, my heart thuds like it's going to burst from my chest. "Hey."

"Hey." I can tell he's smiling; the thought makes my stomach flip. "How are you feeling?"

"Good overall. You?"

"I'm great. How did your mom react when you gave her the jewelry?"

I give him a recap of her shocked and happy reaction. And then I pause, wondering how I'm going to segue into this next part—the whole reason for this call.

"So . . . we kissed." I roll my eyes at just how pathetic that sounds. It's like I'm in middle school again trying to talk to a boy I like.

But his chuckle breaks the tension within me. "We did kiss. And I enjoyed it. Although I gotta say, you end kisses in a hell of an unconventional way. I've never had anyone speed away from me so fast after kissing me. Very memorable, though."

My whole body shakes as I laugh, melting the rest of the tension within me. I don't think I've ever met someone who can make an awkward conversation so comfortable in a matter of seconds like Liam can.

"What can I say? I'm an odd creature."

"Yeah, but I still like you."

"You do?"

"Yes. I like you so much that I'm talking to you instead of taking my preshift nap."

"Oh, shoot, sorry. Right, you work tonight, don't you?"

"It's fine, Chloe. But if you're free tonight, you should stop by and maybe we can chat more about just how much we like each other."

"Okay."

I end the call smiling so wide my cheeks hurt, nerves nowhere to be found.

Chapter Eighteen

This time when I stand in the canned-goods aisle, it's not to spy on Mom. It's to run into Liam. I'm crouched down, checking out the selection of canned fruits, when my legs start to fall asleep. Slowly I stand, then turn around to shake out my legs and bump right into him.

"Crap." I stumble back.

"Sorry." He lets out a flustered laugh. "I was coming up to say hi to you. I should have announced myself."

"It's fine."

"So. Hi," he says when I don't say anything more.

"Hello again." I fidget with my phone and keys in my hand before shoving them in the pockets of my jean shorts. "So."

I shuffle my sneakered feet slightly back and forth along the linoleum floor. The soft squealing noise makes me wince.

"We should probably talk about that kiss," I finally say. "I think I owe you an apology."

"For what?"

"For how I acted after we stopped . . . kissing."

Liam shrugs. "Honestly, it was a pretty awkward moment. Your family was watching us after all."

"Ha. Right." My throat suddenly feels dry, and my hands turn clammy. "Well, I want to apologize for how long I waited to call you afterwards."

"It's really okay, Chloe. You were coming off a stressful and emotional couple of days. I just hope that you don't regret the kiss."

Uncertainty flashes behind his icy-blue eyes.

"I don't regret it at all. I mean, yeah, I was a bundle of emotions. But kissing you felt good. And right. It was exactly what I wanted to do in that moment."

He blinks, looking relieved. "Do you wanna come with me on my break? I usually go outside just to get some fresh air."

"That sounds nice."

A minute later we're sitting next to each other on top of the hood of his car in the grocery store parking lot. We scoot up, then lie back against the windshield and gaze at the night sky. Millions of stars dazzle above us.

"How are you processing things?" he asks.

I turn to him.

If only you knew the things I'm processing in the mess that is my brain. Like, why is it that I feel so comfortable around you—more comfortable than I feel around most people—even though we've only just met?

And how in the world did I get here? Is it time travel? A glitch in the universe? A parallel one? A hallucination?

And how long will my mom be here this time?

"After seeing your dad, I mean," Liam says, pulling me back to our conversation. "Do you feel okay?"

"Oh. Yeah, I do. I don't know if I'll ever feel good or normal when it comes to him. But I feel a sense of clarity I didn't have before."

"I'm really glad to hear that." He clears his throat. "I called my parents the other day."

"You did?"

I can't tell anything from his expression. He doesn't look happy or upset.

"How did it go?" I ask.

"Okay overall, I think. My mom was really happy to hear from me. My dad was a little standoffish at first. But they both said they missed me a lot and were glad that I called."

"That's so great, Liam. I'm happy for you."

"I wouldn't have done it if I hadn't come with you to see your dad. Sorry, I don't mean for it to come off that way, like I was getting something out of watching you go through that difficult moment."

I touch his arm, and he immediately stills. "It didn't come off like that at all. I think that's wonderful you reached out to your parents."

"I know we're not going to automatically be a perfect happy family again, but it's a start."

"How did it make you feel to talk to them?"

"Weird at first. A little awkward with my dad because he's not one to let himself get sentimental. But it felt good to hear their voices. I'm glad I reached out. And I'm definitely going to talk to them again."

He pins me with that warm, icy-blue gaze. "I just wanted to say thank you for helping me get to this point. I don't think I would have called them had you not asked me to come with you to see your dad."

I spend a moment thinking how far Liam has come with his family and how far I've come with mine. I reach for his hand and grip it gently.

"Well, I wouldn't have been able to face my dad without you. So, thank you again."

The longer we stay joined together by our hands, the hotter I burn—and it's not because of the sticky heat coating the atmosphere. It's because that warmth, that connection between us, is resurfacing. It's because I can't remember the last time I shared such an intimate moment where all I did with someone was hold hands but felt like we were as close as two people could ever be.

"I'd like to see you again, Chloe. Like, take you out on a date."

I swallow. "I'd like that too. But"—I take a breath so I can explain myself—"I came home to stay with my mom because I realized that for the longest time, I was taking her for granted. I wasn't spending the time with her that I should have been. For years. I'm trying to make her my focus. And part of me is afraid that spending time with anyone else might take away from that."

"I totally get that. I don't mean to take any time away from her. But seeing me once in a while when she's busy or at work isn't really taking time away from her. Is it?"

The way he explains it, it sounds so simple.

I sigh, then let out an embarrassed chuckle. "You're right. Can I call you tomorrow and we can set up a date?"

The smile that spreads across his face makes me giddy from the inside out.

"Of course."

I hop off the hood of his car and wait for him to get down. When he does, I lean forward and press a kiss on his lips. Much more chaste than the one we exchanged last week. But I like it just as much.

"Good night, Chloe."

"Have a good rest of your shift."

When I go home, I quietly clean up in the bathroom so I don't wake everyone up. I go straight to bed, but sleep doesn't last.

Because soon I'm dreaming. I'm having a nightmare. It's the one where I can't talk or move as Mom stands in front of me with that blank stare on her face. There's a loud crash. And then she's gone.

I shoot up from the bed covered in a cold sweat, panting.

I haven't had this dream in weeks. Why is it happening again?

My mind races as I try to make sense of this. There's no chance of me falling asleep after that, so I get up and walk to the kitchen, down a glass of water, then open my laptop. I email Dr. McAuliffe, asking for a Skype session sometime in the coming days.

Then I tiptoe to Mom's bedroom and peek through the open door. She's snoozing next to Auntie Linda. I watch her chest rise and fall, listening intently to her deep breaths. My racing heart slows the tiniest bit.

And then I walk back to the living room, sit on the couch, and stare out the window to the street in front of the house as the darkness deepens.

~

"Recurring dreams aren't necessarily anything to be concerned about," Dr. McAuliffe says patiently through the screen of my laptop.

"Right, but—I guess I'm just worried."

"Why are you worried? Your mom is safe and healthy. You've been visiting with your extended family too. It sounds like you have a lot of positive things happening in your life right now."

"I guess I still can't shake the paranoia that something might happen to her."

It's two days after my nightmare about Mom, and I still can't rid myself of the terror that plagued me when I woke up from the dream in a cold sweat.

"That's a paranoia everyone has about their loved ones. Are you finding ways to try and manage your stress and anxiety?"

I mention the guided meditation class that Mom and I have been to a few times this summer.

"Have you thought about telling your mom that you're having worrying dreams about her?"

"Oh my gosh, no way."

"Maybe you should."

"I don't want to worry her. She might freak out."

Dr. McAuliffe sighs. "I don't think she will. I remember when you told me her reaction to your dream where you thought she died. I think she handled that pretty well. I think you should give her more credit."

She's right. All things considered, Mom handled that pretty well.

"You should tell her. Maybe speaking about your dream with her will take away a bit of the power from it."

"How do you mean?"

"Sometimes when you let a thought or an idea—or a dream—live inside your head and never talk about it, it feels like this huge, scary thing. But then when you talk through it, it can feel a bit less daunting and more manageable. When you discuss your dream with your mom, it won't feel so much like this big, scary nightmare you had. Just a one-off dream. She could offer some insight too—maybe her take on it will be something you hadn't thought of before."

Like every other time I talk to Dr. McAuliffe, I quietly acknowledge she's right. I think about when I can sit Mom down to do that. She's been gone since this morning, dropping off Auntie Linda and her cousins at the airport, but maybe when she arrives home, we can sit down and talk this out.

"Okay. I'll talk to her about it once she's home."

"How are things going with Liam?"

"Oh, um. They're okay."

"Have you talked to him since you got back from Kansas City?"

"Yes. Once."

"But not since then?"

"No."

"Why is that? It sounded like you started to forge a special bond with him."

I burn up in shame when I think about how I blew my promise to call him and set up a date. The day after I met up with him at the grocery store, I didn't end up reaching out to him. I was too freaked out from my nightmare—and a tiny part of me wondered if seeing him again had something to do with it.

I sigh and acknowledge that I should probably share this tidbit with Dr. McAuliffe.

"I think part of me—the weird, nonsensical part of me—thought that starting something up with him might have had something to do with the nightmare I had about my mom."

Dr. McAuliffe nods like that's not a completely ridiculous idea.

"I understand why your mind might make that connection," she says. "But I think you're mistaken."

"How so?"

"I think part of you is afraid that if you do something for yourself—something that takes you away from your mom for even a little bit—it's going to have a negative consequence."

"Yeah, that's pretty spot-on."

"It doesn't have to be all or nothing, Chloe. You can still care about your mom and stay devoted to her while also doing things for yourself. You've come a long way. You're making some exciting strides in your life. I would hate to see you miss out on a valuable and fulfilling relationship with someone special because of a dream."

Dr. McAuliffe's words ring over and over in my head even after she stops speaking.

"You're right. I need to stop sabotaging myself. Thank you."

We close out the session, and I resolve to talk to Mom the moment she arrives home.

~

It's dark by the time Mom walks through the front door. She drops her purse on the side table next to the couch and waves at me as I finish searing tuna steaks for dinner.

I plate it up for her and set it on the kitchen table while she washes up. As we eat together, I look over at her. It's the first time that we've been alone together in over a week with all the aunties visiting. Now is as good a time as any to talk.

"I've been having some weird dreams lately," I finally say.

"Again? Like what?" Mom says before spearing a chunk of fish with her fork.

"About you."

I carefully explain the recurring dream I've had about her.

When I finish, she squints at me, then her head falls back in a laugh.

"That's ridiculous. So ridiculous," she says through a chuckle.

"Is it?" I'm taken aback at how easygoing her reaction is.

She tucks her hair behind her ears and nods, still smiling. "It's absolutely ridiculous, *anak*." Then she jokingly darts her gaze around the room. "There aren't any invisible loud crashes coming after me, are there?"

She falls into another fit of laughs as I shake my head at her.

"That's not funny," I mutter into my water glass.

She reaches over and pats my hand. "Oh, you know I'm just kidding."

"It scared me to have that kind of a dream about you."

She reins in her smile, her expression softening. "Okay, I understand. But I'm right here. You don't need to worry."

I shake my head and try to explain as she holds my hand. "I know it sounds ridiculous, but it felt so real in the moment. And I don't know, sometimes I think that maybe our dreams are trying to tell us something."

"Like what? Be extra careful when you hear a random loud noise?"

I yank my hand away as Mom chuckles once more, then I stand up and start clearing the table.

"Oh my gosh, okay, I'm sorry. Chloe, look at me."

From where I stand in the kitchen, I turn around to her.

"I didn't mean to upset you. But sometimes you have to realize that dreams are just dreams. Yeah, they're scary, but they're not real. What's real is what you do when you're awake."

She stands up and collects the rest of the dishes while I load the dishwasher and ponder what she's said.

When I finish, I dry my hands and pull her into a hug. "You're right."

She squeezes me back and says she's going to take a shower before heading to bed early so she can catch some extra rest before her shift tomorrow.

I grab my phone and call Liam.

"Hey." His voice sounds almost curt when he answers.

"I'm sorry," I say, skipping all introductions and formalities. "I know I said I'd call you to set up a date, and I totally dropped the ball. I'm officially the worst."

There's a long pause. "Look, if you're not ready for anything like a date, that's okay. I understand. All you have to do is say so."

"No, it's not that. I want to see you again. It's just been so long since I've done this whole dating thing that I sometimes wonder what the hell I'm doing. I freak out, then hesitate and doubt myself. And then I wonder why someone as handsome and kind and wonderful as you even likes me in the first place."

"Don't say that." His tone turns gentle, and it's exactly what I need to hear.

"It's true, Liam. I mean, look at you."

There's a quiet chuckle on the other end of the line.

"Look at me?"

"Yeah. You're a hot, sweet, gainfully employed guy. And you're tall."

My try for a compliment mixed with humor lands well, and he booms out a laugh.

"I still don't understand how a guy like you is unattached."

"I just haven't met the right person yet. It's that simple."

"Is it?"

"Yes. It is."

"I find it hard to believe that you're not being constantly swarmed by available women at the store."

"Swarmed is a strong word."

"I knew it."

"I get approached, but it's not like it happens all the time. And I'm honestly not interested when it happens. I tried dating people I met that way a few times, and it never worked out. So I stopped."

"That's kind of how we met, though. At the store, on your shift."

"You're different."

The gentle tone of his voice combined with the sweet words he speaks has my heart thudding.

"That's smooth."

"Oh yeah?" I can tell he's smiling.

"I'm sorry I let my hang-ups get in the way. Again. It's just . . . I think part of me is convinced I'm going to screw something up—like I did with almost every other relationship I've had. And then there will be this unpleasantness."

"Unpleasantness?"

"Yeah. Because you're my mom's coworker. How weird would it be if things between us fell out, and then you'd have to see my mom almost every day because you work together?"

Liam's soft chuckle echoes in my ear. "I highly doubt you were the only reason your past relationships didn't work out. It takes two people to be together."

I let out a laugh.

"What's funny?" Liam asks.

"Nothing. Just . . . you always seem to know the right thing to say, you know that? You're, like, scarily close to perfect. It kind of freaks me out."

"There's no such thing as perfect. But I like to think I'm pretty damn close."

I grin at the smile in his voice.

"Kidding. Obviously," he says. "Look, I like you, Chloe. Whatever you're feeling, no matter how weird or silly you think it is, you can talk to me about it. At the risk of sounding like a weirdo, I feel like I have this connection with you that I can't really even explain. I've never felt that before."

My heart flutters. "You're not a weirdo. I feel the same about you."

"I don't want hypothetical doubts to get between us if we can just talk through them. We've been through some heavy stuff together already. I think we can handle whatever else comes our way as long as we talk about it. I'm here for you, Chloe, no matter what."

His words linger, landing at the center of my chest, going straight to my heart.

No matter what.

What Dr. McAuliffe said all those weeks ago echoes in my head.

I like to tell my clients that they should have three people they can call at any time, no matter the day, and they know that person will be there for them emotionally. A 'no matter what' person. Who are your three?

Liam might just be another "no matter what" person in my life. And that thought makes me a whole new kind of happy.

"My mom's birthday is in a couple of weeks, and I'm trying to pull off a pretty huge surprise," I say. "Can we meet up to chat about that? I need your help big-time. And I know that's probably the weirdest idea for a date ever, but . . . I'm a weird person. And you said you liked me, so this is what you're in for."

His laugh booms in my ear. "I'm in."

"Good. It's your night off tomorrow, right?"

"Yeah."

"How about I bring Hunan's takeout to your place?"

"Great. I'll have something to drink."

"Maybe around seven?"

"Sounds perfect."

~

My phone buzzes with a text from Liam.

She left five minutes ago, expect her home soon.

I text a thank-you, then finish blowing up the last balloon and drop it on the floor. I glance around the living room and see that the floor is covered in balloons of every color. Not a speck of the tan tile is visible.

"How's it going, Andy?" I ask from across the room.

"Good. I think." He scrambles to tape the last length of streamer against the wall opposite where I'm standing.

I jog over and hold the blue streamer in place so he can tape it.

"Thanks," he says, wiping his brow, which is dotted with specks of sweat.

I glance around the room. Balloons and streamers of every color adorn the living room and kitchen, like a kid's birthday party gone rogue. There's an inflatable palm tree decoration in one corner and two unlit tiki torches propped up against the walls. Cheap mock leis in every color hang off the lamps and light fixtures.

"Think she'll like it?" I ask.

"No doubt."

My heart races as I anticipate the surprise on Mom's face when she sees the setup. Just then, the garage door opens.

I turn to Andy. "Ready?"

"Oh, I'm ready." He grins and tugs at the Hawaiian shirt he threw on over his T-shirt and fusses with the fake mustache he tacked on a bit ago.

The door to the garage swings open, and Mom walks in with grocery bags hooked over both arms.

Before she looks up, Andy and I take identical breaths.

"Surprise," we say softly.

She squints at us, clearly confused, then starts to ask what we're doing. But then her gaze floats around the living room, and her expression morphs to shock. She drops the bags on the floor. "What's all this?"

she asks, walking into the living room. She squints at Andy. "What in the world are you wearing?"

"We have a surprise for you," Andy says before looking in my direction, which is my cue to take over the reveal.

I pull Mom into a side hug. "Your birthday is next week, and we want to do something extra special for you."

"Oh yeah?" Her head spins as she gawks around the room, taking in all the decorations.

I turn her so I can look directly at her. Then I hand her a card. When she opens it, it takes her a second to read the message I've written. Her face goes from a semiserious frown to shocked delight once she processes it all.

"We're going to Hawaii?" She gasps.

"Yes!" Andy and I yell together in response.

Andy mentions that Hannah will be joining us, too, then I say that Auntie Linda, Auntie Lorna, Auntie Kay, Auntie Rita, and Auntie Mel will be coming as well. She cups her hands over her mouth.

"Oh, this is unbelievable!" She pulls us both into a hug.

"It's for real, Mom," I say. "Two weeks in Oahu for your birthday. All you have to do is pack your bags and be ready to head to the airport Friday morning."

She blinks and darts her gaze between me and Andy, then once more around the room.

"Oh, wait. I don't know if I can . . . I haven't asked for time off work, and I don't . . . I can't leave the store for two weeks on zero notice. And what about you guys?" Her expression falls. "Andy, can you even miss that much work? And this is so expensive too. How did you kids manage to pay for all this?"

But then I grab her hands and give them a squeeze. "It's all been taken care of. Right, Andy?"

He nods. "I have all my shifts covered, Mom. You don't need to worry."

She looks at me.

"I talked to Liam, and he talked to your boss," I say. "All the arrangements at work have been made. Everyone at work knows you'll be taking a vacation for your birthday."

She assumes that shocked, openmouthed expression once more. "Are you serious? You mean—you mean everyone at the store knew about this and didn't tell me?"

"Everyone wanted you to be surprised," Andy says.

"Oh, you kids!" Once more she pulls us into a double hug.

Then she pulls away, a determined look on her face, but I stop her before she can argue again.

"Don't worry about the cost," I say. "We took care of it all. You don't have to worry about a thing, Mom. All you have to do is relax and enjoy yourself."

"Is Julianne coming too?" she asks, her eyes hopeful.

I try to keep my smile when I answer her. "She can't make it. She says she's so sorry, but she couldn't get the time off work."

This trip won't feel complete without Julianne. But she helped me plan so much of it that it'll feel like she's there in a small way.

Mom's smile drops as she nods, but only for a second. She claps her hands. "I need to figure out what I'm going to pack."

"Mom, we're not leaving for a few days," Andy says.

Spinning away, she waves a hand at him, dismissing his reassurance. "That's barely enough time."

She scurries down the hall to her bedroom. The sound of her opening her closet door causes both Andy and me to chuckle.

"I think it's safe to say she's excited," Andy says.

"Wait until we get there," I say. "She's going to lose her mind."

My phone buzzes with another text from Liam.

Liam: How'd it go?

Me: Perfectly. She loved the surprise. Thank you for all the strings you pulled at work to make this happen. We couldn't have done it without you.

Liam: It's my pleasure. Everyone here is so excited for her to have some time off finally. She hardly ever takes vacation.

Me: I just hope she has a good time.

Liam: She will. Zero doubt about that. Promise you'll take lots of pictures and show me when you get back?

Me: Absolutely.

Mom ducks her head out her bedroom doorway.

"This is the best surprise ever. Hawaii with my kids. For two weeks! For my birthday!" She blows us a kiss. "Love you both so much."

Even from all the way down the hall, I can tell her eyes are glistening with happy tears. A second later, I realize I'm tearing up too.

Quickly, I blink my eyes dry. "Love you too, Mom."

Chapter Nineteen

"How are you feeling about things now?" Dr. McAuliffe asks.

"Content. But cautious."

I glance from my laptop screen to my suitcase, which is lying open on the floor of my bedroom, clothes spilling out of it like it exploded. It's two days until Mom's Hawaii birthday trip, and I'm in the middle of a Skype session with Dr. McAuliffe.

"Why do you feel cautious?"

"Because everything seems to be going really well. Mom lived past the day that I thought she would die . . ."

The swallow that moves through my throat is hard and painful. I hate saying it out loud, but I'm grateful that it's true.

"She isn't annoyed with me for quitting my job anymore. She's actually happy that I'm at home, it seems like. My brother and his girlfriend are doing well. The rift between my mom and my aunt is repaired. And even though things with my dad are strained, I feel a closure with him I never thought I would. And I'm dating Liam now. That's going well too."

I think back to the first date we had at his house when we planned this surprise for Mom. How hard we laughed, how it ended with more kissing, how he walked me out to my car when the evening was over, how he held the door for me, how he reminded me to drive safely, how he texted me to make sure I got home okay, even though I was less than five minutes away.

And then I think about the two dates we've had since then—one to go to dinner and one to go running together—and relish the way my stomach jumps at just the thought of him.

"It kind of feels like waiting for the other shoe to drop," I admit. "I don't know if any other time in my life things have ever fallen into place like this. It can't last forever."

"Why can't it?"

"Because nothing ever does."

"That's a bit of a fatalist view of the world, isn't it?"

"Maybe, but it's true."

Dr. McAuliffe nods. "You know, Chloe. There's nothing wrong with acknowledging that things in your life are going well and enjoying it for the time being. You don't always have to brace yourself for what's going to happen next. It's okay to live in the moment and enjoy things as they happen."

"I get that. It's just hard to shake the feeling that something out of the blue could happen to my mom when I least expect it—or to someone else, like what happened with Hannah."

"I understand. I really do. But I think it would be best if you tried not to think about what could or couldn't happen to your mom. You get to spend all this time with her now. That's a gift. Cherish it."

Dr. McAuliffe's advice is so simple and spot-on.

"I just want this trip to Hawaii to be perfect for her. She deserves it after all she's been through, after all she's sacrificed for my brother and me."

"Do you feel like you owe it to your mom in a way to give her this big birthday trip?"

Her words nail something deep and unspoken inside of me.

"I don't mean it like that. I just mean that she's a single mom who sacrificed more than I'll ever know to raise my brother and me. I just want to do something to show her that we appreciate that."

"Does that bother you that your mom had to sacrifice certain things to raise you two?"

"Yeah. She deserves so much better than what she's gotten in life."

Ditched by her husband. An unexpected death after a lifetime of hard work, just a few years from retirement.

"You should talk to her about how you feel."

"What do you mean?"

"I think you're carrying a lot of guilt that you don't realize, Chloe. Maybe talking to your mom about what it is that's making you feel that way will help you resolve those feelings—help you find clarity."

I let Dr. McAuliffe's words sink in. I think she's right about this too.

"I'll think about it," I say.

"We're about out of time. Safe travels and have a lovely time in Hawaii. Let me know when you'd like to schedule another session when you come back."

"Of course. Thanks so much, Dr. McAuliffe."

We say goodbye, her words echoing in my head. And then I turn to my suitcase and finish packing.

~

A couple of days later, the universe has conspired to give us the smoothest travel day ever. All flights were on time, there was zero turbulence, zero cranky babies, and zero unruly passengers.

Making our way through the Honolulu airport, I can't help but gawk. Judging from the design of the building, it looks like it hasn't had a style remodel since the 1980s. But I adore the charm of it. When we walk from our terminal to baggage claim, I'm struck by the open design of the corridors and walkways. Every few seconds, a breeze glides through the airport. Salty air fills my lungs. I can't help but close my eyes for a long second and beam. When I open them, I stare at the palm trees I can see so clearly lining the outdoor area of the airport.

When I turn to check on Mom walking beside me, she's got a perma-grin plastered on her face as she takes in the surroundings.

She twists her head to look at me. "We made it! And look how pretty it all is!"

I follow her gaze as she takes it all in.

"It's so warm too," she says. "But not so humid like Nebraska."

She's been grinning nonstop ever since we woke up crazy early this morning to make our flight.

"It feels like home already," she says.

The words sink deep into my chest. Seeing Mom happy, in the place where she longed to live more than thirty years ago, gives me a joy I've never known before.

But before I can dwell too much on it, we run into a crowd several dozen people deep at baggage claim.

"This'll take a while," Andy says with a slight whine to his voice. But then Hannah walks up to him and slides an arm around his waist, cuddling into him. A smile blooms on his face, then he kisses the top of her head.

"No whining allowed unless something legitimately terrible happens," I mock scold him. "I want everything to be perfect for her on this trip. I don't want something like us whining to get her down."

"Your sister's right," Hannah says. "We're in Hawaii! This is so cool already. It's gonna be a blast."

Andy's expression softens as he gazes at Hannah. He promises he'll cool it with the whining and doesn't even make a peep when it takes a solid half hour before we get our bags. Even the long wait for our luggage doesn't chip away at Mom's unflappable excitement. It's in the way she stands straight up and is constantly looking around, as if she doesn't want to miss a single thing happening around her. It's in the way she takes endless photos on her phone of the airport.

I walk up to her and pull her into a hug. "We haven't even made it outside yet, Mom."

She smiles down at her phone screen as she swipes through her photos. "I can't help it. I'm just so excited."

"I can see that."

We make our way to the entrance where we can catch the shuttle to grab our rental car at the other end of the airport. Before we can make it to the shuttle line, I spot a handful of people offering leis to tourists who have just arrived.

I wave one of them down, then point out Mom to my side. The man offers a small smile to Mom before placing a lei over her neck.

"Aloha," he says. "Welcome to Hawaii. We hope you have a wonderful time."

"I already am." She runs her fingers across the plumeria petals that make up the lei. They boast a vibrant fuchsia hue along the edges and slowly fade to light pink, then burst into bright yellow at the center. The shape of the blooms and their color remind me of those shiny pinwheels I used to play with as a kid.

While waiting for the shuttle, Mom turns to me and asks me to remind her when Auntie Linda and their cousins will join. I tell her that they're all due to meet us at the condo rental when their flights get in this evening.

"So what's the plan for today?" she asks, pulling her bright-pink carry-on suitcase behind her.

"Whatever you want, birthday girl."

She squints, as if she's thinking hard about what she wants her first official activity on Oahu to be.

"Let's drop our stuff off at the condo, put on our swimsuits, then go right to the beach."

"You got it."

~

Three days into Mom's birthday vacation, and she's taken "whatever you want" to the max.

The first day was beach lounging at Waikiki and exploring local eateries. Yesterday was spent sightseeing in the North Shore with our rental car.

Today, the morning of Mom's birthday, has been a swim at Waikiki after surprising her with a breakfast in bed of fresh tropical fruit we found at a local market. Now we're having lunch at one of the many busy outdoor food courts in Waikiki, which houses loads of affordable yet tasty eats. Surrounding us are dozens of eateries, delicious smells wafting from each storefront. In the middle of the court is a haphazard formation of tables and chairs. Patrons walk in and out with food orders while people dine around us. Every now and then, a pigeon flies in and waddles around, searching for scrumptious morsels someone may have dropped.

As we sit down at a table and dig into our food, I check my phone. Mom's birthday lunch surprise should be here in a few minutes. While she's busy chowing down on her ramen bowl while chatting with Auntie Linda and their cousins, Andy leans over to whisper in my ear.

"Everything on time?" he asks.

"Should be. The guy said he would be here at twelve thirty sharp."

When I look up from my plate of freshly made yakisoba noodles, I spot him at the edge of the bustling food court, gazing around. Sitting up straighter, I catch eyes with him, then nod my head.

I turn to my side. "Okay, Mom. I need you to stand up with me and close your eyes."

"Why?" She squints at me, suspicion radiating from her black-brown irises.

"We have a surprise for you."

"Another one?" Her eyes widen.

"Of course another one. This is your birthday trip, remember?"

Excited nodding is her response as she stands up. I take her by the hand and lead her to the end of our table. She closes her eyes. I look up at the tall, mustached man standing at the far end of the food court, donning a Hawaiian shirt. I wave him over. He walks to us and stands in front of her.

I stand behind her, holding her by the shoulders. "You ready, Mom?"

She nods again. That smile on her face hasn't budged.

"Okay. Open."

It takes a second for her to process what's in front of her. Probably because she's small and the Magnum, P.I., look-alike is more than a foot taller than her. Her jaw falls, and her eyes bulge.

"Oh my gosh! You're Magnum, P.I.!"

The guy grins wide, dimples deepening as he nods. "That's me." He moves to hand her a bouquet of flowers. "And these are for you. Happy birthday, Mabel."

Mom cups her mouth with her hands. Instead of taking the flowers from him, she lunges forward, pulling him into a hug. Magnum lets out a surprised grunt, but then he chuckles.

I back away a few steps to join Andy and Hannah, who are standing now, too, and observing it all. All of us fail to contain our laughter as Mom gives Magnum another super tight hug that makes him grunt again.

The bustling dining area around us doesn't seem to notice or care about the scene unfolding in front of us. Everyone goes about their day, ordering food and eating, as if it's totally normal for Tom Selleck's doppelgänger to surprise tourists in crowded outdoor food courts for their birthday.

Andy leans over to me. "Where did you find this guy?"

"Julianne found him on Craigslist when she was helping me plan everything. Crazy, right?"

When Mom finally lets him go, she takes the flowers from him and looks at us. "You did this?"

"Tom Selleck was busy, so he sent him instead. Hope that's okay."

"This is way better than okay," she says. "Tom Selleck is much older now." She turns to the fake Magnum. "You're young and handsome—just like the young Thomas Magnum."

Fake Magnum booms out a laugh along with the rest of us. They pose while Auntie Linda snaps a photo. Then Auntie Linda and Mom's cousins swarm Magnum, P.I., to take selfies with him.

Andy darts away to a nearby baked goods booth, then a minute later walks back holding a butter mochi cake that he quietly ordered when we first arrived. A candle sticks out from the middle of it. When he starts singing "Happy Birthday" out loud, Mom's face goes slack in surprise once more.

It must be the familiar song in a public place that gets people's attention. Nearby diners join in and cheer on Mom as she blows out the candle. Applause echoes throughout the corridor when she beams triumphantly at the blown-out candle. Fake Magnum gives her a side hug, then insists she take the first slice, which she does.

Just then, I feel a tap on my shoulder. When I turn and see Julianne standing there in a floral maxi dress, a giant grin on her face, I suck all the air out of the nearby space.

"How the—what are you doing here?" I stammer as I pull her into a hug.

Behind me I hear Mom yell, "Oh my goodness!" Soon, she's at my side, pulling Julianne away so she can hug her.

Julianne gives her a hug, then hands her a small gift box with a ribbon. "Happy birthday, Mabel."

Mom cups her hand over her mouth and opens the box, which reveals a shiny new bracelet with diamond accents.

"Holy sh—" I catch myself before I swear out loud, reminding myself that Mom loathes when anyone curses around her.

I look back at Julianne. "Are those real?"

"Of course they're real."

Mom's eyes dazzle as she asks me to clasp it on her wrist. She turns to show it to Andy as I turn back to her. "Seriously, though, how did you manage this? I thought you were working and couldn't get out of it."

"I told Malcolm I'd be on call for Thanksgiving and Christmas if he gave me these days off last minute."

"You're seriously amazing."

"It's your mom's birthday," she says. "She's worth it."

I pull her into another hug. "You're the best."

I catch Mom staring at her bracelet as the Magnum, P.I., impersonator compliments her on how nice it looks. As I look on, the joy inside me crackles until I'm certain I'll burst. Everyone is here for Mom. Everyone is going out of their way to make sure this birthday is the best that they can make it.

She turns around, flashing me the most dazzling smile I've ever seen her flash. "Thank you, *anak*."

I bite the inside of my cheek to keep it together. "You're so welcome."

~

I stretch out on my beach towel after applying another coat of sunblock, letting a small groan escape. Leaning up on my elbows, I take in the scene on Waikiki Beach around me. The rich-blue waves of the ocean crash in front of us. Endless skyscraper hotels dot the shoreline. In the distance is Diamond Head, its rugged peak jutting against the clear blue sky.

The beach is packed with tourists on every side of me. Dozens of people wade and swim in the waves ahead.

Julianne plops down next to me. Water droplets from her long, lanky body rain over me when she shakes out her hair.

"Hey!" I laugh at the sudden shower.

She chuckles, and somehow that bright-pink lipstick she's wearing isn't even smudged after her swim. "Oops, sorry! Having a nice layout?"

"Yup. Almost dry." I pat my bare stomach. "How am I still full from yesterday's dinner? Boogie boarding this morning should have worked off at least some of it. Will we even be hungry for the luau tonight?"

"We'd better. I heard the food is going to be amazing." She stretches her arms above her head and groans softly. "But seriously, that Asian-fusion restaurant we went to for your mom's birthday dinner was incredible. How did you find it?"

"Magnum, P.I., recommended it. Maybe I should have stayed in the condo and napped like everyone else is doing."

Julianne turns to look at me while wringing out her soaked hair. "I gotta say, Chloe. I've never seen you like this before."

"Like what?"

"So happy. And so much less stressed."

"Really?"

"Yeah. I feel bad for questioning you when you first said you were quitting and moving back home to stay with your mom. Clearly it was the right thing to do."

For a second I soak in what she's said. "I definitely feel more at peace than I used to. God, I sound like that guy from the meditation studio."

We both laugh. Julianne grabs my hand. "Sorry for doubting you. You clearly know what's best for you and don't need me second-guessing you."

"No sorry necessary. You were just being my best friend and caring about me."

She scrunches her hair with her beach towel. "I'll admit, I'm gonna miss you living in the same city as me. You'd better come visit. And you'd better bring that Liam guy so I can meet him one of these days."

My cheeks heat at just the mention of him. "That's jumping the gun a little bit, don't you think?"

"Nope. You haven't been seriously interested in a guy in years—you haven't been out on a date in a year either. And in the space of three months, you meet Liam, open up to him about your mom, take him with you to confront your dad, and make out with him in your car. I'm not saying you have to run out and marry the guy right now, but clearly he's something special to you."

I think back to our date at his place, when he helped me plan this trip and ensured that Mom's shifts would be covered while she's gone.

"He definitely is."

My phone buzzes with a phone call, and we both glance at it. It's Liam.

"Speak of the devil." Julianne winks and stands up, gathering her things. "You and lover boy chat. I'll see you back at the condo."

I answer as I'm waving bye to Julianne. "Hey, you."

"Hey. Are you getting enough sun for the both of us?"

"Of course. How have you been?"

"Good. A little bummed that I haven't gotten a middle-of-the-night visit from you here at the store."

I laugh and scrunch my fingers through my still-wet hair. "Promise I'll come visit you at work when I'm back."

"I'd love that."

He asks how the trip has been so far, and I give him a quick recap of everything we've done.

"I'm bringing you back some butter mochi by the way," I say.

"How did you know I loved butter mochi?"

"Lucky guess," I say through a chuckle. "Or maybe it's that whole 'knowing each other in another life' thing we've got going."

The low rumble of his chuckle sends a wave of giddiness through me. "I think you're right."

"And don't worry, I'm getting you a souvenir too."

"It's one of those wobbling hula dancers I can put on the dashboard of my car, isn't it?"

"Well, now you've just ruined your surprise."

I scan the beach scene in front of me. Dozens of sunbathers lie in the sand while just as many people splash around in the shallow, crystal-blue waters of the beach ahead.

That contented feeling lingers. At the scene in front of me, at the joy a simple chat with Liam is bringing me.

"Can't wait to see you when I get back."

"Likewise. Tell your mom happy birthday for me."

We say goodbye, and I hang up. I take another long scan of the bustling beach scene. Then I gather my things and walk back to the condo to get ready for dinner.

Chapter Twenty

"Ouch! I think I have sand in my eyes."

"That's because you keep touching your face, Kay. Stop touching your face."

"*Manang* Linda, can I borrow your other hat? I didn't know it would be so bright at sunset."

"Is that guy doing backflips in the water? My God!"

I look over to where Mom's cousins, Auntie Linda, and Mom are huddled on their beach towels and chuckle. They're a gaggle of straw hats, flowy dresses, and flip-flops. Their constant conversation and laughter have been the most comforting background noise this entire trip. Even though it's only been a couple of weeks between their visit to Nebraska and this vacation, I've missed them. Maybe we can make their visit to Nebraska an annual tradition.

The whole crew, including Andy, Hannah, and Julianne, is here on crowded Waikiki Beach because it was Mom's idea to watch the sunset on our last evening in Honolulu before flying home tomorrow.

I glance at Mom, who's staring at the horizon as it glows fluorescent orange. Her expression is blissful and peaceful at once, like all the noise and bickering around her doesn't bother her one bit. It makes my heart swell to the point that it's difficult to breathe. I can tell by her smile, by the way she chuckles with her sister and cousins, by the look in her eyes that she's loving everything about this moment. And I hope with everything in me that she'll remember this trip, this time with them, this moment on this beach forever.

The chatting quiets as we watch the sun dip past the horizon. After a few minutes, other people on the beach start to leave.

Auntie Kay adjusts the wide-brim straw hat she's wearing before leaning over to give Mom a hug. "Sorry to be the first to turn in, but I'm exhausted."

"It's all right, *manang*." Mom laughs.

One by one everyone starts to pack up to head back to the condo. I stay sitting next to Mom as another wave of loud chatter hits, everyone trying to figure out whose towel is whose.

Mom laughs as Auntie Lorna and Auntie Rita bicker at each other about getting sand all over the place. Auntie Mel squints at the ground in search of her sunglasses.

"I don't know why you needed your sunglasses, *ading*," Auntie Linda says. "We were watching the sunset, for goodness' sake."

"It's still so bright! Didn't you see?"

I do my best to hold back a laugh. I'm going to miss their good-natured spats when we all leave to go home.

"Here they are!" Julianne hands Auntie Mel's sunglasses to her, and she accepts them with a grateful smile.

"Julianne to the rescue as usual," Mom says. She leans over to give her a hug.

"Thank you for letting me crash your birthday trip," Julianne says.

When they break apart, Mom pats her shoulder. "You didn't crash anything. You're family. I still can't believe you surprised me."

"Anything for you, Mabel."

They share a laugh, and Mom kisses her cheek. Julianne walks over to where I'm sitting on the sand.

"Seriously, thank you for coming all the way out here," I say to her while standing up. "It must have cost so much money to book a last-minute ticket."

Julianne shrugs, still smiling. "I'm a former spoiled rich kid. What else would I do with my time besides flying to tropical island getaways on a moment's notice?"

She heads off to the condo to pack. After a few minutes, Andy and Hannah tell us good night to do the same.

Mom and I are the last ones left, so we settle on the same beach towel, the sky ahead still glowing like it's on fire. People mill around us taking photos of the shoreline against the fiery sky. There are at least three dozen people on this beach who are sticking around past sunset, just like us. An occasional car whizzes past on the street behind us, the sound floating above the soft hum of chatter.

"I guess it's just you and me, *anak*." She pats my knee, then runs a hand through her hair, careful to avoid the bright-pink plumeria she plucked from her lei earlier today so she could wear it on the beach. I'm surprised at how bright and lush it still looks even though it's nearly two weeks old.

I wrap my arm around her, giving her a side hug. "So, was today good?"

She twists to face me. "The best. I couldn't ask for a better day. Or a better vacation."

"Really?"

"Really. This was the perfect day. And the perfect birthday. And the perfect vacation." She gestures to the ocean in front of us. "I'm in the most beautiful place in the world with everyone I love. I couldn't be happier."

I smile at her joyful reply. But after a second, a nagging sense of doubt settles in my chest. What Dr. McAuliffe said before about me carrying guilt when it comes to the sacrifices Mom made for me and Andy lingers in the back of my mind.

"Mom, can I ask you something?"

"Of course."

I take a breath, careful how I phrase things. "Do you ever regret that you never ended up moving here?"

She twists her head to me, the slightest frown on her face. "What do you mean?"

I gaze down at my feet buried under the sugary-soft sand. "I just . . . I know you said before that you're happy now, and that it's not a big deal that you didn't end up ever moving to Hawaii. Or visiting. And that's great, I just feel bad that you had to give up your dream."

"I didn't give up my dream." Her tone borders on shock, as if this thought never occurred to her until I brought it up just now.

"But you said that moving to Hawaii was your dream before all that stuff with Dad happened. Money was always so tight, and you didn't get the chance to vacation out here either."

When I pause, the expression on her face makes me think she knows what I'm about to say next.

"I was just wondering if you ever wished you could have done things differently, knowing now how things ended up."

She shakes her head, laughing softly. "The things you think about when you're young."

"What?"

Turning back to me, she grabs my hand. "I just meant that young people focus on the silliest things sometimes."

For a few seconds we say nothing. I think she's done speaking, but then she turns back to me.

"You're asking if I regret marrying your dad and having kids with him when I could have had a life out here?"

"That's exactly what I'm asking."

"Not at all."

The gentle way she smiles, the way she holds my gaze, tells me there is not one single doubt in her words.

I curl my toes in the sand. I repeat the movement over and over until it becomes a rhythm, like I'm playing a silent song.

"That's good to hear," I say after a bit.

For a minute we sit quietly together as the sky darkens ahead. One by one, our fellow beachgoers stand up, gather their belongings, and leave the beach.

And then Mom speaks. "You know, I can see how you and other people might think otherwise."

"Think what?"

"That I made the wrong choice. That marrying a guy like your dad, who eventually left me and you kids, was the worst thing that could happen to me. And yes, I'll admit it wasn't fun dealing with all of that, especially with his drinking problem."

A wave crashes loudly against the shore. We both pause for a second and look over before Mom starts talking again.

"It's hard when you're alone with two kids counting on you. And you know, if I were one of those people who was on the fence about having kids in the first place, maybe I would have regretted it. But I wasn't one of those people. I always knew I wanted to be a mom. I always wanted kids, more than anything. And when I married your dad, I loved him. I know you only saw us as parents, but before that—when we first met—we were kids in love. We were fun-loving and irresponsible and crazy about each other. We didn't have a care in the world at the time—it was just us. And the good times were wonderful while they lasted. He just changed as we got older. He started drinking more and more, and then it got out of control. Sometimes as horrible as it is, people change for the worse."

I listen, intrigued at how simply she puts everything.

"My dream was to have babies. And I did. I got two of the best babies I could have asked for."

She grabs my hand in hers and squeezes. It makes my throat ache.

"And yes, I was angry with your dad for what he did. Especially that night when he drove drunk with you two in the car. I'll be angry about that forever." She purses her lips together, shaking her head before sighing. "But thank goodness you and Andy were okay. I thank God every day for that—because that's all that matters. And I don't want to spend any more time thinking about your dad when I could be living my own life happily with you and Andy," she says. "You both have made me so proud. You're responsible and smart and kind and you work hard. I don't have to worry about either of you the way some parents have to worry about their kids. You visit me when you can. And you both take care of me, even when I'm stubborn. I'm so lucky."

She turns to me, her brown eyes glistening. "You put your job, your life on hold for me. Because you wanted to spend more time with me. How lucky am I?"

Her voice starts to shake at the end, but then she pauses to swallow before that wistful smile takes over her expression again.

"I can't imagine living my life without you two. You're the best thing that ever happened to me, you and Andy. I wouldn't trade this life with you for anything. Not for Hawaii. Not for money. Not for a different life. Not for anything in the world."

The lump in my throat throbs, even when I swallow. It sends tears to my eyes, but I blink them away before they can fall.

"Thanks, Mom. I love you."

"I love you too."

She pulls me into a side hug. We stay cuddled into each other until it's nearly pitch-black, the nearby streetlights offering minimal illumination.

When we finally stand up to leave, only a handful of people are left on the beach.

"Well, I think I'm ready for some mango," Mom says. "You?"

"That sounds amazing."

I carry our stuff and follow her across the street to our condo. When we walk inside, we go to our respective bathrooms to rinse off. Then I join Mom on the couch where she sits with a plate of diced-up mango.

"What do you feel like watching?" I ask as I reach for the remote and turn on the TV.

"*The Price Is Right*." She settles back against the couch, pulling her feet up and tucking them under her.

She hands me the plate of mango, and I help myself. Together we watch contestants as they scream and cheer their way through the episode.

She rests her head on the back of the couch, her eyelids heavy as she blinks. "This was so much fun, *anak*. Like a dream come true."

Her words land at the center of my chest, right where my heart is. *Dream come true.*

I quickly blink as my eyes water. I look at her as she focuses back on the television screen.

"It really is," I say.

By the end of the game show, I can barely keep my eyes open. When I breathe in, the faintest scent of gardenia hits my nose. Mom's perfume. I turn and see her snoozing. I grab the lightweight blanket from the back of the couch and drape it over her. And then I settle back on my end and drift off to sleep too.

That night I dream a million dreams. Mom and me and Andy sitting in the kitchen, playing cards. And then I dream of the three of us sitting in that room full of pillows again. Everything smells like her perfume. I dream of flowers, of water, of sand, of palm trees, of a sun that never sets. In one dream Hannah and Liam appear. In another is Mom's entire family. They happen one after another with no real sense of flow or logic. But I feel calm and content—everyone does. And that's how I know it's all okay.

~

When I wake, I breathe in deeply. Gardenia again, just like last night. Just like in my dream.

Eyes still closed, I yawn and stretch, then I open my eyes. Everything is blurry.

I blink, letting the haze of sleep pass over me until I'm awake enough to sit up.

When my vision focuses, I realize I'm in my bedroom. In Kearney. What the . . . How did I . . .

An unsettling jolt hits me. It lands in the center of my chest, spreading slowly up and down, to my throat, my legs, my arms, my toes, until I can't move.

Something feels off about today—about this morning.

And that's when I realize what's wrong.

I should still be in Honolulu.

How the hell did I fall asleep in our condo rental in Honolulu and then wake up in my bedroom in Kearney?

I'm dizzy as I gaze around the room but spot nothing out of place. My phone is on the nightstand. My suitcase is lying in the corner of the room in front of the closet. My laptop is on the desk, my power cord is plugged into the nearby outlet. There's a glass of water on the small table by the door, like always. Everything is where it should be.

But there's something in the air. It's thick and heavy, and I can't shake it no matter what I do.

I sit up in bed and swipe my phone from the nightstand. When I run my finger across the screen, I'm frozen. It's May 20.

But it can't be May. Yesterday it was June.

I scramble to the floor and power on my laptop to check the date. It says the same thing. May 20.

And that's when that feeling, that unsettling cloud hanging over me, gets its name.

Dread.

Because if it's May 20, that means only one thing: Mom's gone. And today is her funeral.

No matter how hard I try, I can't seem to catch my breath. I cup my hand over my mouth, huffing against the skin of my palm.

I'm already on my knees, so that means it'll be a soft landing when I inevitably collapse from the shock, from the grief, from the dread that this unexplainable chunk of time with my mom is over.

I cry into my hand, the sound barely muffled.

That's it. She's gone. Again.

I swipe through my phone even though I know I won't find what I'm looking for. Those texts I shared with Mom, with the aunties, with Andy, with Julianne. With Liam. Every single time I scroll through my text messages, it's the same. Nothing.

The most recent texts I have from Andy and Julianne are from May. Liam isn't even in my phone. I can't call him or text him. Even if I did have his number and got a hold of him, it would be no use. He has no idea who I am beyond Mabel's daughter.

I scroll to my messages with Mom. They're dated earlier this month too. Air lodges in my throat and I choke.

Just then, there's a soft knock at my door. I can't answer, but whoever knocked doesn't wait for me to.

Julianne slowly pushes open the door. I can't make out her expression when I look up at her because my vision is so blurry due to the tears flooding my eyes, but I can hear the worry in her voice.

She hugs her body around mine, pulling my face into her shoulder. "Just breathe, okay?" she coaches me in a gentle tone.

It's a minute before I even register what she says.

"I know this is so hard," she says, her own voice trembling. "I'm here for you, Chloe. You're going to get through today, I promise."

Julianne's soothing voice is the calming force I didn't know I needed. Soon I'm breathing at a regular pace again, no longer hyperventilating. I'm still crying, though.

And then she takes my face in her hands and looks at me. "If you can't speak today, all you have to do is say the word. No one will fault you for it, I promise."

My head is a haphazard swirl of emotions and stream-of-consciousness thoughts. I don't know what she's talking about.

"I promise, no one will think less of you if you decide that you can't give the eulogy," Julianne says.

And just like that, I stop crying. "No," I say, my voice hoarse. "I can do it."

"Chloe, it's okay if you—"

I shake my head and fall back to rest against the edge of the bed. "I have to, Julianne. It's for her."

She rests a gentle hand on my knee. "Listen. She of all people would understand if you decided not to."

When I pin her with my stare, her expression changes. It's like she's accepted in that moment there's no talking me out of it.

"I have to do this," I say. "I *want* to."

I wipe my nose with my wrist, then stand up and sit at my desk. I rip a fresh sheet of paper from my notebook and start writing.

It all comes flooding back to me. The memory of trying to put the right words on paper, the frustration and anger that ripped through me every time I couldn't get the sentences to come out right, the pile of crumpled notebook paper littering my bedroom.

But this time, the words flow out of me like a raging river. I can hardly keep up with them all, it's coming so fast.

Julianne gives my shoulder a soft squeeze before moving back to the door.

"I just need a minute," I say, still scribbling. "Then I'll be ready."

Julianne says "of course" before closing the door behind her.

When I finish twenty minutes later, my hands are shaking. I check my phone again to verify the time and make sure I'm not late. And then my eyes catch on a framed photo on my desk, a photo that's sat there for years. It's me as a toddler sitting in a sandbox, building a castle with Mom. I'm laughing; she's smiling.

In a flash, the FaceTime conversation I had with Mom just before her heart attack comes crashing back to me.

How she was looking through baby pictures of me, just like this one.

I think about how I talked to her, hugged her, sat next to her just hours ago.

I glance up at the calendar on my desk, my mind a flurry of confusion as I wonder how the hell I got here again—how the hell three months passed as I slept.

The sound of dishes clanking in the kitchen jerks me out of my stupor. I need to get dressed. It's time to say goodbye.

~

I gaze down at my lap, amazed I managed to dress myself this morning. I'm wearing a long-sleeve black dress that hits at the knee and looked fine in the mirror when I stopped crying long enough to do my makeup.

The rest of the morning was spent silently eavesdropping on all the conversations happening around me to catch up to today. None of it makes sense. Not falling asleep two days before Mom's funeral, and then waking up in March. Not falling asleep in Hawaii in June, and then waking up in May again, on the day of her funeral. If there were any rhyme or reason to this, shouldn't I have woken up the day *before* her funeral?

It's like I was randomly dropped back into this timeline while everyone else was just existing like normal. I'm dizzy just thinking about it all. For a long second I close my eyes and attempt to refocus.

Auntie Linda is staying with Andy and me at Mom's house. So is Julianne. Auntie Linda's sons and Uncle Lyle, along with Mom's cousins Auntie Kay, Auntie Rita, Auntie Mel, and Auntie Lorna—plus their spouses and kids—are staying in a nearby Airbnb since there's not enough room at the house for everyone.

"You need to let me pitch in to help cover the Airbnb, Chloe," Andy says, gripping the steering wheel of his car with both hands as we head to the funeral home. He never drives with both hands on the wheel.

His eyes are red and swollen from crying—just like the first time this happened. Memories of that first time we lost Mom overlay the more recent memories of us in Hawaii, and then other memories of all of us together come flooding in, of us at home with her playing cards and cooking and laughing.

I get so lost and fuzzy-headed as flashback upon flashback layer on top of one another. It's like all my memories are collected in an imaginary box of photos in my brain, and someone has just dumped that box onto the floor. There's no pattern or order—they're all just there.

"No way you're paying, Andy," I finally mumble from the passenger seat when the brain fog starts to clear. "I said I can cover it, and I meant it. So please don't worry."

"You're paying for the funeral, too, though," Andy says. "It's too much."

Big-sister mode takes over. I twist my head to face him. "Andy. It's okay. I would tell you if I needed help. But taking care of this is no problem. I promise."

The frown lines in his forehead ease the slightest bit. We stop at a traffic light, and he turns to face me. "Thanks. Seriously."

He tugs at the collar of his shirt. The black blazer he's planning to wear during the service is hanging in the back seat on a hanger because he doesn't want to wrinkle it while sitting in the car. The longer I look at him, the less he looks like himself. It must be the suit. I'm so used to seeing him in his work polo or jeans and a T-shirt. Like what he wore yesterday in Hawaii.

Yesterday.

Yesterday, his face was boyish and handsome and cheery. Yesterday, Mom cupped his face in her hands and called him her sweet boy when he cooked everyone breakfast in the condo rental right before we all took off for the beach. And now he's . . . now she's—

"Is there something on my face?" Andy asks, interrupting my thought.

"No. I . . . just spaced out for a second there." I turn to gaze out my window.

Andy sighs. "You and me both." From the corner of my eye, I see him look at the rearview mirror. "It was really nice of Julianne to offer to caravan Auntie Linda and Mom's cousins to the funeral so we could ride together."

"It really was."

"She's helped us out so much. I wish there was a better way to thank her other than saying it over and over again."

"What song are we playing at the funeral?" I say out of the blue.

Andy glances at me for a second. "'Here We Are,' that one slow song by Gloria Estefan. You found that instrumental version on Spotify the other day. Remember?"

"Oh. Right."

At the mention of the song, a memory flashes in my head. It's Mom cleaning the blinds in the house, that song blaring in the background. My eyes water.

He swallows, his neck flushing red. "I forgot how often she listened to that song when we were little. But when you mentioned it, it all came back. Thanks for . . ." He stops to clear his throat. "Thanks for remembering it. It's perfect for today."

"Of course," I say, my tone barely above a whisper.

The rest of the ride is a blur. It's like my brain is trying to reconcile everything that happened before today with everything that's happening right now.

We park in the funeral home parking lot. It's a massive brick building with a neatly manicured front lawn. Andy hauls a box of framed photos from the car to display during the service. Just a peek at the images, Mom's smiling face captured endless times in almost every stage of her life, nearly does me in.

She was here. Yesterday. Hours ago, she still existed. And now, she doesn't anymore. Now she's in an urn inside this brick building. I can't hug or hold or talk to her or . . .

When we walk in the building, a memory hits. It's Andy and me walking around and touring the facility. It feels a million years away—but it technically happened a little over a week ago.

My head spins so hard, I start to feel dizzy. It's impossible to make sense of it all.

The director comes out from the back office to greet us, but I can't talk. All I can do is swallow over and over, then hold my breath to keep from bursting into a wave of sobs yet again.

"Hey," Julianne says. She must have come in just now. Concern paints every feature of her face, from her furrowed brow to the way her blue eyes mist. "Why don't you sit down for a sec?"

She leads me to a nearby chair in the lobby and crouches in front of me. "People will be coming soon. I think—I think what usually happens is that family greets the guests, but if you don't feel up to it, I can—"

"No," I cut her off. "I can stand and shake hands and hug people. But I won't be able to say much honestly."

Julianne nods once and squeezes my hand. "It's okay. I'll be right there next to you, so I can do the talking."

The gentleness in her voice breaks me. I yank her into a hug. "Thank you," I say in a barely audible whisper. "Seriously, Julianne. Thank you."

"Always," she whispers back.

When she pulls back and grips me by the shoulders, I already know what she's going to ask. And I already know my answer.

"You sure you feel up to talking in front of everyone today?"

"Positive."

I hope I sound as sure as I feel. Because as much of a mess as I am right now, as confused as I am about what the hell is going on with time and the universe, I know I can speak about my mom. I'm certain I can honor her the way that she deserves.

Julianne frowns slightly. She has her doubts, and I don't blame her. But I've got this.

Just then the entrance opens, and two people walk in and mill around at the front. The first guests. I don't recognize them, but I don't need to. I just need to stand there and say "thank you for coming," and Julianne will help me with the rest.

For a moment, I wonder if Liam will come. My chest squeezes so hard with hope.

I hope he comes—I hope he exists.

Julianne gently touches my arm. "You ready?"

I stand up. "Ready."

Chapter
Twenty-One

Every single one of the seats in the service room has been filled with family, friends, and coworkers of Mom's. There must be at least a hundred people here. Even though I shook hands with a lot of them, I don't have a clear memory of who's even here. It's almost impossible to focus on multiple things in this haze of grief and shock. Especially when I'm channeling all my focus and energy on the speech I'm seconds away from giving.

After the funeral director gives the opening remarks, she turns to me. "And now, Mabel's daughter, Chloe, would like to say a few words."

Tucked between Andy and Julianne in the front row, I dig my speech out of my purse, stand on shaky legs, and take my place behind the wooden podium at the front of the room.

Smoothing out the paper against the wooden surface, I don't dare look up. If I do, I'll lose my nerve.

I take a moment to breathe. No one makes a sound as I take my time.

And then there's warmth, on my left hand. It's like someone is holding it, but there's no one there. For the briefest moment I feel bold. And then I let myself look up at the audience in front of me. It's a sea of faces, of family and Mom's friends and coworkers. The image reads almost like a blur to my eyes. My hands grip the podium for dear life at just how daunting it is to be in front of all these people.

But then the invisible warmth hits me again. I remind myself to breathe.

Always breathe.

I focus my eyes back on my paper. I take another breath. I swallow. I open my mouth. And then I speak.

"Everyone in this room knows how incredible my mom was. I think that's why this hurts so much . . ."

My voice starts to break, so I pause to clear my throat. I close my eyes. In the darkness, I see Mom's smiling face. Her deep-brown eyes— eyes just like mine—that radiated warmth every time she looked at me or Andy. Her pride and joy.

The most recent memories I have of her surface, those impossibly happy moments in Hawaii.

You're the best thing that ever happened to me, you and Andy. I wouldn't trade this life with you for anything. Not for Hawaii. Not for money. Not for a different life. Not for anything in the world.

When I open my eyes, it's back to fixating on my notes. Remembering her words in that moment, sitting side by side on the same beach towel, gazing at the fiery sky ahead, centers me. I can do this. I know I can. And even though she's not here, she knows I can too.

Again I clear my throat, focusing back on the paper, on the words that I wrote just this morning. "I heard something once that I didn't think much of at the time, but it has meant everything ever since my mother passed away. 'The pain is great because the love is great.' I honestly can't think of a better way to describe my feelings and emotions right now. This pain . . . is immeasurable. It's the worst pain I've ever felt. I wouldn't wish it on anyone. But in a way, this pain is a privilege to feel. This pain means the love I have for my mom—and the love she had for me and my brother—was deep and all-encompassing and unconditional. It means that I have endless happy memories and moments to recall when I'm sad."

I blink, and all I see is the gigantic grin on her face when Andy surprised her with a birthday mochi cake in Hawaii.

Another blink and I see her next to me, eyes closed, trying her hardest to relax while meditating as we both lie on the floor in the dimly lit studio at Riva Meditation.

"So many memories. I'm so lucky."

My throat aches at how much I've spoken. There's a sob building underneath all these words, but speaking keeps it at bay.

"This pain means the time we shared together was meaningful and priceless. This pain is a reminder of our bond, both emotional and physical. It's knowing that one hundred percent of her makes up half of me. We shared so much. Our love of food and warm weather, even our stubborn personalities. Apparently we both cross our arms and display the exact same frown when we're being insufferable. That was pointed out to me recently, to my surprise."

Soft, polite laugher follows.

"And as proud as I am to have so much of my mom within me, sometimes that meant we butted heads. A lot."

The stronger chuckle from the crowd this time makes the tightness in my chest ease the slightest bit.

"You know that saying that the apple doesn't fall far from the tree? That was Mom and me. To a tee. But above all, we care about family more than anything. If you're someone we love, be prepared for us to meddle in your life nonstop. Sorry, Andy."

Another soft chuckle.

"Remembering moments like that helps. It's how I've gotten through the past several days. It still hurts, though. It always will. I know I'll never, ever stop missing her. I know that I'll always wish I had more time with her. Because when it comes to someone you love, the only amount of time that even feels close to enough is forever. But the time I did have with her? It was beyond amazing. Every day, every phone call, every 'I love you,' every argument, every hug, and every kiss . . ."

Every road trip she took Andy and me on growing up. Every time she bandaged me up after a fall as a little kid. Every middle-of-the-night FaceTime session. Every healthy cooking class gone wrong. Every time we bickered. Every time she stopped everything to tell me how much she loved me.

"Every moment with her was more than I deserved. But when I think of how many more I wish I could have, the pain—it comes back again."

This time when I blink, a tear falls. I pause, swallowing to steady myself.

"But then I remind myself that I carry her with me always. I carry her in me. Every time I look in the mirror, I see her eyes, her nose, her full cheeks, her wide smile, her hair. Every time I can't drop an argument to save my life, I'll think of her. Every time my forehead starts to ache because of just how hard I'm frowning, I'll think of her. She'd be proud of just how long and how loudly I'll argue a point because that's exactly how she argued too."

There's another soft laugh from the audience. It makes me smile, even through the tears now pooling in my eyes.

"Yes, I'm in pain. I always will be. I know it will get easier to manage over time, but I'll always have it. I'll always battle it. It'll always take my breath away when I remind myself that I don't have a mom anymore, when I remember that the person I love most in the world—the person who loved me and my brother more than anyone else—is gone forever. This pain will always cut me to the core. That will never go away. And that's okay. I don't want it to."

I grip the podium when the ache in my throat and in my chest becomes too much. But it's fine. I'm nearly done speaking. And it's okay to cry. For a just a second, I glance up and see that almost everyone in the room is crying. It's the tiniest comfort to see so many people who loved her too.

"This pain will be a reminder forever that the very best parts of me are from her. And knowing that isn't painful at all. It is one hundred percent joy."

I break completely on my last word. But it's only for a second that I sob. That's the pain. But right behind it comes the flood of memories. There are too many to count. So I just let them roll through me as I make my way back to my seat in the front row.

As soon as I sit down, Andy gives me a reassuring pat on the hand. "That was perfect," he whispers before wiping his eyes with a tissue.

When he lets go, Julianne pulls me into a side hug. "Seriously perfect, Chloe," she says, her voice trembling. "She would have loved that."

When Julianne releases me, I sit up and focus straight ahead. That crack in my chest feels the slightest bit smaller now. My heart isn't threatening to break in half anymore.

The funeral director continues, but I can't hear a word she's saying. It's like I'm in a cloud. All I hear is white noise. And when I close my eyes, I see Mom again. She's smiling. The comfort it brings me is like a warm hug.

And then she speaks. It sounds so real, like she's sitting right next to me.

"*Anak*. You've made me so proud."

～

"You spoke so beautifully about your mom, Chloe."

One of Mom's coworkers pulls me into a hug as she speaks.

"Thank you so much."

"She was such a lovely woman. I'll miss her so much." She holds me gently by the arms as soon as she breaks the hug. Her hazel eyes fill with tears.

I thank her again and she moves to my brother, who's standing just a few feet away. She gives her condolences to him, and he nods and says thank you.

I lose count of the number of Mom's coworkers who showed up for her funeral service today. I'll never be able to remember all of their names or what they said, but what sticks with me is their grief. The sadness etched in their faces as they told me how sorry they were for my loss, how every single one of them told me what a pleasure it was to work with someone so dedicated and caring.

Despite how utterly destroyed from the inside out I feel in this moment, it's a comfort. Mom was loved by so many. She had a family outside of her blood relatives; her coworkers were her family too.

I glance around and see a young woman with long light-brown hair walk up to Andy. I can tell by how close they stand next to each other, this is more than just a polite paying of condolences.

She turns around, and I see her face. Hannah.

They're together now too. Relief and comfort and joy crash into me at once, like a silent tidal wave.

When she pulls him into a hug, I turn away. It feels invasive to stare. But inside, a bit of that pressure in my chest eases. His Hannah is here to comfort him and support him. I'm so happy my little brother has someone—that they have each other.

She turns to me and offers a sad smile. Then she and Andy walk over to me.

"This is Hannah," he says softly.

There's no introduction, no explanation of who she is or why she's here or why she's special to him. It's not necessary. Clearly they're not ready to talk about themselves or make proclamations about their relationship. But it's okay. Because it's clear just how much they mean to each other, and that's really all that matters.

"It's so nice to meet you," I say while shaking Hannah's hand. "I wish it were under better circumstances."

She nods, her eyes welling. "I'm so sorry I never got to meet your mom." Her tone is shaky and delicate. "She sounded like such an incredible woman."

"She really was."

"You gave such a touching speech about her. I kind of feel like I got to know her a little bit with how vividly you spoke of her."

I thank her and, at the same time, think of how she and Mom actually did meet in the timeline I experienced. I think of how well they got along, and how in that other mystery timeline, Hannah was the one suffering loss, and we were the ones comforting her. Now it's the other way around.

The surrealism of it all has my chest tight and my breath fleeting for the briefest moment.

"You know, I actually remember seeing her at the grocery store once or twice when I was shopping late at night. She was always so sweet and helpful," Hannah says.

She turns to Andy. His eyes go watery as he focuses on her, and then he glances at the floor. He's trying to keep it together. When Hannah touches his arm, his shoulders relax the slightest bit.

My eyes well up and a small smile tugs at my lips as I think about how in this world Mom and Hannah managed to meet and get along in some small but significant way.

"She would have loved you," Andy says to Hannah.

I step away to give them a moment alone.

The funeral director walks up to me. "I'm sorry to bother you, dear, but this was delivered this morning," she says in a gentle tone.

I look down at the small cardboard box and open it. When I see it's a familiar rectangular black-velvet jewelry box, my mouth falls open slightly. I know what this is. I open the small card on top of the jewelry box.

For Andy and Chloe. I'm so sorry, Mabel.

—Dad

There's no name or address or any identifying information. But I don't need it. I open the box, and for a few seconds I stare at the gold and diamonds shining under the fluorescent lighting of the funeral home.

More people walk up to offer their condolences, so I quickly close it and set it in my purse.

When they leave, I look around the lobby of the funeral home. Only a few folks linger at the far end, near the door, their backs to me.

I see a guy hold the door open for someone as they leave. When he spins around, I recognize him immediately.

Those enrapturing light-blue eyes zero in on me all the way across the room. He walks toward me, his face solemn, his eye contact hesitant but kind. And then he stops, a respectable foot away.

"Hi." I almost say his name but catch myself. He doesn't know me yet.

"Hi, I'm Liam. I just want to say how sorry I am for your loss."

He sticks out his hand and I shake it, ignoring how unnatural it feels to exchange such a formal gesture with someone who I've been so intimate with.

"Thank you," I say.

"I didn't get a chance to introduce myself when I walked in; you were talking to someone else." He clears his throat. "I met your brother, though."

He tugs at the gray tie knotted around his neck and glances down at the floor. He's nervous.

"How did you know my mom?" I ask.

"We worked together. At the store."

"Oh. That's nice."

His mouth, which is a perfect thick line of light pink, turns in a gentle upward motion. It's a smile, but it's sad. It makes me want to fall into him, to hold him tight and tell him how much it means that he's here.

But I don't. I stay put, feet planted on the ground, hands folded in front of me, trying my best to stay composed.

"You gave a beautiful speech about your mom."

"Thank you so much."

He yanks on the sleeve of his white dress shirt, then rubs the back of his neck. "Sorry. I'm sure you're tired of people coming up to you. I just wanted to say that Mabel was an amazing person. And the best manager. Everyone loved her. She always encouraged people to do their best. She was everyone's biggest cheerleader."

"I remember you saying that."

His brow wrinkles in confusion.

I bite the inside of my cheek at my slipup. "I mean, I remember someone saying that about her before. Sorry, my head is kind of all over the place today."

He expression eases back to tenderness. "That's more than understandable."

"You work overnights, too, then?"

He nods. "I'm one of the shift supervisors." He shifts his weight from one leg to the other. "This is probably the millionth time someone has come up to you and said how sorry they are. It must be a lot."

I shake my head. "It's honestly really comforting to hear all the lovely things people have to say about her. It's—it's nice to know that so many people cared about her."

He lets out a breath, almost like he's relieved. "She was the best boss I ever had. Every month or so she would bring in these really yummy desserts and pretty much force everyone to eat them."

"Really?"

He nods. "I remember, this one night, she made this cake. It was like a super chewy rice cake. That sounds weird, but it was delicious."

"*Bibingka.*"

"Yes. That. She called it that, but so many people were having trouble remembering how to say it. So she started calling it glutinous rice cake. So there she was, shoving slices in everyone's hands, but one of the employees, Jim, has celiac disease. He heard the word *glutinous* and just assumed that he couldn't eat it."

Liam's smile widens. Hearing how happy it makes him to tell this story makes me grin too.

"But Mabel was so adamant that he try it. He kept saying no and backing away from her as she offered it to him. Eventually it turned into her chasing him around the break room with a square of *bibingka*. And he just kept bumping into tables and chairs, politely trying to back away, thinking one bite of this cake was going to end him."

We share a laugh.

"Yup. That sounds like her," I say with a happy sigh. "If she wanted you to eat her cooking, there was no escape."

Liam chuckles. "That's exactly what happened. She eventually backed Jim into a corner and held the dessert up to his face until he took a bite. He did. And when he didn't get sick, he was blown away. We all eventually told him it was gluten-free. After standing aside and having a good laugh at their little scene."

We share another laugh. For a few seconds we just stand and look at each other. The muscles in my neck and shoulders relax. It's the same ease and comfort I felt around him during those times I saw him at the store and when he went to Kansas City with me to confront my dad.

He shuffles his feet, then narrows his stare at me. "This is going to sound crazy, but"—he lets out a soft laugh, ruffling his hair with his hand—"I feel like I've met you before. Have we maybe run into each other at the store?"

The pressure inside my chest loosens. The fact that he feels something—anything—for me means the world.

"I'm not sure. Maybe?" is all I say.

It takes everything in me to keep from telling him everything. But now's not the time or place. Maybe someday, though.

He looks at me expectantly.

"I mean, I've definitely been to the store. Lots of times," I say. "I just—I can't think of a time where we would have met."

"We must have just seen each other in passing then," he says. The way he glances away for a moment makes it seem like he's disappointed.

"Or maybe in another life we knew each other."

When he laughs at my odd joke, I feel at ease. I feel comforted. I feel like this is our millionth conversation and our first rolled into one.

Auntie Linda comes out of the women's restroom and walks over to Andy. My stare lingers on her pinned-up black hair and how different she looks from Mom with it up. I can still see their shared resemblance, though—in her eyes, the shape of her nose, her full cheeks. In that moment, I'm grateful that in addition to their sisterly bond and the endless time and memories they shared together, Auntie Linda has that part of Mom too.

She offers a sad smile as she glances over at me, wipes her eyes, then says something to Andy. He nods, then looks over at me.

"I'm going to run the aunties home and to the Airbnb. You okay taking care of things here?"

I'm about to answer yes when Julianne darts over. "I'd be happy to drive her and Lyle and your other aunties. That way you two can stay and wrap things up."

Auntie Linda smiles at Julianne. "You sure, dear? I don't want to be a bother."

Julianne marches over to Auntie Linda and gently grabs her hand. "You're not a bother at all."

I mouth a thank-you to Julianne, who waves a hand at me like it's no trouble at all.

Liam steps aside just as Auntie Linda walks over to me to pull me into a quick hug. "Such a beautiful and perfect ceremony. Just what your mom would have wanted. You were right to do it this way."

I squeeze her in return, grateful to have her approval.

Mom's cousins walk over from where they were standing and talking at the other end of the lobby and give me tight, tearful hugs. I close my eyes for a moment with each embrace, remembering how they smiled and laughed nonstop during our trip to Hawaii, how they made Mom's last days more special than I could have ever hoped. Every second of darkness behind my eyelids, I picture a different memory: them huddled together on Waikiki Beach, cackling together at the luau, bickering while playing cards and cooking together.

My eyes burn with tears the longer I keep them closed. If only they knew. If only they could share those memories of Mom. If only I could tell them without sounding completely out of my mind.

If only Mom could have actually experienced that extra time with her family.

They all walk over to Julianne and Auntie Linda, then leave the funeral home. Andy turns to ask the funeral director a question, and I turn back to Liam.

"I guess I should take off then," he says, shoving his hands in the pockets of his black trousers.

I open my mouth to say no, to tell him to stay. I want to talk to him more. I want to pick up where we left off.

But I don't say a word. I can't. He has no idea where I'm coming from. He's lived the same reality everyone else has. He doesn't know me at all. And telling him any of this would freak him out.

So instead, I offer the politest smile I can muster. "Thank you for coming."

He lingers an extra second, like he doesn't want to leave. It's good because I don't want him to leave just yet either. I don't know when I'll see him again, but I don't know how to ask him to stay.

With one last small smile, Liam turns to leave. Then he stops and turns around to face me once more.

"Sorry, I didn't mean to make things weird earlier," he says. "For some reason it just feels like we know each other." His cheeks flush pink, and he lets out a laugh. "I know that sounds crazy."

Something tugs in my chest. It feels like a push to say what I'm thinking. "Honestly? I get that vibe too."

"You do?" His eyes brighten.

I nod. "Would you maybe want to meet for a coffee sometime? I'd love to hear more work stories about my mom. If you have more."

The soft smile he flashes me makes my insides melt. I've witnessed it so many times before today. But it feels brand-new, like I'm seeing it for the first time ever.

Which kind of makes sense.

"I'd love that," he says.

He walks over to me, and we put our numbers in each other's phones.

"I know you work nights, so it might be a little hard coordinating anything," I say as I hand his phone back to him.

The smile he flashes is small, but it still makes my heart dance. "I'll make time. No matter what."

No matter what.

I thank him and wave as he walks out the door and to his car.

Chapter Twenty-Two

"Auntie Linda is lying down in your mom's room," Julianne says. She plops down on the couch and kicks off her heels under the coffee table.

I fall down in the seat next to her. "Thank you so much for bringing her back home and for driving everyone else to the Airbnb."

She grabs my hand in hers. "Of course. I was happy to."

I look her in the eye, not sure if I'll be able to make it through this without crying. "I mean it, Julianne. I don't know what we would have done without you running our errands and reminding us to eat these past few days."

Julianne pats my hand.

Andy walks into the living room from down the hallway. He's shed his black blazer and loosened the tie around his neck. He falls into the recliner. "I feel like a thank-you card isn't even close to enough," he says to Julianne.

"Knowing your mom and being part of your family is enough," Julianne says, letting her blonde hair loose from the bun it was in for the funeral.

I pull her into a hug.

Julianne stands up. "I think I'll run to the grocery store and grab some food for tonight."

"You don't need to do that," I say. "Mom's cousins are out shopping as we speak for way more food than we'll ever need to cook for tonight."

Julianne smiles. "Then I think I'll go change and go for a walk, just to get some air, if that's okay with you."

"Of course it is." When she walks by me, I grab her hand. "Seriously. Thank you. For everything."

"No thanks necessary." She leans down and hugs me. "Always here for you. Always."

When Julianne walks out of the house, I glance over at Andy, who's slumped in the recliner, a dazed look on his face.

"This feels weird," I say.

He nods, even though I know he doesn't know exactly what I mean.

Yes, this moment feels weird. This moment where we sit in the living room of our childhood home—our mom's home—overwhelmed with the realization that she'll never step foot in this house again.

But more than that, it's feeling like she was just here. Because she was. And now she's not. And I've had to pretend like I've spent the last several days without her, when in my head and somewhere in my existence, I was with her for much, much longer.

Amid the cloud of confusion I exist in, guilt nags at me. Even though I can't explain it, it still happened. I got an extra three months with her. But Andy didn't. No one else did. Why did it happen to me? How can I sit here and allow myself to feel just as devastated as everyone else when I had that extra time with her?

The longer I look at Andy, the worse it feels. The pain of her loss is etched in his face like a second skin. It's in his eyes that are fixed on his lap, so swollen from crying. It's the upside-down half-moon shape of his mouth, a frown that will probably never go away.

I almost say it. I almost say I'm sorry that he didn't get to see her one last time like I did. Even though he won't know what the hell I'm talking about—even though he'll think I'm out of my mind for saying it, for talking about a chunk of time that I'm sure he'll probably assume is just my own delusion. I have to say something. I can't live with this secret. I open my mouth and start to speak.

But then he looks up at me. "I'm sorry, Chloe."

"For what?" I blink, and a tear falls from each eye.

"That you didn't get to see her that weekend. When you planned to come up."

"It's okay."

He shakes his head. "I just feel so guilty."

"Why?" I gaze at him, perplexed.

The heavy sigh he lets out shakes his entire body. "I got to live with her. I got to see her almost every day." He turns his gaze toward the window nearby. "I know living at home with your mom when you're twenty-five isn't exactly living the dream. But I'm thankful for it now. It meant that I got to have more time with her. And I just . . . I just wish you could have had some extra time with her too. I'm so sorry you didn't."

Just then I'm struck with a thought. It hits so suddenly, with such power, that it feels like I've been slammed by an invisible boulder to the chest.

Maybe those extra three months happened because I didn't get to have every day with her, like Andy did. Maybe something—some force, some entity somewhere in the universe—noticed this and gave it to me.

Or maybe I'm grasping at straws because I'm human, and humans like to have rational explanations for things, even when there aren't any.

And then something else occurs to me. Another thought, but it lands softly, like a cloud moving over my entire body.

Some things don't need to be explained. Some things are a mystery, and that's okay. Because what matters isn't how something happened. What matters is that it happened at all.

The tears in my eyes slowly fade. I give Andy a genuine smile. It's slight and shaky, but I mean it.

"It's okay, Andy. I'm not sorry. I feel lucky for the time I had with her."

There's a new sort of conviction in my voice. My tone is still soft, but there's a steadiness to it. An unwavering confidence that can't be challenged because I'm one thousand percent sure of what I've said, of how I feel.

And I think Andy can tell because the worry and grief that took over his face just seconds ago have now faded away. He looks at me, his expression lighter and happier.

"Besides," I say, "I had seven whole years with her on my own before you came along. I think that counts as extra time."

He lets out a soft laugh. "Good point. So when are we supposed to do the hard stuff?" he asks.

"What do you mean?"

"You know, cleaning out the closets, figuring out what things of Mom's we should get rid of and what we should keep."

I shake my head. I didn't even think about that. "Probably whenever we feel like it."

Andy rubs his face. "She was keeping a bunch of her extra clothes that she wasn't wearing anymore in the closet of your bedroom."

It's like we're both too afraid to make the first move. The longer I look at him, the more I can tell it tears him up to even contemplate getting rid of anything that belonged to her.

"We can go look and see how much stuff there is," I say. "We don't actually have to do anything yet."

He stands up. "Okay," he says with a shaky sigh.

We walk to my bedroom and open the door to the closet. It's packed to the brim with Mom's stuff. Clothes of every color rest on the hangers and on the shelves. There are dozens of pairs of shoes lining the bottom of the closet, along with a pile of purses.

"It's like she robbed a thrift store and was hiding her haul in my room," I say.

Andy lets out a throaty chuckle that warms me from the inside out.

"Where should we start?" he asks.

I shrug. "I have no idea."

"We could ask if Auntie Linda wants anything when she wakes up. And Mom's cousins too," he says. "I'd be happy if they want to take anything of Mom's."

"I think that's a good idea. Oh, wait." I turn around and fetch my purse from my desk, then show him the jewelry box. "Dad sent this to the funeral home today."

Andy scans the note he sent.

"He stole that from Mom before they divorced," I explain.

"Jesus," Andy mutters as he looks at the bracelet and ring. "I wonder what made him send it."

"Maybe he developed a conscience. Maybe he's a better person now than he used to be."

I have no idea who Dad is in this version of the world or if what I say is true. But I hope it is.

"We should show this to Auntie Linda later," I say.

Andy nods yes, then pinches the bridge of his nose. He closes his eyes and sighs, then looks at me. "I think I need to see a counselor. Or a therapist. I think I need to talk to someone about this."

"I think that's a really good idea. I think it would help a lot. It helps me," I say. "If you want, I can ask my therapist to refer you to someone."

"That would be great. I . . . don't know if I'm ready to talk to someone in person, face-to-face, though. It feels kind of daunting, if that makes sense."

"That makes a lot of sense. I'm sure she can recommend someone who can help you in a way that you feel comfortable," I say. "I think it's great you're doing this, Andy."

He mutters a soft thanks before a long beat of silence passes between us.

"Hannah seems nice," I finally say.

He nods, that same small, sad smile from before tugging at his mouth. "She is. She's amazing. I meant to tell you about her—about us—sooner, but then all this stuff with Mom happened and . . ."

I touch his arm. "It's okay, Andy. I'm just glad you have someone who makes you happy."

The big-sister part of me wants to say so much more. I want to tell him that he shouldn't be afraid to lean on Hannah for support if he needs it. I want to tell him that it's okay to call her and tell her to come over to be with him if that's what he wants. I want to tell him that it would give Mom all the joy in the world to know that her baby boy is with someone so wonderful.

But I don't. Because he doesn't need me to say any of that right now. He probably knows all that already.

When I look at him, I see more than just my little brother. When I look at him, I see the person I saw that day when Hannah came over to Mom's house unannounced to talk to her and me. He was protective and watchful and doting and caring. This may be a different circumstance—a different timeline—but he's still the same person. And he'll navigate things just fine, like he did before.

"I wish there were a manual for what to do when you lose a parent," he says after a while. "I feel so clueless."

"I think everyone who goes through this feels the same way."

We stay standing side by side, staring into the open closet.

The longer I gaze at the endless expanse of colorful fabric, the more surreal Mom's absence feels. I spot the flowy purple dress she wore to the luau in Honolulu, and my throat closes. I blink hard to fight back the tears aching to fall.

"There's no rule book," I finally say when I'm sure I can speak without losing it. "We don't have to do this right now. Or anytime soon. Or ever."

Andy glances at me, his expression relieved. "Other than the things that Auntie Linda and Mom's cousins want to take for themselves, I don't want to get rid of anything just yet. I'm not . . . I'm not ready."

I pat his shoulder. "I'm not either," I say, my tone just above a whisper. "Not even close."

Glancing at the ground, he turns to me. There's an expectant look on his face, like he wants to speak but doesn't know what to say.

"What is it?" I ask him.

"You're not seriously quitting your job. Are you?"

I stay silent.

He turns his head to look out the window before looking back at me. "You know that would piss Mom off, you quitting the hospital."

Our conversation comes back to me, landing like a fist to the gut. When Mom died, I didn't care about anything. The memory of me announcing to Andy that I had quit my job while sobbing on the floor of my bedroom resurfaces.

"Oh. Right."

Andy clears his throat. "I thought you loved your job."

"I thought I did too. And then I realized I love other things more." I shuffle my bare feet along the thick carpet. "I know we don't have to figure this out now, but I just want to put it out there. I don't want to sell Mom's house. I want us to keep it. Or one of us to."

"I don't want to sell it either," Andy says. "We can't. Mom worked so hard to pay it off. It's one of the only things of hers we have left."

"Maybe you and Hannah can live here together some day. It'd be perfect for a family."

My heart stops when I realize what I've said. He doesn't know that I know about the loss he and Hannah suffered, if they did suffer it now.

I look back at him, but he seems to rein in his reaction as his stare remains straight ahead. He pauses for a second, then nods before looking at me. The slightest smile tugs at his lips. "Maybe someday. That would be nice, actually."

We both glance back into the closet, staring at nothing in particular.

I turn to him. "When Mom died, I realized just how much time I wasted working my way up at the hospital—and I wasn't even happy. But I promise I'll have a job figured out by the end of the summer. That way you won't have to be embarrassed of your out-of-work older sister."

"You could never embarrass me. And honestly, it would be nice to have you stay here for the next few months. I don't think I want to be alone here right now."

I pull him into a hug. "I'll be here."

When we pull apart, he sighs, fatigue written all over his face. "Auntie Linda had the right idea. I'm going to go lie down."

"I think I will, too, in a minute."

He gives my shoulder a soft squeeze before walking out and shutting the door behind him.

But instead of falling onto the bed and resting, I stay standing in front of the closet, taking everything in once more. My eyes scan every piece of clothing she wore on our trip to Hawaii, the trip that didn't happen. Except it did. Except I can't explain how.

I step forward and run my hands over the endless hangers of fabric. Leaning in, I breathe in and smell the faintest hint of gardenia. It's stale and mixed in with the wooden scent of the closet, but it still hits hard. For the millionth time today, I choke back tears.

It still feels so fresh, so raw, so unreal. Like she could walk through the door at any minute.

Glancing down, I spot the bright-pink carry-on suitcase that she used for every trip. It's tucked away in the corner, peeking out from behind a heavy camel-hued peacoat that Andy got her for Mother's Day one year. I saw her wear it maybe twice ever.

I kneel on the floor and pull out the suitcase, remembering how she brought it with her to Oahu.

Running my hands over the hard plastic, I recall how Mom plucked a plumeria bloom from the lei she received at the airport and wore it in her hair our last night on the island. I remember the grin that stretched across her face when she walked out of the airport, taking in the scene around her.

I unzip the bag and open it, sighing at the empty contents. I don't know why I'm disappointed. I knew there'd be nothing in there.

As I move to close it, something falls out from underneath the fabric flap. A tiny cardboard box. The flimsy kind toy jewelry comes in. I grab it and open the lid. And when I zero in on what's inside, I freeze. I can't breathe or talk or move. All I can do is gawk with wide, disbelieving eyes.

It's the bright-pink plumeria from her lei—the one she wore when we sat together on Waikiki Beach and we watched the sunset.

My hands shake as I cradle it in my palm. It hasn't lost one bit of its luster. My mouth falls open, but the only sounds I can make are shallow, soft gasps. Once again, hot tears cascade down my cheeks.

A memento. It's proof—a real, tangible souvenir from our time together that I can touch and hold in my hand.

It's several seconds before I realize that I'm crying and laughing at the same time. I swallow, remembering that Auntie Linda and Andy are sleeping and I need to be quiet.

So I take another breath. A slow, soothing, calming breath that takes nearly ten seconds for my body to clear.

I'm quiet again, but inside my head is a whirlwind. It feels like a tornado is racing through my skull and leaving behind a tangle of thoughts and feelings. But I know what this means. This flower is proof that the past three months with Mom, *my* past three months with Mom, happened.

It's a thought that sends more tears of utter joy pouring from me. It's a thought that has me shaking with relief and bliss and shock at once. It's a thought that I know I'll come back to countless times when the grief of losing her feels like too much. Those times when I feel like I can't go on without her, I'll look back on this moment and know that she came back when we all needed her the most. And she'll be here to cheer us on through the rest.

The longer I stare at the vibrant pink petals, the surer I feel. When we lost Mom, I never thought I'd feel comfort again. Or hope. Or happiness.

But right now, sitting on the floor of my old bedroom, I feel all three. Maybe someday, I'll wake up and she'll be here again, and we'll get to share another bizarre and unexplainable but utterly wonderful existence together.

Maybe this flower is proof of a new, undiscovered hole in the universe. Maybe this unexplainable chunk of time will happen for us again. Maybe this is a whole new world we're just discovering.

Maybe next time, it'll be Andy who gets to experience more time with Mom. Or maybe even Auntie Linda.

I imagine the shock that would overwhelm them both, how the tears would come, unstoppable at first, but then grateful smiles would follow. Then hugs. So many hugs.

Tears flood me. My heart swells at the thought, at the hope that this can be true. Every muscle, every bone in my body aches for this to happen.

I have to take another calming breath so I don't fall into sobs once more. Because that would be yet another dream come true, a dream that I don't deserve to have in the first place.

My chest rises as I inhale and run my finger over the thick plumeria petals.

But even if none of that happens—even if the past three months were a fluke, a mistake in the universe, a one-off and the last time I'll ever have with her, that's more than enough. I was given more time with my mom. It happened against all odds, against reality, against the entire universe that's structured to move forward in time. I was given something I should never have received in the first place. Every minute was a joy and a fight and a lesson and a dream.

I open the tiny box and place the flower back inside. And then I put it back in Mom's suitcase, zip it shut, and tuck it back into its spot in the corner of the closet against the wall.

Gazing at the bright-pink exterior, I smile.

"Love you, Mom. See you next time."

Author's Note

Even though this book is a work of fiction, I drew from certain elements in my own life. I gave the main character, Chloe, and her family the same background as my own, Filipino American. My mother's family speaks Ilocano, which is the third most widely spoken language in the Philippines after Tagalog and English. It's one of the languages spoken in Luzon, the largest and most populous island in the Philippines, which is where my mother's family is from. I included numerous Ilocano words throughout the book in homage to my family and to remain true to my own experience. They are words and phrases I grew up with and still use, and they are italicized for emphasis throughout the story.

Acknowledgments

There are so many people I want to thank for helping me bring this book into the world. The first is my amazing agent, Sarah Younger. Thank you for the enthusiasm you showed me when I first came to you with this totally off-the-wall idea. I couldn't have written it without you. And thank you to the incredible interns at Nancy Yost Literary Agency who read early drafts and offered such thoughtful feedback.

Thank you to my amazing friend Stefanie Simpson. I was so nervous to write something so far out of my comfort zone, but you reassured me and helped me believe that I could do it. I can't wait to hug the hell out of you and thank you properly for being the most wonderful friend.

A million thanks to my editors Krista Stroever and Chris Werner. You two are so talented, passionate, and insightful, and I feel beyond lucky to work with you. The care and excitement you've shown this story still blows me away. This book wouldn't be what it is without you both.

Thank you to Lake Union for believing in me and this story, and for helping me share it with readers. Thank you to the brilliant copyeditors, proofreaders, and designers for getting *Three More Months* into publishable shape. Thank you to the marketing and publicity team for getting the word out about my book.

Alex, thank you for being the most supportive and amazing partner I could ever ask for.

To my friends and family, thank you so much for loving me and supporting me.

The biggest thanks to you, Mom. I am the luckiest to have come from you, and I owe you everything. Losing you was a nightmare, but your love is a dream that I feel every single day. Thank you for bringing me into this world.

And thank you to everyone who reads this book. It means everything.

About the Author

Photo © 2015 Nick Zielinski and Jessi Reiss

Sarah Echavarre earned a journalism degree from Creighton University and has worked a bevy of odd jobs that inspire the stories she writes today. When she's not penning tear-jerking women's fiction, she writes sweet and sexy rom-coms under the name Sarah Smith. She lives in Bend, Oregon, with her husband. Connect with Sarah at www.sarahechavarre.com.